Wounds of Honour

Marcus took a deep breath.

'Dubnus, you've said it a dozen times in the last week. I *was* a praetorian officer, but I never saw action, so it was just a ceremonial job . . . looking good in uniform, knowing what to say to whom . . . I'm going to need you to help me be a real officer, a warrior leader. What else can I give you in return?'

'I make you a warrior, you'll make me a centurion?'

'Not a warrior. I may yet surprise you in that respect. A warrior *leader*. It's what I'll have to achieve if I'm to survive here.

Or die trying.'

About the author

Anthony Riches holds a degree in Military Studies from Manchester University. He began writing the story that would become *Wounds of Honour* after a visit to Housesteads Roman fort in 1996. He lives in Hertfordshire with this wife and three children. This is his first novel

EMPIRE

WOUNDS *of* HONOUR

ANTHONY RICHES

HODDER

First published in Great Britain in 2009 by Hodder & Stoughton
An Hachette UK Company

First published in paperback in 2010

13

A CIP catalogue record for this title
is available from the British Library

ISBN 978 0 340 92032 9

Typeset in Plantin Light by Ellipsis Books Limited, Glasgow

Printed and bound by Clays Ltd, St Ives plc

Hodder & Stoughton policy is to use papers that are natural, renewable
and recyclable products and made from wood grown in sustainable forests.
The logging and manufacturing processes are expected to conform to the
environmental regulations of the country of origin.

Hodder & Stoughton Ltd
338 Euston Road
London NW1 3BH

www.hodder.co.uk

*To Helen, for unfailing patience and encouragement.
And above all else, for Silloth.*

ACKNOWLEDGEMENTS

By far the most important thanks to be offered by the author must go to my immediate family, Helen, John, Katie and Nick. I suspect that much longer faces would have been pulled that 'summer' day in 1996 if it had been clear exactly what the proposed visit to Housesteads, the site of *Wounds of Honour's* 'The Hill', would mean in terms of my on/off relationship with the manuscript – and therefore to a degree with my loved ones – over the next twelve years.

The guiding influences that led me to put my hands on a word processor with serious intent – even if I wasn't quite sure what that intent was at the time other than a burning feeling that I could do *that* – were, in chronological order; my mother for my letters and the reading habit; my father for fuelling it with his illuminating military history collection and highly informed, unpatronising debate on each fresh subject as I greedily consumed it; and Michael Elliott-Bateman for teaching me how to read the much more interesting stories hidden between the lines. Lastly, with the writing habit already established, the novels of Stephen Pressfield and (of course) Patrick O'Brian particularly stand out as having provided me with signposts as to the level of quality that would be required of my writing were I to stand any chance of publication. Mr Pressfield in particular, his subject matter so close to my chosen time period and with such remarkable skills, left me staring into space wondering whether I should even continue with my half-formed manuscript on more than one occasion. I credit *Gates of Fire* more than any other single book for influencing my eventual writing style.

In writing *Wounds of Honour* I have been dependent on more sources of information than I can recall, but particular influence has been exercised by Kevan White's remarkable website, www.roman-britain.org. Kevan showed me that the dry Latin place names we ascribe to the forts on Hadrian's Wall – and so many other places – hide so much from our understanding what made the Romans tick, essentially and unsurprisingly, like any other human society. The second that Brocolitia (Carrawburgh) became 'Badger Holes' (the literal translation from the Latin) in my head, a good deal else changed in my view of the Wall's occupiers. Kevan's website is an excellent source of information of all sorts with regard to Hadrian's Wall and its occupiers. Any reader with the curiosity to delve behind my necessarily light touch with the wealth of information available on this period in British history could do no better than to start here.

I haven't been an academic for over twenty-five years now, and so my contacts with academia have necessarily been limited, but I must single out for thanks Dr Simon James of Leicester University for his help in understanding the dominant land use patterns along the Wall in the late second century.

Lastly, when it comes to thanking those involved in getting the manuscript out of its long hibernation on my succession of memory sticks, several people have been instrumental. For those fateful words 'my book's doing well' one cold and windy night in a Belfast security office, and for his unselfish encouragement of a fellow author, Gerry Tate, author of *Cappawhite,* deserves special thanks. Buy his book! Daniel Kelly and John Mahon were both encouraging at a time when I was just starting to let people see what I'd been nurturing for so long, and both offered honest and constructive criticism that boosted my confidence in the idea of trying to get it published.

Pivotally, Robin Wade of Wade and Doherty Literary Agency saw enough in the script to have a go at selling it on my behalf, and Carolyn Caughey at Hodder and Stoughton saw enough to want to put it in front of paying readers. I am extraordinarily grateful to both of them. Their acceptance of the script for representation and then publication were revelatory moments for me.

Without all these influences, sources, critics and publishing professionals there would be no *Wounds of Honour,* nor the stories to follow in the *Empire* series as Marcus Valerius Aquila takes his fight for survival and revenge across the length and breadth of Emperor Commodus' imperium. To all mentioned, and to those I have omitted for reasons of space, for either instilling the idea of publication or for helping to make it happen, my heartfelt thanks.

HADRIAN'S WALL

AD 181

~~~~~ HADRIAN'S WALL

🏰 FORT

🏰 THREE MOUNTAINS

🏰 YEW TREE FORT

🏰 RED RIVER

🏰 ROARING RIVER

🏰 FORT COCIDIUS

🏰 HIGH SPUR

🏰 ASH TREE

🏰 THE HILL

🏰 CROOKED GLEN

🏰 WATERSIDE FORT

THE ROCKS

FAIR MEADOW

N

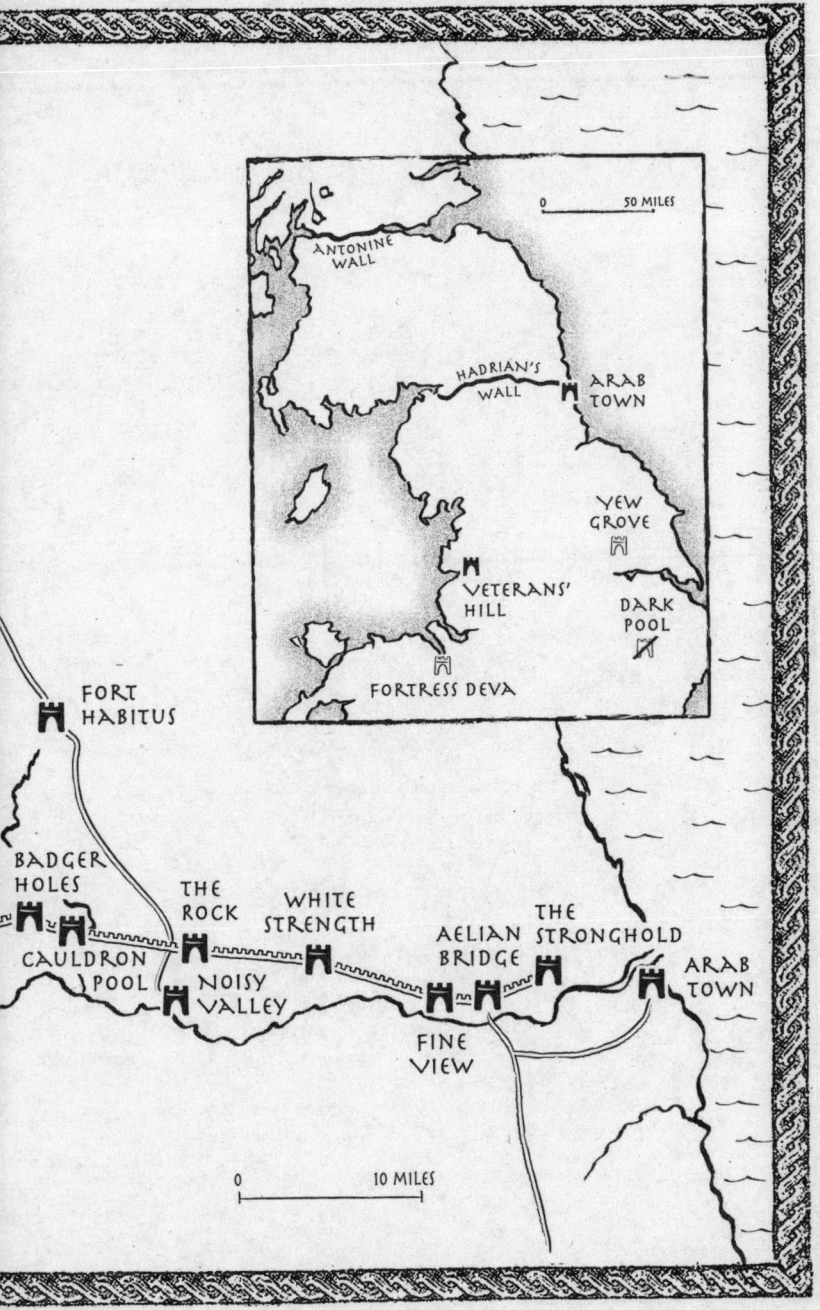

0   50 MILES

ANTONINE
WALL

HADRIAN'S
WALL

ARAB
TOWN

YEW
GROVE

VETERANS'
HILL

DARK
POOL

FORTRESS DEVA

FORT
HABITUS

BADGER
HOLES

THE
ROCK

WHITE
STRENGTH

AELIAN
BRIDGE

THE
STRONGHOLD

CAULDRON
POOL

NOISY
VALLEY

ARAB
TOWN

FINE
VIEW

0   10 MILES

Preface

November, AD 181

A brisk autumnal breeze stirred the leaves lining the forest floor, the sharp gust lifting a handful of discarded foliage into a brief dancing spiral before leaving it to flutter its way back to the ground. Padding softly over the shadow-dappled ground, a small hunting party advanced slowly out of the forest's gloom with spears held ready to throw. The men stepped with deliberate care, each foot lifted slowly and placed back on to the leafy carpet with smooth delicacy. Their movements were unconsciously coordinated, each man obviously familiar with his fellows' actions from long practice. Calgus, tribal leader of the Selgovae and undisputed ruler of the free northern tribes, was doing what he usually did to relax when he wasn't roaming the lands north of the Roman wall, pushing forward his preparations for the coming war. Accompanied by his five-man bodyguard, Calgus was hunting wild boar.

While his rule of the land to the north of the Roman wall that split Britannia into two halves was absolute, by right of both blood and simple domination of the other tribal leaders, the presence of his closest protectors was an obvious necessity. With a brooding imperial presence barely fifty miles to the south, it was prudent to assume the worst even in something as simple as a day's hunting.

'The pigs seem to have our scent, my lord, either that or something else has put them to fright.'

The speaker spat his disgust into the leaves. Another man, stepping softly across the leafy ground beyond him, nodded, keeping his eyes fixed to their front.

'Aye. If this carries on we'll be reduced to roasting hedgehogs.'

Calgus chuckled softly, hefting his spear as if rediscovering its balance.

'You know the rules, Fael. We eat only what we kill in open hunt. If you want to put meat on the fire this evening then keep your wits about you and your spear ready to throw. You might offer a prayer to Cocidius while you're at it. Pray for a big stag to wander our way. And you, Caes, for all that the local animal population isn't jumping on to your pigsticker, you wouldn't want to be anywhere else on a fine crisp day like this, now, would you?'

Caes grimaced, making a stabbing motion with his spear to emphasise his point.

'I'd rather be hunting Romans, my lord.'

Fael smiled across at Calgus, raising his eyebrows into his 'here we go again' face. They were used to the bodyguard's bloodthirsty hatred of their former overlords. Calgus winked at him before speaking, taking his eyes off the surrounding forest for a moment.

'Yes, Caes, as you never tire of telling us. When we finally get the tribes to go to war with them I'll free you from this tiresome duty and put you in the front rank of the warband, give you the chance to swing an axe with the other champions and . . .'

Caes, turning to reply with a wry smile, lurched backwards with the sudden impact of a hunting arrow which punched its vicious barbed-iron head into his chest with a sound like a spear driven hard into a boar's ribs. He stared down stupidly at the arrow's protruding shaft for a moment before dropping first to his knees, then on to all fours. Beyond him, Fael toppled backwards into the leaves with an arrow through his throat, a bright fan of blood spraying across the forest floor.

Calgus turned back to his front and hefted his spear, aware that he was hugely vulnerable whether he fought or ran. The hidden archers loosed another pair of arrows into the men to his left while the remaining bodyguards were still looking for targets for their own spears. His last companion fell as he bounded forward to defend his king, his spear arcing uselessly into the trees in a last desperate throw as he went down with a pair of arrows in his chest. The king waited for a long moment for his turn to come, bracing for the arrows' impact, but none came. Thrusting his spear defiantly into the soft earth, he drew his sword, the scrape of metal loud in the sudden silence. He called out into the forest's deadening gloom, lifting the weapon into a fighting stance.

'Come on, then, let's get this done. Sword, spear or bow, it makes no difference to me. I can go to meet Cocidius knowing that whoever you are, however far you run, my people will hunt you down and gut you slowly for what you do today.'

After another moment's silence, with the only sound his own harsh breathing, figures broke from the cover of the forest's scrubby bushes. Four men stood, two slinging bows across their backs and drawing swords, two carrying spears ready to throw. The latter advanced to within easy throwing range and halted, keeping him under constant threat, while the other two men followed with more leisure. One of them, his face obscured by a deep hood, spoke out while the other, a black-bearded athlete with a long sword at his belt, stood impassively beside him.

'So, Calgus. It seems that we have you at something of a disadvantage.'

His Latin was cultured, almost urbane.

The Briton laughed, disturbingly relaxed in the face of levelled spears.

'So, Roman, you've come to talk. And there I was bracing myself for your blade.'

The hooded figure nodded slowly.

'Oh yes, you're *just* as the stories tell. I've just slaughtered your bodyguard . . . well, most of them . . .'

He pointed to Caes, still helpless on hands and knees, a thin line of bloody drool trickling from his mouth.

'Finish that one.'

His companion flashed out his blade and stepped forward, stabbing down into the helpless Briton's exposed neck, then stepped back with the sword held ready. Calgus stood completely still, watching the act impassively. The hooded man spoke again.

'Better . . . and yet there you stand, as relaxed as if we were your oldest friends and not foreign assassins with your life at the points of our spears and your brother warriors dead at our hands. Well, Calgus, for all your obviously genuine bravado, whether you live or die is as yet not clear. Not even to me . . . A word to my rather rough-edged colleague here will have your guts steaming in the leaves, without very much thought and certainly without any remorse at all. You can be a problem removed for Rome in the blink of an eye, or an ally for one particular Roman over the next few months. Choose the former and you'll end your days here with minimal honour and no dignity. Choose the latter and you'll stand to win a prize beyond that of any king of this land over the last hundred years.'

The Briton narrowed his eyes, seeking to discern the truth in his ambusher's eyes.

'What prize?'

'An eagle, Calgus, an imperial legion's standard, and quite possibly the head of that legion's commander to boot. So, king of "free Britannia", are you minded to discuss a bargain with me, or would you rather negotiate with this barbarian's blade?'

'You seem to leave me without much of a choice. What token do I have of your sincerity, if this is a deal to be made at the point of your sword? And how do you know I'll keep it?'

The hooded man nodded to his companion, who struck at the nearest of the spearmen with unexpected speed and dropped him into the leaves with his throat opened, then reversed his sword and ducked under the other's spear-thrust. He punched his blade's point through the man's ribs with one powerful thrust, then twisted the sword quickly and ripped it free, the open wound spraying blood across his booted feet as the man fell helplessly to the forest floor and started to bleed out.

'You'll be needing some sign of your victorious struggle with your would-be assassins if your people aren't to smell a rat. I trust you can spin a colourful yarn to explain how you cheated your killers? And I know you'll keep the bargain if you make it – the inducements I'm offering are too strong for you to do anything else. Now, make your mind up, Calgus. Shall we be partners in your long-planned war on my people?'

Calgus spat into the leaves.

'For all the bad taste in my mouth, I will entertain your scheme.'

'Good. Now give me that flashy brooch that's holding your cloak closed. Don't worry, you'll see it again in another place . . .'

Calgus unpinned the brooch, an intricately worked gold replica of a shield, decorated with a swirling pattern, a polished piece of amber in place of the shield's metal boss, dropping it on to the outstretched palm. The hooded man turned away, calling back a parting comment over his shoulder while his companion backed away beside him, sheathing his sword and taking the bow from its place on his shoulder. He nocked an arrow and lifted the bow in readiness to shoot, deterring any thought of pursuit.

'You will see me again, Calgus, but not before you have your people in the field with death in their hearts.'

The two men merged with the forest's shaded depths and were lost to the king's eyes. He stood staring after them for a long moment before turning back to his fallen companions.

'Death in their hearts, Roman? That won't be hard to arrange.'

I

Februarius, AD 182

One of the front rank spotted them first, a good three dozen men silhouetted against the afternoon's bright skyline where the road rose to surmount a ridge that crossed their path in its long descent from the Pennines' eastern shoulder. He shouted a warning in a voice made hoarse by urgency. The small detachment's commander, a veteran watch officer with a face seamed by experience, stopped in mid-stride and followed the man's pointing arm, taking a moment to measure the depth of their predicament. When the road had risen to its previous vantage points he'd seen no other troops in front or behind them, just the plodding mule cart they'd passed an hour ago, now far behind them. That many barbarians would make short work of his sixteen men, and the legionaries' heavy armour ruled out any chance that they could outpace their ambushers back down the road to the south. Dropping his pack on to the verge, he drew his sword and pointed with it towards the distant enemy. Unless he kicked his dithering troops into activity quickly the tiny unit would shatter before the barbarians got within spear-throw.

'Piss buckets and shields! Form a line!'

He kicked one of the nearest men in the backside to reinforce his point. Hard.

'*Fucking move!*'

The legionaries shed their pack yokes at the roadside and fumbled to free shields slung across their backs with fingers ed numb by fear, quickly forming a thin line across the road. Helmets, previously hanging round their necks, were slid over their heads, the cheek-pieces adding a much-needed martial brutality to faces suddenly pale with terror. The watch officer stalked out in front of them, sword still drawn.

'Eyes on me! *On me!*'

The legionaries unwillingly dragged their gaze away from the advancing barbarians, now streaming down the shallow slope a few hundred paces away.

'Don't worry, you lot are so pretty compared to the local girls, this bunch are probably looking for a *shag* rather than a fight.'

One or two of them smiled wanly, which was better than nothing.

'And they fucked up by giving us time to get dressed up for the party. So, *when* I give the order, throw your spears, air your blades and get ready for them to hit your shields. *Use* your shields to throw them back! *Don't* leave the line. They want you to fight alone, outnumbered three to one, or to run so's they can spear you in the dog blossom. *Your* best chance . . .'

He slapped a man whose eyes had wandered back to the advancing Britons.

'On *me*! Your *only* chance is to stay in the line, and keep parrying and thrusting like you've done a thousand times in drills. They *will* give it up once they know we won't be a pushover. I will be behind you, and I *will* step in for the first man that falls! Spears . . . *ready!*'

Stalking round to the line's rear, he looked at the ground, gauging from the number of spreading dark patches in the road's dust how many of his men had already lost control of their bladders. There was enough piss steaming in the winter's chill air that their ability even to wait in line for the barbarian charge was hanging in the balance. They would all be dead inside of five minutes, he realised, mentally shrugging his shoulders and getting ready to give a decent account of himself. The men that the detachment was escorting had dismounted from their horses, the stocky veteran and his younger, taller companion something of a mismatched pair. Bloody civilians. At least they had a means of escape.

'If you're going to ride for help, this would be a good time!'

The older man, a legion veteran if the watch officer was guessing correctly, simply smiled back, green eyes twinkling out of a weatherbeaten face still ruddy despite the prospect of imminent death. He was evidently in his late forties, and from the quality of his clothing comfortably well off, cloak pulled across his chest and draped across one shoulder in the military style. While the younger civilian had accompanied the detachment since leaving the fortress at Dark Pool, three days' march to the south, the older man had ridden into the small fort that had sheltered them the previous night, arriving well after the sun's setting. His apparent lack of concern at the danger of meeting robbers on the road had caused more than a few raised eyebrows among the more experienced troops, despite the chain-mail vest beneath his cloak, the short infantry-pattern sword hanging at his waist and the purposeful way in which he conducted himself.

'I'm Rufius, formerly an officer with the imperial Sixth Legion. I never ran away from a fight in twenty-five years of service, and I won't break that habit now ... Besides, we'll see this lot off easy enough.'

The watch officer nodded slowly.

'Fair enough. What about you?'

The younger man shook his head grimly, too tense for humour, drawing a long-bladed cavalry sword with a glimmer of polished iron. The watch officer wondered just how much use that was going to be, given that its owner seemed to be barely out of his teens. His voice when he spoke was strong enough, though, without any hint of the quaver that might have been expected given the circumstances.

'Marcus . . . Marcus Valerius Aquila. I won't be running away either.'

The veteran soldier alongside him nodded approvingly, unsheathing his sword, and gestured to the legionaries' line.

'Shall we?'

The watch officer shrugged, turning back to face the oncoming warband.

'It's your funeral. Stay with me, you're now my reserve. When a man goes down, you go into the line in his place. Right, detachment, spears ready to throw . . . *wait for it!*'

The barbarians' trot had become a run now, closing the remaining distance between them quickly. Half a dozen of them were carrying axes, great tree-cutting blades that would cleave a man down to his waist or lop off a limb, armour or no armour. They were close enough for details to stand out now, lime-washed hair standing stiff from their heads, blue patterns swirling across their faces and jewellery flashing brightly in the afternoon's pale sun, close enough for their harsh battle cries to raise his neck hairs. This was no chance encounter, but a tribal warband dressed and tooled up for a fight, probably fired up by the local beer too, eyes wide and teeth bared in snarls of eager anticipation. The detachment's line shivered, more than one man starting to shrink backwards at the prospect of imminent brutal death. Before their collective breaking point was reached the veteran stepped up to their rear, dimpling the skin of the rearmost man's neck with the point of his sword. He spoke in a matter-of-fact tone, loudly enough for the detachment to hear him above the growing din of the approaching barbarians.

'*Back* in line, sonny, or those blue-nosed bastards won't get the chance to do you.'

More than one man looked round at him wide eyed, while the legionary in question inched forward again. One or two of the older salts, the men that already knew, and with grim resignation accepted, that their lives were about to become short and interesting whether they fought or ran, smiled in quiet recognition and raised their shields slightly in unconscious reaction to the voice of command. The watch officer nodded his head with respect, keeping his eyes on the charging barbarians and raising his voice to be heard above their harsh cries.

'Wait for it . . . Spears . . .'

As the watch officer opened his mouth to order the spears thrown, in the last seconds before the Britons would career into the flimsy shield wall, a sudden flurry of movement at the forest edge fifty paces to their left caught his eye. He snapped his attention back to the more urgent events happening less than twenty paces from his men's shields.

'Throw! *Throw!*'

The legionaries hurled their spears into the oncoming mass of men, dropping two of them in screaming heaps and dragging down the shields of half a dozen others, then drew their swords and braced to receive the charge. With a clash of metal on steel the barbarians' rush collided with his men's defence. Sheer weight of numbers forced the line back half a dozen steps before the desperate legionaries managed to absorb the momentum. Only the slight slope favouring their defence had saved them from being overwhelmed by the impact, the watch officer estimated. He stepped back behind them to keep his position, watching with amazement as armoured men started to emerge from the trees behind their attackers. The initial screaming and shouting of the charge and contact had died away, and both sides fought in almost total silence, broken only by the rasp of laboured breathing and the occasional grunt of exertion or scream of pain.

To his front a man staggered dying out of the line, a two-stepper if ever he'd seen one, his throat ripped out in a fountain of hot blood whose coppery stink filled his nostrils. The men to either side of the sudden gap in the line inched together, unable to properly fill the dying man's empty place. As the casualty sprawled full length on the road's cobbled surface, twitching out his life in a quickly spreading pool of his own blood, Rufius shouldered his younger companion aside, grabbed the fallen shield and stepped into his place. Battering aside a vicious axe blow with the shield, he stepped forward with a speed and grace that belied his grey hair to gut its owner with a swift twisting stab of his short sword as the tribesman struggled to regain his balance. Clutching at his steaming entrails, the barbarian fell to his knees, staring with horror at the horrific wound with a rising wail of distress.

Another of the small detachment went down, an axe buried deep in his shoulder while its blue-painted owner wrestled frantically with the handle, trying to prise the blade free. In a second Marcus Valerius Aquila was in the gap, stooping to grab the fallen man's infantry sword with his left hand even as he slid the cavalry sword up beneath the axeman's ribs in a perfect killing thrust, getting a face full of blood as the price for his successful attack. Chopping away a spear-thrust from his left with the borrowed weapon, he swiftly kicked the dying barbarian off his sword, using the freed blade to hack off the spearman's hand at the wrist before turning his wrist over to swing the long sword backhanded, and neatly sever the head of another attacker on his right. Stepping back into the line to regain his balance, the borrowed infantry sword held forward in his left hand, the longer sword held farther back to level the points of the two weapons, he paused for a moment, breathing hard with the sudden effort, his eyes wide with the shock of combat but still seeking new targets. The barbarians closest to him edged cautiously back from the fight, almost comically wary of the sudden threat from the twin blades.

From the rear of the warband a guttural voice shouted harshly in broken British over the clash of steel, a sword pointing at the retired officer's place in the line.

'Kill officer! Kill *him*!'

Distracted from his open-mouthed appraisal of Marcus's swordplay by movement in the periphery of his vision, the watch officer found his attention dragged back to the detachment's left, where the newcomers from the forest were advancing quickly to combat the barbarian flank and rear. The ten men ran quickly to within a dozen paces, threw their spears into the unsuspecting enemy's rear, then drew their swords, and, screaming bloodlust, went to work on their unprotected backs. Seizing his fleeting chance with both hands, as the tribesmen closer to his men started looking back over their shoulders in bewilderment at the screams from their dying comrades, the watch officer gave the only command possible.

'Counter-attack! Boards and swords, punch and thrust! Get into them, you dozy bastards!'

The response was almost uncomprehending, the product of a thousand mindless practice drills. The legionaries punched hard with the bosses of their shields at the Britons' faces, then stepped forward a pace with a collective thrust of their short swords. Two of the distracted tribesmen went down screaming, while several others edged back, allowing the line time and room to repeat the attack. The warband's leader turned to face their new assailants, spearing one of them with a powerful throw, drew his sword and roared defiance as he advanced into their line. A massive soldier with a crested helmet stepped out to meet him, slapping the sword-thrust aside with an almost casual flick of his shield before lunging his own weapon deep into the barbarian's chest in one swift flowing movement, twisting it to free the blade as he brutally stamped the dying man off its length. A lone tribesman turned and ran at the sight, joined a second later by another. Like the gradual collapse of an overloaded dyke, another two ran after them, then five, at which point the remainder simply turned and fled. They left a dozen dead and dying men on the ground.

The surviving Romans, half of the legionaries sporting a wound of some kind or other, leant breathless on their shields and watched them run, happy enough to let their enemy escape unhindered when a minute before they had been facing impending death. The watch officer walked across to the newcomers, followed at a discreet distance by Rufius, while Marcus dropped the infantry sword beside its dead owner and wiped the drying blood from his own weapon, suddenly exhausted. The other detachment's leader, a dark-bearded athlete of a man with the horsehair crest of a chosen man on his helmet, was staring after the retreating warband with a look that seemed to combine disgust and regret.

'Whoever you lads are, you have the thanks of the Sixth Legion. If you hadn't come out of the trees we were dead meat. You must have balls the size of apples to do what you just did with . . .'

The watch officer's flow of gratitude dried up as he realised that the other man wasn't paying him any attention, but was still watching the retreating Britons. After a moment the chosen man spoke, flicking indifferent eyes over the legionaries.

'You'd better tell your officers to stop sending anything smaller than a full century up the road to Yew Grove. Next time you won't be so lucky.'

He turned to his own men.

'Take heads, then get ready to leave. We'll march to the fortress in company with this lot. You two, you didn't kill anyone that I saw so you can make a sling to carry Hadrun up to the fort. We'll put him underground somewhere he can't be dug up again.'

Rufius caught his arm, stepping back with open palms as the heavy-framed man swung back to face him with an angry look.

'No offence, Chosen, but we're only trying to thank you for what you did. Most men in your position would have given serious thought to letting us get on with things on our own . . .'

Marcus overcame his momentary exhaustion to raise his head and study the other detachment's leader and his troops carefully in the moment's silence that followed, intrigued by his first sight of native troops in the field. They wore chain mail, unlike the plate armour protecting the legionaries, and their weapons and clothing seemed of a lower quality. He noted, nevertheless, the same hard-edged efficiency in their movements, the same lean wiriness. Like their legion colleagues, these were men that had learnt the hard way not to waste energy on non-essentials. The chosen man's eyes narrowed, his face expressionless.

'We're Tungrians, *Grandfather*, and we were doing our duty, nothing more, nothing less. We were moving quietly through the forest, and found that lot waiting by the road before they saw us. After that it was only a matter of pulling back and waiting for someone to come along. When we saw the size of your party it was obvious that we would have to help you out . . . although I doubt it was worth the loss of one of my men.'

Rufius smiled crookedly at the bald statement.

'I understand better than you might imagine. And nevertheless, from one fighting man to another, you have my respect.'

He turned away, clapping an arm round the watch officer's shoulder.

'And as for you, my friend, I'd call that a nice little action. I'll be sure to mention your name to my friends in the camp, see if we can't get you a brush for the top of your piss bucket. For now we'd better get the wounded sorted out and then push on to the Grove, don't you think?'

Sorting the wounded out was easy enough, despite the only bandage carrier in the party having lost three fingers of his right hand to a barbarian sword, which made him of use only in directing treatment rather than providing it. Two men were dead, the two-stepper and the axe victim, the latter with the huge blade still embedded deep in his upper chest. They were stripped of their weapons, armour and boots and hidden from casual view in the trees to await collection by cart the next day. The Tungrians, meanwhile, with pointed remarks about leaving no man behind on a battlefield, ostentatiously rigged a sling with which to carry their own casualty away with them. Of the remaining troops three were incapable of walking, but by putting the lighter two on one of the civilians' horses, and one with a nasty-looking axe wound on the other, they were able to resume their march. The barbarian wounded were finished off without ceremony by the watch officer, his swift economical sword-thrusts removing any chance of their survival. At length Marcus and Rufius fell in behind their legionary protectors for the remaining march, while the Tungrians, several with freshly decapitated heads dangling jauntily from pack yokes by their knotted hair, in turn fell in behind them.

Marcus coughed politely and turned his face to Rufius's after a moment's march. He was tall, overtopping the veteran by a full head, slightly stringy in build but with the sinewy promise of muscle to come.

'Yes, my friend?'

'I'd be grateful to better understand a thing or two. If you'd be willing to talk?'

Something in the younger man's voice made Rufius look at him properly, the taut line of the young man's jaw muscles betraying the fact that he was still dealing with the aftermath of the skirmish.

'Mars forgive me but I'm an unfeeling old bastard. This was your first proper fight?'

The younger man nodded tautly.

'Gods below, how quickly the habits of command leave a man . . . I always made a point of grabbing the first-timers after a fight, to humour or slap them out of their shock at tasting another man's blood on their lips for the first time, and to congratulate them for surviving with the right number of arms and legs. Although I am forced to point out that for a first-timer you did better than just survive. You made a mess of more than one of our attackers without even the benefit of a shield for protection. Those skills won't have come easily . . .'

Above his smile, he raised an interrogatory eyebrow, noting that the younger man's jaw relaxed a fraction.

'You can tell me more about your prowess with two swords later. I believe you had a question?'

'I was wondering why these other soldiers didn't take all of the barbarian heads, if that's the local custom?'

The veteran glanced back at the auxiliary troops behind them.

'The Tungrians? When you know more about the local troops you'll understand better. Legions get moved around. They stay in one place for a year, or even ten, but they always move on again. There's always a campaign that needs another legion, a frontier to be shored up, or just some idiot with a purple stripe on his tunic who wants to be emperor. That means that the legions never stay anywhere long enough to settle into the local traditions, so it's Judaea one year, Germania the next. Besides, serving in a legion is like being a priest for a particularly jealous god – complicated rites, special sacrifices and offerings, your own way of doing things. In a legion the senior officers, the camp prefect and the senior centurions, they make sure that *their* way of doing things always comes first.

'Auxiliaries, though, they stay put where they've been based for the most part, unless there's a major campaign on, and even then they'll usually come back home again. They put down roots, soak up the local lore, start worshipping local gods. Basically they go native. Now *those* lads, they were originally recruited in Tungria, across the sea, but they've been here on the Wall since it was built sixty years ago, more or less, so now there's no real Tungrians, just a lot of their grandsons mixed in with the local lads. They take heads because that's local tradition too, but they also have a code of honour that would shame a six-badge centurion, and they don't, *ever*, take the head of a man they haven't fought and killed face to face.

'Anyway, enough about the Tungrians, I'm sure you'll learn all about them in due course. Tell me, what brings you to the forsaken northern wastes of this cold, wet pisspot of a country . . .'

He looked calculatingly at the younger man, as if assessing him properly for the first time, despite the fact that they had ridden side by side for half the day, albeit mostly in silence.

'Brown eyes, black hair, a nice suntan . . . I'd say you were Roman born and bred, and yet here you are in Britannia getting cold, wet and bloody with the rest of us. Your name again?'

'Marcus Valerius Aquila. And yours?'

'Quintus Tiberius Rufius, once a soldier, now simply a supplier of fine food and superior-quality equipment to the

Northern Command. Soon enough you'll be chewing on an especially nasty piece of salted pork and thinking to yourself, "Jupiter, I wish I had a jar of Rufius's spicy fish pickle in front of me right now." Anyway, now we're introduced . . . ?'

He raised a questioning eyebrow. The younger man shrugged in apparent self-deprecation.

'There's not much to tell in all truth. I'm travelling to Yew Grove to join the Sixth Legion for my period of military service.'

Rufius smiled wryly.

'Exciting stuff for a man of your age, I'd imagine. Cut free from the tedium of your life at home to travel across the empire to the edge of civilisation, and the chance to serve with the best legion in the army to boot? You'll look back on these as the best days of your life, I can promise you that much.'

'I'm sure you're right. What I know for a fact right now is how much I'm looking forward to my first proper bath since we left Dark Pool. This country has altogether too much rain for my liking, and the wind chills the bones no matter how a man wraps his cloak.'

Rufius nodded.

'No one knows that better than I. Twenty-five years I humped up and down this damp armpit of a country in the service of the emperor, getting wet and freezing cold, living in draughty barracks and kicking disgruntled native recruits into shape for the legion. I should mention that I served with the Sixth, second cohort, first century.'

The younger man inclined his head respectfully.

'First century. You were the cohort's First Spear?'

'I was. They were the happiest four years of my life, all things considered. I had six hundred spears under my command, and absolutely no one to stop me turning them into the best troops in the whole of this miserable country.

I was master of my chosen trade, and no one got in my way. No tribune or quartermaster had the balls to disagree with me, that's the truth.'

He tapped the younger man on the shoulder to reinforce his point.

'But let me warn you, this country grows on a man like fungus on a tree, slowly, stealthily, until suddenly you can't imagine life anywhere else. I had the chance to head back home when my term was up, but I just couldn't see the point of having to adapt to a place without a perpetual covering of cloud and a population of blue-painted savages. This place has become my home, and if you're here long enough it'll be the same with you. Perhaps your family has a history of service hereabouts?'

'My father has . . .'

Rufius raised an eyebrow, smiling.

'Connections?'

'. . . *history* in this part of the world. My grandfather commanded the legion for three years before he came back to Rome, and my father was a broad stripe tribune on the Sixth's staff. Military service runs in the family, all the way back to the Republic. Although my father wasn't really a military man, even by his own admission, and much to my grandfather's disappointment. He's a man of words, not action. Mind you, I've heard that he can reduce a man to silence without even raising his voice when he speaks on the floor of the Senate. I wish I had the same eloquence.'

Rufius nodded sagely.

'Two senior officers in the family, and both of them served with the best legion in the empire. You're a young man of even greater privilege than was at first apparent. Which reminds me . . .'

'Yes?'

'I caught a glimpse or two of you back there, in between

fighting off pissed-up barbarians who were convinced I was still under the eagle. I'm still curious as to where you learned to throw your blade around like that?'

Marcus blushed slightly.

'When it was decided that I would serve with the Sixth, almost before I can remember, my father decided to make sure I wouldn't make a fool of myself with a sword in my hand. He paid a freed gladiator to teach me a few things . . .'

Rufius gave him a sardonic look.

'A few things, eh? Well, new friend, if we get any time to spare in Yew Grove, you can teach me one or two of your "few things" . . .'

Just over an hour later they marched through the fortress's town, across the river bridge, and stopped in front of the massive main gate. Standing to one side to allow the wounded to be lifted groaning from their horses, Tiberius Rufius exchanged a few words with the gate guard, then took Marcus firmly by the arm.

'You can't report to the legatus yet, he's out on manoeuvres with part of the legion. Why don't we sort the horses out, then visit the bathhouse, get a decent meal and see how much the local food has improved since I was last here? On me, as celebration of our survival this afternoon. We'll stay in an inn owned by an old friend of mine, like me discharged and unable to leave the place after so many years. He joined all the other poor bastards that have taken root here for want of anywhere better to be, and now he runs the best guest house in the Yew Grove vicus.'

He smiled easily with the memory.

'Petronius Ennius was standard-bearer of the second cohort when I was First Spear, built like a fortress latrine, just like most statue-wavers. We made a fine pair when we could

work a leave pass at the same time, had the women squirming
in their seats when *we* passed by! I get the time to stay in
his inn all too rarely these days. Come on, let's go and get
the blood washed off these chariot-pullers and see they're
fed and watered, I feel the sudden need for a bath and a
drink.'

The innkeeper greeted Rufius warmly, clapping him on the
back with a hand the size of a dinner plate.

'Back already, Tiberius Rufius? Only a few days ago you
were telling me that the quality of my wine was only fit for
removing rust from armour, now you can't stay away from
the place. Although I can see from the state of your tunic
that *someone*'s upset you recently. Well then, what's the story?'

He listened intently to Rufius's retelling of the ambush,
laughing quietly when his friend recounted having to threaten
the Sixth's legionaries to keep them in line.

'Nothing changes, does it? I remember you having to do
much the same thing to keep one or two of our weaker-
kneed sisters in their places when the blue-noses had their
last little revolt.'

At the end of the story he pursed his lips, whistling to
show his appreciation of their escape.

'You were lucky, old friend, very lucky. If that tent party
of auxiliaries hadn't chanced on you . . .'

Rufius nodded sagely, a dark look in his eye.

'I know. We were carrion. Mind you, if that was good
fortune I still wonder just what chance put those tribesmen
in our path.'

'Yes . . . Well, enough of your boasting, you haven't
introduced me to your bloodstained young friend . . .'

'This is Marcus Valerius Aquila. A fellow traveller from the
south, and soon to be a brother in the service of Mars, all the
way from Rome itself. And, despite the slightly travel-worn

appearance of his clothes, not to mention the fine pattern of dried blood across his face, a man of influence, promised a position on the Sixth's staff.'

The innkeeper turned back to Marcus with a gravely inclined head.

'My apologies, a young *gentleman*. So, will you both be staying, sirs?'

Rufius pulled a mock grimace.

'Despite the hideous expense of your lodging, the mediocre quality of your board and the watery nature of your wine, yes, we both need lodging for the night.'

'Excellent. My man Justus will see to your horses and take the baggage to your rooms. You take a couple of hours to sweat out that blood, and I'll have two of my very best roasted duck waiting for you, cooked in their own fat and served with a sauce of wild honey, red wine and herbs. And for you, Rufius, because I know your needs of old, I'll crack open my last amphora of a rather special Iberian red. How does *that* sound?'

As the pair made their way through the town towards the fortress baths, clean tunics under their arms, the familiar sound of hobnailed boots clattering against the road's surface swelled behind them, echoing through the narrow streets until the sound and its reverberations merged into a constant roar. The windows of the buildings to either side of the road, shutters closed against the cold, were quickly opened to allow the curious to look into the street. Several of the female onlookers obviously shared a keen professional interest in the arrival of a body of soldiers at the fortress to judge from the way that hair was hastily let down and, in at least one case, breasts placed on open display. The standard-bearer and leading century of a legion cohort swept around the corner behind them at the march, heading for the fortress gates in the dying light of dusk. Rufius pulled Marcus into a doorway and off the street as the leading troops poured past, rank after rank of soldiers pounding up the street with their heads back to suck air into their bursting lungs, belting out a bawdy marching song.

... my brother keeps a restaurant with bedrooms up the stairs, but none of them will talk to me 'cause I'm a legionnaire!

Rufius smiled with fond memories, his lips moving to the song as the legionaries kept coming in a seemingly unending column. Centurions and chosen men stalked alongside their centuries, shouting commands at their men to carry their fucking spears straighter and stop eyeing the bloody prostitutes, while century after century pounded past. As had been the case with the troops who had escorted him up the road from Dark Pool, Marcus found their appearance disappointing after the spit and polish he'd got used to in the Guard. Shields were clean, but not shining, armour and weapons lacked the finely detailed workmanship to which he was accustomed, and their clothing was utilitarian – rough leather boots, heavy woollen tunics and coarse woven leggings all spattered with mud from the road.

His eye was caught by a group of horsemen, however, whose equipment looked every bit as fine as that he was used to, their polished cuirasses tied together with clean ribbon. Tiberius Rufius pointed at them and put his mouth close to Marcus's ear to shout over the din, coughing at the dust kicked up by the units' passing.

'It must be at least half of the Sixth, out for fitness training. That's the legatus and his staff, with an escort from the legion's cavalry. They're drafted in from an Asturian cohort from up north on the Wall, but most of them are German.

Funny how the roughest barbarians always look the smartest once they're given uniforms . . .'

Marcus nodded distractedly, watching the legion's commander ride past in the midst of his staff tribunes, grim-faced cavalrymen to their front and rear. The man's head turned as his horse passed the doorway, and he nodded recognition at Tiberius Rufius as he passed out of sight. Marcus looked at the older man, his eyebrows raised.

'You know the legatus?'

'I've sold the Sixth locally bred cattle, and given him a little information about the border region. What else can an old soldier do but help out his former mates?'

They stood in silence as the rest of the column ground past, waiting until the last century had passed over the bridge and into the fortress before leaving their doorway and stepping out into the near-dark street and continuing on their way. The garrison's bathhouse was as large as was necessary to cope with the cleansing and leisure needs of several thousand legionary infantry, the imposing halls lit with hundreds of large torches.

Changed out of their battle-stained clothes, the two men oiled their naked bodies and slipped on wooden-soled bath shoes to protect their feet from the hot floors. They went through the chilly frigidarium and into the steam room, finding seats among the dozens of soldiers who sat perspiring in the clammy heat. Tiberius Rufius pointed to a floor mosaic depicting Mars in full armour, and brandishing an infantry sword.

'That's your first god for the next few years! Who were you brought up to respect the most?'

'The household shrine is dedicated to Mercury, so that's who I always prayed to first.'

'A good choice in a merchant's house. Mercury won't begrudge Mars your attention while you're in the service, though. Always be sure to seek his blessings before you embark on any course that may end in battle. *Jupiter*, it's hot. I can *feel* the dirt being forced out of me. Scraper! Over here, boy!'

They endured the clammy heat for another fifteen minutes, luxuriating in the pleasure of a good sweat, and the chance to get the last of the barbarian blood out of their skins. Climbing into the hot bath for a moment to remove any residue, they went through to the hot room and settled down again. Tiberius Rufius bought them a small flask of wine and a small cake apiece, 'just to get our appetites up', and they sat in companionable silence, watching off-duty soldiers, some lifting weights in one corner of the room, others content just to play dice and drink wine, each man loudly invoking Fortuna's divine help before tossing the bone cubes. Almost dozing in the oppressive heat, Marcus opened an eye lazily as a magnificently muscled black-bearded man walked across the room, settling on to the bench opposite their resting place. He nudged Rufius with his elbow.

'Isn't that . . . ?'

'Yes, our saviour from this afternoon. Dubnus, wasn't it?'

'He looks like an ugly piece of work.'

Rufius frowned.

'I suspect there's more to the man than you'd guess from his outward appearance. You might find a chat with him educational. Perhaps he'll join us for a cup.'

He beckoned the other man to come across and join them. The Briton rose, padded across the floor and settled on his haunches facing the two, his thick black eyebrows raised in question above hard grey eyes. Marcus estimated his age to be about twenty-five years. The Briton nodded to Rufius, acknowledging his presence, but gave no sign of greeting to the younger man. Rufius returned the compliment, gesturing to the wine flask alongside him on the bench.

'Chosen, we were wondering if you would be willing to join us in a cup of wine, as recognition of your actions of this afternoon?'

The Briton regarded the pair with a level gaze before replying.

'I will not drink with a Roman.'

To Marcus's surprise, Tiberius Rufius's face muscles did not move as much as a twitch.

'You disappoint me, but it *is* your choice. Tell me, what is it that you have against my friend's illustrious city?'

The Briton's face twisted at the question.

'Your question surprises me. You've been here a while, to judge by your appearance. Surely you can see what they've done to this country – taken our lands, killed our forefathers and fucked our women.'

'So why do you serve in our *army*?'

The words were out of Marcus's mouth before he could control his reaction. The Briton swivelled his head to face him.

'I serve in the First Tungrian Cohort, *not* in your army. I defend my people from attack by the northern tribes. My people have no defence against them without the presence of the auxiliary cohorts.'

'No defence? With three legions within a few days' march?'

The man facing him smiled without mirth.

'Your legions defend Rome's interests – your mines, your farms, everything which makes *your* people rich. My people have grown soft in the time since you conquered us, and become used to living on the scraps from your table. Without men like me on the Wall, the northern tribes would raid our settlements many times in each year. Your legions wouldn't lift a sword until *Roman* interests were in danger. My thanks, Tiberius Rufius, but I will *not* drink with you today.'

Rising smoothly from his squatting position, the Briton

walked back to his former seat, settled on to the bench and closed his eyes. Tiberius Rufius watched him for a long moment, cocking an eyebrow at Marcus's pale, angry face.

'Hmmm. That *is* an interesting man, and I think we can now officially discount any possibility that he's stupid. Come on, let's drown that irritation in another cup of wine . . .'

Their bath complete, the two men dressed in their clean tunics and walked back to the inn for dinner. The duck promised by Ennius was brought to their table roasted to perfection and coated with a delicious sauce, and the red wine he poured for them was of the quality Marcus had become used to drinking at his father's table. Rufius poured cup after cup for him until, with a belated realisation that his face was suddenly feeling numb, and that he was losing the power to string together a coherent sentence, the younger man decided it was time he was in bed. As he staggered unsteadily up to his room, half carried by his new friend, he recalled, with the needle-sharp random insight of the truly drunk, a comment his companion had made hours before.

'Rufius . . . you said that Mercury was a good hous'hold god for a merchan'. *I* didn't tell you Father was a merchan' . . .'

The fact that he got no answer seemed to be of little importance at the time.

After putting the drunken Marcus to bed, Rufius, having deliberately rationed his wine intake to keep his wits intact, slipped back down the stairs. He handed Ennius a coin and left, strapping on his sword and taking up his pack. He walked through the torchlit streets to the river bridge and across, to the fortress's main gate. Challenged by the gate guards, he stood his ground confidently in the teeth of their levelled spears.

'You'd better fetch the duty centurion, boys, and look

lively about it. I've got an appointment inside, and it doesn't pay to keep Calidius Sollemnis waiting.'

The duty officer marched up, took a look at the veteran and waved him through the gate, raising a sardonic eyebrow to his deputy. At the entrance to the headquarters building he was brought up short at the main entrance by a tall blond man dressed in mud-spattered armour coming out past the sentries, his plumed helmet dangling by its chinstrap. Rufius stepped back, inclining his head with careful respect.

'Tribune Perennis, salutations. You've had a full day on the road, it appears.'

The other man dropped his hands to his hips in a confident stance.

'Tiberius Rufius. Well, don't you always manage to turn up when things get interesting? Doubtless merely coincidence, just as always seems to be the case. And yet we never see you out in the countryside, no matter how carefully we look.'

Rufius smiled gently, keeping his face neutral.

'Yes, Tribune, well, I like to move around with a degree of caution. You can never be sure just who's waiting to jump out on you in these troubled times. Only today I heard a man with a surprisingly German accent exhorting a bunch of drunken Brits to carve out my liver.'

The officer laughed quietly, with a faint smile that failed to touch his eyes.

'German, eh? How very interesting. Well, never fear, senior centurion, my Asturians will take care to look out for you on the road. Our paths will cross one day soon, of that I'm quite certain. Goodnight.'

Rufius watched him walk away with hard bright eyes, muttering so quietly under his breath that even the sentries' straining ears were frustrated.

'Not if I see you coming first, you cocky young bastard.'

★

A beaker of water in the face served well enough to wake Marcus from a seemingly endless nightmare of roads and hills. Rough hands pulled him from the bed, still dressed in the tunic and leggings he'd worn the previous night, putting him on his feet and holding him upright while his head swam. A disgusted voice cut through his daze.

'*Pissed!* Throw some more of that water over him.'

The sudden cold sting shocked him into a degree of consciousness. A pair of armoured and armed legionaries were holding an arm apiece to keep him vertical, while a centurion watched impatiently from the doorway, an oil lamp in one hand throwing unsteady shadows against the walls. He considered vomiting, but fought the impulse down after a moment of awful physical indecision.

'Waking up, are you, you little shit? Good, you've got two minutes to pack. After that, anything you haven't stowed gets left behind. You, take that sword and make sure he doesn't get a chance to grab it off you, he's dangerous behind a blade from what I've heard.'

The marble-hard face left no room for argument. Stuffing his travel clothes, left dirty on the room's chair for washing in the morning, into his saddlebag, Marcus checked that his purse was still in place at his belt.

'Ready? Right . . .'

His voice returned, hoarse from the wine's bite.

'Wait . . . where are you taking me?'

The centurion stepped across the tiny room to put his face close to Marcus's, close enough for his sour breath to register, and for grey whiskers to stand out of the black of his beard. He reached out a hand and, with cold, hard fingers, took the younger man's jaw in a firm grip.

'For a short and painful interview with the legatus, cumstain. After which I'd be happy to go a round or two with you in a closed room, you fucking traitor!'

'*What!?*'

'Shut your face! *Bring him!*'

The innkeeper was waiting grim faced outside the room. The centurion nodded to him.

'Pay your bill.'

Marcus numbly dropped coins into the outstretched palm.

'Petronius Ennius ... my friend Rufius ... ?'

Ennius shot him a hard stare, his mouth set in a grim line.

'Left straight after dinner. And well away from you, from the looks of things.'

The soldiers hustled him from the inn, moving briskly through the town's dark streets. Across the river bridge, through the main gate's man-sized wicket gate and into the fortress they marched, past sentries waiting at the parade rest for their dawn relief. A building loomed out of the torchlit gloom, the door watched by another pair of legionaries. Inside there was warmth and light, a mosaic floor and painted walls, pleasant enough to take the chill away from Marcus's skin in the few moments that he waited, still under close guard, in the house's hallway. Waiting for the officer's return, he spent several moments examining the quality of a wall painting representing the goddess Diana hunting with two dogs, but all the while he stared at the artist's handiwork, trying to affect an indifferent air, his mind raced frantically, trying to account for the sudden turn of events that saw him under armed guard where he should have been greeted as an equal. It was a circumstance for which he was completely unprepared, and he was sure that his disquiet was showing beneath the attempted veneer of confidence. Resolving to remain silent as to his mission for the time being, although the desire to end the charade pressed heavily on him, he awaited the officer's return, concentrating on a studied ignorance of the guards' curious stares. The centurion eventually returned, motioning the soldiers to stay where they were.

'Keep his belongings here and *don't* touch them, they might contain evidence against him. You, come with me.'

He followed the officer past yet another guard into a large office, hearing the door shut behind him. The centurion pointed to a spot on the room's floor, sliding his sword from its scabbard.

'Stand there and don't move. If you do move, I'll put my iron through your fucking spine. And don't speak unless you're asked to!'

Seated at the heavy wooden desk was a tired-looking man in his mid-thirties, his white tunic edged with the thick senatorial stripe, his black hair cut somewhat longer than was the formal military style. Marcus found his face strangely familiar for some reason, and wondered distractedly whether they had met before. Another, younger man, whose tunic bore the thinner equestrian stripe, lounged against the room's far wall, casting a calculating gaze over Marcus. Blond hair and piercing blue eyes hinted at northern European ancestry somewhere in his not too distant past. The seated man sat in silence for a moment, then spoke with a swift and practised formality.

'Marcus Valerius Aquila, I am Legatus Gaius Calidius Sollemnis of the Sixth Imperial Legion. This is Titus Tigidius Perennis, my senior tribune, who I've asked to attend this interview to act as a witness to my decisions. I've had you brought to my residence since I didn't want to do this in the headquarters building – too many eyes and ears, I'm afraid. Before we go any farther in this matter, I will declare an interest in your case – I was at one time a close friend of your father's, although we haven't spoken for some five or six years now. You look very much as your father did at your age . . .'

He raised a hand in pre-emption of any question.

'No, you're here to listen. Marcus Valerius Aquila, do you know why I ordered you to be brought here at this time?'

The opportunity was irresistible to a young man in desperate need of reassurance.

'No! Sir, I . . .'

The flat of the centurion's sword slapped his arm hard in admonishment.

'Answer the legatus's questions with a simple yes or no!'

'No.'

'So you have no idea of events in Rome of the past weeks?'

The urge to be sick returned, held in check only by the sudden return of the concerns he had managed to put to the back of his mind over the weeks of travel.

'No.'

'I see. Then I must inform you that your father was arrested three weeks ago, for the crime of plotting to assassinate the emperor. When did you leave Rome?'

Marcus's skin crawled with the revelation, and with the equally sudden realisation that he was in desperate danger. It was time to shed the deception that had accompanied him from Rome, to reclaim his identity before this went any further.

'The fifteenth day of the month of Januarius. Sir, I have . . .'

The blow fell again, harder this time.

'*Silence!*'

'I see. You arrived here only a day after the courier bearing the news of your father's crime. Good timing for the legion, though, to have the opportunity to arrest a traitor . . .'

'Arrest . . . ?'

Marcus thought he saw a brief narrowing of the legatus's eyes, but the man's face itself was set hard against him.

'Indeed. The son of an old friend you may be, but an

enemy of my emperor is an enemy of mine. I have no choice but to send you back to Rome to beg for the mercy of the throne. Do you have anything to say?'

'*Yes*, sir. Sir, I am a praetorian officer on detached courier duty, bearing a private dispatch for you from the emperor himself. I have been instructed to travel incognito, in order to ensure that the message remains confidential. My saddlebag contains a message container bearing the imperial seal, to be opened only by you. I know nothing of the events you describe, and have been following the direct orders of my superior officer in making this journey.'

The tribune leaning against the office wall spoke for the first time, his voice heavy with irony.

'Correction, citizen, you *were* a praetorian. The praetorian prefect rescinded your commission as soon as your absence *without* leave was linked to your father's crime. Your tribune was interrogated, and admitted taking money from your father in return for sending you away from Rome on a false errand. A very large amount of money, as it happens. He has already paid the appropriate penalty for consorting with enemies of the throne. The seal on your message container is nothing more than a good fake, and the container itself holds nothing more than a last letter from your father . . .'

'*Thank* you, Tigidius Perennis . . .'

The legatus fixed the tribune with a dark-eyed silencing stare. He held the stare until the younger man looked down at his boots, clearly intending to win the brief clash of wills with his junior.

'Perhaps your father expected that I would be in a position to protect you . . . but if he did it was a misguided expectation. In the light of his crime, you must return to Rome immediately to face trial in connection with his offence. You will be escorted to the main gate, where your horse will be waiting for you. You are instructed to return to Rome by the most direct route, deviating from that road for no reason. Failure to present yourself at the praetorian camp by a date no more than six weeks from now will result in your immediate loss of senatorial rank, and the declaration of your *entire* family as proletarians, to the most distant cousin, with confiscation of all assets. I'll send a message back by fast courier warning the praetorians of your return, and when they should expect your arrival. That is all.'

The centurion, sensing the numbness of shock in the young man's hesitation, grasped Marcus firmly by the upper arm, leading him out of the office and back to the waiting escort. They marched back out to the main gate, where the watch was being changed with all the usual noise and disturbance. The centurion looked around him at the ordered chaos, and then pulled Marcus into a small guardroom, dismissing the legionaries inside with the order to go off duty with their fellows. In the meagre yellow light of the oil lamps that lit the stone-walled room he seemed larger than he had in the brightly lit commander's residence, squat and menacing in the bulk of his armour. Marcus found his voice at last, slowly starting to recover from the initial shock and finding anger where there had initially been only fear.

'Is this where I get the beating you promised me earlier? Don't you need your men with you to make it completely one sided?'

The other man swept his helmet off, dropping it on to the table with a clatter, running a hand nervously across his balding scalp.

'Button it. We've got less than five minutes before your horse is ready, and I've had to bribe the stable master to get that much time.'

The sudden change in his tone put Marcus, who had been readying himself for a fight, off balance once more.

'What . . .'

The centurion prodded a broad finger into his chest, urgency fuelling his irritation.

'Shut up and *listen*! You're being turned loose, alone, before dawn, to make your disposal as easy as possible. You think it's usual for enemies of the state to be sent back to Rome alone, no matter what threats might be made to their families? Most criminals would think of their own necks before those of their loved ones. This is just a set-up to get you out of the way, out into the dark. You were *supposed* to get killed on the road yesterday, but the locals apparently managed to cock that one up. The men waiting out there for you now won't make the same mistake. You ride out of here alone, and you'll be lucky to get five miles before that bastard Perennis's tame cavalry cut-throats take you and slit your throat, steal your purse and your horse, and leave you in the dirt for the morning patrols to find. Do you fancy that for an epitaph, "Killed by robbers"?'

'No.'

'Well, that's a start. You know how to use a sword and shield on horseback?'

'Yes. I was trained in . . .'

'I know. Listen, half a mile down the road you'll come on a stunted tree growing over a large rock, on the right. Look behind the tree and you'll find a cavalry sword and shield. Ride on, as fast as the moonlight lets you, and stop for *nobody*. At the two-mile marker you'll be met by . . .'

A solid knock rattled the room's wooden door.

'Centurion! The traitor's horse is ready.'

The officer nodded at Marcus, grabbing his helmet and replacing it on his head before replying.

'Good! I'll bring the little turd out.'

He cocked a solid-looking fist.

'. . . you'll be met by friends. Sorry, but this needs to look like the real thing.'

The swift punch stung Marcus's right eye; the heavy slap that followed cut his upper lip against his teeth. The officer pulled him to his feet, whispering urgently in his ear.

'*Stop for no one until the two-mile marker!*'

'But who's meeting me?'

'You'll know when you get there! And once we're outside keep your mouth shut, unless you want me nailed up alongside you.'

He paused to fill his lungs.

'Right, you bastard traitor, let's be about it!!'

He slammed the door open, propelling Marcus through it with a hefty shove in the back.

'Here he is! Take a good look at a *traitor*!'

The incoming watch's centurion goggled at Marcus's face.

'You've had a go at him!'

'Yeah, but it was no fun. All he did was beg me to stop. Even *you* wouldn't have enjoyed it at all.'

The other man put his hands on his hips and laughed uproariously.

'I see what you mean. I doubt he'll offer any fight to the first robbers he meets.'

'Yeah, and since those Asturians are bum boys to a man it might be quite a morning for our friend here.'

He reached out, pushing Marcus's saddlebag at him.

'Go on, take your bag. It'll be a small compensation for the boys that have been out half the night waiting for you. Now get on your horse and bugger off. Open the gate!'

Marcus climbed on to the beast's back, eyeing the soldiers that surrounded him with a sense of complete powerlessness. A scent of violence filled his nostrils, the energy generated by men eager to deal out pain. The main gates opened with a ponderous swing as half a dozen legionaries strained against their weight. The centurion pointed out into the darkness beyond the gate's flickering torches.

'Right, piss off. I only hope they get the time to do a proper job on you! *Go!*'

He slapped the horse's rump, and the gate towers were suddenly behind Marcus as the animal bolted out into the pre-dawn gloom, across the bridge, past the houses and shops of the town and away down the dark road, pursued by the shouted insults of the gate guard.

2

Out on the open road, even without the magnifying effect of the tightly packed buildings, the sounds of Marcus's horse's hoofs on the road sounded deafening. He steered the animal on to the softer grass verge, diminishing the staccato clatter to a gentle patter. When the stunted tree loomed out of the slowly lightening murk he dismounted, finding the promised sword and shield hidden in a tangle of roots that curled sinuously over the massive boulder around which the oak had flourished. His father, he mused, would have paid a fortune for such a decoration in the house's courtyard. His father . . .

The sword's edge glittered slightly in the moonlight. Marcus touched the blade, his fingers snagging against a razor-sharp line of minutely ragged steel, rough-sharpened for combat, rather than the smooth steel of a peacetime weapon. He'd heard of the practice from old soldiers, but never seen it carried out. Someone expected him to need every small advantage that could be put his way. He remounted, riding cautiously on with an ear cocked for trouble, holding the reins with the hand that gripped the sword's hilt. Shadows moved and swirled in his vision, purple and black, each eddy in the night's mist taunting his senses.

At the one-mile marker he thought he could just make out the distant sound of horses' hoofs in front of him. He halted his own mount to listen in silence, but could hear nothing other than the wind's moan. Another five minutes of uninterrupted progress relaxed him a little, and he started to worry more about exactly who he would find waiting for him at the two-mile marker than what might happen in the intervening stretch of road. He reached down to pat the horse with the back of his sword hand, as much seeking as offering reassurance.

Looking up, he saw them materialise out of the mist to either side of the road, a pair of horsemen with swords held upright like cavalry troopers on parade. Wanting him to see the weapons, he guessed. He started as a voice spoke in the murk behind him, the Latin made crude by the edges of the man's German accent.

'Give up now and we'll make it easy for you. Run, and these two will have their fun with you before you die.'

Three, or more? Marcus let the sword and shield, already held low from stroking the horse's mane, slip down against the animal's flanks, hopefully invisible in the dim grey light of approaching dawn. Curiously unafraid, although his heart was pounding at his ribs with the force of a blacksmith's hammer, he gently spurred his horse with his boot-heels. Riding steadily towards the horsemen he allowed his body to slump in the saddle, reassuring them that he was already in their grip. Behind him, hoofs clattered on the road's surface, a fast trot designed to close the distance and put the third man within striking distance. Marcus kicked the horse hard, shouting encouragement into its ear as it surged forward into a gallop. He lifted the sword and shield from their resting places on the beast's flanks, and into the positions his father's bodyguard had made him practise thousands of times.

'He's armed!'

Bracing himself against the saddle's projecting horns, and clamping his feet to the horse's flanks, he pulled the beast towards the man on the right, flinching as something flicked past his head with a vicious whirr. The arrow's passage was close enough for him to feel the wind of its passing. The men to his front spurred their own horses forward, but his burst of speed caught them by surprise, closing the gap before they could manoeuvre to meet him as they might have wished. Punching out with the shield at the man to his left, he felt the jar of a heavy sword blow-hammer his left arm into numbness. His own weapon, the point thrust forward towards the centre of the other horseman's indistinct mass as they came together, rang with contact on metal. The sword's hilt moved in his hand as the blade struck something softer. The pain of the wound was enough to make the horseman wheel his mount away with a shout of anger, leaving a gap through which Marcus's steed burst with its gathered momentum, too swift for the other man to get in a second attack.

He rode for his life now, crouching low to avoid any more arrows, looking back for any sign of his pursuers in the greyness behind him. A frantic clatter of hoofs behind convinced him to keep the horse at the gallop, angry shouts lending urgency to his efforts. The shield fell from his numb left hand, its layered wood and leather deeply scarred by the sword-blow. Without its protection the blade would almost certainly have taken his arm off.

The horse was starting to pant heavily with the exertion when a figure appeared out of the dawn's murk at the roadside. In a second Marcus pivoted his mount to put the new threat on his right-hand side, within his sword's striking arc. He pulled the blade back for the sweeping cut he'd been taught up on the wooden practice horse in the villa's sunny courtyard almost a decade before, high above the rooftops and fume of the city.

'*Marcus!*'

He allowed the weapon to drop from its slashing path, pulling the panting horse up with a hard pull at the reins.

'*Rufius?!*'

He jumped down from the saddle, following the older man's frantic beckoning to bring the horse into the deeper shadow of a small copse that crept close to the road's edge. The animal, unimpressed by the events of the previous minutes, baulked at moving into the trees' threatening gloom. Marcus dug his feet in and pulled, and for a second it looked as if they might succeed in finding cover, but the horse's resistance had removed the slight time gap between him and his pursuers. The two horsemen who had attempted to block his path before rode out of the darkness, as the two men hesitated between fight and flight into the trees. Marcus grabbed for his saddlebag, releasing the horse's bridle as his hand gripped the oiled cloth, allowing it to bolt into the darkness. Tossing the bag aside, he dropped into a wide-legged fighting stance with the cavalry sword extended, ready to fight. Rufius stepped to his side, unsheathing his shorter infantry sword and lifting a round gladiator's shield from the ground where he had let it fall. The horsemen slowed their advance and crowded in closer, leaning out of their saddles with swords held ready to strike down at the two men.

At the last moment something flew past Marcus's head, thudding into the nearer man's chest and pitching him prone on to the dark road. A moment later a spear arced out of the trees, forcing the other rider to twist in his saddle in desperate evasion, his horse hesitating as the trees' shadow loomed. As the rider wrestled with his mount's reins a powerful figure stepped swiftly past an amazed Marcus, swinging a heavy sword in a single brutal blow at the animal's legs. With an awful scream the animal fell to its knees, hurling its rider untidily on to the ground, where the horse's assailant finished him with an efficient thrust to the throat. Another blow silenced the animal's agony in a steaming flow of its blood. The silent attacker stepped back into the trees, vanishing wraith-like into their dark shelter.

The third rider trotted slowly out of the slowly departing night, an arrow ready to loose from his taut bow. The arrow's point arced slowly across the bloodied scene in search of a target. Marcus shrank back towards the trees, Rufius pulling him into the shield's inadequate protection, but the archer saw their movement while they were still a good ten feet from the deeper shadows. Straightening in his saddle, he swung the bow to bear on them, bending the bow the last few inches before loosing its arrow. With a berserk howl their rescuer broke from the trees again at a dead run, throwing himself into a forward roll as the mounted archer loosed the arrow at him in a split-second reaction. As the rider's left hand plucked another arrow from his quiver his attacker rolled out of his dive and sprang forward with his sword, gutting the horse with a single turning thrust. The rider went down under his screaming, dying mount, trapped beneath its dead weight. The massive figure stepped over the dying animal's trembling neck, lifting his sword for the final kill.

'*Dubnus! No!*'

The sword froze in mid-strike, and then withdrew. Tiberius Rufius strode across to the man, slapping him on the back in congratulation.

'Excellent work, man, worthy of celebration by mighty Mars himself! What a sacrifice you have made to him! Marcus, come and renew your acquaintanceship with my good friend Dubnus!'

Marcus walked across the road to where Rufius and his companion stood over the fallen horse and rider. The other man turned to face him, one hand exploring the muscle of his forearm, and the arrow shaft that protruded from it.

'The *Tungrian* . . . ?'

'Indeed it is. And isn't he magnificent? I told you that this was a man who knew how to fight, but I had no idea that he would be so *good*!'

Marcus looked into the Briton's eyes, seeing there a wary expression, but one lacking the hostility he'd noted there previously.

'You're wounded.'

Dubnus shrugged impassively.

'It didn't hit anything important, or there'd be more blood.'

He grasped the arrow and adjusted his big fingers experimentally around its shaft, taking a steadying breath. A swift push tore the arrow's head, narrow but evilly barbed, through the undamaged skin at the back of his arm, the arrow protruding from both sides of the limb. The Briton growled at the pain, a rivulet of blood snaking down his arm to drip from the spread fingers. With a casual twist of the shaft, the arrow broke into two easily removable halves.

'I wiped . . . the point . . . with my shit . . .'

All three turned to look at the fallen horseman, panting for breath as the injuries inflicted by his dead horse's weight tightened their grip on his life. Dubnus laughed at him, pulling a bloody finger across his throat.

'You're a dead man, I've already killed you. I can clean this wound, use herbs and maggots to remove any poison, but *your* leg is broken. Badly broken, probably bleeding inside. I've seen it happen before, takes an hour or so. Perhaps I should help you to die?'

'Fuck you . . . blue-nose.'

His eyes found Marcus, widening with recognition.

'You . . . traitor . . .'

Marcus stepped forward, the long cavalry sword still hanging from one hand.

'You were sent to kill me.'

'Would've . . . been easy . . . except for him . . . keep looking . . . over your shoulder . . . no hiding place . . . for you.'

Rufius gently pushed Marcus to one side.

'Dubnus, do what you must to make your wound safe for travel. We have to be away from here in ten minutes, no more. Take him with you.'

He squatted down next to the trapped horseman.

'I need a few minutes with my friend here . . .'

He waited until the Briton had shepherded Marcus away before slipping an ornately handled dagger from its sheath, and addressing the fallen rider in a quiet conversational tone.

'Yes, we're old friends all right. I'm the "officer" you were shouting for those blue-noses to kill yesterday on the North Road. And in fact for a long time I was an officer, and a good one too. I spent several very nasty years patrolling the Tava valley, up past the northern wall, before you idlers gave up our hard-won ground and moved back south to old Hadrian's Wall. One of the things I learnt to do with *complete* expertise during my time in that forsaken place was to persuade the local tribesmen we captured to tell us the things they didn't want to tell us. And now, before you die, I'm going to share that skill with *you*. So, where shall we begin . . . ?'

Dubnus dropped a heavy hand on Marcus's shoulder, pulling him farther away from the scene.

'You don't want to see that. Stay here and watch my pack.'

He drew his sword and walked to the closest of the fallen horses, pausing to wrest his throwing axe from the chest of his first victim before turning to the man's horse. Practical necessity overrode any qualms he might have felt about either the man's death or the use he was about to make of the dead horse. From the moment he'd agreed to do what the former officer had asked of him he'd been working out how to make good their escape, once the Roman was safe from the threat of murder. The veteran officer had disturbed his sleep earlier that night with the request, one that had made him laugh out loud with its audacity once his irritation at being awakened before the dawn call had worn off.

He'd stopped laughing when a bag full of gold had landed on the bed in front of him. The former officer, it seemed, was determined to have his help, and was willing to pay handsomely. It was enough money, Tiberius Rufius had told him, to buy every man in his cohort a decent coat of mail. He'd stopped laughing all right, but the look on his face had made it clear enough to the veteran centurion that he wasn't going to pick the money up from where it had landed, at least not without a good reason. Which Rufius had proceeded, with a half-smile that signalled how well he understood the Briton, to matter-of-factly provide.

His task complete, Dubnus returned to find Marcus waiting where he had left him. He stuffed the carefully wrapped bundle into his pack and then led the way deeper into the copse, searching in the half-light until he found what he was looking for. The plant glistened in the grey light.

'Woundwort. Good.'

He ripped a handful of the plant away from its stem, squeezing it hard in a straining fist until a milky fluid dribbled from between his fingers on to the arrow punctures, then reached into his pack, hidden at the foot of a tree, for a strip of cloth.

'The juice will help to stop the bleeding. Help me to tie it.'

Dubnus wound the cloth around his bulky forearm and allowed Marcus to knot it. A slow red stain seeped through the layers.

'Tighter . . . good.'

A shrill scream made Marcus start. The soldier shrugged, regarding the temporary bandage with a professional scrutiny from beneath his heavy eyebrows, a slight smile crossing his face.

'He'll talk soon, that German. It's inevitable. Our friend Rufius will offer him either a quick death or a slow one. Any man that runs from a fight before it is lost will take the easy way out when there's a knife probing the root of his cock.'

A flush of anger ripped through Marcus's body, part reaction, part frustration at the uncontrolled spiral of events, and part hot burning disgust at what Rufius was doing to the fallen rider. Spinning, he thrust his face into the soldier's, snarling his anger into its indifference.

'Why did you come here? Why save me? You *hate* Romans!'

'You're an outlaw now. The German called you a traitor. You're not one of *them* any more.'

The simple reversal of judgement infuriated Marcus, as much for the smug simplicity of its verdict as its perpetuation of the injustice done to his family.

'I am *not* a traitor!'

Dubnus pointed into the darkness, to where the screams had sounded.

'German or not, he's a Roman. A cavalryman. One of their elite. Why was he hunting you? *He* must think you are a traitor.'

The Briton watched Marcus as he frowned at the simple verdict, attempting to gauge the man's mettle, whether he would stand up to the rigours of the coming days. He'd wondered whether the Roman would even be able to make effective use of the weapons they'd hidden for him by the roadside, after they had slipped out of the fort through a hidden door concealed in the wall. The thick oak door had answered the first of his objections, as to how they were going to get out of the fortress without word getting back to Titus. It was faced in stone to match the walls around it, with heavy stone slabs inside the wall poised ready to fall and block the tiny entry if small wedges restraining them were knocked away. He would never have known it was there if he hadn't been guided to its precise location.

'It's designed to allow troops to get out and attack besiegers, or messengers to leave in secret,' Tiberius Rufius had told him as they forded the river between the fortress and its town on carefully placed stepping stones that lay beneath the river's slow-moving surface. 'But it's a good thing it hasn't rained hard for a week or so, or the river would be trying a lot harder to pull us off this little bridge.'

They had skirted the town and headed down the road to the two-mile marker, while he hefted his spear and thought darkly about what he was going to do to the German cavalryman if he got the chance. Tiberius Rufius had made the connection for him, pointing out that the man shouting orders to kill him over the din of their little battle could not have been a tribesman with an accent like that. It had been all the bait needed to get the big Briton off his bed and into his mail coat, intended murder in his heart, revenge for the man he'd lost the previous day.

In the event, seeing the Asturian decurion trapped beneath his horse had put out the fire of his bloodlust in an instant. Knowing that the man was doomed to die in agony, his leg shattered under the horse's massive dead weight, had been enough for him. He had still smiled to himself when the screaming started, though. A man made his choice and lived with the outcome.

Tiberius Rufius appeared out of the dawn's murk, wiping his dagger with a tuft of grass pulled from the roadside.

'Well, at least that was easier than it might have been. We must leave this place, and quickly. Dubnus, we need to make good speed, but be well away from the road before the first patrols get this far. Lead us, if you will.'

The Briton nodded, turning away towards the indistinct hillside above them and picking up his pack pole and spears.

'Come.'

For a wounded man he made good time, grinding across the hard winter ground at a pace that had Marcus breathless inside ten minutes, their path climbing steadily up and away from the road. He glanced back at Rufius, bringing up the rear with an alert eye to all sides, to find that he was striding out without any sign of trouble. Returning his energy to putting one boot in front of the other time after time after time, he concentrated on the Briton's muscular back. Weeks of travel, by sea and on horseback, had done little to help his fitness. After about fifteen minutes of increasing physical torture Dubnus stepped off the line of their march, leading them into the shade of a small huddle of trees. A patch of scorched earth in the middle of the tiny grove showed where a fire had burned quite recently. Dawn had come and gone, and the first glint of sun was edging the horizon. Below them the road was still, trees along its verges casting stripes of dark shadow across the landscape. The Briton gestured down towards the road.

'This is a good place to camp, the fire shows as much. A moving man is easily seen from here in the dusk or dawn, his shadow will stretch across the land. It is a good defence for us, but will make us vulnerable if we move any farther until the sun gets higher. We'll have to wait here until the sun clears the horizon.'

Marcus stood with his head back, sucking in the cold morning air with his eyes closed. Somewhere in the gloom a crow cawed hoarsely, echoing his mood. Dubnus prodded him in the stomach.

'You're *soft*. A soldier has to march all day, then dig out a camp before eating or sleeping.'

Marcus opened his eyes and grimaced in return, looking

up at the Briton's relaxed posture. Only the slight rise of steam from his skin in the half-light gave any hint of his recent exertion.

'I *am* a soldier . . . I've just been without real exercise for too long.'

Rufius raised a sympathetic smile, almost hidden in the dawn's meagre light.

'If it helps, my legs ache too. It's been too long since I had to cover country at that pace, but Dubnus has got us away safely, and that's what counts. Now, let's talk, you and I. Dubnus, do me a favour and keep watch.'

The Briton took the hint, moving quietly away to the edge of the small copse to watch the road below their hiding place. Tiberius Rufius took Marcus by the arm, pulling him down into a conspiratorial squat. The Roman huddled into his cloak, shivering as the sweat cooled on his body.

'You met with the legatus, I presume?'

Marcus snorted, his lip curling.

'The legatus? Yes, he had me thrown to those wolves.'

Tiberius Rufius nodded his head.

'Indeed he did, and he no choice in doing so. Calidius Sollemnis did no more than he had to in order to be sure that he looked the model servant of Rome. In all truth it was his tribune Perennis who set the Asturians on you, the same way that he ordered the attack on us yesterday. I would have been sure of *that* even if our deceased Asturian friend back down there hadn't just confirmed it. Forget the carefully posed interview, consider what else has happened in the last few hours. The legatus had a trusted centurion pick you up from the inn and stay with you all the way to the gate. Without that safeguard it's likely that you would have been conveniently knifed before getting anywhere near your horse. Sollemnis also had me leave you the weapons that saved you from the Asturians, and wait for you down the road at a place where we might escape into the forest and evade pursuit. He knows what Perennis is capable of, and he took every step possible to fend off the man's efforts to have you killed.'

'And the Briton?'

'The first time he saved your life was pure luck, and fortune of the finest quality given the fact we'd have been dead men without his intervention. I'd say Fortuna smiles on you, Marcus Valerius Aquila. The second time, well, that was my own doing. People who plan for the worst have a tendency to survive when it actually happens, so I took steps to make sure that I was using my own dice for the game.'

He paused for a moment and looked the younger man square in the eye, as if weighing up his state of mind.

'And now, Centurion, there are things you have to know before we leave this place. None of them are pleasant, but then you find yourself in a difficult place with very limited options. You must fully understand your situation before you can decide how to face it.'

Marcus met his gaze with a level stare.

'I've been sent across Oceanus to the very edge of the world on a fool's errand, ambushed twice in two days by men I do not know intent on my murder, and informed in casual terms of the downfall of my father, previously a respected senator of Rome. I'm not sure you can make that picture very much bleaker, Tiberius Rufius, but if there's more to tell then I am ready.'

'Bravely put, Valerius Aquila. And you can drop the formalities. My forename is Quintus, and I'd be proud to count you as a close enough friend to use it. Now then, where to start? Legatus Sollemnis received a message from your father twenty days ago, stating that he feared for your family's safety in the current political climate in Rome. The senator wrote to warn Sollemnis of his decision to have you sent as far away from Rome as possible. He asked Sollemnis to hide you away from his enemies, as a last favour to a friend. This, of course, was no idle request – he was asking his friend to defy the throne and harbour a man who would swiftly be named as a traitor.

'When I met with Sollemnis last evening it was already clear to him that Tigidius Perennis would be his main problem. You've probably guessed by now that he's the son of your praetorian prefect, a man closer to the throne than you may know. What you don't know is that his appointment as a tribune on the Sixth's staff was imposed on Sollemnis last year. At the time he took it as a clear signal that Emperor Commodus, or at least the men who stand behind him, intended to be assured of his loyalty. After all, three legions and a dozen auxiliary cohorts *is* a lot of spears, the biggest single concentration of troops in the entire empire, and that could be an irresistible temptation to a man of the senatorial class with ambition. Sollemnis mistakenly thought that Perennis had simply been appointed to spy on his actions, but since his arrival this new tribune's actions have gone well beyond simple spying. He's subverted the Asturian cavalry to do his dirty work, and Sollemnis is convinced that he's planning to take command of the legion if ever he gets the chance.'

Marcus raised a sceptical eyebrow.

'A tribune? Unseat an imperial general officer? How likely is that?'

'With the right authority? With a scroll of authority embossed with the correct seals, and with the legion's most senior officers in no doubt as to their fate if they jumped the wrong way? Easier than you might think, I'd say. When, at the right time, Tigidius Perennis brings out his letter of authority, complete with the imperial seal, half a dozen men find themselves harking back to quiet conversations with the man. Flattery, offers of promotion and veiled threats to loved ones from a clever young man of the highest influence and absolutely no scruples. I'd put good money on Sollemnis finding himself at the wrong end of the spear very quickly in such a situation. He knows that he has very good reason to behave in a manner that provides no opportunity for Perennis to make his move.

'So, the legatus originally thought that it would be relatively simple to send you across to the Twentieth Legion at Deva, under the supervision of *their* legatus, if he could just keep you from Perennis's attention. The Twentieth's man owes him a favour or two, apparently. A second messenger arrived, two days ago, an urgent dispatch from Rome, and carried by a courier I've met a few times before. Once I got a few drinks into him he was happy enough to discuss the stories he'd heard around the palace before he left. Your father had been arrested for the crime of conspiracy against the throne, and was . . . questioned on your disappearance, but even *in extremis* refused to give any clue as to your whereabouts. All they could wring out of him, after days of suffering, was that he'd sent you to the ends of the empire, out of their reach. His remains were scattered for the crows, denied the burial rites to avoid there being any rallying point for your family's supporters. You should be proud of him, Marcus Valerius Aquila; by dying in such ignominy, but with such dignity, he brought great honour to your name. But suspicion obviously fell on your tribune, and he told Commodus's men everything they wanted to know as soon as they came for him. Hoping to save himself from torture, it seems. Fool. It would have been easier on him if he'd just fallen on his own sword while he had the chance. The elder Perennis was so furious that you slipped from his grasp just as he was ready to move on your family, he had his thugs torture Tribune Scarus to death just trying to prove his story false.

'The instructions from Rome were simple enough. As far

as Sollemnis was concerned, you were to be detained and returned to the capital at the first opportunity, day or night. A private message for Perennis was delivered by the same courier, and it wasn't too hard to guess what orders that contained. Once the senior officer at Dark Pool fortress reported you as being on the road to Yew Grove, I was sent south in secret to find you. I was to provide you with whatever protection I could until you reached the city. In the meantime Sollemnis decided to take five cohorts out into the country on a no-warning exercise, to avoid your walking into the fortress before he was ready to receive you. He knew I'd keep you out of trouble until he got back.

'When he arrived back at Yew Grove late last night, Sollemnis had no choice but to "deal with you", and provide clear evidence of his loyalty to the throne, but he had time to set me to work again, preparing your escape from the death that Titus Tigidius Perennis had planned for you . . .'

Rufius looked at him for a long moment before reaching out a hand, patting his shoulder in a gesture of reassurance that was not mirrored in his troubled eyes.

'Marcus, there comes a moment in every man's life when he must shoulder the full burden of his fate, accept his own death or, worse, the death of those he loves. This, I regret, is your moment. Read the scroll you were ordered to bring here.'

Marcus cut away the protective wax seal and opened the box containing his father's last message, turning the unrolled parchment to the morning's slowly brightening eastern horizon.

My son, may the gods have remained with you, you are by now safe in northern Britannia, and far distant from the throne's vengeance. You are reading this message at the suggestion of the man to whom I have entrusted your fate. By the time you reach

Britannia, I expect that Commodus and his supporters will have laid formal charges of treason at our family's door. I will have been tortured for information as to your whereabouts, then killed without ceremony or hearing. I can only hope that my persecutors will have been kinder with your mother and our other children and relatives, although I doubt it. This emperor brings evil out from under the stones that have long concealed it, and few men display less honour in their deeds than your praetorian prefect, Perennis. Whatever the ugly detail of their ending, our kindred will be taken and killed out of hand, our honour publicly denounced, and our line almost brought to an abrupt full stop. You are almost certainly all that remains of our blood.

My purpose in bribing your tribune to send you to my friend is a simple one. He will, I am confident, undertake to send you deeper into that harsh and difficult country and hide you among his friends, out of sight of the throne's hunting dogs. I apologise gravely for not sharing my intention with you, as should have been the case between men. Your sense of honour, so carefully instilled by years of patient teaching, would only have tripped you before you could fly. Our conversation on the night of your sister's birthday proved to me that you had no comprehension of the fate looming over our proud house. I chose therefore to make your flight one that required no such understanding.

So now you are in Britannia, if all has gone well. You must think hard now, despite your sorrow, and act with decision and courage. You are the last of our line, the only blood left unspilt from a once distinguished family. Your task now must be to preserve that blood, to hide it from the hunters until the chase is abandoned, perhaps even until the man on the throne has changed. You alone must judge the right time to emerge from hiding, and how much vengeance to seek at that point, depending on your circumstances. Remember, my son, revenge is a morsel best savoured at leisure, rather than hot from the oven, lest you burn your own mouth. In truth, it would be enough for me to know that our blood will be passed on to later generations. For our honour to be restored would be more then I could expect.

I only ask, for your grandfather's sake if not for mine, that you do not despair of this last request. I know that you loved the old man, and would like you to know that your military training and position were mostly at his request, a promise I gave him on his deathbed. Certainly I had no will to resist the last desire of a dying man, as I hope will now be the case with this request I make of you, since I am most certainly doomed.

I wish you, and the future of our line, the best of luck. May Mercury guide your steps and Mars strengthen your sword-hand.

Your father, Appius Valerius Aquila

Marcus looked up from the scroll and stared bleakly at the older man. Rufius took a deep breath before speaking again.

'Sollemnis tells me that your father had the misfortune to be both wealthy and a man of honour and intelligence at a time when both made him a target. No emperor can afford to leave any survivors when he removes a perceived threat to his greatness, for the fear of their becoming a rallying point for discontent. Worse, most guard commanders will tell you that almost anyone can be killed, *if* the assassin has no concern for his escape once the deed is completed – if he has nothing left to live for. It's a usual precaution for the emperor to order the death of all males in any family he moves against, an essential task of the praetorians, I'm afraid . . . I'm sorry, but your father is almost certainly dead. Did you have any brothers?'

The younger man nodded, swallowing painfully.

'A younger brother. He's . . . was . . . ten . . .'

'I'm sorry . . . So you see, this is that moment of which

I spoke. You are the only surviving male of your family, the last of your bloodline. If you die, your father and grandfather's line will be snuffed out for ever. But you're going to have to take a part in your own protection. Neither I nor Dubnus can run around looking after you for the next ten years, and so . . .'

Marcus nodded his understanding, took a deep breath and got to his feet, stooping to pick up the razor-sharp cavalry sword.

'And I certainly won't knowingly endanger either of you any further. You've both already done more than enough. I'll find some way to escape the pursuit . . .'

Rufius looked up at him with a gentle smile, shaking his head in bemusement.

'Brave enough talk, my lad, but likely to see you dead before dusk tonight. What's needed now isn't nobility, but *mobility*. You need to be somewhere else, as far from here as can be managed. And, much as it pains me to tell you this, you must also become someone else, another man entirely, and take on a name as far removed from the one you've used with pride all these years as possible.'

Dubnus turned to face them across the grove. Marcus met his frank stare with a shrug.

'You're right. This is your country, not mine. So tell me, where should I go?'

Rufius exchanged glances with Dubnus, and then continued.

'What I was *going* to say was that neither Dubnus nor I can be absent from our usual routines for long. I would quickly be missed, and suspicions about my role in all of this will already be high enough, and Dubnus is expected back on duty with his unit on the Wall in a few days. We do, however, have an idea of how we can spirit you away from under your enemies' noses, and hide you in a place they'd never consider. Your part will be to do everything and anything Dubnus tells you to, from now until he delivers you to your destination. Perhaps you can find a way of repaying him . . .' He lowered his voice. '. . . although I'd advise against offering him money.'

Marcus nodded slowly, his face still white from the shock of reading his father's message.

'I will do whatever I have to. I have no choice. My name . . .'

Rufius grimaced.

'It's never easy to jettison something as close to your identity as the name your father gave you, especially under such circumstances, but you have no choice. You need a simple name, one to let you fade into the background of this bloody story and be lost to view from Rome. Your forename should remain the same, there's no sense in risking your being caught out in your deception when there's no need. As for clan and family . . .'

He pursed his lips in thought for a moment, then thrust a hand into his bag.

'For a clan name, I suggest this . . .'

Resting on his outstretched palm was a device constructed of four metal spikes heat-welded together, their points bright iron teeth.

'It's a tribulus. Strew a few thousand of these in front of a cohort and you've removed any danger of cavalry or chariot attack. See, no matter how you drop it to the ground, there's always one nasty little point sticking up to wreck a horse's hoof, and it'll make a mess of a blue-nose foot too.'

Marcus picked up the vicious device.

'It's bent.'

Rufius nodded, taking the tribulus and wrapping his fist around it.

'My own modification. See, a small change to the spikes'

angles makes it the perfect close-combat weapon if you lose your sword.'

A single spike protruded from between his fingers, two more poked out from either side of his fist, while the last stuck straight out from his palm.

'However I choose to punch a man with this I'll always have a nice length of iron in front of my fist. This one's yours, I've got another one in my bag, and you never know when you might find that little toy your only weapon. So, for your clan name I suggest "Tribulus". Seems quite appropriate, given the way you keep fighting back no matter which way up fate throws you. As for a family name . . .'

The distant crow cawed again, its harsh call cutting through the crisp morning air. Marcus lifted his head, looking out across the bleak landscape laid out below them.

'There's your answer – "Corvus" – it will serve to remind me how my father was mistreated even after his death. And it's as good as any other name if I have to abandon the one my ancestors have used with pride since the expulsion of the ancient kings from the city . . .'

Rufius put a hand on his shoulder.

'You're not abandoning anything, just burying it here for a while, along with everything else that can betray you to your pursuers. Work the new name through your mind until you consider yourself as Marcus Tribulus Corvus. If the right gods smile on you, you'll be safe at the Hill in a matter of days, and once there you'll have to be comfortable with your new identity.'

'The Hill? Where's that?'

Rufius's face creased in a rueful grin.

'Where's the Hill? At the end of the world, that's where. Dubnus, it's time for you both to leave . . .'

The Briton pondered for a moment. To their west rose the Pennine mountains, still snow-capped with retreating winter, a bleak killing field with little cover if the inevitable searching cavalry patrols came upon them. A long climb would take them to the peaks, another day's march would drop them back on to the lowlands on the far side. There they would find safer ground, another legion's territory, although he knew that the ripples from the slaughter he'd inflicted on the Roman's pursuers would still spread wide. Taking the fugitive to the north, on the other hand, would take them off the road, but into the forests, dangerous beyond belief for a pair of men, one in the hated armour of Rome, the other very much an unknown quantity. Even if the cavalry sword in his grip was edged with blackened dried blood.

'I will take him over the mountains to the west.'

Rufius nodded agreement.

'And I need to be back about my business, away from the pair of you, at least for now.'

He embraced Marcus briefly, stepping back to appraise the younger man one last time.

'Farewell, then, Marcus Tribulus Corvus, we'll meet again in the north, Mars willing. My horse is safe in the woods below, so I'll leave you to it.'

He nodded to Marcus, clasped hands with Dubnus and started back down the slope. The Briton turned to face Marcus, unwrapping a bundle that Rufius had left behind.

'Clothes and boots, as worn by my people. Rufius bought them for you in Yew Grove. Let's hope they fit. Also, a blanket, and a nice heavy hooded cape to keep you dry in the rain.'

Fit they did, although they were a rude surprise to Marcus after the quality of his own clothing, rough material and ill-made boots that chafed his feet before he'd even started walking. They buried his tunic, cloak and boots to prevent their discovery, wrapping his gold cloak pin and the message from his father in their folds, and marked their position with a small pile of rocks. Dubnus strapped the cavalry sword to his right hip.

'Better I throw it to you if it comes to a fight. What would a roughly dressed peasant like you be doing with such a fine weapon? You can have it back when we reach the Hill.'

He wiped mud across the younger man's face to complete the transformation, standing back to admire his handiwork.

'You'll pass. Your hands are too soft, you need to get some dirt under your nails, and your hair is too short, but we'll cut it even shorter once we've got the time, make it look military. You're a tribesman now, my nephew in fact, and I'm taking you to join my cohort at the Hill . . . Cocidius forgive me. Anyone talks to us, you keep your mouth closed, your head down and you let me do the talking. Very well, let's march.'

He turned to leave, shouldering his pack pole and spears. Marcus tested his new boots by walking a few paces, grimacing at their fierce grip on his feet.

'So how far is it to the Hill?'

'One hundred and fifty miles, seven days' march for a legionary. We're going to march at that pace, like legionaries. Your legions use the roads they build to move fast and concentrate dispersed forces to gain superior strength before they attack, it's their strongest weapon against the rebel tribes because it multiplies their strength. Now we're going to use their roads to get you away from their patrols.'

Marcus nodded his acknowledgement of the point.

'I'm impressed with your knowledge.'

Dubnus snorted, his nostrils flaring as he looked at the bedraggled Roman.

'You look at me and see a barbarian in Roman armour. You view me with Rome's contempt, or something close to it, because that's what you've been taught. I'm an educated man, and a soldier in a country where soldiers are guaranteed to see action several times over their term of service, even if only in dirty little skirmishes with locals. Let me tell you, you can die in a skirmish just as easily as in a full-scale gang fuck unless you're trained and ready. I will start to train and ready you as we travel north.'

Marcus smiled wanly.

'At the speed you promise to travel you may kill me first.'

The Briton shook his head slightly, the ghost of a smile touching his eyes.

'Far from it. Instead I'll give you the stamina of a Tungrian by the time we reach the Hill.'

Marcus rolled his eyes to heaven in mock despair.

'Or kill me trying. Gods help me!'

Dubnus, unable to retain his outrage, replaced it with an evil smile.

'Roman gods won't save you now. You belong to me, and you're just a recruit as far as I'm concerned, and therefore subject to a new god. My god, *Cocidius*, a warrior god, a hunter god. So run, master recruit. *Run!*'

They ran, Marcus gulping the cold upland air deep into his bursting lungs. Between education and exercise it threatened to be a long week.

3

That evening, as the sun dipped slowly towards the horizon, Dubnus broke off the line of their march and climbed a short distance into the forest before lowering his pack to the ground. The fugitives had avoided the road for much of the day, moving cross-country on game paths that threaded through the thin scatter of copses decorating the mountain slopes. Having avoided the first angry heat of the inevitable cavalry sweep for the murderers of Perennis's men, they had returned to the road when the sun was quite low in the sky. The Briton gestured to the small hollow he had found, sweeping his arm in around to indicate the sparsely wooded land around them.

'We need to light a fire. It should be safe enough here, hidden from the road. You look for some kindling, dead stuff only, mind you, we don't want to make smoke. And stay out of sight of the road. Keep within shouting distance, there are wolves in these hills.'

By the time Marcus, limping from the pain of his blisters, had found sufficient wood to make a good-sized pile of dry twigs and sticks, the Briton had cut and lashed branches to form a spit above the spot where the fire would burn. A large chunk of meat was in place, ready to cook. He examined the wood carefully, nodding sagely.

'Good enough. If you're wondering what the meat is, I cut it from one of the horses I killed this morning. If that bothers you, you have a choice – eat horse or go hungry, tonight and tomorrow. I took two pieces like this. While you think about that you can go and find twice as much wood again – we'll need to burn the fire through the night in this temperature. Thicker branches, mind you, to last longer.'

Dubnus had the fire glowing hot by the time Marcus returned with his last load of wood. His boots were off, and he had the horsemeat turning over the flames. They sat a while in the evening's peace while the meat started to cook, drops of fat falling on to the flames and burning in bright flares. The aroma tormented Marcus's empty belly until he broke the silence, as much to distract him from his hunger as from any desire to talk.

'Dubnus, who taught you to fight so well?'

'My father. He was a hunter, killed animals for food and skins, then traded the skins with Roman traders like Rufius. Former soldiers usually. He taught me to fight, and to track and hunt . . . how to live off the country for months, with no need go back to our village. The land has everything required for survival if you have the right tools. Here, take a spell turning this meat.'

Marcus shuffled over to the fire to do as he was asked.

'So why did you join the army?'

The other man's eyes clouded for a moment.

'You ask a lot of questions.'

'I'm sorry. I had no intention of . . .'

'I joined the army because my father sent me to the Tungrian fort when he was dying, told me to ask the recruiting centurion to take me. He said that the army would be the best place for me when he was gone . . .'

'Were you sad to leave home?'

'Sad? Yes, I was sad. Leaving the land was difficult. Life in the army was very different.'

'Hard?'

'No. Nothing they could throw at me bothered me. My

centurion beat me with his vine stick to get my attention and drum in the lessons. I told him to keep it up, told him I loved it. He broke it on my back and called for another one.'

The big man sat in silence for a moment.

'It wasn't any harder than what I was already used to. It just wasn't home.'

Marcus fell silent, eyeing the meat critically. He could imagine the huge Briton as a younger man, little different from how he was now, silent and proud. Every inch warrior blood. What a challenge to his first centurion, a man expected to turn him from barbarian into trained soldier. The meat was starting to crisp above the fire's heat, almost ready to eat.

'Dubnus?'

'Yes.'

'What will I do when we reach the Hill?'

'Rufius has a plan. He'll tell us when we meet.'

'When *will* we meet again?'

The Briton shrugged indifferently.

'Somewhere on the road north. Let's eat that meat before it burns.'

He scraped the horsemeat from the spit and on to his wooden plate with a swift movement of his dagger, dividing it equally before passing one portion to the Roman. Marcus nodded his thanks, his nostrils flaring in anticipation of the meal as he gingerly sank his teeth into the hot meat, eating the first mouthful open mouthed to avoid burning his palate. The taste was divine after a day's hard exercise without food. Fat ran down his chin unnoticed as he ate. He nodded at Dubnus in between mouthfuls.

'I never expected to be eating horse . . . or for it to taste so good.'

The Briton swallowed a mouthful of his own portion.

'You'll be surprised what you can do when you have to. Now it's your turn to speak of your past. Tell me about your father.'

Marcus thought for a moment, chewing reflectively on his meat.

'He was a good man, I think, but he never learned how to keep his thoughts private, even when they were a danger to him. Not even when my mother threatened to take the children to her sister's house in Naples if he didn't stop goading the emperor. His views were dreadfully old fashioned. He believed that imperial rule was a dead end for Rome, doomed to produce ever more feeble leaders until the whole thing came crashing down. He believed that a republic, and rule by the Senate, voted into power by the people, was the only answer. My uncle Condianus once told me that his brother was too liberal with his opinions, too quick to share his beliefs. He told me that my father mistook the indulgence of the last emperor for approval, and mistakenly believed that the old man would come to renounce the throne and restore the Republic. Which, of course, was never going to happen. Uncle Condianus feared it would lead to all our deaths, but I suppose I could never quite believe that his fears were justified . . .'

He paused for a moment, remembering.

'All the time the storm clouds were gathering over us, and I never knew it was happening. Or *wanted* to know, I suppose. I did try to speak to my father a few days before I was sent away on this fool's errand, after a dinner to celebrate my sister's birthday. We sat down for a cup of wine together after the meal, and it all came out again. His disgust for the emperor, his hopes of restoring the Republic. I warned him to be more careful with his views, that the new emperor wouldn't necessarily share his father's tolerance. I told him that he certainly shouldn't be speaking ill of the throne to a man sworn to protect its occupant with his life . . . but of course he wouldn't listen. All he would say was that he thought it was a bit rich for me to be warning him about loyalty to the emperor when it was his money that had put me in my fine uniform. And that was that.'

Dubnus nodded, snorting quiet laughter past a mouthful of meat.

'Fathers. They always have a way to put you in your place, no matter how big your boots get.'

They shared a quiet moment before Dubnus broke the spell by pointing to Marcus's feet.

'Show me your blisters.'

Marcus put down his plate and examined the sores, swollen with fluid from the day's friction against rough footwear.

'You won't be able to walk tomorrow unless we do something with these. Here.'

Marcus looked at the knife questioningly.

'Do what the legionaries do. Pinch the blisters, slice off the top and expose new skin beneath. It'll hurt for a moment or two once you get walking, then you'll feel nothing much. After a day or two you'll start to grow leather. Then get some sleep. We'll watch for two hours at a time, and keep the fire burning.'

Marcus did as he was bidden, smarting as the raw flesh beneath his blisters protested at its exposure. He curled up in his blankets underneath the heavy cape, and lay for a moment listening to the howling of distant wolves hunting in the hills about them. There was comfort to be taken from the fire's protective circle of light, and from Dubnus's reassuring bulk as the Briton sat out the first watch, before sleep took him. When his time to watch the fire came it was uneventful enough, apart from tossing the occasional branch on to the blaze, and fighting off his urge to sleep. He was petrified that he would make a fool of himself in front of the Briton.

At dawn the next morning, they were ready to move. Dubnus carefully brushed the fire's ashes away into the grass with his feet before spreading fresh earth over the burnt ground, cautious despite his eagerness to move on. He made one last critical examination of their surroundings then turned away, satisfied with his precautions.

'We weren't here. March.'

Marcus forced his protesting leg muscles up to Dubnus's speed, realising with dismay after a moment of torture that while the other man was setting a slow pace, he was gradually accelerating their rate of progress. Gritting his teeth and digging into his willpower to match his stride, he searched for something to distract him from the physical torment. Memories of Rome that he had previously suppressed flooded back to fill the emptiness created by exhaustion, and he stopped in his tracks, resting his hands on his knees as the memories cascaded out from the place into which he had roughly pushed them in the aftermath of his arrest and escape.

His older sisters taking turns to amuse him with rag dolls as a toddler. His younger brother Gaius playing with the cup and ball he'd given the ten-year-old as a present, turning excitedly to grin his thanks. The girls would likely be dead by now, according to Rufius, quite possibly horribly so, and it was inescapable that the boy would have been killed out of hand. A family traceable back to the time of the Second Punic War simply expunged from existence. A pair of booted feet appeared in his vision. He spoke without raising his gaze.

'Kill me now, Briton, save us both the trouble of dragging my weary body across this ghastly land. I have little enough reason to live . . .'

A powerful grip took Marcus's rough shirt, pulling him up to stare into the warrior's grey eyes. Dubnus held him there for a moment, looking deep into his soul through its only window on the world.

'You grieve for your family. I told you before, it's right to grieve, at the right time. Grieve now, and say farewell *now*. I'm marching north, whether you come or not.'

Grief and rage tautened Marcus's jaw, making him force out his words between gritted teeth.

'They're all dead, Dubnus, my father, my mother, sisters. My little brother!'

'So Rufius told me. Was your father stupid?'

'What?'

'When you talked about your father last night it was clear that he couldn't betray his principles, but was he a stupid man? Unwise? Lacking in intelligence?'

Marcus thought hard, grateful for something other than death on which to ponder. On balance, while being the first to accept that he was not the soldier his grandfather had been, his father had been no kind of fool. Bribing a praetorian tribune to send his son away before the impending storm broke proved that.

'No ... I believe he was not.'

'He sent you to safety. Perhaps he did the same with his other children?'

Marcus felt his heart lift a little at the possibility.

'Perhaps ... but ...'

'But?'

'But I have to assume that my entire family is gone now, and that I'm all that's left.'

'So *you* are the family now. You're the only keeper of your family's blood. And so ... ?'

'And so I must do whatever I have to, if I am to keep that name alive.'

The Briton nodded his head gravely, placing a hand on Marcus's shoulder for a second, in a halting effort at comfort.

'Yes, you do *whatever* you have to do. And the first thing you have to do is to march. *Now.*'

'In a moment. Wait for me, please.'

He walked away from the path, feeling the barbarian leggings rubbing against his legs. A sore patch was developing between his thighs, skin unaccustomed to the contact of the rough homespun cloth. At Dubnus's suggestion he had rubbed fat from their meal on to the sores, which would harden, given time, and the discomfort would have to be borne in the meantime. As, he mused brokenly, would his heart's pain at the presumed loss of all he had loved in his past. What, he wondered, would his father and grandfather, both soldiers in their time, have expected of him? The answer came without conscious thought, as if familiar voices spoke in his memory. Take the chance you've been given. Survive. Continue our proud line. He turned back to the road, his heart lighter than it had been five minutes before. Dubnus poked him in the chest, hooking a thick thumb over his shoulder in the direction of their route.

'Good. *Now* we'll march. No stopping until midday, and perhaps we'll buy food at a village. Even praetorians need food!'

Smiling at the Briton's attempt to lighten his mood, Marcus stepped back on to the track, ignoring the pain in his calves and thighs. Another thought sprang unbidden to his mind, alongside the nobler concepts of protecting the family's survival. Revenge. He marched away to the north behind the seemingly tireless Briton, savouring the thought of making the men who had destroyed his family pay in blood for their crimes, no matter how long his wait for that revenge might be. He muttered the word quietly to himself, savouring its implications.

'What?'

He smiled bitterly at Dubnus's back, his thoughts suddenly washed clear by the heat of the new emotion.

'Just something I was thinking about. A morsel best savoured at leisure. And I have plenty of leisure, it would seem.'

Every step that the pair took to the north, through pale sunshine, frequent rain and once through an eerily quiet day of gently falling snow, made a tiny reduction in the likelihood of their being taken by the units searching for the murderers of the rogue cavalrymen. Still, even as they drew nearer to the wall that divided empire from barbarian waste, and farther from likely pursuit, Dubnus remained cautious. What sustenance he took for them from the land was supplemented with food purchased with Marcus's money from the farms and villages they passed. Dubnus skirted round each settlement with great caution, leaving Marcus in cover while he went to make their purchases. As they went north, the Briton quizzed Marcus as to the nature of his military experience. Before long he had evidently decided that while the Roman clearly knew how to run a century, the lack of any combat in his short career, other than the brief skirmish on the road to Yew Grove, greatly diminished any value that experience might have had.

'You're a barracks officer. This place needs a man who can face the tribes with a drawn sword, not just a head counter.'

No amount of argument, or attempts by Marcus to discuss the great campaigns of history and show his understanding of either strategy or tactics, could change the Briton's gruff opinion. As far as Dubnus was concerned, his new companion was quite simply not a fighting man, praetorian or not, at least not until he'd proved otherwise. The skirmish on the road to Yew Grove apparently didn't count.

The strangely matched pair reached the Wall late in the morning of the ninth day of their march, a morning of fitful rain from a uniformly grey sky having given way to intermittent gloom and sunshine while towering walls of cloud rolled west in stately procession. The road from the south ran to the walls of a fortress set a mile back from the Wall before forking past its walls to the east and west. They halted a little way from the imposing structure while Dubnus drew a map in the dust with his dagger, pointing to each fort on their route in turn.

'This fort is The Rocks, home to the Hamians. The next fort to the west is High Spur, that's the Thracians. To the east there's Ash Tree, that's the Raetians and Fair Meadow is next, again set back behind the Wall, home to our sister cohort, the Second Tungrians. Then we'll reach the Hill.'

The last fifteen miles of their journey took them along roads busy with military traffic, and for a while Marcus quailed at the appearance of each new patrol. He soon realised that the troops they passed, recognising the colour of Dubnus's tunic, were more interested in passing snide comments than looking for fugitive Romans. Another ten-man patrol passed in the opposite direction, one brave soul calling out, 'Who's your girlfriend, Chosen?' once the distance between them was sufficient for safety, and his fear evaporated, replaced by a sudden feeling of superiority.

'I don't see much discipline here . . .'

Dubnus laughed over his shoulder.

'Oh, they've got *discipline*! They're tough, better than most legionary soldiers, better trained, harder trained. All they know is fighting, unlike the legions where every man seems to have a trade first and a sword as an afterthought. They have to be ready to fight at any time, since their enemy is everywhere around them . . .'

He was silent for a moment.

'Their enemy is their own people. Can you imagine what that feels like, knowing that you might have to put your own brother to the sword if it came to war? You're not a *fighting* soldier, you wouldn't understand . . .'

Marcus closed his mouth, considering the statement. Perhaps the other man was right. The only soldiering he'd known *was* in barracks, the continual watch over Rome that was intended to keep a boot on the city's throat rather than to protect it. What would it be like to face enemies both outside and inside the empire's walls, a situation perhaps as confusing for the local troops as it was dangerous?

A mile later they saw more troops marching towards them, a full century in campaign array, each man with a heavy pack on his carrying pole and two spears. Dubnus stopped in the road, putting his hands on his hips and smiling broadly.

'Those men are the best soldiers on the Wall. Those men are *Tungrians*.'

Their centurion was marching at the head of his men with his helmet buckled to his belt, a big, scar-faced man with a full black beard. A distinctive white streak ran from forehead to collar through his wiry black hair. He recognised Dubnus at some distance and trotted forward from his place, clasping arms with him as if he were an equal before turning and barking orders at his own chosen man to halt the column and give the men a five-minute break. They talked animatedly for a moment or so in their own language before Dubnus turned to Marcus.

'This is Clodius, centurion of the Third Century.'

The other man nodded carefully, taking in both Marcus's native clothing and his distinctive physical appearance with a glance. Eyes hard with suspicion momentarily bored into Marcus's before he turned away to his men. The soldiers treated Dubnus with respect during their brief halt, their body language betraying his apparently dominant position within their small world. Marcus tried to fade into the background, conscious of the troops' inspection of him. He wondered what they would make of his worn boots and rough local clothing, his jet-black hair and darker complexion. Most of them had the fair local colouring, while only a few had black hair like Dubnus and Clodius.

The century marched away to the east after a few moments, leaving them to resume their own journey. They had passed Fair Meadow, a mile south of the Wall, by mid-afternoon, its whitewashed stone sides standing out from the country around like a ship at sea. Turning north for a short distance, they climbed a shallow ridge, at the top of which the fort for which they were heading came into view. Shaped in the usual rectangle, it butted up to the white line of the Wall at the top of the next ridge, an untidy cluster of town buildings huddled against its lower rampart.

'The Hill,' Dubnus confirmed.

At the gate he was greeted with the same mixture of respect and deference that Marcus had noted on the road, and told the sentries to call for the officer of the watch. The centurion arrived quickly, listened to Dubnus for a moment, and then, apparently expecting the arrival, led Marcus away to the headquarters building in the centre of the fort. Dubnus nodded farewell, turning away to rejoin his own unit without any show of emotion. At the entrance to the headquarters, Marcus was delighted and relieved to find Rufius waiting for him.

'Well, young Corvus, here you are, then! Looking a little thinner if that's possible, although it suits you well enough. Makes you look more determined, and that's no bad thing in your situation.'

He dragged the younger man into the entrance hall, away from the sentry's straining ears, pulling a wax tablet from his tunic.

'I have a formal request from Legatus Sollemnis to the prefect here, backed up by a quite astonishing amount of gold for the cohort's burial fund, asking him to take you in . . . no, don't smile yet, man, that's only a start. Even if he says yes, which I believe unlikely, I expect his First Spear will fight the idea tooth and nail. I know I would in his place. So, before we go in to see the prefect, here are the two rules that you must follow if we are to see you safe. One, keep your mouth shut and let me do the talking as much as possible. I know these people and you do not. Two, if you're asked a question, keep your answer direct and simple. If you strike them as anything other than what I've described, you won't get past the door. Understand?'

The cohort's prefect was a dark-faced man, from the north coast of Africa by Marcus's best guess, and looked to be in his early thirties. He kept a remarkably straight face when Rufius handed over his message from Sollemnis, scanning the tablet for a long moment before tossing it back on the desk in front of the retired officer, one hand distractedly teasing his thick brown beard. Rufius stood impassively in an unconsciously adopted parade rest, uncomfortably aware of both the man's stare and his unquestioned power inside the garrison's small world. He made no move to retrieve the message. After a long pause the prefect shifted his gaze from Rufius, sizing up Marcus in a single glance of his dark brown eyes before speaking in a well-educated and reasonable tone.

'So, it's better if I don't know his real name, he's officially declared traitor, his family are either all dead or in hiding, and yet the commanding officer of the Sixth still sees fit to send him into *my* care and invites me to betray the empire alongside him. He looks like all the other failures my First Spear rejects each year during recruitment, and yet Gaius Calidius Sollemnis commends him as "intelligent and resourceful" and asks me to take him under my wing. As a *centurion*! I'm not sure I have sufficient education to express my amazement . . .'

Rufius, having taken pains to convince Marcus to remain silent, no matter what the provocation, had the luxury of time in which to draw out a carefully calculated silence of his own before responding.

'Prefect Equitius, this man is a trained praetorian centurion. He and I fought together on the road outside Yew Grove, when tribesmen surprised our party, and I saw no lack of courage in his eyes on that day. He also wounded an armed horseman in mounted combat during his escape from an ambush outside Yew Grove. He *also* marched from Yew Grove to this fort in nine days, thirty miles a day. Yes, he is tired, dirty and footsore, but he has courage and determination that you and I should be grateful to call our own. With the right guidance he . . .'

The prefect's calm voice trampled over his sentence, used to being heard with deference under most circumstances.

'Guidance? And that would be imparted by whom, in your opinion? I've got a civil war brewing to both north and south of my sector of the Wall and only four of my centurions with recent combat experience. I've got problems enough without having to nursemaid an untrained officer. Besides, my First Spear would laugh in my face – just as *you* would in his place.'

Rufius shifted his position slightly, weighing his last weapon of persuasion before throwing it.

'Your chosen man Dubnus seems to think reasonably well of him . . .'

Equitius's eyes narrowed at the name. He stood and walked around the desk, stopping in front of Rufius to speak softly into the retired officer's right ear.

'Dubnus? Now you *do* trouble me. What part does our very own Brigantian warrior prince play in this tale?'

Rufius thought quickly, praying that Marcus would remain silent.

'Dubnus and his tent party intervened to save our lives when the barbarians attacked us on the road. Then he chanced upon me and the young man as we were being hunted through a murky dawn, by killers hired by the imperial appointee at Yew Grove. Only his impressive skills in combat saved us both from swift and ignominious death at the hands of those heartless mercenaries . . .'

'I was coming to that. And you can keep the fancy language for the next time you want to overcharge Annius for a consignment of fish pickle. As *I've* received the news, a decurion of cavalry from the Second Asturian Horse at Cauldron Pool and two of his men, part of a detachment serving with the Sixth on attachment, were ambushed by *this* man and his cronies. Murdered before they had time to arm themselves. All three of them were left dead at the roadside, apparently, and to add insult to injury two of their horses were butchered for their meat. You're telling me that Dubnus was a part of *that*?'

Rufius allowed himself to bridle slightly.

'That he defended our lives at the risk of his own, taking us for innocent travellers beset by robbers, yes. That he attacked defenceless cavalrymen, *no*. These men were without uniform or insignia, and attacked us without hesitation. Your excellent chosen man saved both of our lives.'

Equitius stared hard at the retired officer, his face set hard.

'The decurion, in the reports I received, showed signs of torture. A small blade had been used to inflict severe pain upon him as he lay trapped and dying underneath his dead horse. The Asturians have sworn bloody revenge on their altar to Mars. You wouldn't know anything about *that*, I suppose?'

Rufius shrugged, his face remaining impassive.

'More robbers would be my guess, Prefect. Desperate to have the decurion's money perhaps? He made the mistake of abandoning his uniform and, since he looked like any other traveller, he paid a severe price.'

The other man turned away, his face shadowed by disbelief.

'Hmmm. And Dubnus brought him here.'

'Only as the result of a request from Legatus Sollemnis, passed on by me. I work for him in a minor capacity . . .'

The prefect spun back to face Rufius, speaking into his ear so quietly that Marcus could barely pick out the angry tone of his voice.

'I *know* the capacity in which you work, Tiberius Rufius, assessing the Wall units' readiness and reporting on the situation beyond the frontier to Northern Command. Don't assume that everyone this side of the Wall is simple minded enough to mistake you for a trader. You should beware your secret reaching the wrong ears on the *far* side.'

He paced away to stare out of the room's open window, his hair ruffled by the fresh breeze.

'Very well, I'll accept your version of these unfortunate events, despite the fact I don't trust a single word. I'll also try to accept Gaius Calidius Sollemnis's request of me, since I do trust *his* judgement, and since I still owe him a very substantial debt of gratitude. As for the money he sent you to offer . . . I'll use that to buy my men some decent equipment, if those incompetents over at Noisy Valley still have anything worth bribing out of their stores. Quite *how* I am to discharge this responsibility is at the moment, however, beyond me . . .'

He sat down behind his desk, surrendering to thought, idly pulling at his beard again. Rufius craned his head around, giving Marcus another warning stare of instruction to remain silent. At length the prefect spoke again, his sharp eyes boring into Marcus's.

'I presume that you are an educated young man?'

'Yes, Prefect.'

'And I presume that you speak little or none of the local language?'

'Very little, Prefect.'

'What weapons training have you received?'

'Ten years' training with the sword and general skill at arms, six years' horsemanship, and seven months' as a praetorian centurion, Prefect.'

The officer got out of his chair again and walked round the desk to look yet more closely into Marcus's eyes.

'Young man, while I respect the Guard's renowned abilities on the battlefield, I'm not stupid enough to suppose that you actually *learnt* any of the art of modern warfare during your time in their ranks. I hear that it is the practice these days for a certain number of the sons of the aristocracy to be bought positions as praetorian officers each year. I hear that they serve with the Guard for a period, usually in ceremonial roles, and are shepherded at all times by experienced subordinates. Shepherded, young man, to ensure that they do nothing to degrade their unit's fighting capabilities.'

Marcus winced inwardly at the memory of his clashes with his former chosen man Apicius, who he had often accused of being too harsh a disciplinarian.

'In return they earn the right to enter the army as senior centurions, usually over the heads of men with much greater experience and ability, and can then return to Rome after a short period of service. Lucrative positions are open to such men, in the urban vigiles or even as praetorian tribunes. Often, it is said, such young men do more harm than good in their first years of command, and keep more capable men out of the positions they have earned by their efforts and successes.

'To be blunt, Marcus Tribulus Corvus – and trust me, I really don't want to know your true name – you have been trained to perform the tasks of a *ceremonial* officer. You know how to ensure that your men look smart on parade; you know the etiquette to be observed on palace duty. Doubtless you know how to address the emperor's favourite mistress should you chance upon her being serviced by a gladiator during your rounds of the palace. I doubt very much, however, that you have the first idea as to the requirements of an officer on active service. Hmm?'

To Rufius's relief, Marcus kept his eyes firmly fixed on the wall in front of him, and said nothing.

'Do you *really* want to make the attempt to gain a centurion's rank in this unit? Do you want it badly enough to accept *any* terms I place upon allowing you to convince my First Spear to accept your candidature?'

Marcus hesitated for a moment, sought Rufius's eye and, receiving a nod from his friend, took a breath before speaking.

'Prefect, my family is destroyed, my honour stolen, and I am declared traitor. This is my last chance to save myself *and* be of service to Rome. If I fail to convince you to let me have this chance, I will have little option except that of suicide.'

Equitius laughed softly, but without malice.

'Hmm. Stirring words. But I'm really not the person you need to convince.'

The cohort's First Spear was adamant in his refusal, turning to glare out of the office's window at the rolling hills beyond the distant parade ground in the at-ease position, as if addressing a gathering of his centurions. The individual rings of his mail shone with a high polish across his broad chest, while his moustache curled in a magnificent glossy arc down his upper lip. He ran a hand across his head, reflexively seeking to smooth hair which had long since fallen out or been shaved close to his skull to leave him almost perfectly bald. A large man, but constant exertion ensured that his body was all muscle, given no chance to run to seed.

'No, Prefect, no man in this cohort's one-hundred-and-twenty-year history has ever attained the rank of centurion without first serving in the ranks as a soldier. Usually for at least ten years, often a good deal longer. I have no intention of changing a tradition that has served us well for that long.'

'I . . .'

'Sir, with respect, I've seen combat beyond the rampart. I *know* what it's like when the blue-noses charge into the shield wall with their swords swinging. We never stop telling those boys about the superiority of our way of fighting, about the fact that they only need to jab the point of an infantry sword in four inches at the right point of the body to kill a man in seconds. We train them day after day to do just that, until they'll kill and kill again on instinct alone in the horror of a battle. And it *still* scares the shit out them to have some hairy great bastard swinging a battleaxe and running at full speed into their line. The main thing that stops them from running when they're blasted from head to foot with blood, when the man to each side has been either killed or is trying to hold his guts in, is me, and the other ten officers they know will fight alongside them to the death. Will stand and fight even if they *do* turn and run, even if only to cover their backs. They hate us and they fear us in equal portions, but mainly they *respect* us. Very few men of nineteen summers have that kind of leadership potential. Praetorian or not.'

He turned back to face his superior, determined to give no ground to the suggestion. Equitius stared back at him, his expression unrepentant.

'As I was *trying* to say, I agree with you completely.'

'Then why ask me even to speak to him?'

The prefect stood up, walking around the desk to join his senior centurion at the window.

'Three reasons, Sextus. Firstly, I took that rascal Quintus Tiberius Rufius to one side once the boy had said his piece, and asked him why the Sixth's commander was willing to risk his life for this matter.'

'And?'

'The young man doesn't know it, but the legatus is his real father. Nor in my opinion must he find out, after the shocks he's had. Apparently our colleague in arms and the senator were friends in the service, tribunes in one of the Hispania legions, and when Sollemnis got a local girl pregnant, it was Valerius Aquila and his new wife who took responsibility for the child. And, as you'll be aware every time you look at the equipment our troops use, we owe him more than one favour.

'Secondly, if we don't give the man the chance to try, he'll walk out into those hills and fall on his sword. I've seen enough men in that situation, and he has the same look in his eyes . . .' He paused for a moment, staring into space at nothing in particular. '. . . without hope, beaten down by circumstance but still determined to stay in control of his destiny. I have some respect for that attitude, as you may be aware.'

A long silence ensued, until the centurion spoke again.

'And your third reason, Prefect?'

Equitius paused for a moment, his lips pursed in thought.

'I just wonder if there isn't more to the man than we might suppose. You're the judge of men – *you* decide.'

'And if I still decide against?'

'Then Tribulus Corvus will have to work out his preferred means of taking his own life.'

★

Marcus and Rufius jumped to their feet at the sudden opening of the prefect's office door. The senior centurion stepped through the frame, stopping in front of the younger man and looking him up and down with slow care. He saw, through the shadows of exhaustion, a hard face with a determined set, its hawkish aspect enough to make a stranger approach with care.

'Are you tired, candidate?'

'Yes, First Spear.'

'"*Sir*"' will be enough for the time being.'

'Yes, sir.'

'Do your feet hurt?'

'Yes, sir.'

'Are you hungry?'

'Yes, sir.'

'Could you march another ten miles if your life depended upon it?'

'Yes, sir.'

'Very well, we'll march.'

The officer accepted his cloak, sword and helmet from a soldier who had run to fetch them, handing over his vine stick while he buckled the weapon to his body. He looked inside the helmet to check the position of the woollen cap that nestled inside the bronze dome, catching Marcus's sideways glance.

'My one concession to advancing years. The old pot can be painful to wear in the absence of hair, even with the issue liner, and we don't wrap rags round our heads under the helmet in *this* cohort.'

He secured the helmet by its chinstrap, taking his vine stick back from the waiting man.

'Dismissed, soldier. I believe your century have drawn duty cleaning the bathhouse.'

They walked up the fort's slope, past barrack buildings

and staring soldiers, to the Wall itself, towering twelve feet above the fort's stone roads. First Spear Frontinius led the way up the ladder of one of the two gate towers, bringing Marcus out on the rampart. The sentries looked on in surprise while he gestured for the Roman to look out over the scene beyond the Wall. A hundred-foot drop, almost sheer, fell away from the Wall's base to the plain below, a mighty natural defence that must have made the military engineers salivate with its potential when the rampart's line was first planned.

The escarpment ran in both directions as far as the eye could follow its sinuous path, the whitewashed wall that topped its line clearly visible for miles. Below the Wall the ground was more or less flat, until it swelled into shallow hills a mile or so distant, their slopes heavily forested.

'We cleared away the trees from the land in front of the Wall.'

Marcus nodded his understanding. Such open ground would make any covert approach to the fort almost impossible. A fair-sized lake fed the Fort's bathhouse, the water flowing down from its location on the higher part of the plain. A notch had been cut in the escarpment by the stream over the ages, and here, a hundred yards past the eastern wall of the fort, and behind the Wall, he could see the high-domed roof of the bathhouse. Frontinius tapped him on the shoulder, recapturing his attention.

'This view shows our place and role here more clearly than any speech I might make. On this side of the Wall, there is order. Order, discipline, cleanliness, the right way of things. On the other side there is nothing better than barbarism, surly tribesmen with an appetite for Roman goods but little desire to enter our society. The tribes to our immediate front, the Selgovae, Votadini and Dumnonii, number at least a hundred thousand. The tribes from beyond Antoninus's

Wall, farther north, Maeatae and Caledonii, barbarous tattooed animals all of them, as many again. Even the people to our rear, Carvetii and Brigantes, would cheerfully put a dagger between our shoulder blades given half a chance, for all their veneer of civilisation. We on the Wall are ten thousand men in a sea of hostile spears – even the northern legions are several days' march distant. If the natives decide to fight, which currently seems inevitable given that their leader Calgus has spent most of the last year whipping them up for it, we'll have to face down several times our own number until the legions can get forward. And they won't get here at all if the tribes in their own operational areas decide to join the fun. Life here is as dull as it gets most of the time, but it could quickly become a lot more exciting than any of us would wish.'

He led Marcus back down through the fort, out of the massive southern gate and through its small collection of houses and shops. Women and children in the street stood respectfully as the officer passed, even a couple of hard-faced prostitutes favouring him with smiles.

'They depend on us for their livelihood. If the prefect decided that the Hill would be more secure without the hangers-on, they would be destitute. Mind you, there are so many men with women and children in the town now that I suspect they form no risk to our security.'

They marched over a bridge spanning the massive ditch that separated the civilian and military zones, Marcus readjusting to the renewed pain in his feet. The road fell away steeply towards the parade ground's expanse, across which several groups of men were training with swords and shields. The older man marched briskly past them, barking directions to individuals whose performance caught his eye.

'You, yes, *you*, with the red hair, lift your shield higher! You're supposed to be stopping blue-nose spears, not protecting your bloody ankles! Chosen Man, show him what I mean, he clearly can't understand . . . Well done, *that* man, excellent sword work!'

They passed the final group and left the parade ground behind before he spoke to Marcus again, talking at the air in front of him rather than turning to face the younger man.

'Recruits. In two months we'll have knocked them into rough shape, and toughened them up enough to give them a good chance of surviving a battle, and in six they'll be every bit as good as any legionary. We've got men serving with ten and twenty years with the cohort, some who fought in the last uprising. What I'm being asked to do is put you in command of eighty of those men, all of whom, since they grew up playing at soldiers in the woods and fields of this area, have more idea of *real* soldiering than you do. The very idea of it makes me feel sick. This is *my* cohort, *my* fort and *my* parade ground. I was passed the leadership of them all, every man that serves here, by my predecessor, and when I retire I'll bring the best centurion in the cohort down to that parade ground. I'll make him promise me, and the shrines of Cocidius, Jupiter, Mars and Victory, to maintain the traditions we live and die by. I'm responsible for those traditions now, and for making sure that my decisions are made in the best interests of the unit. *My* cohort.'

He turned his head to look at Marcus's face for a moment, checking for any reaction. The road ran arrow straight up to the next fold in the land, making Marcus open his mouth to increase his air intake, but he kept his eyes fixed on the horizon.

'The prefect knows very well what his role here is, and so do I. He's here for two or three years, to represent Rome, and make decisions as to the course of action the cohort should follow in Rome's service. I've been here for my entire adult life, and I'll stay here until I retire, or die in combat.

My word as to the ways in which those decisions are carried out is final, although since we respect each other's judgement he will usually issue orders upon which we've agreed jointly. I also make all decisions as to who is allowed to enter service, based on what centurions tell me and on what I see with my own eyes. And from what I see and hear, *you* represent a good deal of trouble to both the prefect and this unit. If it were a simple "yes" or "no" on those grounds I wouldn't even be taking this trouble to understand you better.'

He fell silent for a moment as they marched on side by side, and then spoke again.

'The prefect, however, sees something in you that he encourages me to consider before making that decision. Your threat of suicide found a chink in his armour you may not have appreciated. His uncle fell on his own sword after losing most of a cohort just like this one in the German forests twenty years ago, but not before writing to tell his nephew why he was doing it. Prefect Equitius still has the tablet. Consequently, his sense of honour is his prime motivation when he considers your case. Would you do the same?'

Marcus blinked for a second at the unexpected question.

'Yes, sir. I would have no other remaining choice.'

'Very well.'

Frontinius stopped walking under the shadow of a lone tree growing by the roadside and drew his gladius with a swift movement, holding it towards Marcus with the hilt foremost. The sun eased one corner of its disc out from behind the cloud that had obscured it for much of the day, caressing the landscape with a slender strand of light.

'Take the sword.'

Marcus did so with a sudden feeling of utter detachment, hefting the weapon with one hand, judging the weapon's fine balance and razor-sharp blade.

'It goes with the responsibilities I bear, passed from each First Spear to his successor. It's an old weapon, forged in the Year of the Four Emperors over a hundred years ago, and it belonged to a prefect who rewarded an act of bravery in battle which saved his life with the gift of his personal weapon. The courage you've shown to get this far entitles you to fall on a blade whose honour is indisputable.'

He stood in silence on the empty road, watching Marcus intently, his body taut in its readiness for action, with one hand resting lightly on his dagger's ornately decorated handle. Marcus looked at the weapon's blade for a long moment before speaking. His senses sharpened perceptibly, the tiny sounds of bird calls and the breeze's ruffling of his hair suddenly catching his attention, although the colours of grass and sky seemed to fade to dusty, washed-out shades.

'Thank you, First Spear, for at least providing me with a dignified exit. I must now look to find revenge for these wrongs in the next life.'

Clamping his mouth firmly shut, he steeled himself for the act, placing the sword's point firmly against his sternum, and taking a last deep breath before throwing himself forward. A strong arm whipped out and grabbed his rough shirt as he fell towards the ground, turning him in midair. He hit the road's surface hard on his back, losing his hold on the sword's hilt and letting it fall. Frontinius looked down at him, holding his hand out, with a new respect in his eyes.

'You *meant* it. That's something.'

Marcus reached up and took the hand offered by the officer, climbing back on to his feet. The officer's sword was already back in its scabbard.

'I'm sorry, that was deliberately cruel, but I had to know if you had the stomach for what you threatened.'

Frontinius was intrigued by the look he received in return

for his apology, the dark eyes seeming to skewer his soul. Perhaps, if the man were trained to *use* that ability . . .

'What would you have done if I had failed to use the sword, or turned it upon you?'

A laugh cracked Frontinius's face, despite the gravity of the situation.

'I'd have cut your throat with this.'

He pulled the dagger, cocked his wrist and threw the short blade, putting it cleanly into the centre of a truncated branch that projected a foot out from the tree's trunk at head height, lopped off by a work gang when it had grown to obstruct the road. He reached to retrieve the knife, speaking over his shoulder.

'They're not made for throwing, but when you practise enough anything's possible. As you may discover. Now march!'

They walked on along the road's arrow-straight path, passing an eight-man detachment patrolling back towards the Hill.

'Keep marching.'

The older man turned back for a hundred yards, marching alongside the detachment and studying each man's uniform in turn before turning once more, calling over his shoulder to the tent party's leader.

'A very good turn out, young man, we'll make a chosen man of you yet!'

'Thank you, First Spear!'

He jogged back along the road to catch Marcus, barely breathing hard with the effort. Slowing to a brisk walk, he resumed the conversation.

'My cohort, less than a thousand men, is expected to keep the peace along this sector of the line, out to a range of fifty or so miles either side of the Wall. We are the only law this country has, both in front of and behind the rampart. We control two tribal gathering points, the only place those peoples are permitted to come together, and then only under the supervision of an officer of this unit. They hate us with a passion, more so since we are their own people turned to the empire's purpose, and within our area of control there are *fifty* of them for every soldier within our walls. Our strength, the thing that counterbalances that disadvantage in numbers, is our discipline, the strength of our resolve. We dominate the ground, we know its secrets, and we *own* every fold and seam. They know that, know that we'll die to keep it ours, but that many more of them will have to die to take it from us. Yes, there are legions within a few days' march, but we'll have to meet any attempt to dislodge us alone, most likely us and the other ten thousand or so men like us along the frontier.

'Men join this unit at an average age of fourteen summers, serve most of their adult lives in the ranks, most of that time doing boring or dirty jobs unless they get the chance to become an immune, with a few hours of death and terror thrown in every few years. Some of them, the better soldiers, rise to command tent parties, or if they're really effective, to the position of watch officer, and even fewer to chosen man, deputy to their centurion, responsible for keeping the century aligned and pointing the right way in battle. The best of them, the boldest and the bravest, ten men in eight hundred, reach the position of centurion, with their own rooms, high rates of pay, but most of all with the privilege of leading their century into battle in the proud traditions of the Tungrians. What makes you think you can live up to their ideal?'

Marcus took a moment before replying, weighing his words carefully to avoid his earnestness being mistaken for desperation.

'I can't promise you that I will. But I can promise you that I will do everything in my power to make it so . . .'

The older man stopped, trying hard to suppress a smile as he cocked a sardonic eyebrow.

'So we'll do for you for now, will we, until the issue of your legal status is forgotten? What then, I wonder?'

Marcus's nostrils flared with his anger and he turned swiftly, making the other man tense involuntarily and extend a stealthy hand towards his sword's hilt as a dirty, broken-nailed finger tapped his armoured chest.

'*Enough!* I've been hunted across this country, questioned by you and your prefect as if I *were* a criminal, instead of an innocent man whose entire family has been slaughtered, and had my honour and my ability doubted one time too many. I've put up with it all because I've been in no position to argue with the men judging me, and perhaps that's still the case, but for now I've tolerated just as much as I can. So, make your mind up, First Spear, either give me the chance I crave or cut my bloody throat, but you *will* stop playing with me, one way or another!'

Folding his arms, he glared back at the officer, clearly at the end of his patience. Frontinius nodded slowly, walking around him in a slow deliberate circle until he once again faced the younger man.

'So there is anger in there, it just needed a spark to light the tinder. Just as well too, you'd be no good to me if you didn't have fire in your guts, although you'll be sorry if you ever speak to me that way in front of any other man. Very well, I'm decided. I'll go against tradition, break the rules and offer you a bargain. I'll give you a position as centurion, probationary, mind you, and with the decision as to your suitability entirely mine, on the condition that I get something I need. Something my cohort needs more than anything else, right now.'

'You've *accepted* him?'

Equitius's eyes widened with genuine surprise.

'Yes. He's being issued with his equipment now.'

The prefect smiled quietly.

'Thank you. You've allowed me to discharge a debt to Sollemnis.'

The senior centurion grimaced.

'We'll see. All I've agreed to is to give him a chance. One I fully expect him to fail to grasp. In return I get two centurions for the price of one. Or, more likely, one very good centurion and a corpse for quiet burial . . .'

Equitius stared at him questioningly. His First Spear smiled grimly in return.

'Well, you didn't think I was going to let a fully trained legion centurion slip through my fingers, did you? I had a quiet chat with Tiberius Rufius earlier today and he made me an interesting proposition, given our current dearth of trained centurions. It's a deal I resolved to accept only if there was a hint of talent in young Corvus – which, to be fair, there is. Your friend the legatus gets a hiding place for his son, and in return I get the use of his man Rufius until the first snowfall of next winter. Sounds like fair barter to me.'

4

Marcus didn't realise how his place with the Tungrians had been secured until the soldier ordered to take him to the fort's stores for equipping pointed him through the door into their twilight world. Quintus Tiberius Rufius stood waiting for him beside the long wooden counter, a pile of equipment and clothing stacked next to him. Marcus paused in the doorway for a moment, adjusting to both the gloom and his own surprise.

'Quintus, what are you . . .'

The older man grinned sheepishly, clearly torn between his pleasure at being back in uniform and what his presence said for the provenance of his friend's recruitment.

'I've taken the salt again, lad, accepted the offer of a centurion's berth for a year, or more if it works out well.'

Marcus made the connection, and his face creased with sudden anger.

'So I get a chance to make a new start at the cost of your service? Well, it isn't going to . . .'

He stopped speaking, brought to a halt by Rufius's raised hand.

'Just a moment, lad. *You!* Come here!'

The store's clerk detached himself from the rack of spears behind which he'd been lurking, and unwillingly presented himself at the counter's far side. Rufius shot out an arm, grasping him firmly by one ear and dragging his head across the broad expanse of age-polished wood.

'Interesting, was it, our conversation?'

The head shook vigorously, or as much as possible with one ear pinned to the counter. Rufius drew his dagger, and slid the point under the pinned ear's flesh, allowing the steel to caress its curve.

'Good. Let's be clear, if I hear anything about the last minute of my private conversation with my friend here repeated I'll have this ear off your head within the hour. You might be an immune, but it won't protect you from my blade. Got it?'

The head nodded frantically.

'Good. Now go and hide in the back of this shed, and don't come back out until I tell you to.'

The clerk vanished into the gloom without a backward glance. Rufius turned back to his friend with a wry smile.

'One thing you learn early on, everything you say in a cohort's stores is public property, just as sure as the stores officer is the richest man in the fort if he has an ounce of wit about him. Now, you were in the middle of telling me how you weren't going to tolerate such treatment, my being blackmailed to serve with the cohort in return for your safety?'

'I . . .'

Rufius raised his hands again, silencing the other man.

'One moment. Before you say any more, I think I should make *my* position clear. When Sollemnis asked me to bring you here, he warned me that Prefect Equitius is desperately short of experienced officers. He cautioned me that Equitius, or more likely his First Spear, might try to induce me to serve here. And do you know, when he told me that my heart fairly leapt in my chest. You think I'm being blackmailed, and yes, Frontinius thinks that he's extorted a bargain from me that serves him well, but the real winner here is *me*.'

Marcus frowned his lack of understanding.

'But why? Surely you've earned an easier time after twenty-five years of service?'

Rufius reached into the pile of his new kit, pulling from it his vine stick, the twisted wood shiny from years of use.

'See this? A simple piece of wood with no more value than kindling for a fire, until I pick it up. In my hands, however, it becomes the symbol of my authority. For fifteen years I carried another, very much like this, all over this country, until it was like part of my body. It was the first thing I reached for in the morning, and the last thing I put down at night, and let me tell you, I *loved* that life. And do you want to know the worst day of my twenty-five years under the eagle?'

Marcus nodded, his anger fading to a sad resignation. Rufius gave a faraway look, his eyes seeing something other than the storehouse walls.

'My worst day . . . it wasn't the first one, at the recruiting camp in Gaul where I joined up, where they cut off all my hair and my new centurion chased us round the parade ground until we puked our guts up. It wasn't the day when my century was ambushed in the Tava valley, and seventy-seven men became fifty-three and a collection of dying men and corpses in less than ten minutes. Brigantia forgive me, it wasn't even the day that my wife died before her time, taken from me by the cold and the damp, although it's a close-run race . . .'

He took a deep breath.

'No, my very worst day in all that time was the very last one, when I had to hand my vine stick back to my legatus. It was a misty day, and the entire legion was on parade, centuries stretching away into the grey until they were invisible. All I had to do was march up the line of my cohort, take their salute, march to the legatus, hand him my vine stick, salute, about-face and watch the legion parade off. It seemed to take for ever, and yet it was over in the blink of an eye. I stood there beside him as the legion stamped off the parade ground, watching my cohort under the command of another man, a friend that I'd been grooming for the job for years, chosen from among my centurions. It was like watching your wife on another man's arm . . .'

He turned from the memory, fixing Marcus with a serious stare.

'So, *Centurion*, when Sextus Frontinius smiles at you, and you know full well that he's thinking that he's got an experienced officer at the expense of your troubling him for just as long as it takes to find a reason to declare you a failure, here's what you say to yourself – Quintus Tiberius Rufius is as happy as a pig in the deepest shit he can find. And you, my lad, are not going to fail. Not with me here to keep you straight. Got that?'

Marcus nodded, blowing out a pent-up breath.

'Got it.'

'Good. Now, have they told you who your chosen man's going to be? I only ask because Frontinius made a special point of telling me on the way down here. He seemed to think it was quite funny.'

Marcus nodded again, his lips pursed with foreboding.

'So would I, if I didn't think it was going to be *so* damned difficult . . .'

To the Roman's huge surprise Dubnus took the news of Marcus's appointment as centurion to the cohort's 9th Century, with himself as the new chosen man, with perfect equanimity. He waited until they were alone in his centurion's quarters before tackling the subject head on. Dubnus looked at him without any obvious emotion, shrugging his shoulders.

'You're worried that I'm angry about this, but you don't need to be. I'm not angry, and I don't want to talk about it. Now get into uniform and let's go and look at what we've got here.'

Marcus persisted, not willing to believe it could be that simple from the big Briton's perspective.

'We *need* to talk, Dubnus, and it won't wait. I . . .'

'You're a centurion. I'm a chosen man. I'll do as you command. This is not a problem.'

'But you're a warrior, a true soldier. I walk into your fort, already owing you a life, and get promoted to centurion just like *that*? You should want to put your fist through my face! How can you take this so easily?'

'Perhaps you'll be a real centurion. I content myself with being the best chosen man in the cohort instead, better than half of the officers, and they know it. But I'll never be a centurion, I've already been told as much.'

Marcus realised in a flash what was holding the man back, stunned both by the insight and the way the other man had been held from his potential.

'You've been told that you won't be an officer so many times, you've stopped even trying. What my father used to call a "self-fulfilling prophecy". Look, the First Spear told me all about your father, and how he was deposed from his throne when you were still a boy, how he sent you here when he was dying. He told me that he doesn't believe you'll fight your own people when the time comes, that he believes you're the best soldier in the cohort to satisfy your wounded pride, not because you want to serve. He doubts your commitment, Dubnus, not your abilities . . .'

The other man just shrugged. Marcus smiled, giddy with relief at making the mental leap to see through the bluff soldier's reserve.

'And he's told you you'll never make it to centurion so many times that you've started to believe it. I can change that. You can be a centurion – if you *want* to . . .'

Dubnus stared into his eyes for a long moment, testing the sincerity of the words.

'You'll help *me* to become a centurion? Why?'

Marcus took a deep breath.

'Dubnus, you've said it a dozen times in the last week. I *was* a praetorian officer, but I never saw action, so it was just a ceremonial job . . . looking good in uniform, knowing what to say to whom . . . I'm going to need you to help me be a real officer, a warrior leader. What else can I give you in return?'

'I make you a warrior, you'll make me a centurion?'

'Not a warrior. I may yet surprise you in that respect. A warrior *leader*. It's what I'll have to achieve if I'm to survive here. Or die trying.'

'Perhaps.'

Marcus noted that the Briton wasn't smiling.

The century's barrack block was primitive in comparison with the facilities his men had enjoyed in Rome, but Marcus ignored the condition of his quarters as he got into his new uniform. The red tunic was savagely rough in comparison to the fine white cloth he'd worn as a Guard officer. Thick woollen leggings tickled his legs and made him sweat in the building's shelter, although he guessed that their warmth would seem little enough on a cold winter morning. He bent to examine his armour and weapons, laid out across his bed, noting with dismay the patina of rust that dusted the mail coat's rings. His helmet was slightly dented on one side. Pulling his sword from its scabbard, he peered closely at the blade.

'Blunt.'

Dubnus nodded unhappily.

'Annius keeps his best equipment for those willing to pay. You get second best.'

It was true. The clothing he'd been issued was, on closer inspection, well worn.

'I see. First things first. Inspection.'

They marched into the first of the eight-man rooms, troops scattering with surprise from their game of dice.

'Attention!'

The soldiers froze into ramrod-straight poses at Dubnus's bellowed command, shuffling to make room for Marcus to walk into the cramped room. He looked slowly around, taking in the dirty straw scattered haphazardly across the barrack floor and the poorly stacked weapons and shields in the outer room. Noticing the squad's food ration for the day, waiting next to the small oven in and on which all cooking was done for the eight men, he turned to shout through the open door.

'Chosen!'

'Sir!'

Dubnus stepped into the room, looking at the food to which Marcus was pointing with his vine stick. A couple of the men cast him sidelong glances of amazement. Nobody had warned them that they had new officers, never mind that one of them was the man they called 'the Prince' when they were sure he wasn't listening.

'Is that quality of food normal for this cohort?'

The salted fish looked green in parts, the fresh vegetables riddled with holes from the attentions of parasites. Only the bread, fresh from the fort's oven, invited closer attention.

'No, sir.'

'I see. Chosen, what's the normal size of tent party in this cohort?'

'Eight.'

'So why are there *nine* men in this barrack?'

Dubnus growled a question at the nearest soldier in his own language.

'He says that one soldier has taken a whole room for himself. They're all scared to fight him . . . including the acting centurion.'

Marcus stiffened with anger, as much at the acquiescence of so-called fighting men with this act of bullying as with the offence itself.

'So a man has to sleep on the floor? Take me to that barrack.'

They marched down the line of doors, the frightened soldier pointing to the offending door. Dubnus put his long chosen man's pole down on the floor, flexing his powerful hands and clenching them into fists. He spoke to Marcus without taking his eyes off the barrack's door.

'I'll do this.'

It was a statement rather than a request, a baldly stated invitation for Marcus to step back from the physical side of his role, and it tempted him more than he had expected. It would be so easy to let the Briton pull this miscreant from his room and discipline him . . .

Shaking his head in refusal, Marcus pushed him gently but firmly aside, rapping on the door with his vine stick.

'*Inspection! Open this door!*'

A clatter sounded from inside, the door bursting open to reveal a half-clad man wielding a wooden stave. Long hair hung lank across his shoulders, pale blue eyes staring insolently from a hatchet face.

'You tosser, Trajan, I'll . . . what?'

Surprised by the appearance of an unfamiliar officer at his door, he hesitated the crucial second that Marcus needed. Taking a quick step forward, he jabbed the stick's blunt end forcefully into the Briton's sternum, dropping him to the ground in writhing agony. Dubnus stepped forward, collecting the stave with a sideways glance of surprise at his new centurion before effortlessly lifting the soldier to his unsteady feet. Marcus tucked his stick under one arm, forcing himself to give off waves of confidence. With an audience of a dozen or so of his new command's rank and file, he couldn't afford to get this wrong.

'Name?'

The soldier, his initial shock starting to wear off, glared at him from beneath heavy black eyebrows. Dubnus, still holding him up by one arm, flexed his fingers and squeezed the bicep hard, communicating without words.

'Antenoch . . . ah! *Centurion.*'

'Chosen, do you know this man?'

'A good warrior, a poor soldier. He lacks *discipline.*'

The soldier sneered at his face, disregarding the pain in his gut.

'What I *lack*, Dubnus, is any vestige of respect for your authority. And even more so his . . .'

He nodded in Marcus's direction. The Roman raised a hand to Dubnus, preventing the explosion of rage he saw building on the big man's face, keeping his voice dead level.

'Like it or not, I'm your new centurion, soldier, so you'll follow my instructions to the *letter.* Which begin with my telling you to return that barrack to the men you evicted to take possession, and return to your given tent party. If you don't like taking orders from me, you can *try* to take it out on me on the practice field tomorrow morning, but until then, move your gear. *Now.*'

The other man locked eyes with him momentarily, found steel in their gaze, and shook his arm free, slouching off into the empty barrack.

'Chosen, which of this disorganised rabble was responsible for discipline until our arrival?'

The Briton turned, pointing to one of the men gathered

in silent amazement at the turn of events, his face blank with the shock.

'Chosen Man Trajan. In temporary command of the century while there's no officer available.'

Marcus swivelled to regard the man with a glare of contempt.

'Trajan, step forward.'

'Centurion.'

The man stepped white faced from the throng, coming to attention and pushing out his chest.

'This century is a disgrace to the cohort. You are hereby reduced to the rank of soldier. Chosen, find this *soldier* a tent party. You might also want to discuss the matter of the quality of the century's rations at some length, along with the possibility of a donation to the funeral club. Perhaps you could take him over the Wall for a short patrol in the forest . . . later. Now I want a full parade of the century, here.'

'Centurion.'

Dubnus strode away, beating at each door in turn and shouting *'Parade'* at the top of his voice. Men flew from each barrack, pulling at hastily donned items of clothing as they fell in to the rapidly swelling unit. Within a moment the parade was complete, the demoted Trajan pushed carelessly into the line to more astonished glances while Marcus stood in front of the wide-eyed soldiers, biding his time. Several window shutters on the quarters facing the 9th's barrack quietly opened just enough for their occupants to peer through the gaps but remain out of view, hidden from Dubnus's searching eyes.

Once Dubnus had commanded the gathering to 'shut your fucking mouths' Marcus gave a cursory inspection, noting the poor repair of almost every man's tunics and boots, and the generally unkempt and undernourished look that predominated. Returning to his place in front of the parade, he called to Dubnus.

'Translate for me, Chosen, let's make sure everyone understands.'

'Centurion.'

'Soldiers of the Ninth Century, I am your new centurion, Marcus Tribulus Corvus. From this moment I formally assume command of this century, and become responsible for every aspect of your well-being, discipline, training and readiness for war.'

He paused, looking to Dubnus, who drew a large breath and spat a stream of his native language at the troops.

'One *fucking* smile, cough or fart from any one of you cock jockeys, and I'll put my pole so far up that man's shithole that it won't even scrape on the floor. This is your new centurion and you will treat him with the appropriate degree of respect if you don't want to lead short and very fucking interesting lives.'

He turned to Marcus and nodded, indicating that the Roman should continue.

'I can see from the state of your uniforms that you've been neglected, a state of affairs that I intend to address very shortly. I have yet to see your readiness for battle, but I can assure you that you *will* be combat ready in the shortest possible time. I do not intend to command a century that I would imagine is regarded as the laughing stock of its unit for any longer than I have to . . .'

Dubnus cast a pitying sneer over the faces in front of him before speaking again, watching their faces lengthen with the understanding of his methods, passed by whispered word of mouth from his previous century.

'You're not soldiers, you're a fucking waste of rations, a disgrace to the Tungrians! You look like shit, you smell like shit and you're probably about as hard as shit! That will change! I will kick your lazy fucking arses up and down every hill in the country if I have to, but you *will* be real soldiers. I will make you ready to kill and die for the honour of this century, with spear or sword or your fucking teeth and nails if need be!'

Marcus cast a questioning look at him, half guessing that the chosen man was deviating from his script, but chose not to challenge his subordinate.

'You'll have better food, uniforms and equipment, and soon. Your retraining starts tomorrow morning, so prepare yourselves! Life in this century changes *now*!'

Dubnus smiled broadly, showing his teeth with pleasure.

'Your hairy white arses are mine from this second. Get ready to grab your ankles.'

Marcus turned to Dubnus.

'Once you've had a conversation with *Soldier* Trajan, you are to ensure that all barracks are cleaned out, fresh flooring is distributed, and that all men have practice equipment ready for morning exercises. I'll see you on parade in the morning. Dismissed.'

'Sir.'

Dubnus turned on his troops, spitting a stream of orders in all directions. Marcus walked away towards his quarter, only a tremor at the corner of one eye evidencing the exhaustion washing through his body. Sweeping the equipment off his bed, he collapsed gratefully on to the lumpy mattress, closed his eyes, and slept.

Later that night, as Equitius settled into bed alongside his wife, he replayed the day's events in his mind. A rueful shake of his head caught her attention.

'Well then, you've been in a world of your own all evening. What is it?'

'Eh? Oh . . . nothing. I received a replacement officer this morning . . . well, two, although one of them is a nineteen-year-old aristocrat fresh from the Grove. A gift from our good friend Gaius Calidius Sollemnis.'

'Really? Did they bring news of the legatus and his family?'

Paccia was a close friend of the legatus's wife and missed her visits to Yew Grove, recently made impractical by the growing enmity of the local Brigantians. Equitius was already wondering whether he shouldn't pack her off down the North Road to the fortress and its relative safety from the border area's uncertainties.

'Again, of a sort . . . look, these new arrivals aren't good news, not for Sollemnis and not for us. He sent them to us as a means of hiding a fugitive from the emperor.'

His wife propped herself up on one elbow, her forehead furrowed.

'But *why*!? That's treason, Septimus!'

'Exactly. The lad's his son, and that's a pretty good reason for Sollemnis not to want him delivered for justice, plus he's the adopted son of a Roman senator who was unjustly accused and executed by Commodus's cronies as a means of appropriating his land and wealth.'

'And therefore the son of a declared traitor. And you've agreed to harbour him inside *this* fort?'

'I've made him a centurion, actually . . .'

Paccia sat up in bed, her eyes wide with fear and anger. He raised a hand to forestall her outburst.

'*Listen* to me, Paccia, and listen well. I've served the empire in a succession of commands in places that neither of us really wanted. Do you remember Syria? That heat? The sand that got absolutely everywhere? The rain in Germania, and the cold? No man can accuse me of ever stinting in my loyalty to the throne, even when I could just have walked away to relax as a civilian. The boy is an innocent victim of imperial greed, and the gods know that should be enough for us. He is also the son of a man to whom I have a sworn debt of honour. He's *also* a trained officer, praetorian in fact, and he brought an experienced legionary centurion here with him as well. That could be invaluable in the next few months.'

'Septimus, I . . .'

'No, Paccia, and I've never done this to you before, but *no*. The decision is made. When men in authority turn a blind eye to the iniquities of a misguided ruler all hope will be lost for the empire. He stays.'

He turned away on his side, setting his face obdurately against any further protest. And prayed to his gods that this was not a decision for which he would pay with both their lives.

In the non-commissioned officers' mess, Dubnus was sitting in a dark corner, nursing a leather cup less than a quarter full of the thick, sweet local beer. Morban, the 9th Century's standard-bearer and in both age and rank his superior, came through the door, his squat frame filling the frame for a moment while he searched out his friend. Finding his man, he raised an arm in salute, grasping the passing mess steward by his arm, propelling him towards the serving counter with a command for 'two beers, and make them full to the brim this time', before waddling across the room to plump himself into the chair facing Dubnus.

Together they represented the 9th's heart and soul. Morban, as the century's standard-bearer, was also the treasurer of the funeral club that ensured each man a decent burial, whether serving or retired. Squat and muscular, ugly, balding and approaching the ripe age of forty, with twenty-two years in the cohort, Morban was at the same time the 9th's greatest cynic and the fiercest protector of its currently flimsy reputation among the other centuries. More than one soldier had found his head locked under Morban's thick arm while the big man went to work at a brief but effective facial rearrangement.

'Dubnus, you great oaf, good to see you back. Not so

good, however, after a long day locked away in an audit of the funeral club records, to find that spotty little oik of a trumpeter waiting as I came off duty. What's so urgent that I didn't even have the time to nip over and see my lad on guard duty? Not that I mind the chance to put a beaker or two away . . .'

The steward ambled up with full beakers, managing to spill a good splash down Morban's tunic in the process of handing them over. The standard-bearer gripped him by the front of his own tunic, pulling him down to face level, almost bent double.

'Very fucking funny. These just became *free* beers, or you can clean my tunic with your tongue.'

The retired soldier scuttled away, cursing under his breath. Morban scowled after him to reinforce the point, tipping his beaker back for long enough to put half its contents down his throat.

'Right, lad, what's your problem?'

Dubnus drank from his own measure, setting the beaker down and staring at his friend for a moment before he spoke in his own language.

'You've not heard, then?'

'Heard what? I told you, I've been knee deep in records scrolls all day.'

Dubnus took a drink, drawing the moment out.

'You've got new officers, Morban, a chosen man and a centurion.'

'Chosen man *and* centurion? Who's the chosen?'

'I am.'

The burly standard-bearer's face lit up with pleasure as he leaned over the table and slapped Dubnus's shoulder in congratulation.

'*Excellent*, best news I've had all day. Be good to have a real soldier stood behind the Ninth for a change . . .'

His face became sly, sudden realisation dawning.

'And I presume this means that halfwit Trajan got his marching orders?'

Dubnus smiled evilly, dropping a bag of coins on to the table.

'*Soldier* Trajan has declared his eagerness to make a donation to the funeral club, as atonement for all the money he fleeced from the Ninth's rations budget in league with that greasy storeman Annius. Our new centurion actually *ordered* me to take him over the Wall on patrol and give him the choice, cough up the cash or take the consequences, at which point he coughed up quickly enough. A pity really, I would've enjoyed cracking his nuts . . .'

Morban drained his beaker, waving imperiously to the sulking steward for a refill.

'Well, Dubnus, lad, you as our chosen, Trajan back in a tent party . . . which one, by the way?'

'Second.'

'The Second! Perfect! I imagine he's biting on the leather strap even as we speak! Now, make my day complete, Chosen, and tell me who our new centurion might be, eh?'

Dubnus drank deeply again, eyeing the other man speculatively over the rim of his beaker, then put the drink down and took a deep breath.

'That, Morban, is the bit I need your help with . . .'

Marcus woke at Dubnus's rousing before dawn the next morning, blinking into the light of a small lamp placed next to his bed.

'You report to the First Spear at dawn with all the other centurions. I've got your report here for you.'

The Briton watched while he washed in a bowl of cold water in the lamp's tiny bubble of light, dragging a sharp knife across his stubble to reduce the growth to a tolerable shadow.

'You don't have to fight Antenoch. I'll talk to him, tell him it wouldn't be . . . *wise*. He'll see reason soon enough . . .'

Marcus paused in his shave, cocking an eyebrow at his friend.

'And when none of them respect me, seeing me hide behind your strength? What then? I have to do this, and I have to *win* if I'm to command here. All of the other centurions rose from the ranks, took their beatings and gave them back with interest, Frontinius made that perfectly clear to me yesterday. I have to prove that I can control my men by my own efforts, not simply through yours. But thank you . . .'

Dubnus shrugged, slapping a writing tablet into Marcus's hand.

'Your choice. Now, get dressed, tunic, armour and weapons, and go to the principia. Make your report. I'll wake the century.'

Outside the cold dawn air was freckled with drizzle, a swirling curtain of wind-blown moisture soothing the heat in his recently shaved face. The headquarters building was quiet, a pair of soldiers standing guard at the entrance beneath the usual reliefs of Mars and Victory. Inside, at the far end of the basilica, stood another pair keeping the eternal vigil over the cohort's inner sanctum, the Chapel of the Standards. Behind their swords lay not only the cohort's battle standards, its very soul, but the unit's pay and savings chests, heavy with the accumulated coin of the soldiers' spending money and burial funds. Following the sound of voices, Marcus found the space outside the prefect's office crowded with uniformed officers, bearded faces turning briefly to regard him with combinations of indifference and hostility, probably noting the threadbare nature of his tunic and the poor condition of his mail coat, before turning pointedly to ignore his presence.

Rufius emerged from the group, clearly already at ease

among men whom he would naturally consider his equals, and walked across to Marcus's side.

'Morning, lad. Ready with your report?'

Marcus showed him the tablet.

'Good. Speak up nice and loud, don't let this lot put you off. You can't expect them to accept you overnight . . . Now, I hear that you're intending to demonstrate some of those "few things" again this morning?'

Marcus nodded, glum faced, making the veteran officer smile despite himself.

'Don't look so worried. All you've got to do is imagine that he's a blue-nose looking at you down three feet of iron and I'm sure that the rest will come to you easily enough. Just remember, keep it simple. No fancy stuff, mind you, just put your toy sword into his ribs nice and hard and teach the stupid Brit some respect.'

He smiled encouragement before sidling back towards the group of centurions, nodding at some comment Marcus was unable to make out. One man, his hair and beard equally bristly in appearance, favoured him with a tight smile, and seemed about to open his mouth to speak when Sextus Frontinius stepped out of his office and called the gathering to attention.

'Unit reports, gentlemen! First Century?'

One of the throng considered his writing tablet, solemnly intoning his report.

'First Spear! First Century reports seventy-seven spears, three men on annual leave, nine men detached for duties beyond the Wall, two men sick and sixty-three men ready for duty.'

'Second Century?'

'First Spear! Second Century reports seventy-nine spears, five men on annual leave, one man sick and seventy-three men ready for duty.'

With the exception of the 6th Century, which had a detachment of fifty men escorting a delivery of weapons in from the main depot at Noisy Valley on the North Road, fifteen miles to the east, the reports were much the same. Marcus managed to stammer out his report when the time came, attracting more hostile glares from the other officers, then waited with burning cheeks for the session to end and allow him to escape. When it did the centurions milled about in idle conversation in the few minutes before the morning parade, leaving him to stand awkwardly to one side like the proverbial spare guest at a wedding for a moment before walking quietly away from the gathering. Whatever he'd expected, a friendly welcome did not seem to be on the agenda, and Rufius had clearly decided that he must find his way into the group without any obvious help.

'Centurion Corvus!'

He stopped and turned back, coming to attention as he recognised the First Spear's booming voice.

'First Spear.'

The other man walked up to him, ignoring the curious stares of the other officers, standing almost toe to toe in order to speak in quiet but fierce tones.

'I hear that you've invited an enlisted man to try his luck this morning?'

Marcus swallowed, more afraid of the other man than of the morning's coming events.

'Yes, sir, a troublemaker called Antenoch. He'll get his chance to see what his new officer's made of.'

Frontinius stared at him without expression, gauging his new centurion's composure.

'As will we all ... It was bound to happen, of course, since they've no way to measure you against their own standards. I wasn't expecting it quite so soon, though ...'

He turned away, leaving Marcus uncertain as to whether

he should wait or walk away. Frontinius turned back, nodding his head slightly.

'At least you had the sense to call his bluff. One piece of advice, though, Centurion . . .'

'Yes, sir?'

'*Win.*'

Half an hour later the cohort's centuries marched out into the dawn's growing light, down through the tight little township that clung to the fort's skirts. Dressed in their training rig of tunics, leggings and boots, they carried shields and wooden swords in readiness for the morning's training exercises. A few windows opened to allow curious children to peer out at the marching men, searching for the men their mothers had pointed out to them on other occasions. The drizzle was still falling, whipped into misty curtains of tiny silver droplets by the eddying wind, making the air both cold and damp. Rufius strolled alongside his century, conversing with his standard-bearer with a carefully calculated indifference.

'I hear that there's a score being settled on parade this morning?'

The muscular standard-bearer nodded quickly, keeping his eyes fixed firmly to his front.

'So we all hear, Centurion. Apparently the other new officer has decided to let one of his men try to take him down with sword and shield.'

Rufius stole a sideways glance at the other man.

'Really? And who is this soldier that's so keen to test my colleague?'

A snorted laugh gave him a clue as to the man's likely loyalties.

'Test? Antenoch will break his ribs and send the boy packing back to Mummy in under a minute. The man's a lunatic, except he doesn't need the full moon to release his madness half the time. Your young friend had better know what he's getting into!'

Rufius lifted an eyebrow.

'*My* young friend? All I did was arrive here at the same time he did. Besides, if he can't look after himself . . .'

The standard-bearer nodded approvingly at the sentiment, and Rufius pressed on with his gambit.

'I *also* hear that a man can place a wager with you and expect the bet to be honoured?'

The other man looked at him warily, taking his eyes of the road for the first time.

'No, man, I'm not about to interfere with your business, far from it. I just wondered what odds you're offering this morning?'

The standard-bearer frowned at him, almost tripping over a loose cobble in the road.

'Odds? You want to place a bet on another officer getting a beating?'

Rufius grinned at him in reply.

'I think you'll find, Standard-bearer, that I'm a little more financially aware than the average officer. Now, odds! Unless you want to find your opportunities to fleece your fellow soldiers somewhat more restricted than they are now . . .'

The standard-bearer's eyes narrowed.

'I'm offering five to four on the lunatic, five to one the centurion.'

'And how's the betting so far?'

'Heavy on Antenoch, which is no surprise, and not a single coin on the boy.'

Rufius nodded.

'No surprise at all. I think I ought to have a small sum on my colleague, show my solidarity . . . shall we say a nice discreet twenty-five denarii on the officer . . . ?'

The standard-bearer's eyes widened, and Rufius stared back at him levelly.

'And, before you blurt out anything we might both regret, the deal is this. You don't tell anyone I wagered with you, to avoid spoiling my reputation, while I keep my bet strictly between us, to avoid spoiling your odds. You still make a nice profit, you keep your business intact, and I might just make some money. It might be an idea to ease the centurion's odds in a little, though, just in case he should actually be quicker with a sword than you've given him credit for . . . And smile, man. If I'm right I'll be the only person you pay out to today.'

Marcus's 9th Century was at the rear of the column, under the watchful eye of the First Spear, who marched this morning alongside Dubnus, in the chosen man's place at the century's rear. Marcus winced inwardly as the Briton cursed his way down the hill, sufficiently enraged by the poor standard of marching discipline to dive into the ranks and pull one offender out to walk alongside him, slapping the miscreant with every misplaced step.

Reaching the parade ground, spread across the floor of the valley below the steep approach to the fort, the cohort broke into century-sized groups, as the centurions and their senior soldiers marshalled the troops into their parade positions. Marcus stepped out in front of his century, suddenly calm in the moment of decision. Turning, he found Dubnus's face looming over the century in his accustomed place to the rear of the ranks of soldiers, his long brass-knotted chosen man's pole shining dimly in the early morning's pale light, and took strength from its stolid set.

A shouted command floated down the ranks of men, ordering the unit to commence the set routine of warm-up exercises that would prepare them for their morning training session. Grateful for the distraction, Marcus watched the centurions to either side carefully, copying each new bend and stretch, taking pleasure in the physical exercise. His new command, he noticed, were less enthusiastic. After fifteen minutes the order to commence training was passed down the line. Marcus braced himself and stepped forward, closing to within a few paces of his front rank, meeting the suspicious and hostile gazes of those of his men that he could see with a careful mask of indifference.

'Good morning, gentlemen. Normally we'll start the morning by rotating the tent parties between sword, spear and shield training. Today, however, since I'm new to most of you, we'll start with a demonstration of the kind of swordsmanship I'm going to expect from you. Do I have a volunteer to help me demonstrate?'

Antenoch shouldered his way to the front rank, his long plaited hair matted by the falling drizzle. He stepped out in front of Marcus, his mouth set in an implacable white-lipped slash.

'I volunteer for that *privilege.*'

Marcus ignored the sneering note in the other man's voice, taking his wooden practice sword from its place at his waist, then called for another, hefting the practice weapons as if testing their relative weights. His lips were suddenly cold in the chill air, and his fingers slightly numb, as they'd been that afternoon on the road to Yew Grove. And then, in the instant of settling the swords into their accustomed positions at his sides, ready to lift into the long-practised fighting stance, having the handle of a weapon in each hand was suddenly, mercifully, the most natural thing in the world. He felt an almost blissful return to the simple disciplines drummed into him during the thousands of sunny afternoons of his childhood, and a moment of simplicity in the heart of his personal confusion. *I can do this*, he suddenly thought to himself, and the spark of belief lit a cold fire that ignited in his belly, something deeper than anger, calmer than rage. Cold, rational, calculating purpose filled the place where doubt and confusion had circled each other, events slowing to a more relaxed pace as his brain adjusted to its unexpected confidence. I *can* do this, he told himself with surprise. *I grew up doing this.*

Antenoch took his weapon and shield, wristing the sword in blurring arcs clearly calculated to impress the watching troops, dropping into a brief leg stretch before jumping back to his feet. Looking to his right, Marcus could see that half of the neighbouring century was watching with poorly disguised excitement. Antenoch threw him a mock gladiatorial salute, pulling his shield and sword into position.

'Ready? You'd better find a shield, Centurion, or this will be even quicker than we're all expecting.'

Marcus stepped into sword reach, unconsciously adjusting the swords' positions until the points of the practice weapons were aligned, rock steady, less than a foot from the Briton's shield. The soldiers watching stirred at the sight, their first intimation that all was not quite as they had expected, and a ripple of whispered comments like wind through tall grass spread through their ranks. Marcus's eyes, stone-like in their concentration, locked on to Antenoch's the way he'd been taught, watching the eyes, not the weapon, for the first signs of an attack.

'I'll stick with the swords if it's all the same to you. We don't use body protection for sparring, I see?'

Antenoch smiled sourly from behind his shield, half turning his head to share his ridicule with the ranks of silent soldiers.

'No, *sir*, this isn't Rome. This is a *real* fighting unit.'

Marcus shrugged without visible emotion.

'Oh, I'm not concerned for myself, I just don't want to injure you too badly. Guard your chest . . .'

'*What?!*'

The enraged Briton sprang in to the attack, swinging his sword in a brutal overhand chopping blow down on to Marcus's quickly raised left-hand sword, the defending weapon's edge splintering slightly at the blow. Marcus allowed the sword to give downwards with the blow, absorbing its force, and stepped back to further soften the impact, encouraging Antenoch to strike again rather than punching with the shield. Again the sword chopped down at Marcus's raised defence, and again he retreated, lowering the sword slightly more this time, and once again Antenoch lifted his weapon to strike, sensing the Roman's apparently feeble defence beginning to fail under his sword blows. As the sword reached the zenith of its attacking arc Marcus dropped his rear leg a little farther back, turning the foot to gain maximum purchase on the parade ground's hard-packed surface, while the other sword stirred stealthily in his right hand, easing back into position for attack.

Antenoch chopped down again, exerting his full strength in a blow intended to smash the left arm down and open Marcus's defences. The Roman met the descending sword with a suddenly rigid defence, braced off his extended back leg to stop the blow dead. Simultaneously, he threw the other sword in backhanded, smashing aside Antenoch's almost disregarded shield and opening the soldier's body to attack. The momentary gap in his adversary's defence was enough for Marcus to strike again with his right-hand weapon, chopping mercilessly at the other man's right wrist and sending his weapon tumbling from suddenly nerveless fingers on to the wet ground before hammering the left hand sword into the Briton's ribs. The counter-attack left Antenoch clutching at bruised ribs while Marcus stepped back, keeping the twin swords raised. He watched Antenoch trying to both cradle his wrist and rub his stomach for a moment, calling softly to the Briton.

'I *told* you to guard your chest. Enough?'

The other man glared back at him, hefting his weapons back into their positions.

'Fight!'

Taking the initiative, Marcus stepped back into his opponent's sword reach and went to work with clinical skill and speed, his swords a sudden whirl of blurring arcs as he attacked with pace and technique for which the Briton had no answer. Half a dozen swift strikes put the other man off balance, allowing Marcus to smash at his shield with each sword in turn until the third blow, delivered with his left-hand sword, wrenched the shield from Antenoch's hand and left him unable to defend himself as the other wooden blade smacked across his back, dropping him to his knees with sudden agony in his kidneys. Marcus stepped away from the writhing figure and turned to address his troops, noting that more than a few were watching the squirming Briton with the slack-jawed look of men who were finding it hard to believe what they saw. Dubnus stared over their heads, one eyebrow raised in silent comment. Farther down the line he could see Rufius out in front of his 6th Century, his fist held clenched below a smile of congratulation.

'Disappointing, gentlemen, if that's the best we have. You evidently need a great deal of training. Speed and technique *will* disarm the strongest and bravest of opponents. You will have noted that the use of the shield in attack is as important as the sword. You will learn to fight this way, as well as in the standard formations and drills. You *will* be the best century in this cohort with your personal weapons, or I and my chosen man will want to know why.' He dropped the practice weapons to the ground, reaching to collect his vine stick.

'*Bastarrrrd!*'

Marcus swung quickly to face the shout, taking in a split-second image of Antenoch, his face distorted by rage, charging at him with a flat dagger held out towards him, held ready to strike. Holding his ground, he waited until the last possible second before sidestepping the blade, pivoting on his left foot to swing his body away from the thrust. At the same time, he lifted his left arm, bent double, to point the elbow at Antenoch, gripping his left fist in his right hand as he leant back to avoid the knife's point. As the blow went past his neck he stepped smartly back in, jabbing his elbow into his onrushing assailant's face and stopping his charge dead, following up with a viciously powerful side-fisted hammer blow that spun the reeling Briton on to his back, his eyes glazed. Out of the corner of one eye he saw the First Spear moving from his position at the far end of the line of centuries at a dead run, his clerk trailing in his wake. He crouched close to the other man's head, bending over to whisper urgently into his dazed face.

'*Stupid*, with the First Spear watching. Now, decide, do you want to live?'

'Eh . . . ?'

The Briton's eyes struggled to focus, and for a second Marcus was afraid he'd done too good a job of stopping the attack, and left Antenoch without the ability to save his own life.

'Everyone dies. You have the opportunity to cross the river this morning, or stay a while longer. Decide which you want, *now*.'

He prised the dagger from Antenoch's unresisting hand and stood up to meet the First Spear as he arrived on the scene, allowing the weapon to dangle casually at his side. Frontinius looked livid, his eyes wide with shock and anger.

'I was watching from the review stand, Centurion, and I clearly saw this man attempt to strike you while you were disarmed.'

He pointed down at the prostrate Antenoch, whose wits were returning as the threat he was under became clear.

'Sir . . .'

'Shut your mouth! I'll have your head on a pole above the main gate for this, you *scum*! Attempting to strike a superior officer carries the death penalty, which I . . .'

'First Spear, with respect?'

Frontinius turned on Marcus, his eyes narrowed with premonition.

'*Centurion?*'

'Sir, I *asked* Soldier Antenoch to attempt a surprise attack upon myself, to show the rest of my men the standard of ability and speed I'll be expecting from them.'

'And why did he call you a bastard at the top of his voice while doing so?'

'Enthusiasm, I'd expect, sir.'

'Enthusiasm. Very likely, Centurion, he felt *enthusiastic* about the idea of putting a knife between your ribs. An illegal weapon too, I'd say, not our standard issue, although no doubt you *lent* it to him. You're defending this man from a charge of assault upon you?'

The watching soldiers tensed visibly, waiting for the answer.

'Yes, sir. I believe that Soldier Antenoch is a valuable member of the century. He's agreed only this morning to act as my orderly and clerk, and to provide advice as to the best way of getting things done in this cohort. Isn't that right, Antenoch . . . ?'

The Briton started up open mouthed at his officer, realising with sudden resignation that he'd been backed into a corner that had only two exits, acceptance or death.

'Yes . . . Centurion . . .'

Frontinius smiled then, without mirth, his eyes locking with Antenoch's.

'Good. *Very* good. I shall look forward to hearing reports

on your progress, Soldier Antenoch. Let us hope that you demonstrate your abilities sufficiently well that I forget all about this interesting episode. In the meantime, I'll keep a pole sharpened above the gate . . .'

He turned to return to his place, brushing close to Marcus in the process and hissing a whispered comment at him.

'Don't push your luck, Centurion . . .'

Marcus turned back to his men, squaring his shoulders and glaring across the lines of suddenly fixed faces.

'Very well, Antenoch, back into rank. We can discuss your new duties after morning exercise. Now, let's examine what happened there. There are a couple of basic techniques for close combat that I want us to practise this morning . . .'

Morban smirked up at the lanky soldier standing next to him, enjoying the sick look on his face.

'I believe that's *fifty* you owe me, sonny. Did I forget to mention that our new centurion was a member of the imperial bodyguard before he asked the emperor if he could come and see the blue-noses at first hand? Never mind, since you'd only have spent it on whores at least it'll end up in the same purse. Even if they'll have a harder time earning it!'

Off parade, Dubnus drew Antenoch into Marcus's quarters with irresistible force, pushing the defeated soldier into the room in front of him. Marcus, waiting in his chair with his sword unsheathed across his knee, nodded to the chosen man, who pushed the soldier into the middle of the room. With the shutters closed against the rain and cold, and the room only dimly lit by a pair of oil lamps, the young centurion's face looked brooding, lit with menace. Antenoch turned and glared at him, putting his hands on his hips in carefully calculated insult. The big chosen man bared his teeth in a half-snarl, half-sneer, pulling the dagger from his belt.

'I'll go and sharpen the stake over the main gate. It'll be waiting for you.'

He looked over at Marcus as he turned to leave, shaking his head.

'Do *not* trust him. Keep your sword ready.'

When the door was closed, Marcus reached into his tunic, holding out the other man's knife. Antenoch took it from his outstretched hand, looking closely at the blade for a long moment, staring past it at Marcus.

'Wondering if it'd be worth another try at planting that thing between my ribs?'

The Briton said nothing for another moment, pursing his lips as he slipped the weapon back into its familiar resting place.

'No.'

'Because I spared you even after you tried to kill me?'

'No.'

'Then why?'

'Because I don't think I'd get close enough . . . They've got a nickname for you, those cattle out there, they always do with officers. It was going to be Wetnose, until this morning. Now it's Two Knives!'

He spat the words out. Marcus smiled levelly.

'Two Knives? Like the gladiator? It could be worse, for a man in my situation.'

Antenoch's eyes narrowed.

'The rumours are that you're the son of a rich man, just stupid enough to want to slum it with us for a while.'

'Rumours you'll encourage if you want to be my clerk . . .'

The Briton bristled at the suggestion.

'*Want* to be your clerk? Fuck *you*!'

Marcus sat back, laughing gently at the incensed soldier, tapping the hilt of his sword.

'Sit down, Antenoch, and *think* for a moment.'

He waited until the other man had slumped gloomily on to his bed before continuing.

'You're obviously an educated man, well spoken in a language which is not your native tongue. You should be an administrator to some local official, or a trader, not a common soldier on the Wall, miles from anywhere with decent food and women you don't have to pay for. What happened?'

'Mind your own fucking business!'

'Come on, man, what can it hurt to tell me? I won't be sharing the story with anyone else.'

'You'll tell Dubnus, and he'll tell Morban, and he'll . . .'

'You have my word. I've little else of value, so it should be of *some* note.'

The quiet response silenced Antenoch far more effectively than a bellowed command might have. Strangely, his face softened as if with repressed memories.

'I was adopted by a merchant in the wool trade when I was young, after my mother died, and raised as his son, alongside his own boy. I never knew my father, although I often wondered if I was actually the merchant's bastard child. Taught to read and write, and to speak well. I imagined that I would find some place in his business, until my "brother" took it into his head that I was supplanting him in his father's affections. He poisoned the old man against me, slowly but surely, and I ended up on the street with a handful of coins and their "best wishes". So . . . I decided to earn the one thing they never could buy, for all their money, and become a Roman citizen. I planned to go back to them after my twenty-five, as an officer, of course, and snap my fingers at them as second-class citizens in their own country. Cocidius help me, I was so *stupid*!'

'And now you're stuck here.'

Antenoch looked up, his eyes red.

'And you're so clever? The only difference between us seems to be one of rank, Centurion, since you apparently have nowhere better to go than the arse-end of your own empire!'

Again Marcus's response was instinctively gentle, defusing the Briton's anger.

'And that should make us more likely *allies* than enemies. Will you work with me or against me? You'd make a first-class centurion's clerk, and with a little polish you could be one of the best swordsmen in the cohort. Besides, I could do with someone to watch my back . . .'

He tailed off, his persuasive skills exhausted, and wisely waited in the unnerving silence rather than spout nonsense to fill the silence. Antenoch levelled his stare, his face set hard.

'And if I won't, you'll set that bastard Frontinius on me. What choice do I have?'

Marcus shook his head emphatically.

'No, the choice has to be yours. Besides, nobody does my dirty work for me any more. Look, I need a man I can trust behind me in a knife fight, not one waiting for the chance to carve my shoulder blades apart. What do *you* need?'

The response was slow and measured, the Briton thinking through his position aloud.

'I need a chance to be something other than the wild man those fools have labelled me . . . I'd *like* to learn some of those fancy tricks you pulled on me this morning. I want that bastard Dubnus to speak to me with a little respect, rather than looking at me as if I were something he scraped off the bottom of his boot.'

He looked up at Marcus, calculation written across his face.

'What's the pay?'

'Standard pay, but I'll make you an immune. You'll never have to shovel shit away from the latrines again, just as long as you're my man.'

Antenoch pulled a face and nodded.

'Very well, we have a deal . . . but you should beware one small fact, Centurion Two Knives.'

Marcus grimaced in his turn.

'And that is . . . ?'

'I promise always to be honest with you. Always to speak my mind, whatever my opinion. Whatever the likely effect. You may find my views hard to accept, but I won't spare you them.'

'And your view as of this moment?'

'You look too young for credibility with men who don't happen to be looking down the length of your sword. Put into Frontinius for permission to grow a beard. You *can* grow a beard?'

5

Rufius came through the storehouse door first, impaling the clerk with a fierce glare and gesturing with a thumb over his shoulder. The soldier, remembering his close encounter with the veteran officer's dagger the previous day, made for the door, finding himself restrained by a muscular arm, as the centurion bent to whisper in his ear.

'We're all going to have a little chat with Annius about the quality of his rations. You're going to stay outside and keep nosy people from trying to interrupt us. If anyone does disturb our discussion, we'll set *him* on you.'

Antenoch stood in the doorway, locking his cold bruised eyes on the clerk's for a moment before turning away to lift an axe handle from the wall, hefting it experimentally to test the wood's weight. Behind him came Dubnus, in turn momentarily filling the doorway, his eyes flicking across the clerk without any recognition of his existence before he strode into the store. Released, the clerk bolted for the door willingly enough. Annius never cut him in on any of his swindles, so there was no reason to argue with anyone in his defence, much less *that* lunatic. He almost ran into the other new centurion in the entrance, shrinking back again to let the hollow-eyed officer walk through, the man not even seeming to notice him. Which suited the clerk well enough. What a combination – the freshly recruited veteran centurion he had already learned to fear and an officer the fort's collective opinion had suddenly decided probably *was* man enough for the job, after all. He closed the door to the stores building and leant on it in what he hoped would appear a nonchalant attitude.

Rufius walked to the counter, dropped a bundle of equipment and clothing on to the wooden surface and smacked his hand down with a flat percussive crack.

'Storeman!'

Annius bustled out of his office, looking about him for his clerk, then, pausing uncertainly at the sight of the new centurions, pasted an uncertain smile across his features and advanced to the counter. His jowly face and high forehead glistened minutely with pinprick beads of sweat.

'Centurion Rufius! What a pleasure! Always good to have experienced officers join the cohort. And Centurion Corvus! All of the camp has heard of your prowess with the sword this morning, quite remarkable! How can I be of service to you and your, er ... colleagues ... ?'

Finding his bonhomie unrewarded by Rufius's stern expression, he looked uncertainly to Marcus, found no comfort there, and returned his regard to the older officer, his instincts muttering loudly in his inner ear to play things *very* carefully with this unknown quantity. How much could the man have discovered in less than a day? He cursed his own stupidity for letting that fool Trajan convince him to push the usual rake-off to such a high percentage.

To his surprise it was the younger man who stepped forward, raising a patrician eyebrow and curling his upper lip to complete the air of dissatisfaction.

'This equipment, Quartermaster, issued to myself and my colleague Tiberius Rufius yesterday, is quite clearly defective in numerous regards. The mail is surface rusted, the sword is blunter than my grandmother's butter knife, and even the tunics seem to have seen better days. I trust that you'll want to remove them from service after what has clearly been a long and illustrious history, to judge from their condition.

Oh, and I'm used to a longer sword than the infantry gladius, so see what you've got that'll suit my style better, eh?'

Annius swallowed nervously, feeling a trickle of sweat running down his left temple. He scuttled back into the store, returning within a minute with two sets of officer's equipment, his best. He would usually charge a new centurion two hundred and fifty for their full rig, unless they wanted somebody else's leavings, but this was an occasion, he judged, to forget to mention payment.

'I hope that these meet with your approval, centurions, and solve the problem. You'll understand that errors sometimes occur, but that's soon amended. I'll have to discipline that blasted clerk, issuing such shoddy gear to an officer.'

He reached a hand out to take the bundle of rejected kit, only to find Marcus's hand there first, closing over his podgy fingers in a firm grip. Rufius leant on the counter, resting his chin on a bunched fist, a half-smile playing on his lips, his eyes boring into Annius's. Behind them, Antenoch lounged against the wall, pointedly studying his fingernails for dirt, while Dubnus prowled around the room, casting dark glances at the stores officer. The younger man spoke again, his voice quiet and yet shot through with steel.

'If only it were that simple. You see, when I discovered the poor quality of my own equipment issue, I was prompted to check on the welfare of my men. You'll be as surprised as I was to learn that I found many of them apparently undernourished. Their food is both insufficient and of a disgusting quality, and has been so, I'm told, since Soldier Trajan was appointed temporary centurion several months ago. Interestingly, when my chosen man offered to take Trajan out over the Wall for a short patrol into the forest last evening, he insisted that this purse of gold be a contribution to the century's funeral club.'

He released the other man's hand, pulling a leather bag

from his tunic and spilling its contents carelessly across the counter, watching the fear grow in the other man's eyes. The coins rattled on to the wood, each spinning gold disc reflecting tiny flickers of yellow light as it sank into stillness across the flat surface. A long silence stretched out, as both men stared at the small fortune lying across the counter.

'Apparently, he wanted to make amends for his previous greed. It seems he was foolish enough to have participated in a scheme to make money by supplying his men with substandard rations, and sharing the profits with *somebody* in your department . . .'

Annius shifted uncomfortably, opening his mouth to deny any knowledge.

'I . . .'

'No, don't tell me, you don't want to incriminate any of your staff. We understand completely, any good officer would wish to protect his men from bad fortune, even that of being caught committing a capital offence. Of course, if *I* were to discover the identity of that person, I'd have them in front of the First Spear the same hour, and see them pay the maximum penalty possible. Don't you agree, Chosen Man?'

Dubnus spoke over his shoulder while he leaned over the counter to examine a mail shirt hanging from a rack close to the wide desk, fingering the leather jerkin to which the rings were fastened.

'No, it'd be too quick just to have his head lopped off. I'd take him into the great forest, give him a one-hundred-count start and then hunt him down through the shadows. I'd pin him to a tree with my throwing axe and leave him there to die.'

Annius looked from Marcus to his men, realising with horror the game they were playing with him, not doubting for a second any of the commitment behind their words.

'That's still too good,' came a voice from behind them.

'I'd just break the bastard's arms and legs and leave him out there for the animals. The wild pigs would make a mess of him before he finally died.'

Antenoch flipped the heavy axe handle as he spoke, juggling the three-foot length of wood with impressive nonchalance as he shot a hard stare at the stores officer. Annius had heard about the way the young officer had turned the man's rage to his own advantage on the parade ground, and suspected that he had a good deal of frustration to unleash upon the first convenient target. He looked away, attempting to feign an indifference that he was far from feeling.

The young officer smiled down at him without mirth, his jaw set hard.

'So you see feelings are running high. Soldier Trajan is already feeling the wrath of his former subordinates by all accounts, although I suspect that a protracted revenge holds more savour for the troops than anything hasty. Of course, he was only the dupe of your man, from the relatively small amount of money he handed over to us . . .'

An opening?

'I could . . . *pay* you . . . to keep my clerk out of trouble?'

The four men stared at him in silence, waiting. He plunged on.

'I could take the man's profits, give them to you, for use in making amends with your unit, of course. Gods, the fool might have made as much as five hundred from his ill-advised swindle . . .'

Rufius leant across the counter, putting his face close to Annius's.

'Three thousand. Now. You can reclaim the money from *your* man at *your* leisure.'

Annius stared at the officer aghast. That was almost twice as much as they'd actually raked off . . .

'Perhaps we could . . .'

'Suit yourself. Pay now or I'll put the matter in the hands of less forgiving judges. You know the story: new officer finds evidence of fraud and feels compelled to take the proof to his superior officer. Frontinius might turn a blind eye to your profit-making activities; I never yet met a senior centurion who didn't, as long as there was a healthy contribution to the burial club every month. My last camp prefect used to call it "balancing the books", said some men were born to make money, some to lose it, and this way at least he could guarantee every man a decent funeral. What he couldn't ignore, though, would be the brand-new, "wet behind the ears" centurion who had discovered how his men were being fleeced, and who would of course be filled with righteous anger. So the price is three thousand – pay up or suffer the consequences. You can think while my young friend buckles on that nice new sword. I've seen him take a man's head off at six feet with one just like it.'

Annius hesitated, weighing up the alternatives he saw in Rufius's pitiless stare. A simple death sentence was his only choice apart from cooperating without question; none of his men would hesitate to lay out everything they knew of his various business activities if required to do so by Frontinius, no matter how well they had been paid to take part.

'Of course, to spare a good, if misguided, member of my department, I could probably find the money . . .'

Rufius flipped the hinged section of the counter and walked round behind him.

'Get the money. I'll come with you.'

Unable to argue without running the risk that he'd end up face down in the deep forest with a spear between his shoulder blades, Annius huffed into his office, prising up the floorboard beneath which he kept his money. Three of the five leather bags went into the centurion's waiting hands, the other man sneering his disgust into Annius's face. Out in the storeroom, he was alarmed to find that Marcus and Antenoch were on the wrong side of the counter, and were examining his inventory with considerable interest. The centurion lifted a mail shirt from its hanger, holding the rings up to a window's meagre light and rubbing the soft leather undershirt between his thumb and forefinger.

'You're right, Chosen Man, this is *very* nice mail. Much better than the standard-issue rubbish. Annius, you must have enough here to equip a whole century.'

'I . . . I have to keep enough stock to supply each new intake of troops, and spares.'

Dubnus loomed over his shoulder.

'He keeps the stock all right, but only sells good mail shirts to men who don't want to repair their own, or want softer leather.'

'I see. How much?'

The businessman in the stores officer took over, not seeing the trap into which he was running.

'One hundred each.'

'Hmm . . . A fair price would be . . . sixty, Antenoch?'

'Fifty.'

'Very well, Annius, let's call them forty sesterces apiece, as my discount for bulk purchase. I'll take your whole stock. And tunics, let's say two apiece for my century at five apiece. Now, what else do you have for sale, before we discuss how you're going to make sure that my men eat like prize gladiators from now on?'

He turned away from the dazed quartermaster, threading his way deeper into the darker recesses of the store. Regaining his equilibrium, Annius weaved after him, panting his petulant outrage.

'Oh no, Centurion, you're not going to steal my stock as well as my money! That's just not *fair* . . .'

And quailed back against a rack of spears as the Roman

spun, his sword flashing from his waist and arcing up to rest against his neck. Marcus's face scared him more than the weapon's fierce bite against his flabby throat. Even Rufius's eyes widened momentarily, before a wolfish grin crept across his face.

'Not *fair*, storeman? Not much *is* in these days. My men probably weren't too impressed at the way you and Trajan fed them shit every day for the last three months. Your choice, one you're lucky to have, is to bite on the leather and take your punishment. Of course, you could go to the prefect, and see if he'll accept your word against mine. Shall we go to him now? It might be entertaining to see which of us appears the more credible.'

Annius shrank farther into the forest of wooden poles, his face red with fear, but said nothing. The sword swung away from its harsh grip on his life, dropping back into its place on Marcus's belt. Rufius pushed him out of the way, the smile on his face broadening as he headed for the rear of the store.

'I spy amphorae back here! How much for the wine, store-keeper ... ?'

Annius smiled through the pain, knowing he lacked any choice in the matter. If the young bastard chose to shit on the store floor and then ordered him to clean it up with his tunic, he would have to do as he was told. Later, however, he promised himself, when the new centurions had taken their leave of him, probably in possession of half his stock, bought at knock-down prices with his own money, he would sit silently in his office, brooding over his revenge. That, and the ways in which he might learn more of the enigmatic new arrival's past.

Rufius opened the door of the centurions' mess an hour later, meeting the stares of the officers present with a careful smile.

'Gentlemen . . .'

He waited in the doorway. Marcus stood in view behind him, both of them acutely aware that they had to be invited in for their first visit. The shortest of the cohort's centurions, a bristly-haired man whom Marcus recognised as the least unfriendly of the gathering for morning report, had apparently just reached the punchline of the joke he was telling. He turned back to the others.

'So the centurion says, "Well, Prefect, normally we just ride the horse to the whorehouse!"'

He turned back to Rufius.

'Come on then, Grandfather, in you come.'

Rufius winced, giving Marcus a dirty look as the younger man hid a smile behind his hand. The speaker beckoned again, looking over Rufius's shoulder.

'And you, young Two Knives, and let's have a proper look at you.'

One of the speaker's companions snorted derisively, turning away to study the wine jug behind the serving counter, one hand teasing at a knot in his heavy beard. The man next to him appraised Rufius and Marcus through eyes that seemed permanently half closed, peering down a nose that had clearly seen better times. Their host smiled openly, showing a selection of crooked teeth in the bristly thicket of his beard.

'Don't worry about our colleagues here. Otho's wondering whether he could take either of you in a fair fight, as opposed to the knife-in-the-dark methods that got him to where he is today . . .'

The battered face split into a happy grin.

'While my good friend Julius already knows from your performance this morning that he'd have no more chance against you than *I* would.'

His good friend Julius snorted his disgust again, peering disdainfully down his nose.

'Pretty swordsmen don't necessarily make good officers. Especially when they have no idea about soldiering. He'll give up soon enough, once the Ninth sees through him.'

He sized Rufius up with a swift up-and-down glance, nodding with some measure of respect.

'I hear you've done your time with the legions – come and see me in my quarter if you'd like to talk soldier to soldier.'

He strode from the mess, slamming the door behind him. Marcus swallowed his anger, forcing himself to smile again.

'This morning . . . ? I was lucky that Antenoch was stupid enough give me a warning. I'm still rusty from too long on the road.'

The bristly-haired officer raised an eyebrow at him.

'Still rusty, eh? In that case old Otho had best jump you while you're still polishing up! I'm Caelius, by the way, centurion of the Fourth Century, although my men call me "Hedgehog" when they think I'm not listening . . .' He paused and stroked his prickly scalp for effect. '. . . can't imagine why! Otho here, also known as "Knuckles", although you might have guessed that from the state of his face, has the Eighth. Julius, not unreasonably known as "Latrine" since he is, as you can see, built like the cohort shithouse, has the Fifth. Your chosen man was his chosen man until you arrived, hence his sulking demeanour. He's having to work for a living now, instead of lounging around here and letting the Prince get on with doing the hard work for him.'

He waved an arm around the other centurions.

'As for the rest of your colleagues, there's Milo, or "Hungry", since he's forever eating and still skinny as a spear, he's got the Second, and Clodius the "Badger", both for his hair and his temper. He keeps the Third in a permanent state of terror.'

The centurion Marcus and Dubnus had encountered earlier on the road inclined his head in an impassive nod.

'Brutus has the Seventh, and has seen more action than the rest of us put together with never a scratch on his baby-soft skin, which is why he answers to "Lucky". Lastly there's Titus, or "Bear", he's got the Tenth, which is our century of axemen. When we're in the field they specialise in tree-felling and field defences, and they fight with their axes like barbarians, so they all have to be great big brutes like him. "Uncle Sextus" has the First Century, but you already know that. Anyway, introductions made, will you join us in a drink?'

Wine was procured by the steward, which Rufius tasted and instantly judged to have come off second best to the long journey from its birthplace.

'Actually, it was wine I came to discuss with you, apart from making our introductions. You see, we made a deal with your deeply unpleasant storeman just now, included in which were a dozen large jars of a rather nice red from Hispania. Perhaps the mess could use them? As a gift from the new boys, you understand.'

Caelius smiled at them with renewed warmth, knocking back a large swig from his own beaker and wiping his moustache with the palm of his hand.

'Well, after six months of drinking this issue filth, your gift would be as welcome as bread to a starving man. That slimy bastard Annius never even told us he had anything of the sort. Now, one good turn deserves another, so here's a word of friendly advice for you, young Two Knives . . .'

He paused significantly.

'If you want to keep the cold out up here, and look like an officer . . .'

He paused again portentously, making it clear that he was about to do his new colleague a great favour. Rufius raised a cautionary eyebrow over the man's shoulder.

'What you need to do is grow yourself a nice thick curly beard. You can grow a beard . . . ?'

6

The cohort's long stay in winter quarters began to draw to a close a fortnight after their arrival. The onset of warmer weather heralded the opening of spring's campaign to revitalise the land. The change was much to the relief of officers at their wits' end with containing the fallout of boredom and indiscipline that the winter's long inactivity had bred in their troops. Marcus had already had one case to deal with from within the 9th, a tall, darkly surly, one-eyed soldier who went under the official name of Augustus and the unofficial title of 'Cyclops'. It seemed that the name had as much to do with his poor temper as any more obvious reason.

Called out in the early hours by the duty officer, he found the man slumped, bruised and still bleeding from his nostrils, in a headquarters holding cell. The duty centurion, with some good fortune Caelius, who, Rufius excepted, was still his only real friend among the officers, shook his head more in sorrow than anger.

'He's known for it, I'm afraid. All it takes is for someone to find the right lever to tug at, the right jibe to set him off, and he goes off like a siege catapult. He's been warned, fined, beaten, put on punishment details for weeks . . . nothing works. If this goes to Uncle Sextus he'll get another beating, a really bad one this time, perhaps dishonourable dismissal too . . .'

Marcus looked in through the thick bars, weighing up the

man slumped before him. While he'd learned a few names, and the characters behind them, the man was no more than an imperfectly remembered face in the cohort's second rank on parade.

'And what was the lever this time?'

'We don't know. He won't say, and the men that beat the snot out of him are sticking to a story that he jumped them in the street outside the tavern they'd been drinking in, without warning or reason. Which is probably at least half true. You might not be surprised to learn that they're both Latrine's men.'

'Hmmm. Open the door and leave me with him.'

Caelius shot him a surprised look.

'Are you sure? He broke a man's arm the last time he was in this state.'

'And you think I couldn't handle him?'

A sheepish grin spread over the other man's face. He took a lead-weighted rod from his belt, tapping the heavy head significantly against his palm.

'No, well, when you put it that way . . . Just shout if he gets naughty, and I'll come and reintroduce him to the night officer's best friend.'

He opened the door, drawing no reaction from the prisoner. Marcus leant against the door frame, waiting until Caelius was out of earshot in his tiny cubicle. In the guardroom next to the office a dozen men were dozing, sitting up on their bench, packed in tight like peas in a pod. The building was quiet, eerily so when it was usually so vibrant with activity during the day.

'Soldier Augustus?'

The words met with no reaction.

'*Cyclops!*'

The soldier started at the name, looking up at his officer. He stared for a moment and snorted before putting his head down again.

'How many times *is* this, soldier? Three? Four?'

'Six.'

'Six, Centurion. What punishments have you suffered as a consequence?'

The recitation was mechanical, the question often answered.

'Ten strokes, twenty strokes, twenty-five strokes and two weeks' pay, thirty strokes and two weeks' free time, fifty strokes, fifty strokes and three weeks' free time, fifty strokes, a month's pay and a month's free time . . . Centurion.'

His head came up while he recited the litany of punishment, his one eye, previously dulled by pain, seeming to regain some of its spark.

'None of which has stopped you from fighting . . . So, then, Cyclops, why *do* you fight?'

The other man shrugged without expression, almost seeming not to comprehend the question.

'I take no shit from no one.'

'From what I've heard, you take "shit" from almost anyone. You let them get under your skin and goad you to the point of starting a fight, at which point you usually get both a beating *and* a place at the punishment table for starting the fight.'

Marcus shook his head in exasperation.

'So what was it this time?'

Augustus's eye clouded with pain again, and for a moment Marcus thought he was going to cry.

'Phyllida.'

'A woman?'

'*My* woman. She left me, went to a soldier from the Fifth. Him and his mates took the piss out of me . . .'

'Mainly because it gives them an excuse to batter you, I'd say. Did you give some back?'

'I hit them a few times.'

'Want to hurt them some more?'

Cyclops looked up at him again, suspicion in his good eye.

'How?'

'Simple. Just tell me who else witnessed these men baiting you.'

'I won't speak against them.'

'I guessed that already. I'll deal with this my way, *unofficially*, but I need a name to start with.'

Cyclops paused for thought, as much to consider the request as to recall any detail. At length he spoke.

'Manius, of the Fourth, he was in the tavern. He's from my village.'

Marcus went to wake up Dubnus, waiting until the man had splashed cold water on his face before detailing the problem. The Briton's response was simple.

'Leave him to rot. Let Uncle Sextus deal with him. The man's a liability, bad for discipline.'

Marcus leant back against the small room's wall, rubbing his stubble wearily.

'No. Leaving him to the First Spear's discipline says we have no ideas of our own. That we don't look after our own. How well do you know this man "Cyclops"?'

'Well enough. His heart is poisoned, full of anger.'

'Is he a warrior?'

'He's fierce enough in a fight, but he lacks . . . self-control.'

'So if we could make him behave, he'd make a good soldier?'

'Ye-es.'

Marcus ignored the grudging tone of agreement.

'Good. In that case I need your help. Let's give him a real chance to change his ways this time.'

The Briton looked at him with a calculating expression.

'You want to wake up Grandfather for this?'

Marcus shook his head.

'No, although I'd dearly love to have his advice. He has to be neutral in this, and if he knew about it he'd find it hard not to get involved in some way. This is a Ninth Century problem, and the Ninth will handle it. *Our* way.'

'Which is?'

'First we have to talk to a man in the Fourth. It's a good thing Caelius is captain of the guard tonight, saves us waking him up too.'

Julius was woken from sleep by a hammering at his door, climbing bleary eyed from his bed to answer the insistent banging. His bad-tempered scowl became a snarl of distaste when he saw Marcus in the doorway, just recognisable in the night's bright moonlight.

'What do you want, puppy?'

Marcus gestured to an unseen person to his right and then stepped aside. Dubnus stepped into view, a semi-conscious soldier grasped firmly under each arm, his biceps bulging with the effort. One of his eyes was slightly closed, but otherwise he appeared undamaged. He dropped the men on the ground between them, making the centurion step back as they crumpled at his feet, and spoke for the first time.

'I must be getting slow. A year ago neither of them would have laid a finger on me.'

Julius spluttered with fury, stepping out into the cold air without noticing its icy grip on his skin and squaring up to Dubnus.

'What the *fuck* have you done?'

Marcus stepped in alongside his chosen man, his eyes narrowed with anger.

'What he did, *brother* officer, was exact a very precise retribution on the men that beat up one of my troops earlier this evening. I have a witness who has sworn to me that Augustus was provoked, just as they knew he could be from happy experience. All we've done is even the account. If you attempt to take any further action on this matter he's promised to come forward and tell his story.'

'You're bluffing! No man in this cohort would inform on another.'

'Your choice. The only way to know is to try me. It can stop here, Julius, this quiet war on my century and your attempts to make them turn against me. From now, everything you start comes back to you twofold, no matter what it is. However many of my men suffer, twice as many of yours will receive the same punishment . . .'

The younger man stepped in closer, putting his face into Julius's, the set of his jaw and flare of his nostrils rooting the older man to the spot.

'. . . and if you want to make it a little more personal, I'll see you on the practice ground for a little exercise, with or without weapons. If you have a problem with me, you can take it up with *me*!'

He turned and stalked away. Dubnus raised an eyebrow in silent comment and turned to follow, leaving the 5th's centurion for once lost for words.

The next morning, after early parade, Prefect Equitius and the First Spear sat to judge Cyclops's case, running through the facts with the offender standing to attention in front of them. With the bare facts of the case established, Frontinius asked Cyclops whether he wanted to make any comment before sentence was passed. The soldier's response was mumbled at the floor, but no less of a surprise to officers used to the man's customary stony silence at the punishment table.

'Sir, I ask my centurion to speak for me.'

Prefect and First Spear exchanged glances.

'Very well, Soldier Augustus. Centurion?'

Marcus stepped forward, helmet held under his arm, and snapped to attention.

'Prefect. First Spear. My submission on this man's behalf is simple. He claims provocation to fight, but that is beside the point. He has a worse record of indiscipline than any other man in the Ninth, and I've already told him that I won't tolerate it. I believe that he can make an effective soldier, but only if he can learn to control himself. My recommendation therefore is this: no beating, no loss of training time, in fact nothing that will keep him out of training. Instead, take away as much of his pay as you see fit and as much of his free time as appropriate. If he offends again, dismiss him from the cohort – he'll be no use to me or any other officer if he can't control his temper.'

Frontinius mused for a moment before turning to the tribune.

'I agree. I've seen enough of this man at this table for one lifetime. Soldier Augustus, you are hereby fined one month's pay, deprived of one month's free time with bathhouse duties as further punishment, and restricted to the fortress for three months unless on duty with your century. One more appearance here, for any reason, and I will accept your centurion's recommendation without hesitation. Do you understand?'

Cyclops nodded curtly.

'Very well. Dismissed.'

Outside the headquarters Dubnus collared Cyclops, poking a long finger into his chest for emphasis, lapsing into their shared native tongue to be sure he was understood.

'That was the officers' version. Here's mine. The centurion put his balls on the table for you in there, made his prestige with the First Spear a matter of your behaving yourself in future. You make one more mistake, you won't just embarrass my centurion, you might be the reason he gets kicked out of the cohort. So, if you do fail to change your ways it won't just be you out of the service. If that happens I'll boot your punchbag so fucking hard your balls will never come down again. *Do. You. Understand. Me?*'

The one-eyed soldier stared back at him with an expression Dubnus found hard to decipher.

'I'll be a good boy from now, but not for you, Dubnus, I'm not scared of you. I'll do it for the young gentleman.'

He turned and walked away towards the baths to start the first day of his punishment work routine, leaving Dubnus standing, hands on hips, watching him with a thoughtful expression.

With the beginning of the gradual change from winter into spring the cohort accelerated its training programme. Sextus Frontinius, listening to the reports of a slow flame of resentment burning steadily brighter in the northern tribes, was keen to get his men into the field and training towards peak fitness, ready for the campaign he made no secret of believing they would fight that year. Twenty-mile marches became a thrice-weekly event, rather than the freezing misery inflicted on the cohort once a fortnight.

Marcus's and Rufius's centuries, the former properly re-equipped and both suddenly the envy of the cohort, eating the best of rations and appropriately vigorous, responded to their commanders' different styles of leadership well. Whether it was Marcus's blend of humanity and purpose, or Rufius's legion training methods, quietly imparted to Marcus in conversations long into the night when their duties allowed, both centuries grew quickly in fighting ability and self-confidence. The 9th were driven relentlessly by Dubnus and his two new watch officers, hand-picked older men who understood what would be required of the century if it did come to war. With the open backing of the influential Morban the 9th quickly coalesced from a collection of indifferent individuals into a tightly knit body of men, and set about rediscovering the pleasure of testing themselves alongside men they were coming to regard as brothers. Rufius had put the idea to his friend in the officer's mess one evening after their day's duties.

Otho and Brutus were playing a noisy game of Robbers in another corner of the room, on a black-and-white chequered board painted on to their table. 'Lucky' was failing to live up to his title, as the boxer chased his few remaining counters around the board. He was picking them off one by one and laughing hugely with each capture. Rufius tipped his head towards the two men, lowering his voice conspiratorially.

'And let that be a warning to you. Our brother officer might be called Knuckles, but don't ever think he might be punch drunk. That's the fourth game in a row he's taken off Brutus, and there's no sign of the streak being broken. A good game for the military mind is Robbers, teaches you to think ahead all the time. The only mistake dear old Lucky's making is to worry about where his counters will go next, not where he wants them in three moves' time. He plays aggressively, pushes for the straddle, while Knuckles, he knows the art of steady play, how to gently ease the opponent's counters into position for the attack. There are lessons for life in the simplest game, but some lessons are harder won . . .'

He took a mouthful of wine, savouring the taste for a moment with a sideways glance at his friend.

'Which leads me to a subject I've been pondering the last few weeks, watching you and Dubnus turn your lads from a rabble to something more like infantrymen. I don't doubt for a second that you'll teach your boys enough about sword and board work to make each one of them an effective fighter, but I can tell you from grim experience that isn't the key to fielding a century that will grind up anything thrown at them and come back for more.

'Let me tell you what happens when we fight the blue-noses. Before the battle, when our men are trying to keep from soiling themselves with fear, the barbarians stop just outside spear-throw and start shouting the odds like vicus drunks, how they're going to carve off our dicks and wave them at our women before they fuck them to death, how we'll soon be staring at our own guts as they lie steaming on the turf, all that rubbish. However, take note of a man that's been there – it works. There's a natural reaction I've seen in many a century and cohort when the barbarians are baying for blood, and that's for each man to sidle to his right just a little, looking to get just a little more protection from his mate's shield. Before you know it the line's half a mile farther to the right than the legatus wants it, and the fight's half over before it begins, just from sheer fear . . .'

He drank again, signalling to the steward for a refill.

'The secret to winning battles, my friend, isn't fancy sword work, or how well your boys can sling a spear, important though those skills are. It's actually much simpler than that, but harder to achieve. All you have to do is to make the lads love each other.'

He sat back, cocking a wry eyebrow at the Roman.

'And no, before you laugh at me, I don't mean all that arse-poking in Greek pornography, I mean the love a man has for his brother.'

He paused again, judging the moment.

'There's only one way to explain this to you, and I apologise for the necessity. You had a brother in Rome, right?'

Marcus nodded soberly, finding the memory painful, but less so than before.

'Well, what you would have done had you been in a position to fight his killers?'

The younger man's nostrils flared with remembered anger.

'I would probably have died with a bloody sword in my hand, and a carpet of dead and dying men around me.'

'Exactly. And *that*, friend Marcus, is the love we need to get into the hearts of our lads. When one of your tent parties is in trouble, whether it's a punch-up in a vicus beer shop or a desperate fight against hordes of blue-nosed bastards, their mates to either side have a choice, to look to their front and ignore their mates' peril, or to dive in to the rescue. Orders don't make that happen, and you can't teach it on the parade ground, but if you get them to love each other, they do the rest for you, without even thinking about it. When you get it right a man will use his shield to protect the man next to him when he falls, and ignore the risk he runs in doing so, knowing with complete certainty that his mate would do the same for him without a second's thought.'

He smiled conspiratorially at his friend.

'And, to be honest, when me and my lads are knee deep in guts and shit, with the spears all thrown and our shields splintering under blue-nose axes, I want your boys to be straining at their collars, to be looking to you for the command to take their iron to our enemy, just for the love of my lads. If we can achieve that, we'll *both* have a better chance of seeing next winter . . .'

The 9th's tent parties exercised and practised against each other, each time striving to win for some inconsequential reward or other, their bonds growing stronger with each victory or defeat, vowing to do better in the next contest, the weaker helped and cajoled by the stronger. The trick was repeated with multiples of tent parties, the groupings changed each time and soldiers judiciously exchanged to equalise their relative strengths, until each octuple was used to fighting alongside every other, and knew their abilities. In the evening, watching their men down in the vicus, Dubnus and Morban reported back a new spirit, the other centuries quickly coming to recognise that taking on a single man from the 9th was offering a fist to every one of them, no matter what the odds. The respect in which they were held rapidly increased, to the point where it was rare for fights involving the 9th's men to be anything other than between themselves, combat quickly over and insult swiftly forgotten as they closed ranks.

Marcus and Rufius, who had played exactly the same game he had preached with his own men, repeated the trick with their centuries, again exchanging soldiers, ostensibly to add strength or skills where they were needed, but in truth to build the same spirit of comradeship between the two units. At length, one night in early May, a tent party from Rufius's 6th waded into an unfair fight on behalf of a pair of beleaguered 9th Century soldiers. It was the first sign for the two friends that they had achieved the breakthrough they were looking for.

Prefect Equitius returned to the Hill from a senior officer's conference in Cauldron Pool that same evening. He called for the First Spear to join him in his office shortly thereafter.

'It's war, Sextus, there's no longer any doubt. Sollemnis's spies tell us that the call has gone out for the tribes to mass north of the Wall, probably within a short march of Three Mountains Fort. From there it's only about two days' march to the Wall, and the blue-noses can knock over two more single cohort forts on the way just to get their spirits up. He's not interested in defending the outlying forts against a force of between twenty and thirty thousand men, since that's clearly what Calgus will be hoping for. Our defence will focus on holding the Wall while the legions from Fortress Deva and the far south slog their way up the country to join us.'

Frontinius nodded reflectively.

'So the outlier cohorts march back behind the Wall in good order rather than being slaughtered to no purpose. At least our leader seems to be taking a practical approach to the situation. Does that mean we get the Dacians from Fort Cocidius joining us?'

'Not this time, despite the fact it seemed to work well enough in last summer's exercises. No, the Dacians will make a temporary camp down at Fair Meadow and form a two-cohort force with the Second Tungrians, ready to reinforce any of the western Wall forts that get into trouble.'

'Perhaps some of their professionalism will rub off on the Second. And how long does the legate reckon it will take for the Second and Twentieth Legions to reach us?'

'That depends who's asking. To anyone else in this cohort, up to and including the officers, the answer's fifteen to twenty days. For your information only, I happen to know that Sollemnis called them north nearly two weeks ago, and asked his brother officers not to spare the boot leather, so they ought to show up within a week. With any luck that will give Calgus a nasty shock and put Fortuna on our side rather sooner than he might have expected. Sixth Legion is already deployed, of course, although he was pretty tight lipped as to exactly where they are. Whether it's accurate or not, the rumour in Cauldron Pool is that he's got them camped fifty miles back at Waterfall Fort to give him the flexibility to move to the north or west as the situation develops.'

The First Spear shook his head in exasperation.

'West? Calgus isn't going to make a push for Fortress

Deva. The legion should already be in position to defend our supplies at Noisy Valley. Mind you, rather them than us, if there really are thirty thousand men massing under Calgus.'

Equitius nodded silently, reaching for his cup.

'We'll be moving inside the week, I'd guess. There's no point leaving the Wall units all divided up into cohorts when we can form a legion-sized battle group with two or three days' marching. So, First Spear, are we ready?'

Frontinius nodded.

'Ready enough. There's still the question of completing the assessments, but I think we'll have time enough for that if I pull the schedule forward.'

'And our new centurions?'

Frontinius stretched out his legs, pursing his lips in consideration.

'A timely question. Rufius is everything I expected, tough, professional, more than up to his task. A gift from Cocidius. As for the Corvus boy . . .'

The prefect took another sip of wine, raising an eyebrow. 'Yes?'

'To be honest, he's surprised me in the last few weeks. He seems to have an excellent grip on his century, Prince Dubnus is backing him to the hilt, he's converted more than one complete waste of good rations into an effective soldier, and his reputation in the cohort seems to be stronger than I could ever have imagined. He's a cunning young bastard too.'

'Cunning? Not quite what I'd expected.'

'Nor I, but I can't find any other way to describe a man who hides his men's abilities from his brother officers. His men run faster than any other century in the cohort, certainly faster than I can keep up with. He hides this, however, with overlong rest breaks to hold down their average speed, or else he takes them on detours to make their performance look slower than it is. I find that very interesting.'

'And so do I. I wonder what else he has hidden away from view?'

The First Spear reached for his helmet.

'Exactly. I think it's time to give him a chance to show us.'

Ordering the guard centurion to assemble the officers, Frontinius installed himself in the principia to wait their arrival, mulling over his thoughts on the subject of his youngest officer while the two men standing guard over the cohort's treasury stared uneasily at the wall above his head. He was still brooding when the officers started to enter the praetorium in ones and twos, the first arrivals dragging him back to the moment at hand. Rufius arrived in the company of Caelius and Clodius while Marcus and Julius made predictably solitary entrances. When all nine men were gathered in front of him, Frontinius roused himself to their briefing, sending the duty guards out to stand watch at the door.

'If we wanted to pilfer the pay chests we'd have done it a long time ago. Nobody, with the exception of the prefect, enters without my permission. This briefing is for officers' ears only.'

He waited theatrically until the doors were closed.

'Brother officers, the prefect came back in from Cauldron Pool an hour ago, as I'm sure you've all heard by now. The message from the boys in the purple-edged tunics is simple enough – prepare for war. There's a Brit called Calgus mustering thirty thousand painted maniacs somewhere not much more than two days' march from here, and very soon now they'll come south with fire and iron, looking for a fight . . .'

He paused, catching more than one eye riveted to his gaze.

'A fight they'll get – eventually.'

'Eventually, First Spear?' Rufius's eyes narrowed with professional interest.

'Eventually, Centurion. Calgus will muster more spears than the Wall cohorts and Sixth Legion could cope with, even banded together to our full strength, unless he was stupid enough to throw them at us piecemeal. And on the subject of our enemy's wits I have intelligence of my own for you. Calgus isn't that stupid, in fact he isn't stupid at all. I met him five years ago at a gathering of the tribal leaders north of the Wall. I was the supervising officer, with half the cohort behind me to keep the peace between them and make sure it didn't get out of hand, and it was still, I can assure you, a bloody uncomfortable experience. Not only were the tribesmen a fairly ugly bunch, but Calgus could dispute with Minerva and not come away ashamed.

'He was recently crowned at the time, and still finding his feet as king of the Selgovae, but where his father was a sly old sod, a master of the knife in the back, the son was clearly a man of a different nature. He's a clever brute, a barrel-chested, red-haired bear of a man, born to swing a battleaxe but blessed with his father's silver tongue for all that. He would insist on seeking me out for arguments about the justification for Roman rule of the land south of the Wall. Of course, in the end I had little option but to end the discussion on the grounds that since we're the ones with our boots on the ground there was little point to it. I expected that to be the end of the argument, and to a degree it was. However . . .'

He lowered his voice slightly, reliving the moment.

'. . . Calgus just stood there and looked at me for a moment, then reached out a hand and tapped me on the chest with one finger. My escort had their iron aired and ready to go in a flash, growling like shithouse dogs, and I reckoned we were a hair's breadth away from a bloodbath, but Calgus never faltered. He just tapped me gently on the chest again and said, "Just as long as you can fill those boots, Centurion." Not enough to give me a pretext to have him for inciting rebellion, of course, and half the North Country's tribal elders were hanging on his words, as dry as tinder if I were stupid enough to provide the spark. Enough to make his point, though, and while I didn't like him I had to admire the size of his swingers. I've been waiting for his name to reach this far south ever since, and now that it has I can assure you all that we have a very worthy opponent. So the word, Centurion Rufius, is most definitely "eventually". I'll show you what I think will happen.'

He turned to their sand table and sketched in a few swift lines with his vine stick.

'Here, east to west, coast to coast, is the Wall. Calgus can't go round it. He has to go through it if he's going to make any impact other than burning a few outlying forts that we can rebuild before next winter. Here, north to south, is the road from Yew Grove to the northern forts, crossing the Wall at the Rock. There are the outlying forts north of the Wall up the north road, Fort Habitus, Roaring River, Red River, Yew Tree Fort and the tip of the spear, Three Mountains. They'll be evacuated by the time Calgus can get his warband limbered up, and their cohorts will retreat back to the Wall in good order, leaving the forts to the blue-noses. They'll steal everything that's left behind and torch the buildings, but they won't have the time to destroy the walls and so, to be frank, who cares? Those three cohorts will muster at the Rock, most likely, making a force of about three thousand men when combined with the local half horse cohort.'

Knuckles raised a hand.

'What about our Dacian mates at Fort Cocidius?'

Frontinius dotted the sand twice with the tip of his vine stick.

'Good question, Otho, you clearly haven't had all of your wits beaten out of you. Here's us at the Hill, on the Wall, and here's Fort Cocidius five miles to our north-east. The Dacians will also pull back behind the Wall, bringing with them, before you ask, all of their altars to Mars Cocidius. They're going to squat with the Second Cohort down at Fair Meadow, and we can only hope that they don't pick up too many bad habits while they're there. That's another two thousand men ready to move wherever they're needed, another reserve force like the one at the Rock. Add to that the ten thousand or so lining the Wall's length and we've half the number of spears we expect Calgus to muster. The difference is that we have to stay spread out for the time being while he can concentrate his power in one place, which means that the trick will be for us to avoid actually fighting the warband until the legions come into play . . .'

He paused for effect.

'All I can tell you about the heavy boys is that the Sixth are already somewhere close to hand, and the Second and Twentieth are footslogging up from their fortresses in the south, which means we won't see them for the best part of a month. The general isn't going to want to engage in pitched battle without at least two full legions in the line. That way he can face off the tribes and still have a nice big reserve to manoeuvre into their flank or rear if he plays it smartly enough.'

Rufius nodded agreement.

'So we can expect a month or so of marching round the country avoiding a fight?'

'Yes, that's about the size of it. Although it might be closer to the truth to say "avoiding a fight if we're lucky". Calgus will be desperate to bring us to battle early, to set his dogs on us before the legions get themselves cranked up ready to fight. If he can destroy the Wall garrison, or better still take

Sixth Legion out of the campaign early enough, the southern legions would be severely handicapped, fighting at a numerical disadvantage against fired-up tribesmen on ground they don't know. Calgus knows that, and he'll do whatever he can to force an early battle. If we can stay on our toes and avoid a fight for the next month we'll have done very well, in my opinion. Very well indeed. You'd best be generous making your offerings to Mars Cocidius tonight, we're going to need all the luck he sees fit to grant us. Now, the cohort assessments . . .'

He paused to allow the initial muttering to die down.

'. . . will still be held, but just to a different timetable. We still need to know who's going to guard the cohort standard this summer. Given that time is of the essence we'll dispense with the usual parade-ground tests, I've been scoring your men on their sword and spear work over the last few weeks, just in case, but we can't ignore the main test. So, all units on parade tomorrow morning at first light, last five centuries for the speed march, first five for the ambush force. Dismissed!'

The next morning dawned just as fine, with a warm and dry day in prospect. The First Spear paraded his cohort an hour after dawn, taking pleasure in the cool morning air, and announced the pairings of marching and attacking centuries with a slight smile, delighting Julius by tasking his 5th Century with ambushing Marcus's 9th Century during their speed march. The veteran centurion strolled across the parade ground to watch the 9th's departure, standing to one side with his arms folded and his face set impassively, drumming impatiently with his fingers against the iron rings of his mailed shoulder. While some of Marcus's men cast anxious sidelong glances at the officer, Morban stared back impassively beneath the century's standard, muttering to the nearest soldiers without taking his eyes off the scowling officer.

'Rumour says our old friend Julius and the glorious Fifth Century are going to give us a right kicking today, put young Two Knives in his place and take the standard for another year. In fact rumour had us paired with the Fifth long before Uncle Sextus announced it. I had a drink with their silly bastard of a standard-bearer in the vicus last night, and I had twenty denarii with him that we'd come out on top today, so you turd burglars had better wake your ideas up.'

Both Marcus and Dubnus ignored Julius for the most part, by prior agreement as to their tactics for the day. Dubnus, unable to resist the temptation, caught his eye, looked down to his thigh and extended his middle finger down the muscle. If Frontinius spotted the gesture as he strode up to Marcus he gave no sign.

'Are your men ready, Centurion?'

Marcus saluted, snapping to attention.

'Ninth Century ready, First Spear.'

The senior officer nodded, beckoning the younger man by eye as he walked slowly away from the century, out of earshot.

'Well, Centurion Corvus, your time of judgement is nearly upon us. This cohort goes to war tomorrow, and it must have officers that I can trust to lead their men to the gates of Hades if that's where fate takes us. Every day since your arrival I have asked myself whether you're that sort of officer, despite your age, despite your alleged treason, and in all those days I've never yet found an answer I can trust. You're quicker with a sword than any man I know, your century seem to love you well enough, and yet . . .'

Marcus met his eye levelly.

'And yet, First Spear . . . ?'

'And yet I am still not convinced that you will be capable

of giving this cohort what it needs in time of battle. So this is your day, Centurion, the last day in which that question can be answered. When you take your men out of those gates take one thought with you, and keep it in your mind all the way back here, no matter what happens.'

'Sir?'

'The good of the cohort, Centurion, simply that. Dismissed. Go and show your brother officers what you've been hiding from them these last two months.'

Marcus frowned at the last comment but had no time to reflect on it. With the trumpeter blowing the command to commence the exercise, and the first hourglass turned, the 9th were out of the fort at the double march. Away to the west they marched, along the military road behind the wall, their iron-studded boots stirring the dust into tiny clouds. The road ran along the northern lip of the vallum, the massive ditch that divided military and civilian ground, and its elevation allowed a cooling breeze to dry the sweat from the marching men's bodies as they pounded away from the fort in the early morning sunshine. A mile from their starting point a track branched south over a bridging point across the vallum, in the protective shadow of a mile fort, before starting a shallow climb into the hills to the south. It was the route by which they were to cover most of their march. Once he was certain that the century was out of sight of any watcher, Marcus trotted out in front of his men, turning to walk backwards for a moment to be sure that they were no longer observed, before signalling to Dubnus in his usual position at the century's rear. The big man's voice boomed across the marching ranks, making heads rise and backs straighten in anticipation of the coming order.

'Ninth Century, prepare to change pace! At the run . . . *Run!*

The soldiers lengthened their stride together, long accustomed to hauling their bodies and equipment across the undulating countryside at a fast jog. They went south at a fast pace for another two miles before dropping back to rest at a fast march for a mile, then stepped up the pace again. The troops were sweating heavily now with the effort of running in armour with full campaign kit, each man humping his armour, sword, shield, two spears and his pack, with only the pointed wooden stakes made to be lashed together into obstacle defences missing from their loads. They were working to a timetable known only to Marcus and his triumvirate of advisers, Dubnus, Morban and Antenoch, who had planned the day over a jug of wine the previous evening. While Dubnus still lacked any trust in Antenoch, he remained polite enough to the other man's face, and had tolerated Marcus's insistence on his being involved in their preparation.

The wind dropped, allowing the day's heat to get to work on bodies that were tiring and starting to dry out, but still they ground on, Dubnus relentlessly driving them on with shouts of encouragement and threats of a faster pace if any man flagged. Five miles out from the Hill, Marcus pointed to the roadside.

'Ten-minute rest and briefing. Get your water bottles and drink, but do it *quietly* if you want to know what we're about to do!'

Breathing hard, his men forwent the usual playful push and shove of the rest stop, drinking eagerly from their bottles while their centurion explained what they were about to attempt. His command of the British language had progressed a long way in the time available, but he spoke in Latin now, pausing for Dubnus's translation, to ensure complete understanding.

'The usual way of things in this event is for the marching

century to concentrate on getting around the course as quickly as possible, to win points for ground covered before the ambush. When they are ambushed, as they always are, a practice battle results. A few minutes' fighting, one of the two centuries is declared the winner, and then they finish the march together, all good friends again . . .'

A few heads nodded knowingly. *This* was the speed march they had come to expect.

'Not *this* time. Not *this* century.'

They stared back at him, eyes widening at the heresy.

'How many of you would *knowingly* walk into an ambush, or even the risk of one? We've trained to march fast because we'll use that speed in the field to *avoid* ambushes, or to put ourselves into the best positions before an enemy can reach them.'

He paused, allowing Dubnus to translate, although he could see from their faces that the majority had understood his words.

'This one's real as far as I'm concerned. What about you, Chosen?'

Dubnus nodded grimly, staring dispassionately at his men, daring anyone to disagree. Marcus continued.

'Julius wants to teach me a lesson, take me down a peg, and he wants to do this at the expense of your pride. That, and your reputation as soldiers. You might not have noticed it . . .' He knew they knew all too well, were basking in the glory of their meteoric rise. '. . . but we're second in the standings. The century everyone wrote off as useless. You want to keep that reputation? Be second best?'

A few heads shook slowly. Morban roared at them, his challenge lifting the hair on the back of Marcus's neck as he shook the standard indignantly at them.

'I'm not taking *second* place to any bastard without a fight! You're either in this or you can turn round and fuck off back to the Hill and apply for a new century. One that takes losers.'

Marcus watched their reaction carefully, gauging their sudden enthusiasm as men turned to their neighbours to see the excitement reflected in their eyes. The standard-bearer grinned proudly at Marcus, tipping his head in salute to hand the century back to his centurion.

'So shut the fuck up and let the centurion tell you how we're going to pull Latrine's beard for him.'

7

Julius lengthened his stride, eager to reach his chosen ambush site. Alongside him, moving with an easy grace that belied his age, Sextus Frontinius matched him step for step. The centurion would have avoided taking the First Spear out on the ambush march if he could have found a way, but his superior was all too well aware of the potential for the event he had staged-managed to get out of control. He had made a point of politely requesting his permission to accompany the 5th Century, a courtesy Julius had no choice but to return through gritted teeth.

'So you've decided to attack them at the Saddle, eh, Julius?'

Julius, tempted to ignore the question but with enough sense to avoid the pitfall of failing to acknowledge the innocent enquiry, nevertheless waited a full five seconds, taking his response to the margins of insolence, before answering.

'Yes, First Spear.'

Sextus Frontinius smiled inwardly, keeping his face a mask of indifference.

'A little early in the march, isn't it? His men will still be relatively fresh. I'm surprised you're not going to wait for them farther into the route. What's wrong with the usual places?'

Stung by the implied criticism, Julius wiped sweat from his eyebrows, shaking his head in irritation at the unusual warmth.

'I'm not allowing any rest stops until we get there, so we'll get there first. The Ninth will never suspect a thing until we're down the slope and on top of them.'

'If I didn't know you better I'd have to say you're taking all this a bit too personally.'

The centurion spat into the roadside dust to clear his throat.

'And, First Spear, if I didn't know you better I'd have to say that you've rolled over for this Roman with the rest of them.'

Frontinius glared at the soldier marching alongside him, who redoubled his efforts to be seen not listening.

'March out front with me, Centurion, let's show these nosy bastards of yours how to cover ground.'

He waited until they were ten yards clear of the marching century before speaking again.

'I think it's time we discussed this properly. Our rules, not First Spear and centurion. Just Sextus and Julius.'

The other man glanced over at him.

'And if I don't want to discuss it?'

'But you do, Julius, you've been quacking away about it ever since he got here. Come on, man, let it out!'

'Our rules?'

'Absolutely. The same as the day we joined.'

'Don't say you haven't asked for it. He's a traitor. An enemy of the man who rules the world, and of the empire you swore to serve. And yet you've gone out of your way to make him welcome.'

The First Spear shrugged unconcernedly.

'I'm not convinced by all this "traitor" talk. You've heard the same stories I have, Julius, you know how this new emperor's behaving and who pulls his strings. As far as I'm concerned our man's guilt isn't proven.'

'Not your call, Sextus. If the empire says he's a traitor, then he's a traitor.'

'And if it was you, old mate. What if you were unjustly accused?'

'Then I'd run a thousand miles to avoid hurting my friends, and . . .'

'And end up somewhere like here, dependent on strangers for justice. Not negotiable, Julius, I won't hand over an innocent man to that kind of evil.'

'And if they come for him? If they nail you and the prefect up and decimate the rest of us for hiding him?'

'It won't come to that. Besides, we'll be at war in a few days. We could all be dead in a week, so some unlikely discovery by the empire doesn't worry me overly right now. Next?'

'He's a snotnose. He's never commanded so much as a tent party in action, and he'll fall to bits the first time he sees a blue-nose warband.'

Frontinius snorted.

'Rubbish. He killed on the road to Yew Grove, he fought again on the road here, he faced down that headcase Antenoch with his bare hands, and he seems to have faced you down well enough since then.'

Julius turned furiously, still walking.

'That was Dubnus!'

Frontinius pursed his lips and shook his head.

'Sorry, but that's not how I heard it. The version that reached me was that he got right in your face and practically offered you the dance floor.'

'I was half awake and unprepared . . .'

'Rubbish, man. I've never known you not ready to fight, day or night. Admit it, there's something in the young man's eye that would make any of us step back and take guard. And I don't mean the sword skills either. He's lost something in the last few months, some carefully instilled self-control, an edge of civilisation that his father probably worked on all his life. What I see in him is a dangerous animal that's been given every reason to want the taste of blood, and now those early disciplines have been stripped away there's only cold calculation keeping that rage in check. The pair of us could take him on two on one with swords and boards and I'd have money on his opening us both up from chin to balls in under a minute.'

Julius lifted exasperated hands to the sky.

'So he's dangerous. Enraged. He's a goat-fuck waiting to happen. Put him in combat and he'll go berserk and take his century with him.'

Again the First Spear shook his head.

'No he won't. He's the model of self-control. Think back to Antenoch, that first morning? Came at him with a knife and ended up with it tickling his own ear? Did you see a single drop of blood on the fool? Because I was there in seconds and I didn't. No, Centurion Corvus will have iron control right up to the second where he chooses to let it go. Just don't be on the wrong end of his sword when that happens.'

He took a deep breath as they marched on side by side.

'You know as well as I do that you're not competing for the honour of carrying the standard along the Wall to the games this year. What you're looking for is the opportunity to fight off every blue-faced bastard between here and the River Tava who thinks it would look nice on the wall of his mud hut. Every century in this cohort is going to need strong leadership, and the Ninth isn't any different from any of the other centuries in that respect.'

'So give them to the Prince. He'll give them strong leadership all right.'

'You know my thoughts on that individual. He's no more proven than young Corvus as far as I'm concerned.'

He took a deep breath.

'I'll tell you what, I'm just simply bored with pondering the whole thing, so I'm going to delegate the decision.'

'Delegate it to . . . ?'

'You. But . . .'

He raised a hand to silence the astonished centurion.

'Yes, I know, you already know the answer, except I'm really not sure either of us have actually seen what's in Centurion Corvus's heart yet. So, you can make the decision, but only when this day's events are fully played out.'

Julius grunted his satisfaction.

'My opinion won't change, you can be sure of that.'

Sextus stared fixedly ahead as they marched on.

'Perhaps it won't. You feel betrayed and undermined by your old friend, the man you joined up with all those years ago. I've allowed an inexperienced outsider into our close circle of brothers, an action that might spell disaster for us all. On the other hand, oldest friend, Corvus might just have a pair of stones larger than either of us appreciates. So let's wait and see, eh?'

The 5th made good time, taking their water on the march rather than stopping, and reached a position with a clear view of the Saddle by the middle of the day. Julius called a halt, sending a scout past the feature to make sure that the 9th were not about to hove into view just as he deployed his men into their positions for the ambush. The man ran back a few minutes later to confirm that the road was clear to the grassy horizon, provoking the first smile the 5th had seen grace their commander's creased face all day.

'Excellent! Even-numbered tent parties to the right-hand hill with the chosen man and into cover, odd numbers with me to the left. And remember, any man that shows himself before I give the signal loses a month's pay!'

The century split quickly into two disciplined groups, hurrying down the slope from their vantage point and starting the climb up to the twin hills. Their equipment rattled and clattered noisily, while the soldiers talked among themselves about the afternoon's entertainment, planning individual acts of revenge for real or imagined slights upon their century's good name by members of the 9th. Thus it was, with nobody looking too carefully at the greenery that crowned their objectives, that it took a bellow of challenge from Dubnus to draw their attention to the previously well-hidden troops who had risen like forest spirits out of the undergrowth of the right-hand hill's heavily wooded crown.

The 5th's soldiers hesitated for a moment, caught between their orders and the shock of finding the Saddle already occupied, the short pause enough to cause a chorus of abuse to shower down upon them from the hills. The 9th had taken their objective first, and showed every sign of being in the mood to defend their ground. Julius stepped out in front of his men, drawing his sword and sweeping it over his head, ready to slash it down to point at the twin hills and issue the command to attack, ready to start a full-scale battle if it was the only way to restore his face. As the sword started to move in the downward arc, Sextus Frontinius stepped out of the century with his arms in the air.

'*Hold!*'

Ignoring Julius's red-faced fury, he turned to the Saddle's hills, his voice bellowing out across the landscape.

'Ninth Century, form ranks for parade *here*.'

The 9th's troopers came out of the trees and streamed obediently down the hill, while Frontinius paced back a dozen steps, pushing soldiers aside without ceremony, and pointed to the ground again.

'Fifth Century, form ranks for parade *here*.'

The 5th's grumbling men pulled back, still reeling from the shock of their centurion being so comprehensively out-thought. Julius, restraining himself by an act of supreme willpower, stamped back down the hill to the designated place, bellowing at his subordinates to get the fucking century on parade. The two units lined up opposite each other, scowls and sneers along both opposing lines of men, while the First Spear paced equably between them and watched the clouds scudding along in a clean blue sky, enjoying the breeze's cooling caress. When both centuries were lined up, and the harsh shouts of the chosen men and watch officers had died away to silence, he turned slowly to look at both centuries, taking in Julius's set scowl and Marcus's white face, ready to fight, his lips thin with determination over a tight-set jaw.

'In all my days I swear I never saw two sets of men who wanted so *badly* to kick the balls off each other. If I were to let you dogs loose now I'd end up with a dozen or more broken limbs, and as many men with the wits knocked out of them. Well, you mindless apes, let me remind you that there's a great hairy-arsed tribal chief by the name of Calgus mustering a warband the size of five legions to the north. Whether it's sunk into your thick skulls yet or not, we will most likely be at war within a few days. You need to learn to work together, side by side in the line, either century ready to perform whatever manoeuvre is needed to support the other. Even if it'll cost lives. And the time that you need to learn to do this is *now* . . .'

He turned away from them and stared for a moment across the rolling countryside, taking a moment to enjoy the sunshine's gentle touch on his bare scalp.

'We do need a winner from this competition, if we're to have a century to guard the cohort standard, but *without* spilt blood. The answer is single combat, with, *before* anyone jumps forward, combatants chosen by the person here best qualified to make that judgement. Which would be me.'

The silence became profound as he paused again, every man straining to hear his decision.

'And I choose Centurions Julius and Corvus. Prepare for combat, exercise swords and shields.'

Marcus passed his vine stick to Dubnus, leaving the sword at his waist in its scabbard and taking the heavy wooden practice sword from his other hip. The Briton fussed at his helmet fastenings for a moment, leaning in close to look at the offending buckle, murmuring into Marcus's ear.

'He's weaker on his left side, shield dependent. Don't go in too close until he tires, though, or he'll try to smother you with his strength. Stand off and use your skill, you can cut him to pieces easily enough . . .'

Frontinius walked over to face him, dismissing Dubnus with a pointed nod to the 5th's ranks. The senior centurion stared away into the distance, speaking in a matter-of-fact tone.

'I'm awarding your century three points for ambushing the Fifth, which puts you level with Julius before the result of this event. If you win, you'll take first place, and carry the standard through the campaigning season. If you draw, and finish level on points, I'll award the prize to the Fifth as the previous champions . . .'

He paused significantly, shooting Marcus a sudden glance.

'I'll give you no guidance, young man. This is an opportunity for you to exercise some judgement. I'll simply remind of what I said to you this morning.'

Marcus nodded, moving his shield into a comfortable position on his arm before stepping out into the space between the two units. Julius stepped out to meet him, glowering from between the cheek-pieces of his helmet, its red crest riffling slightly in the breeze. Frontinius held them apart for a moment, speaking softly into the silence that had descended upon the hillside, as the opposing centuries waited for the spectacle to commence.

'I want you both in fighting condition when this is finished. I'll deal with the man that injures the other *personally* . . .'

They stepped apart, saluted formally with their practice swords before moving together again, each eyeing the other over the edges of their shields. Julius crabbed around to his left, searching for a weakness in the younger man's defence, striking without warning in a powerful lunge, his sword hammering on Marcus's shield as his opponent stepped away from the strike, his studded groin apron whipping about with the movement. The Roman moved in low, swinging his weapon in an arc that whipped past Julius's forward leg with a fingernail's width to spare, and then drew back as quickly, looking for another opportunity to strike. The fight lasted the length of a five-minute sandglass, each man alternately attacking and defending, seeking to land one disabling strike on the other. The soldiers watching made Marcus the better of the two but unable to land the killing blow, several times just a split second too late to press his advantage on an overextended and tiring Julius. At length Frontinius raised his hand, stopping the bout and declaring a tie. The two men stepped apart, both breathing hard from their exertions. Frontinius ushered them back to the ranks of their centuries, waiting for them to take their places before speaking again.

Antenoch, in his customary place next to the centurion, spoke from the corner of his mouth.

'Well, Centurion, I had no idea you were a politician.'

Marcus ignored him as the senior centurion started to speak again.

'We started the day with the Fifth Century leading the Ninth by three points. I have decided to award the Ninth three points for a successful ambush on the Fifth, which places both units level. These scores will be officially confirmed, and awards made, on formal parade, but since I'm the final judge of the competition, you can take this pronouncement as final. Since both units finish level, last year's champion century, the Fifth . . .'

Julius's century erupted into cheers and roars of delight, men punching the air with the joy of their victory. Only their centurion seemed subdued, standing in front of his unit to a rigid attention.

'Silence!'

The harsh command, combined with Frontinius's furious body language, was enough to promptly silence the Fifth's celebration.

'. . . will retain their position as cohort standard-holders, *unless* of course there's any repeat of that undisciplined outburst.'

He paused to allow time for the threat to sink in before continuing.

'In recognition of their achievement in tying the contest, and their improvement on what was until recently a very poor standard of performance, I *also* award the Ninth Century the task of lead century for the season. The standard will be carried in its wartime position in the column's centre this season, rather than at the front, which means that I need a good century to lead the cohort. Let us hope that none of you have cause to regret winning these positions of merit, which will leave you *all* holding the bloody end of the spear if we go to war with the tribes this summer . . .'

They marched back to the fort at a steady pace, Frontinius keeping their minds busy by ordering both centuries to belt out their lewdest marching songs in unison until they tramped over the final hill and drew up on the parade ground. The senior centurion walked down their ranks, taking the measure of his tired but erect men before calling them to attention.

'Soldiers, you represent the cream of this cohort's fighting skills. I've nothing better in my armoury than the one-hundred-and-sixty-odd warriors mustered on this parade ground. You are trained and disciplined fighting men, every one of you ready to stand in line and shed blood for the cohort. Now I suspect that there are a few scores waiting to be settled in these ranks, things that have been said and done that can hardly wait to be avenged. It'll start with fists and boots, some fool will pull a knife, and I'll have my two best assets at war with each other . . .'

He paused significantly.

'And that is not going to happen. *I* will not allow it to happen. So here are the rules for these two centuries. Any man brought in front of me for fighting a member of the other century will suffer the maximum penalty I can apply under the circumstances. Up to and including dishonourable dismissal without citizenship. No excuses, no leniency, and no exceptions. So *you* choose.'

He strolled away across the parade ground for a few paces before turning back with a sly look on his face.

'Of course, the situation might be different to that I imagined. You might march back into the fort as the two best damned centuries in the cohort, both so good I can't separate you. You might take pride in your shared excellence. You might *even* take the attitude that it's the others that take second place to *you*, not either of you to the other. Whatever you decide, collectively you are my best weapon. And I make a point of keeping my weapons razor sharp. Don't test me. Centurions, take your units back to barracks. Dismissed.'

Marcus marched his men back into the fort, left Dubnus to chivvy them down to the bathhouse, and went to wash the dust from his feet, musing on the day. Antenoch had vanished, and for once the centurion was happy to be spared his presence, knowing that his clerk had already guessed the truth behind the result of his contest with Julius. The sound of his quarter's door opening made him turn swiftly, as Julius came in without waiting for an invitation. He looked to the bed, where his belt gear and sword lay discarded, wondering whether he could reach the weapon if the older officer intended him harm. In the enclosed space of the quarter he doubted that he could resist a determined attack by the larger man without being forced to try to disable or even kill him. Julius held up his hands, seeing the swift glance.

'No, I'm not here for a rematch. But we do need to talk . . .'

Marcus nodded, reaching for a flask of wine and two cups. Julius stayed silent while the wine was poured, tipping half the offered cup down his throat with a sigh of satisfaction.

'Thanks. I should thank you for this afternoon's performance as well. You could have put me down half a dozen times this morning. I knew it, I could *tell* that you were holding back from connecting with your attacks. You're faster, and better trained than I am, and that's all there is to it. You're the better swordsman, although time will tell if you're the better *warrior* when the shit really starts flying. You should have taken first place, and we both know it . . .'

He stared at Marcus until the younger man nodded slowly, letting out a sigh of release from his internal pressure.

'Why? You earned that victory, built up your men to taking it from under my nose. Why didn't you take it?'

Marcus frowned, starting to speak and closing his mouth again. After a moment he tried again.

'You'll laugh at me . . . I did it for the cohort. Uncle Sextus told me to think about what would be the best result for the cohort, and when I did, it was obvious that you had to win. If I'd beaten you, you'd be sitting in your quarter now, plotting revenge on me. As it is, you're just puzzled. The cohort gets undivided leadership, Frontinius doesn't have to deal with a series of running battles between our centuries . . . everyone wins.'

Julius looked at him for a moment without speaking.

'Except you.'

'Perhaps.'

The older man shook his head, resting a hand on the hilt of his sword.

'Except *you*. Frontinius gave me something this morning, something I've wanted since the day you arrived. He gave me the responsibility to decide your fate. Said he was tired of pondering whether you have what it takes or not. And if I say you're gone, boy, just a fading stain on this cohort's proud history, what then? If I tell you that where you go is of no concern to me, and that all that matters to me is that you leave, and don't come back? What do you say to that, eh?'

Marcus gazed back at him for a long moment, then nodded his head, half turning away to speak woodenly at the room's wall.

'I'm not surprised. I've known deep down that you and your brothers wouldn't be able to accept me. This cohort can't operate with a rejected officer at its heart, and I've developed too much affection for this place to risk that rejection turning into casualties. As to where I go, don't worry yourself. I'll be in another place before dawn, and that's all you'll be wanting from me. I'd be grateful if you could find a way to overlook the last few months, and recommend Dubnus to command the Ninth?'

He gestured to the door.

'And perhaps now you could leave me in peace. Let me get on with what I have to do.'

The burly officer stared at him a moment longer, then shook his head wryly.

'I'll have to apologise to Sextus. I told him I was going to come here and say those words to you, and he told me you'd bite on the leather the way you did.'

Marcus turned back to face him, his face hardening, his eyes flicking again to the sword lying on the bed alongside him.

'If you think that I'm going to let you stand here and calmly discuss my personality traits now that you've had your way you'd better look to your blade, Centurion, because in about ten seconds you're going to be getting a very close look at mine.'

Julius opened his hands again, backing away slightly and talking quickly.

'Hold! It was your last test, to see if you cared enough for the cohort to accept the hardest decision. You'll do for Sextus, and, while it's hard to admit, you'll do for me too. Quite how we're going to keep a swarthy bugger like you any kind of secret when we march to war is beyond me, but Sextus gave me the decision and I've made it. You stay.'

Marcus's eyes narrowed, and Julius realised with a shiver that his temper was fully alight.

'And if I don't accept your gracious offer after this last little test? If I take that sword and fillet you like an old bull, then spill my own blood?'

The other man smiled, holding his ground and keeping his sword hand rock steady six inches from the hilt of his weapon.

'I don't doubt that you could spill my guts, although we'd have some fun finding out within these four walls, without much space for fancy sword work. I probably deserve it too, the way I've been hounding you and your men. But you won't. The other thing Sextus has you nailed for is iron self-control. And, given that you're now the centurion of the cohort's lead century, likely to be first into the shit and last out of it, you're going to need it. Get some sleep, young Two Knives, you've a hard month in front of you. But before you do, fill me up with a little more of that dog-rough piss you're drinking, I can't drink a cup to your success if my cup's empty.'

He passed his cup back for refilling. A hammering at the

door made them both jump, Antenoch thrusting his head through the opening, breathlessly ignoring the frown on Marcus's face. Clearly Julius's presence was no surprise to him, and Marcus suspected he had been lurking close by, ready to come to his assistance if necessary.

'Centurion Julius, you've an order to join the First Spear at the north gate. Something to do with a bonfire.'

Julius downed the wine in a swift gulp and turned to the door.

'I'll see you later . . . *Centurion.*'

In a woodland clearing well to the north of the Wall, beyond the reach of the units nervously manning the forts along the North Road, the leaders of Britannia's remaining free tribes were gathered in their first war council. Seated around a crackling fire in the cool light of dusk, the half-dozen tribal chieftains eyed each other soberly as they waited for the arrival of their leader. Each of them was very well aware that they were about to step hard on the tail of a very dangerous animal. When Calgus, tribal leader of the Selgovae, made his entrance, it was without fanfare. He shrugged off a cloak of wolfskin and walked to the fire to warm his hands. He spoke without turning away from the heat, his voice a deep rumble.

'Leaders of the northern tribes, our men are poised to attack down what our oppressors call the North Road, straining for release into battle like a hunting arrow bent and ready to fly. The Romans' scouts have been put to flight by our horsemen, and there is nothing more substantial between here and their Wall than a few pitiful forts. One word from each of us, and our men will fall on Three Mountains and put it to the flame . . .'

He turned away from the fire, opening his arms to encompass the gathering.

'It simply remains for us to make the decision to attack. But before we do so I want you all to be very clear about exactly what we're committing ourselves to. You all know very well that I was educated in "Isurium Brigantium", as the Romans have named that great tribe's historic home, now trapped behind their Wall and made slave to their empire. You know that I speak Latin, and that I spent my childhood absorbing their history and culture, and I know for a fact that many of you still mistrust me as a result of that education. In truth you should thank Cocidius for my father's insistence on that education, since it woke me to the danger to our tribes that has brought us all to this point of decision.

'I was sent south by my father when I was in my eighth year, and I stayed in the south until my fifteenth summer, learning their language and their ways. I hated every waking moment, brothers, with a passion that grew stronger with every year, with every fresh lesson that taught me how they have spread their rule across the world in a restless search for new peoples to enslave. And with each year my eyes opened wider to the state of the Brigantian nation, once proud rulers from the mountains to the sea for a hundred miles to the north and south of "Isurium", now castrated lapdogs to their rulers. So helpless that even their ancient capital has a Roman name. At fifteen I returned home for the summer and told my father that I wouldn't go back and live among slaves for a single day more. I expected harsh words or a beating, but he simply smiled at me and told me that in that case my education had served its purpose. He'd sent me south in order to open my eyes to the Romans, and their lust for expansion. He'd sent me south to harden my heart against their insidious persuasion. He'd dedicated my childhood to opening my eyes to Roman deception, making me a fit successor to his rule.

'So, brothers, let me outline our alternatives. We face a

stark and simple choice: either we try to live in peace alongside their rule, and suffer eventual defeat and enslavement, or we fight now and push them off our lands. We can still gain a lasting peace on our own terms, but the Romans will only ever respect strength. Offer them weakness and we will all be in chains inside five summers.'

He fell silent, watching the faces in front of him. After a moment the chief of the Votadini, an elderly man whose eldest son stood behind him to steady his arm, spoke out softly.

'You give us convincing words, Calgus. We all know of the Romans' desire to take our lands, we all lost sons and brothers the last time they tried to pen us up like cattle. We all wish to avoid this, and we would be willing to fight in response to your summons even were we not bound to follow you into battle. But still I fear their legions. Three generations before us have failed to defeat them in open battle, even with the advantage of superior numbers. Our victory in forcing them from the northern wall was the result of many attacks on small detachments of their soldiers, a war of striking and hiding and having the strength to ignore their reprisals. It was a victory, but it was not won on any field of battle. How will our warriors deal with their way of fighting if we take the field against them now?'

Calgus inclined his head with respect for the wisdom of the question.

'By dealing with their strength one unit at a time, Brennus. First we'll smash their forts along the North Road, and bring the Wall cohorts to battle by attacking the wall itself.'

The old man tilted his head.

'And if they decline to fight us? If they choose to keep us at arm's length, and wait for their reinforcements?'

Calgus laughed sharply.

'Exactly what we must expect them to do. Only a fool

would throw a single legion and their auxiliary rabble into battle against our great forest of spears. Which is why I have formed a plan to ensure that they have no choice but to engage us, and most likely in groups of less than their full strength. A plan, my brothers, of the utmost simplicity. Yes, a swift strike down the North Road by our eastern warband, burning out their forts all the way down to Noisy Valley. By destroying Noisy Valley we deprive them of supplies, we keep them on the back foot, and we strengthen our arms with whatever we can take. While they dither as to our next move, we'll split the warband to left and right, burn out the forts to east and west, then pull back into the north, taking what plunder we can carry. We can trust in our unexpected retreat to drag them along behind us, hot for vengeance. At the same time our second warband, and our main strength in horsemen, will strike at their undefended forts in the west. They will burn out Fort Cocidius and cross the Wall to destroy the Hill and Fair Meadow. This threat in their rear will fix the auxiliaries and prevent them joining with the legion. Brothers, we must put them off balance and keep them that way, continually rushing their forces to the newest point of danger. And when the opportunities present themselves, as they will, we will strike hard and destroy their cohorts piecemeal.'

Another of the tribal kings spoke out, stepping into the firelight.

'We agree, Calgus, although I still say that this is a strange kind of war to fight . . .'

'I understand. In past days we would have gone straight for their throats, dashed ourselves against their shield wall as we have a dozen times before, and lost warriors by the thousand in futile battles that could only end one way. We know their legions are meat grinders, made to fight in one way and only one way, in a battle line where they slaughter our warbands from behind their shields. They will never choose to fight man to man, because man to man they know they can only lose.

'This way we avoid confronting their legions face to face until the moment is right, when we've bled them a dozen times, razed their forts to the ground and made them charge round the land in search of us. We strike where they are weak and we avoid their strength until we're ready to deal with them, when they march into a trap of our patient making. Then, my friends, we will take so many heads that we'll make mountains of their skulls. After that there will be no choice for them but to negotiate a settlement. Their southern legions will be needed in their own areas soon enough, or the entire country will go up in flames. Victory, and peace on our terms – I trust that would meet with your approval?'

The Dumnonii chief nodded reluctantly.

'Where you lead I will follow, Calgus. Just don't wait too long to bring my tribe some glory, or all the promises of future slaughter I can make to them won't keep them in hand.'

Calgus laughed, putting a hand on the other man's shoulder.

'Caradog, you need wait no longer. I've put you and your tribe at the tip of the spear tonight. You'll be beheading Romans before the sun rises again, even if it's only the pitiful few that haven't already run off down the road to the Wall.'

Brennus snorted.

'And their Sixth Legion will sit idly by and let all this happen?'

Calgus's smile broadened.

'Ah yes, the infamous Sixth Legion. I have something special planned for Legatus Sollemnis and his men.'

One of his retinue approached respectfully, whispered

into the tribal leader's ear and withdrew. Calgus pulled an amused face, raising his hands in apology.

'I must ask you to excuse me. I have a visitor.'

He left the circle, his bodyguard of picked Votadini warriors clustering around him as he made the short walk back to his tent. At the door he was met by one of his advisers, an elder of proven wisdom who had stood alongside his father in his day.

'It's a Roman. He rode up to the scouts and asked to be taken to you, said that you would be expecting him. I have him under guard inside, two spears at his throat. If he twitches in the wrong way our men will kill him immediately . . . I asked him what he wanted, but he refuses to talk to anyone but you. Shall I have his throat slit?'

Calgus shook his head quickly.

'Not this one, Aed. This one's the key to our victory. I knew that he would come to me at this time – in fact I've been depending on it all these weeks. So pass the word, the man that so much as looks at him the wrong way will be joining his ancestors after a long session under my knife. This one gets safe passage, and no questions.'

Nodding his thanks, he entered the tent. The newcomer was standing at the far end, the two warriors tasked with his control watching him down the shafts of unwavering spears. Crossing his arms, Calgus looked the newcomer up and down, taking in his air of complete relaxation.

'I've been expecting a visit from a Roman these last few days, but if you're that man you'll know I have no way to be sure you're the same person.'

The Roman tossed a small object to him. Catching it, Calgus recognised the gold shield brooch that had been taken from him after their first meeting in the forest months before.

'Proof enough. I have to salute your courage. Not only

putting yourself in my hands when I might well still be smarting for vengeance for the murder of my companions, but riding into this camp, at this time . . . ? Brigantia herself must be smiling on you for you to have got this far without losing your head.'

The other man smiled confidently.

'Fortuna smiles on the man who knows when to take the right risk. I've taken that risk to offer you a bargain we can both profit from. Your gain, you will recall, will be two things you'll value over any other prize. A legion's eagle standard, and the head of a Roman general. If you kill me now you'll never see either, or hear the information I've brought to convince you of my sincerity. If you're still interested.'

The Briton stared back impassively.

'Interested? If there's a way that I can be guaranteed you're not just the high-risk end of a plot to mislead me at this critical time, yes, I'm still interested. But to gain my trust, Roman, you'll need to give me two things. Firstly, I want some proof that you can deliver me the prizes you offer so blithely. Secondly, and much more importantly, I want to know *why*. Start talking.'

The Roman shrugged.

'Proof that I can deliver you what I've promised? Where shall we start? Why not with who I am. My name is Titus Tigidius Perennis, and I am a tribune with the Sixth Imperial Legion's staff. You want proof? I can tell you that the supply depot at Noisy Valley is being emptied out even as we speak. By the time you get there the place will be a collection of bare cupboards, with nothing of value to sustain your army in the field. I can tell you that the other two legions, The Second and Twentieth, have been on the road north for over two weeks, and will be here long before you're expecting. You see? I can tell you that your options are becoming more and more limited with every day, and you haven't even made your first move yet. I'm your best hope for victory, probably your only hope.'

Calgus nodded slowly, raising a sceptical eyebrow.

'I see. And as to my second question?'

'Yes, why would I be doing this? That's simple. There is a cancer at the heart of the Sixth Legion, a seed of disloyalty to the emperor and his closest advisers, and I intend removing it in any way I can. The ends will more than justify the means.'

Later that evening, well after dark, with the 9th either settled for the night or, in the case of a few lucky men with dependants in the vicus, on a one-night pass out of the fort, Marcus went for a walk up to the Wall. He'd looked for Rufius, hoping to benefit from some measure of the older man's imperturbability by discussing the situation with him. The veteran officer was nowhere to be found, however, and his chosen man had simply shrugged apologetically at the question. Standing above the north gate, with the wind tugging at his tunic, he drank in the hour's quiet peace. Away to his right he could just make out the lake by the faint ripples kicked up by the wind's touch, while the forest wall made a darker line against the landscape. The distant flickers of torches inside the treeline betrayed the presence of some part of the garrison, clearly camping down for the night in barbarian territory. Most likely one of the night familiarisation exercises that Frontinius ran from time to time, he decided without interest, leaning against the parapet to enjoy the moment. The guards below were talking, their words drifting up to him, sometimes audible, other times too low to be discernible.

He listened for a few minutes, hearing hopes and fears expressed more in the voices themselves than by the words used, taking strength from an uncertainty that seemed to match his own. On the verge of turning to walk back down into the fort, he heard his voice being called from below.

Leaning over the inner parapet, he saw Caelius standing below.

'*There* you are! Message from the First Spear, you're to join him at the treeline as soon as possible.'

Marcus frowned down at his colleague.

'Why? I was about to go and get some sleep.'

'How the bloody hell would *I* know? Look, I'm not tired yet, I'll walk out with you. Come on, you don't want to keep Uncle Sextus waiting any longer than you have to.'

They strode down the steep north face of the escarpment, leaving the gate guards nodding knowingly at each other once they had passed, and made their way across the flat plain below the fort's walls. Away from the fort's reassuring bulk the darkness seemed deeper, pregnant with uncertain futures. Caelius's presence at his side was more reassuring than he'd expected.

'War's coming, Two Knives. Are you ready?'

Marcus paused for a second.

'We're ready. They're fit, good with their swords . . .'

'No. Are *you* ready?'

The pause was longer than before.

'I think so. I know I can fight, I can take my century where I want it to go, fight the way I want it to fight. Yes, I'm ready.'

'Ready to kill? To drop a man's guts out of his belly and see the life fade from his eyes?'

Marcus stopped in the darkness, looking up at the brilliant blaze of stars.

'I fought on the road to Yew Grove, you know, and killed more than one man. All I haven't done is face a full warband in a battle line. Everyone gives that so much weight. I've caught the other officers looking at me, weighing up how

I'll perform when it comes to a real fight. Even Dubnus seems reserved now, part of another world. And all they've ever done that I haven't is fought in a full-scale battle. What's so difficult about that?'

Caelius walked back to face him, starlight dimly illuminating the harsh lines of his helmet, its shadows reducing his face to a death mask between the cheek-pieces.

'That depends on the man. I've known some who've called the odds in barracks but shat themselves at the sight of a half-dozen angry farmers. Others, the sleepy-eyed men that you wouldn't trust to chase cattle out of a cornfield, go wild in battle and paint themselves black with enemy blood . . . You *need* to be ready for it, *you*, not just your men. You don't get a second chance in a real fight – you hesitate for a second and some big blue-nosed bastard with a tenth of your skill will have your guts steaming in the dirt. When we meet the enemy, you remember what I told you, eh? And offer a prayer to Cocidius for me when you come out alive?'

He swept his hand past Marcus's face, as if catching a delicate butterfly from out of the air, holding the closed fist up in front of him.

'That's life, grabbed from nowhere, easily lost. Don't throw yours away.'

Marcus put up his own fist, tapping Caelius's gently in the gesture of respect common between the cohort's soldiers. They walked on in silence, drawing closer to the torches moving in the trees, until Marcus saw that they were held by soldiers standing facing into the forest, as if on guard duty. A figure materialised out of the darkness, with a walk that was familiar even in the near-darkness, pure arrogant power in the strides.

'Julius?'

'Two Knives.'

'What . . . ?'

'There's no time. Come. And whatever Sextus asks of you, you just say "Yes, First Spear".'

Both men took an arm, propelling the mystified Marcus towards a darker shape that loomed large in the gloom, until its unseen bulk blocked all view of the lights in the trees. Julius abruptly put a hand on Marcus's chest to stop him, giving a soft whistle to signal his presence. Another voice spoke out of the darkness.

'It is time. Light the fire.'

For a moment nothing seemed to be happening, although Marcus sensed the presence of men around him, one or two darker spots against the darkness. Then, the flames creeping round the sides of the massive pile of brushwood and branches, fire applied on its far side took hold, gradually illuminating the scene. Almost a dozen men stood around him, all of the cohort's centurions, all with faces set in solemnity, although Rufius did manage a crafty wink of greeting. Frontinius stepped forward, speaking clearly so that all could hear him above the fire's growing crackle.

'Welcome, Centurion. Until today you were probationary, under the assessment of these men, your brothers-to-be. For all our initial doubts, it is our belief that you will make an excellent addition to our number, and provide leadership for your century that will be sorely needed in the coming days. This is your moment to renounce your past and join your brother officers in our chosen duty . . .'

He paused significantly, giving Marcus an interrogatory stare.

'Do you wish to become a part of the cohort's brotherhood, in spite of the heavy weight of responsibility that the position brings, renouncing all that has gone before in your life?'

Julius nudged his arm.

'. . . Yes, First Spear.'

'Do you swear to uphold the traditions of the cohort, even at cost of your life?'

'Yes, First Spear.'

'Will you give faithful service to the cohort until death or the end of your service?'

'Yes, First Spear.'

'Will you fight and die as commanded by your superiors?'

'Yes, First Spear.'

'Will you demand the same of your men if required?'

'Yes, First Spear.'

'And will you pay appropriate respect to the cohort's chosen god, mighty Cocidius the warrior?'

'Yes, First Spear.'

'Very well, Marcus Tribulus Corvus, I formally and irrevocably appoint you a centurion of the First Tungrian Cohort. Your previous life ends in this place, purged in the fire. Your new life begins here, forged in the fire. Remember your vows well, youngest brother, for the time for you to fulfil them will come when you least expect it. Be true to your words.'

He walked forward, offering Marcus his hand, and the other officers crowded round with congratulations and slaps on his back.

'Now, brothers, there is one last matter with our new brother officer before we give thanks to Cocidius for his meeting our high standards. Within a week we'll be camping alongside the other Wall units, some of them cohorts of doubtful honour and with many sharp ears besides. If it becomes obvious that we have a Roman officer serving with the cohort, that information might reach the wrong people. The men who destroyed our brother's family and made him outlaw for no good reason would come for him, and that would most likely bring death and dishonour on all of us, and our families, and upon the prefect for that matter.

Understand me clearly, we have taken a calculated risk in accepting this man into our family. From this moment he is to be referred to only as "Centurion" or by the unofficial title that his century has seen fit to give him. Make sure that your deputies are all aware of the rule, and their soldiers. From now, this man is to be known only by the name of Two Knives.'

8

Legatus Sollemnis arrived on the Wall at the Rock with the Sixth Legion's cavalry detachment shortly after darkness fell two nights later. The rest of the legion was more than thirty miles back down the road to Yew Grove, encamped after a day slogging their way north at the forced march, and still a day away. He had raced forward to take control of the Wall forces on receiving word from his Asturian scouts, ranging across the frontier zone under Perennis's command, reports that the barbarian warband was already in the field. Their latest dispatches had Calgus poised to strike down the North Road towards his main eastern strength, and a much greater prize besides. Once past the Rock, the Wall's eastern gateway, it was less than a five-mile march south to Noisy Valley, his main supply base for the Wall units. This, he suspected, was the prize for which Calgus would commit his strength.

Jumping down from his horse, he hurried into the fort's headquarters, acknowledging the sentries' salutes with a distracted wave of his hand. As he'd hoped, not only the cohort's grim-faced prefect but also his own senior tribune Appius were waiting for him in the lamplight, a map of the area spread across the table in front of them.

'Gentlemen, I suspect we haven't much time so I'll forgo the usual formalities. What's the situation?'

Appius swiftly painted a picture for him, pointing to the key points on the map.

'Calgus has thrown at least two-thirds of his force straight down the main road, with no attempt at concealment whatsoever. They're about ten miles out right now and coming straight on. They've already burnt out the fort at Three Mountains, Yew Tree and Red River, and we expect them to do the same to Roaring River very shortly.'

'What about the garrisons?'

'The cavalry detachment attached to the Three Mountains garrison seems to have attempted a defence of the fort. A few survivors have straggled in, but from their reports we shouldn't expect to recover the unit. The Brits seem to have a substantial cavalry force in the field, perhaps five hundred horses.'

'Fools! Of all the times that we can least afford to lose horsemen . . . and the detachments at the other forts?'

'Falling back in good order, sir. It would seem that the sight of burning forts on the horizon got their attention.'

'At least we can count them into our covering force. What about the Twentieth?'

'A messenger arrived three hours ago, with bad news, I'm afraid sir. Twentieth Legion won't arrive for another five days; they've had problems of their own with the local tribes. The Second has caught up with them as planned, but they've still only got as far as Veterans' Hill.'

Sollemnis frowned at the news.

'Still several days out, then, yet how I long for their arrival. Until they join us Calgus has the initiative, and from the way he's acting I'd say he knows it. I should have put the Sixth in play three days ago, instead of which they'll arrive footsore and in need of rest late tomorrow.'

He rubbed at tired eyes, shaking his head wryly.

'I gambled that the delay was compensated by my flexibility to move either side of the mountains if Calgus's move down the North Road were a feint to distract me from the west.

It was a poor guess, despite the strategic sense it made, and so here we are scrambling to catch up with the game.'

He rubbed at his weary eyes again before slapping the table with decision.

'We shall have to manage with what we have. Prefect Galen, have your men ready to pull out within the hour, and burn everything that will burn. Calgus won't stop at Roaring River; he needs to keep his men on the move if he's going to try what I think he intends, so I expect the warband to be knocking at your gates before daybreak. You're to pull back to the east and link up with the auxiliary battlegroup forming at Cauldron Pool. Appius . . .'

'Legatus.'

'Send riders to the Sixth, I want them moving up the road at first light and no later, forced march. Send riders to the prefects at White Strength and Cauldron Pool; warn them that the Rock and Noisy Valley are being abandoned, and that they're on their own for the time being. They're authorised to pull cohorts from the Wall units farther down the line in both directions if they see fit to form larger formations, but I don't want fighting men thrown away defending ground needlessly. As far as I'm concerned Calgus can mess about on the Wall as much as he wants – the forts are just wooden walls for the most part. We built them once, we can build them again. Men are more important than ground at this point, make that *very* clear.'

The officer nodded his understanding, scribbling notes on a wax tablet.

'Good. I'm riding south to Noisy Valley with my bodyguard, we'll have to prepare what's left of their supplies for the torch if we're going to deny Calgus that stepping stone, but I want to get as many more wagons away as possible beforehand. You're to stay here and help make sure the local boys get away in good order, and that the fort is burned out in good time. I don't want to be fighting outside these walls when we come north again.'

'Yes, sir. What do you think Calgus intends after he gets south of the Wall?'

'If I was Calgus, I'd have my eye fixed on two prizes. Firstly I'd want to take Noisy Valley intact, with its supplies and weapons. That way he can keep his men moving without having to forage for food, either south for Yew Grove or west to roll up the Wall forts. Then I'd be looking to destroy our legions one at a time, overwhelm them with sheer numbers before we get a chance to build up a proper sized army that can grind his warbands into mince. Either way I reckon he'll come looking for the Sixth, hoping to roll us over before The Second and Twentieth arrive. Noisy Valley he's welcome to, he can play in the ashes of those empty sheds as long as he pleases, but as Mars is my witness, I'm damned if I'll let him anywhere near my eagle until it's accompanied by two others just the same. Let's be about it, gentlemen!'

The first indication to the Tungrians that the warband had struck was a distant glow against the eastern horizon. On being called by the sentries, Julius, as that night's guard captain, took one look and called for the cohort's senior officers. First Spear and Prefect stood on the fort's high wall for several minutes, watching the minute flicker of light in silence. At length the senior centurion turned away from the view. Taking no pride in the vindication of his professional opinion, he turned to Equitius.

'That will be the Rock burning, at a guess. The warband must have come down the North Road during the night and attacked the fort without much warning. Impressive discipline to make a move like that in the dark with untrained savages . . . sentries, watch for another fire, a little to the south of the first. Duty officer, enter orders in the night report that all men are to parade at dawn and be ready to leave the fort at short notice. Pull the mile fort units back in after breakfast, but leave a fast runner at each point to keep watch for any activity over the Wall.'

He stamped off back to his bed, leaving the guards to watch for any further sign. It came an hour before daybreak, another tiny flicker of light in the distance, and the dawn revealed a distant plume of black smoke that rose in concert with that of the original blaze, and once again the senior officers grimly gathered to view the scene. Julius, off duty but unwilling to sleep, grimaced at the sight, chewing morosely at an apple while Marcus stood silently alongside him, not quite able to fully comprehend what was happening on the horizon. Julius shook his head sadly.

'Noisy Valley. There goes the forward supply station. We can only hope that Northern Command had the good sense to get all of the weapons and grain out before the barbarians decided to strike. I don't much fancy tackling thirty thousand blue-noses if they've all got a belly full of our bread and half a dozen of our spears apiece to repatriate.'

After breakfast the cohort's women started their journey to the safety of Waterside Fort on the west coast, thirty miles in the opposite direction from the horizon's grim signs of battle, the older women and small children riding in mule carts while the remainder walked alongside. A courier galloped up to the walls minutes later, his horse and those of his four escorts lathered in sweat from the speed of their journey. Equitius hurried down to the gate to receive the dispatch, calling the officers together in his office. The courier party, their horses watered, rode away to the south-west, heading for the Second Tungrian Cohort at Fair Meadow.

'The Rock and Noisy Valley are burnt out, but their units are largely intact and falling back to the west to hook up with the units gathering at Cauldron Pool. Northern Command has given orders for the prefect commanding Cauldron Pool to exercise local initiative, but to avoid any last stand that would result in heavy loss of trained men . . .'

The centurions waited imperturbably, wondering how they would have reacted to an order to abandon the fort. Cauldron Pool was only nine miles distant, with only the fort at Badger Holes between them to block the barbarian progress to the Hill.

'Early reports are that two warbands of about ten thousand men apiece have been deployed through the gap in the Wall, one turned east and driving for White Strength, the other advancing south. That leaves something like another ten thousand men as yet uncommitted somewhere in their rear, and a lot of options still open for Calgus to exploit. We're directed to deploy forward to Cauldron Pool and join the Second Asturian Horse, the Batavians, the Raetians and the Thracians, plus our neighbours the Second Tungrians, to form a strong combined blocking force. The general's intention would seem to be that of deterring any westward movement by the forces already identified, while we wait for the legions to move in from their forward camps. After that we'll start trying to find the warbands, and destroy them one at a time. Anything to add, First Spear?'

Frontinius rubbed his scalp, stepping out in front of the centurions.

'Brief your men that we're marching east to take a blocking position along with other cohorts from the line forts. *Don't* tell them that the total strength of the blocking force between the rest of the line forts and the blue-noses will only be five hundred cavalry and three thousand infantry. *Do* tell them that we'll be away from the fort for a long period, and that we are very likely to see combat. No, tell them that we are certain to see combat. Be ready to march as soon as the sentries are back in, guard commander to sound the recall. That's all. Centurion Corvus, a word.'

He drew Marcus to one side.

'What I didn't mention yesterday, when I gave your century the reward of being first in the line of march, was the role traditionally played by the leading century in this cohort in time of war.'

'Sir?'

'The first-placed century gets all the kudos, carries the standard about and dies gloriously in its defence if all is lost. The *second*-placed century, on the other hand, gets all the dirty jobs, scouting in front of the cohort, diversionary tasks and the like. In other words, all of the fun. Are you game for a little *fun*, Centurion?'

Marcus straightened his back, pushing his chin out.

'Yes, sir!'

'Good. In that case I've got just the job for you . . .'

With the 9th Century detached for the First Spear's speculative mission, the cohort marched from the fort seven hundred men strong, Julius's 5th Century marching with the standard at the heart of the column that snaked out on to the military road and headed purposefully away to the east at the double. Marcus waited in front of his men until the last were clear of the vicus, then turned to address them over the diminishing clatter of hobnails on the road's surface. His farewell to Rufius had been hurried, his friend simply clasping arms and tugging his head down to whisper into his ear.

'Keep it simple, Marcus, and don't be afraid to ask Dubnus for advice if you're uncertain about anything. I expect to see your pretty Roman features within a day or two, so don't disappoint me.'

Marcus nodded to himself without realising it, then turned to face the century, drawn up in parade formation.

'Very well, Ninth Century, we're on detached duty until our present task is finished and we head for Cauldron Pool to rejoin the cohort. Let's go hunting.'

Four hours later, having slipped through the wall at a now unguarded mile fort, far enough from the Hill to be out of sight of anyone watching the fort, the 9th stole quietly back towards their camp in the steady light of a cloudy afternoon. The emphasis now was upon stealth rather than speed across ground, the soldiers picking each footfall with care to avoid snapping fallen branches, their passage marked by nothing noisier than the buzzing of disturbed flies in the oppressively heavy air. Dubnus, long accustomed to the hill country's weather, looked at the sky for the tenth time in half an hour, working out how long they had before the inevitable rain started falling. The century was stretched across the rough country in a half-mile-wide net, each tent party spaced across its own hundred-pace frontage, the men at each end keeping sight of their opposite numbers in the neighbouring parties. Marcus and Dubnus moved silently in the rear, waiting for any sign that their men had made contact, their backs covered by a watchful Antenoch. If the Hill were under observation, for whatever purpose, they would know soon enough. At length, later than Dubnus had predicted, a steady rain began to fall, slowly growing heavier until water had penetrated down everyone's necks, no matter how tightly capes were fastened.

'At least the rain will cover any noise we're making.'

Dubnus snorted at Marcus's comment, flicking water out of his beard.

'You've officially been here too long when you start finding reasons why it's good for rain to fall.'

In the early afternoon, after an hour or more of painstakingly slow progress in the continuing rain, a flurry of hand signals rippled down the line of soldiers, who, as instructed, went to earth once the message was passed on. Marcus and Dubnus made careful haste up the line until they reached the soldier who had raised the alert, behind the cover of a thorn bush. He pointed forward, then pointed to his nose and sniffed audibly. Marcus sampled the air, finding the slight tang of wood smoke on the breeze, and nodded to Dubnus, who leant in close to whisper in his ear above the rain's pattering.

'I'll take the two closest tent parties in.'

Marcus nodded. The rest of the century would stay in place until the order was given to move again.

'We're too far from the Hill for this to be the watch point. Try to do it silently, and we'll get the watcher as well . . .'

After a whispered conversation with the two tent party leaders, their men gathered behind the thorn bush. Dubnus whispered a command and the group split up, one tent party remaining with the officers, the other snaking away on their bellies to move around behind the source of the smells that had betrayed their quarry.

Marcus and Dubnus crept up to the edge of the copse from which the cooking smells were emanating, allowing time for the men making their way around to the far side to get into position. As they slowly eased in between the trees the guttural sound of native conversation grew louder. Clearly the hidden men did not fear discovery. Raising his head with a hunter's patient stealth, Dubnus peeped through the top of a bush, then sank back into place. He whispered to the nearest man, Marcus straining to pick up the words despite his proximity.

'Three men, one well dressed, one poorly dressed, one old. Kill the young peasant, spare the others if you can.'

The whispered command was passed around the group, and a man wormed around to brief the other tent party,

while the soldiers readied themselves to spring. Dubnus
hefted his throwing axe, then stepped out of the shade of
his bush, barking a low challenge at the startled Britons as
Marcus came to his feet. A rough circle of bare ground
had been created in the copse's middle, half a dozen trees
having been felled to clear enough space for a shelter of
branches and turf to be erected in its middle. To one side
of the clearing a man of about twenty years, dressed in
rough woollen leggings and tunic, was tending a cooking
fire protected from the rain by a crude turf roof, over which
were suspended half a dozen gutted hares, his shocked face
an upturned white blur. An old man of fifty or so, sitting
on the stump of one of the felled trees, was looking up at
the last member of the group, a man in his early middle
age and dressed, as Dubnus had indicated, well enough to
be a local noble of some kind.

The cook leapt to his feet, reaching for a sword propped
against his cooking spit. A spear blurred out of the trees
behind him and thudded into his body, arching his back and
dropping him across the fire face first. The other two men
drew swords, spinning back to back as the rest of the hunting
party burst into their hiding place, snarling defiance at their
attackers.

'ALIVE!'

Dubnus stepped into the clearing, smashing the noble's
sword from his hand with a sweep of his axe, following up
with a shield punch that knocked the man out cleanly. Faced
with half a dozen armed troops, the older man's resistance
crumbled, and the soldiers disarmed him without a struggle.
Marcus strolled into the copse, eyeing the dead cook, whose
rough clothes were smouldering.

'Get him off that fire. There may be others close at hand.
We need to know what these men were about, and quickly
. . .'

'Yes. Put the knife to the older man.'

Marcus turned to find Antenoch at his shoulder.

'Why him?'

The subject of conversation glowered up at them, crouched in a kneeling position under the swords of a pair of soldiers, his wrists and ankles bound firmly. Antenoch squatted to look into his eyes, smiling at him without any change of expression in his own eyes.

'He's seen more than most, to judge from his age. Probably fought in the uprising of '61, killed, saw men die horribly . . .'

'Wouldn't that just harden him?'

'For a while, but as a man grows older his own mortality begins to press upon him. I can get the information we need. But I'll have to shed blood to get it quickly enough.'

Marcus hesitated.

'Centurion, they wouldn't think twice about skinning *you* alive if they captured you.'

'And we have to descend to their level?'

The other man shrugged.

'Depends whether you want to win or not.'

Marcus nodded.

'Take the other one away, out of earshot. I don't want to risk him hearing any of this.'

Dubnus nodded, gripping the unconscious Briton by the arms and dragging him from the clearing. Marcus squatted down alongside Antenoch as his clerk drew a small dagger. If he condoned the act of torture he could hardly walk away from its consequences. The Briton stared unhappily at the knife, only his eyes and nose visible above the heavy cloth gag that had silenced his muttered protests. Antenoch tossed the blade from hand to hand, staring at the older man until he dragged his attention away from the weapon and returned the gaze. The soldier spoke in the British language, gesturing with the knife to emphasise his point.

'You know that you're going to die, don't you?'

Marcus was perturbed to see the other man nod impassively.

'But then you're not that far from dying in any case, five or ten years at the most. Better to go this way than slowly, with no teeth and depending on the help of your sons to eat and shelter, eh?'

Again the nod. The Briton had clearly come to the same conclusion.

'In fact, the only thing between you and a nice clean death is the fact that you know some things that I need you to tell me. You talk, I slit your throat and make sure you're buried too deep for the wolves to find you. How's that for a deal?'

They waited while the Briton digested the suggestion. At length he shook his head unhappily, pulling a deep breath into his lungs, in preparation for what might be to come.

'Shame. You see, I reckon you're a respected warrior, with many heads on your walls. I think you've earned the rewards of the afterlife, all of the good things you denied yourself to live a life of training and devotion to the sword. The women will be oiling themselves up in the great kingdom over the river, ready for your arrival. Be a shame for all of you when *you* arrive without your manhood.'

Without warning he reached down and unfastened the bound man's leggings, pulling them down to reveal his genitalia.

'Not bad, not bad at all. Think what the girls upstairs are going to miss out on.'

He grasped the Briton's testicles, separated one from the other and, with a flourish of the knife, neatly sliced it from the captive's body, holding the bloodied organ up for him to see. One of the watching soldiers vomited noisily into a convenient bush, earning a glare from Dubnus, who had returned to witness the interrogation.

'Show some respect.'

The Briton's howl of pain and anguish was muted by the gag to a low moan, his eyes bulging with the pain. Antenoch stopped him from slumping to the ground with an outstretched hand, holding him up as the waves of pain washed over him, waiting until the man's eyes opened again.

'Now, from here it can go one of two ways. Either you can be sensible and tell us what you know, or I can remove the rest of your manhood and send you on your way incomplete. I'd imagine even one ball and your cock would be of more use to you in the afterlife than nothing whatsoever . . .'

The older man nodded, honour satisfied. Antenoch cut his gag away, keeping the knife close to his throat once the obstruction to speech was removed. The Briton spoke through gritted teeth, fighting back the pain with a conscious effort.

'You'll kill me cleanly, and put my body where the wolves can't drag it to pieces?'

'My word. And his.'

He gestured over his shoulder to the silent Marcus, who nodded gravely.

'I will tell you what you want to know. But first, there's a woman . . .'

Antenoch frowned.

'What woman?'

The warrior sighed and shook his head at a memory, his breath still shaky with pain.

'I warned him not to take her, I told him that no good would come of it. It offended Cocidius. She's one of *his* people . . .'

He nodded his head at Marcus.

'. . . although I can't say if she still lives. Or what's been done with her.'

The confession and burials took another two hours, during which time Dubnus took three tent parties and found the watcher's hide post betrayed by the Briton, leaving the lone watcher's head tied to a branch by the hair as a calling card. The century took a swift meal of bread and cheese from their packs, then headed north-east in early evening's half-darkness, dragging the unwilling noble with them and using their intimate knowledge of the terrain to make reasonable progress under a fat full moon.

When they stopped five hours later, within thirty minutes' march of their target, Marcus and Antenoch took the noble off into the dark, a tent party of soldiers shadowing them in a watching arc to ensure that no unfriendly strangers interrupted. Dubnus busied the century with the task of camouflaging their faces with saliva-moistened mud, each man painting broad stripes across another's features to break up the large area of pale flesh. Out of sight of the halted century Antenoch pushed the man to the ground, and pulled his knife, finding Marcus's hand on his shoulder.

'My turn. Translate.'

He squatted next to the noble, pulling his regulation dagger from its place at his side.

'I always thought I'd never use an issue weapon for a dishonourable purpose. This country is changing my mind in all sorts of ways. We're a mile from your farm where, I'm told, you have a Roman woman captive . . .'

The other man shrugged at the translation, spitting at Marcus's feet.

'We offered your companion the chance to change his mind earlier. My bodyguard here only cut off *one* of his balls, and then allowed him to think again about telling us

what he knew. He told us that you had already taken the
woman by force, and that you intend giving her to your men
as a celebration of the great victory to come.'

Another shrug.

'*You* don't get that extra chance to change your mind.
You *will* die here, either intact and quickly, or no longer a
man and in terrible pain, and *very* slowly. I expect that the
wolves will find you quickly enough if we slit your belly and
peg you out for them. Take a moment to consider your choice,
but don't expect to get an opportunity to make that choice
more than once.'

The nobleman looked from Marcus to Antenoch, who
nodded slowly to emphasise the threat. He coughed noisily
to clear his throat, then glared up at Marcus. His Latin,
roughened by lack of practice, was nevertheless clear in its
emphasis.

'Better to die without my manhood than to betray my
people. You should understand that. Do what you must.'

Marcus turned away, his mind thousands of miles and
several years distant. On a windy afternoon late in the year,
training inside the house to avoid dust stirred up by the
gusts outside, his trainer, sensing boredom in his student,
had suddenly dropped his sword to the floor, and indicated
to him to do the same.

'Sometimes you won't have a blade to defend yourself
with, Master Marcus. In the arena I've had my blade smashed
from my hand more than once, but still won the fight.'

'How?'

'Ah, got your attention now, have I? Simple enough, young
man, know where to strike a man, and how hard to strike
him. If you're fast enough to get inside his defence and land
a blow, you can choose to put your opponent on his back
or simply take his life. Just hit him here . . .'

Pointing a finger to touch Marcus's throat.

'. . . and you'll stop him breathing. You choose how long for. A little tap will put him down for a moment, short of breath and helpless. A decent thump, carefully measured, will probably knock him out for a few minutes. Anything harder will almost certainly kill him. Since swords obviously don't entertain today, let's practise that killing blow, eh?'

He raised an arm, pointing to the back of his wrist.

'Strike here, as hard as you like . . . no, boy, I said *hard*. Your opponent just smiled at you and stuck his sword into your guts. Pick a point a foot behind the target and punch at that . . . Good, excellent follow-through! Again . . . Excellent! Now let's work on the harder job, just knocking the man down for a little while . . .'

He spun back and struck the kneeling man's throat with the dagger's hilt with killing force, dropping him choking into the grass. After a moment or so the spasmodic jerking slowed, then stopped altogether. He knelt, and put two fingers to the man's neck.

'Dead. He'll meet his ancestors a complete man, and I didn't dishonour the blade.'

Antenoch frowned in the moonlight.

'Why didn't you torture him?'

'Because he wasn't going to talk. And we don't have the time to waste carving one man when there's a job to be done. Come on . . .'

He turned back to the century's waiting place, leaving his clerk staring quizzically after him in the darkness.

The Tungrians made a silent approach to the farm, advancing down the dark hillside that brooded to its south until the black shapes of its round huts and fenced enclosures which surrounded them stood out against the stars. A stop group of three tent parties moved carefully around the buildings, heading for their position at the farm's rear to catch any escapees, while the rest of the century dropped their packs into a large pile and advanced to the walls, still silent behind their shields.

In the darkness a dog awoke, smelt strangers and barked indignantly, joined a heartbeat later by half a dozen others. Marcus drew his sword and jumped the wall, sprinting across the empty animal pen and kicking hard at the door to the main building. It resisted his attack, and he stepped back to allow a pair of soldiers to shoulder-charge through the barrier, moving through the shattered doorway in their wake and peering into the gloom over the top of his shield, sword ready to strike.

A man charged out of the darkness, a faint light reflecting the line of steel brandished high above his head, and without conscious thought Marcus stepped forward into the brace and punched his shield into the contorted face, stabbing his sword upwards into the unprotected chest. He stepped back again, watching the body crumple back into the darkness. A shriek sounded from the far side of the hut as another point of resistance was extinguished. Dubnus moved swiftly past him, stepping over the sprawled body of his kill, and headed away into the darkness. Marcus followed, through a wooden archway and into a smaller hut, this one lit by a candle in whose puddle of light huddled a woman and her three children. Dubnus grabbed a soldier, pushing him at the terrified group.

'Watch them. Kill them if they try to escape.'

On the hut's far side, barely illuminated by the candle, was a heavy door, secured by a bar. Dubnus tossed away the bar and heaved the door open, then ducked away as a wooden bowl flew past his ear. A cultured female voice spat Latin imprecations at them from the darkness within.

'Come on then, you *bastards*, come and get me!'

Dubnus backed away from the door, gesturing to Marcus to try his luck. Marcus peered around the frame, quite unable to make out anything in the dark.

'Chosen, get me some light. Ma'am, we are the Ninth Century of the First Tungrian Cohort, Imperial Roman Auxiliary forces. You're free . . .'

A slight scraping movement inside the room made him duck instinctively, but the wooden cup caught him neatly under the eye, making stars flash before him for an instant.

'*Jupiter!*Where's that bloody light? Captured Roman citizen or not, if you throw *one* more thing at me I'll . . .'

Dubnus ducked back into the hut with a blazing torch, careful not to let it catch at the straw roofing. Marcus sheathed his sword and took the light, holding it carefully in front of him as he stepped back into the doorway.

'Take a good look. Armour, helmet, shield. I am a Roman soldier. Satisfied?'

The woman stayed where she was, crouched behind a small knife in the far corner of her cell. Her dark hair was in disarray, straggling across a dirty face, out of which shone piercing green eyes above a snub nose and small mouth. Her chin, wobbling slightly as she fought back the tears, was delicately pointed. She was dressed in a woollen shift and little else, her feet crusted with scabs from previous cuts and scrapes, her clothes and shoes presumably stolen on her capture.

'Very well, suit yourself. We'll leave you here for the blue-noses to find when the fire brings them running.'

He turned away, winking at Dubnus.

'*No! Wait!*'

He opened his mouth to invite her out of the cell, just as a sudden scream sounded from outside the hut. Dubnus chose the fastest way out of the structure, hacking fiercely at the wall to make a small gap through which he burst in a shower of dried mud and horsehair into the night. In his wake Marcus drew his sword, shouting at the soldier already guarding the still-terrified family to watch the woman as well. Outside, the fighting had already all but ended with two of the 9th's men down, one not moving, and half a dozen native men in rough woollens sprawled in the light of Dubnus's torch. Two remaining enemy were falling back under the advance of a dozen of Marcus's men, through whose line Dubnus charged in a blaze of light, tossing the torch at one of them even as he ran another through with his sword. Leaving the sword buried in the dying man's guts, he ripped the axe from his belt and hurled it into the distracted tribesman's throat, a froth of blood sheeting out from the wound as the man dropped to his knees, then pitched headlong to the ground. Marcus grabbed the nearest man that wasn't vomiting, demanding to know where the barbarians, clearly too well equipped to be farm peasants, had come from.

The soldier, still wide eyed from sudden combat, pointed vaguely out into the darkness. His voice shook with fear, rising as if a shriek was waiting to explode from his body.

'Came from out there. Might be more!'

Marcus took the man by the throat, pinching his windpipe hard to get his attention and putting his face in close.

'*Steady!* There aren't any more of them or they'd be all over us by now. Dubnus, get these men ready to probe forward!'

He looked at the wounded soldier, seeing a great dark stain blacken the man's right legging above the knee, a bloody spear lying near him. The man lay back against the cold earth, his eyes closing as if to sleep.

'Bandage carrier!'

A calm voice spoke behind him, assured in its tone.

'I'll treat him. You concentrate on doing your job.'

He turned to find the woman at his arm, her eyes locked on the fallen soldier.

'*You . . . ?*'

'He's going to die, Centurion; the wound has pierced the great artery. Let me comfort his last few moments.'

He turned away in wonder, pushing a pair of soldiers towards her and telling them to watch over her, and get her a cloak, then stalked off to find Dubnus.

'Chosen, are these men ready to scout forward?'

'Yes, sir, I . . .'

'Good, then go and organise the searching of the farm and get the rest of the century ready to move out. We'll be back inside ten minutes.'

Dubnus stared at him hard in the gloom, then turned away to his task. Marcus looked his men over. Most of three tent parties, twenty-five men, all looking jumpy enough to run if a small boy with a wooden sword came out of the darkness.

'Right, we're going forward to look for signs of where those barbarians came from. We're going to move in a line, and I want you to look for anything that might give us a clue as to what a party of warriors was doing hanging around a latrine like this.'

That got a laugh at least.

'Form a line, two-foot spacing, and follow me. Oh, and by the way . . .'

They stared at him, a mixture of curiosity and dread distorting their faces.

'. . . you won that one, yes? Be proud of yourselves, you're all *warriors* now.'

He ignored the fact that half of them had probably stood watching in amazement when the fighting started. That was for those that had actually fought to take advantage of later. What he needed now was for them to take courage and, for the most part, they did, some of them actually standing taller under the praise.

He led them forward, using his drawn sword to feel ahead

into the darkness, a tinge of purple in the east betraying the approach of sunrise, only an hour away. Not a good time to delay, in the face of an enemy of unknown strength and disposition. Fifty paces brought them to a fence, which Marcus vaulted with a bravado he was far from feeling, grateful to hear the grunts and thuds of his men crossing the obstruction even as he hissed at them for silence. Ten paces past the barrier he heard a tiny sound, a scraping rustle against the ground that made him duck into his shield and advance the sword, wrist cocked arena-style, ready to strike. A heavy breath puffed against his cheek, making him jump backwards in shock, a muted bellow of greeting bringing his heart into his throat.

The soldiers started to laugh, one of them walking forward to get a better look.

'Cattle, sir. *Lots* of them!'

Marcus sheathed his sword in disgust, taking a closer look. The animals jostled around them, hoping for food. The ox that had startled him crowded in closest, nudging at his hands with its massive snout, like an overgrown mastiff, and his heart lightened as he realised that the biggest threat was being trampled if the animal thought there might be fodder somewhere behind him. Beasts like these became used to being pampered, hand fed with the best food that could be found for them, anything to make them fatter and glossier for the day when the army's purchasing officer came to call. Children tended to get the job of looking after them, and, as children do, ended up domesticating them into pets. He sighed at the thought, and how his men, many of them the children of the local farms on both sides of the Wall, might react to what he already knew was his only course of action.

'Very well, farm boy, they seem to like you well enough. Take a rough count and let me know how many there are.

You, get me some light. You, get the chosen and bring him here, *quickly*!'

Dubnus arrived just as the count was completed, roughly fifty fully grown animals standing silently in the dark field. Dubnus stroked his beard.

'I left two tent parties guarding the farm. Those enemy troops must have been guarding *these*, heard our noise and ran into our men. There's flour in the farm, enough for thousands of loaves, and big hearths built into the walls, firewood too, and pine pitch and staves for making torches, lots of jars. Fifty oxen are enough to feed ten thousand men. This is a supply dump, waiting for a warband the size of a legion . . .'

He stared sadly at the cattle, their breath steaming in the torchlight. Marcus nodded agreement. But where was the enemy – within marching distance and hungry for supplies before they went at the Wall, or was this just a contingency, an option prepared for an eventuality that might not come to pass? They looked at each other, sharing a moment of understanding.

'How many jars of pitch?'

'Enough.'

'Very well, let's get it over with.'

The chosen nodded, then shook his head ruefully.

'War makes for unhappy tasks . . .'

He swung to face the waiting troops

'Odd-numbered tent parties, fetch firewood from the barn. Three loads each, bring them here to me. Even numbers, to me.'

The slaughter was grimly efficient, farm-raised soldiers reluctantly leading the oxen out of the enclosure one at a time, to be greeted by a party of the stronger men, who gently penned each beast in their ranks, using gentle hands and words to soothe the animals. Dubnus and two of the older soldiers, one of them a butcher's apprentice in his youth, all of them bloody spectres after the first few animals, calmed each animal further with soft words, then dispatched each one with a swift twisting thrust of their long knives beneath the massive jaws. The soldiers dragged each fresh corpse away with ropes taken from the farm, building a pyre of their bodies with the firewood piled around them. Soon they too were liberally streaked with the animals' blood, as it worked deep into scalps and fingernails.

The man who had first gone forward into the herd, gently touching and caressing the oxen as he counted them, turned away and wept at the spectacle. To Marcus's astonishment, not only did his colleagues keep a respectful distance until his eyes were dry again, but Dubnus wrapped a bloody arm around his bony shoulders and spoke a few private words of comfort. After a while, tired of the smell of the animals' blood, Marcus went back down to the farm buildings while the cull was completed, finding the Roman woman sitting quietly, the dead soldier's head cradled in her lap while the men set to watch over her squatted on either side. She looked up at Marcus, her dirty face streaked with dried tears.

'He regained consciousness for a few moments. He called on Brigantia to take his spirit . . .'

She sniffed quietly.

'Thank you for staying with him.'

She stood, gently placing the dead man's head on his shield.

'Centurion . . . ?'

'Valerius Aquila.'

The response was automatic, the word hanging in the air between them as her eyebrows rose with interest, visible in dawn's first light.

'A famous name in my childhood. Your family are a powerful force in Rome.'

'No more, lady, it seems. You're a native Roman?'

'Until I was thirteen, and my father was posted to thc Wall. So how does the son of a famous family come to be an auxiliary officer, rather than choosing to serve with the legions . . .'

Her voice came to a stop as his response sank in. Marcus bent closer, whispering in her ear.

'I'd be grateful if we spoke no more of my *former* status until we have the privacy for a frank conversation.'

'I see. But I . . .'

A soldier ran up to them, his armour crusted with blood, saluting respectfully with more than half an eye on the woman's body.

'Centurion, the chosen says to tell you that the cull's finished. We're ready to burn them.'

Her eyes ignited with fury, scalding Marcus with their sudden flare of anger.

'Not the oxen. *Tell* me it isn't the oxen!'

He marched stony faced back up the hill, the woman running at his shoulder. When she saw the lifeless humps of flesh littering the mist-wreathed ground her anger was kindled anew. She rounded on Marcus with a snarl that made the soldiers closest to her step back involuntarily, their minds jerked back to distant memories of angry mothers.

'You *bastards*! Every one of those cattle represented life or death to a crofting family, and you've slaughtered them without a second thought.'

Dubnus stepped forward, interposing himself between them before Antenoch had a chance to take umbrage.

'These cattle were either taken or purchased from the crofters to feed a *barbarian* warband. Either way, we're denying food to the enemy.'

He turned away, accepting a torch from one of the soldiers sadly staring at the scene.

'Pour on the pitch!'

A dozen men hefted heavy jars, pulling their stoppers and pouring the sticky, viscous pitch, half liquid, half solid, over the dead animals, then repeated the act with fresh jars, until the pungent aroma spread across the field. More men stepped up with further jars, pouring until the fumes made Marcus's eyes sting and water. Dubnus stepped up to the nearest corpse, muttering a swift prayer under his breath as he lowered his torch to the dead animal's sticky fur. The pitch smoked for a long moment before catching fire, the flames slowly spreading across the pile of dead animals. The flames sent a pungent scent of roasting hair to assault their nostrils, the 9th's soldiers standing in reverential silence at the destruction of such great wealth. Smoke from the burning beasts created an artificial fog to replace that burnt away by the heat, making the men cough, and cover their faces with their sweat rags. The century watched the growing blaze for a few moments more, every man taking a drink of beer from jars found in the farmhouse as reward for their efforts with a prim-looking Cyclops posted to ensure that nobody drank more than would be prudent so far into unfriendly country. Once everyone had taken their share, and several had been turned away with bristling indignation by the beer's custodian, Marcus shook himself from his tired reverie.

'Time we weren't here. Century, form ranks for the march!'

Men ran to assume formation, transforming chaos into ordered ranks with a practised ease, half a dozen men holding the halters of ponies taken from the farm's enclosure. Marcus turned to the woman, his smile tight lipped with fatigue and residual anger at her outburst.

'Well, ma'am, would you care to ride or walk?'

She glared at him, then stalked away and mounted one of the ponies.

'Ninth Century, at the quick march . . . march!'

They moved quickly down to the farm. The flour intended for loaves to feed the oncoming warband had been stacked in the farm's main room, and doused with more jars of the aromatic amber pine pitch, ready for burning. Dubnus tossed a torch in through the door with a sad smile, then led them back up the hill on the far side in grim silence. At the crest he halted them temporarily, turning them to look back into the valley as the first rays of the rising sun lit the hilltops around them. The reek from the burning oxen and the newly fired farmhouse was rising in a thick dark column that would be visible for twenty miles. If there were a warband heading for the farm, its leader would shortly be doubling his efforts to reach the scene, and probably throwing whatever he had by way of mounted scouts forward at their best speed to investigate the reason for the fire. Marcus turned to face his men.

'Ninth Century, this is a major victory. There's almost certainly a large enemy warband within a day or two's march of this place, probably marching in the expectation of replenishing their supplies in preparation for an attack on the Wall. Perhaps even on the Hill . . . What they will find, thanks to us, is their meat destroyed, the pitch for their torches burned and their flour gone up in flames with it. Unless they have an alternative source of supply, their leader will be forced to fall back on more friendly territory in search of food.

'Now . . .'

He paused for effect, aware that every eye was locked on him, their sensitivities about the destruction of so many fine oxen forgotten. The responsibility of bringing the century back to its parent unit intact weighed him down for a moment.

'. . . now we have to think of ourselves. There might well be scouts heading for the farm even as we speak, quite possibly in numbers that would overwhelm us on open ground. My intention is that we should make a forced march for the Wall, and get it between us and any potential threat.'

He grinned at them wolfishly.

'Now's the time that we get some return on all that training. We'll eat breakfast once we're back on the civilised side of the Wall. We move in two minutes, so make fast and get ready to run.'

The soldiers set to work, tightening fastenings and making sure that their boots were secure. Once the century was on the move, any man who dropped an item, or whose footwear loosened, would be forced to drop out, then run twice as hard to catch up again. He pulled Dubnus to one side, speaking quietly in his ear.

'We need to know what happens here in the next couple of hours. Choose a good distance runner, share his kit out and have him find a sheltered spot to watch the fire. He waits until mid-morning, then pulls out and follows us back to the Wall.'

The chosen nodded silently, walking away into the century's activity. The morning air was a cool relief as the 9th jogged towards the Wall; it was too early for the sun to be uncomfortable. Looking back, even ten miles from the farm, Marcus was amazed at the size of the pillar of smoke that rose into the heavens, shearing suddenly to the west where it met a high air current thousands of feet above the ground. He smiled wryly at the probable effect of the sign on his own side of the Wall, and what it might be mistaken for. At least he could expect to meet friendly faces once the 9th had crossed the border. Scout units would in all likelihood be racing for the spot from both east and west.

They reached their original crossing point at mid-morning, and set up a temporary camp on the southern side of the Wall. Marcus gave the command for field rations to be opened, and luxuriated in dried meat and the last of the previous day's bread issue, with a little pickle from a jar that Antenoch had slipped into his pack. Climbing the rampart to survey the ground to their north, he saw that the pillar of smoke was lightening, the fire presumably having consumed the farm buildings. Its top stretched, a dirty stain in the clear blue sky, for a dozen miles or so to the west, slowly dispersing in the gentle winds. The ground in front of the Wall climbed gently for a few hundred years before falling away towards a distant line of trees. From the ground on that slope, he mused, it would be impossible to see the Wall.

He made his way back to the ground, and walked over to where the woman was taking a solitary breakfast, still guarded by the same soldiers who had shared her vigil over the dying man at dawn. Dismissing the men, Marcus squatted on to his haunches when she showed no sign of standing to meet him. Her face, seen for the first time in the daylight, bore the marks of a heavy beating within the past week, bruises past their first lividity still evident as shadows on her cheekbones and jawline.

'Ma'am, we've had no formal introduction . . .'

She looked up at him with a quizzical gaze, then offered her hand. He noticed the wedding ring.

'Your husband must be worried . . .'

'I doubt that very much. He's the reason I'm here.'

He caught the tone in her voice, and skirted away from the subject.

'Marcus Valerius Aquila at your service . . . although that isn't a name I've spoken to anybody else these last three months.'

She smiled for the first time, perhaps at his formality.

'When I left Rome the Valerius Aquila brothers were among the most respected senators in the city. My father spoke of them frequently. What relation are you to them?'

His eyes must have clouded, since she reached out a hand to touch his arm with an unnerving concern.

'I'm sorry . . .'

He smiled at her, feeling another layer of his mental scar tissue fall away.

'That's all right . . . It's just that you're the first Roman to ask me that question. I always wondered what I'd do when the time came – lie, and protect myself, or tell the truth and honour the dead.'

He took a deep breath, grateful that she waited patiently for him to gather himself.

'My father was Senator Appius Valerius Aquila. He fell victim to a palace intrigue led by the praetorian prefect, and, from what I've been told, my entire family was murdered to prevent any danger of attempts at vengeance. I was a praetorian centurion . . .'

Her eyes widened momentarily as the irony dawned on her, then softened with sympathy.

'. . . my father managed to bribe a tribune to send me away on a false imperial errand to this country. He told me that I was carrying a message for the legatus in Yew Grove, but it was really a last message from my father . . .'

'I'm sorry.'

'Thank you. I escaped two attempts to finish the job by killing me, thanks to the efforts of two men I count my as closest friends, and now I fight under the name Marcus Tribulus Corvus. Only five other men know of this deception and so now, lady, you hold the power of life and death over me. A simple denunciation will be enough to have me imprisoned and executed within days. Won't you return the compliment by telling me your name?'

She smiled briefly, her face lighting up with the expression.

'With honour, Centurion. I am Felicia Clodia Drusilla, daughter of Octavius Clodius Drusus and wife of Quintus

Dexter Bassus, the prefect commanding the Second Tungrian Cohort at Vindolanda. A name with which I would far rather not have fouled my mouth!'

She glowered at the ground for a moment.

'Forgive me, Centurion. An unhappy marriage is neither your business nor your concern.'

'Except, perhaps, when it results in the abduction and . . . mistreatment of a Roman citizen?'

She laughed again, a strange reaction in someone who had endured the torments attributed to her captivity by their first informant.

'I wasn't *mistreated* in any particular way, and these bruises predate my time in captivity. I probably would have been raped senseless if the warband had arrived before your rescue, but those people were more embarrassed than excited by my presence. I ran away from my husband's fort when his cruelty and violence towards me became too much to bear. I persuaded my serving maid to disguise me as one of her own once we were out of sight of the fort. We slipped through one of the mile fort gates a week ago, and were caught by the master of that farm a day later, heading for my maid's home village. He locked me up, probably wanted to force himself on me, but his wife was too fiercely opposed, said it would bring the legions down on them. I think she took pity on the state of my face.'

'She might well have been jealous too.'

She smiled again, ruefully this time.

'Thank you for your gallantry. They still hadn't decided what to do with me when you arrived. What made you come?'

'We captured the husband spying on our fort at the Hill. One of his men told us that he'd already . . .'

He paused, embarrassed at the word's implication. Touched by his embarrassment, she put her hand on his arm.

'I'd guess he boasted in public to maintain his reputation. I . . .'

A shout from the Wall's top grabbed Marcus's attention. Dubnus beat him to the ladder, the pair of them bundling breathlessly on to the flat surface atop the mile fort's structure. In the middle distance, half a mile or so from their gate, a single man was running across the wind-blown grass.

'That's our scout!'

Dubnus nodded grimly.

'Yes, and he's running too fast for my liking . . .'

He turned back to look down at the resting soldiers.

'Ninth Century, stand to! Fighting order.'

Even as he spoke, a dozen horsemen broke from the cover of the trees to the north, another mile or so behind the running figure.

Dubnus hurled himself down the ladder, while Marcus scanned the distant trees for any more movement. He turned to look down at the century, each man holding his shield and javelins at the parade rest, their faces filthy from the night's impromptu camouflage of dirt, their armour and bodies covered with dried blood. Get them moving first, his instincts told him, and then explain the dangers.

'First tent party, open the gate!'

Marcus slid down the ladder, drawing his sword, which flashed in the sunlight.

'Follow me!'

He ran through the open gate, turning to watch his men charge through the opening four abreast. Jogging backwards and watching their faces, he saw fear and determination written in equal proportions. He gestured with the sword, catching their attention with its flashing arc.

'Ninth Century, we have a comrade in danger. There may be more cavalry lurking in ambush, waiting until we're clear of the Wall. If there are, we might all die seeking to rescue one man, but think how *he* feels seeing us coming out to him. We're going out to him, we're going to bring him back with us, or they'll have to cut every one of us down to take any one of us.'

More than a few faces stared at him in disbelief, though their legs kept them moving away from the Wall's shelter. He sensed the situation slipping away from him, and felt the first touch of panic grip his mind. Suddenly he had no words to reassure or embolden them. He turned his back on them, mutely waving the sword forward in another flashing arc that pointed to the enemy cavalry galloping across the grass. From the century's rear another voice sounded, deep and harsh, booming across the open space.

'Ninth Century . . . at the run . . . *Run!*'

Where the appeal to reason had faltered, the whiplash of command took the soldiers and threw them forward into a headlong run without any conscious thought process. The century put its collective head back and ran, the ranks opening out slightly as men opened their legs for the task. Marcus looked gratefully back at Dubnus, but the big chosen simply waved him forward to do his job, and in that second he understood and embraced what he had to do if they were to succeed, the adrenalin kick giving his words an unaccustomed savagery.

'Run, you bastards, no fucking horse boy beats me to one of my own!'

Grabbing a deep breath, he ran to catch the front rank, then matched strides with them and started to accelerate, pulling them out across the murderously empty ground in a race with the barbarian cavalry. They crested the gentle ridge and ran down the slope on its far side to reach the exhausted scout with seconds to spare, bundling him into the hollow square that Marcus had shouted for as he fell into their arms. The small cavalry band, shaggy-haired men on hardy ponies with long spears and round wooden shields, simply parted to either side of the square and rode around them, clearly not willing to tackle so many infantrymen readied in defensive formation. The 9th jeered and waved their spears, shouting abuse at the circling horsemen, venting their relief at the stand-off. As he stood in their midst watching the native cavalry circle impotently, Marcus felt a pull at his shoulder.

'Oh, Brigantia! Gods help us . . .'

Marcus looked at the point to which Antenoch pointed, his face suddenly pale with the sickening realisation that there was in reality no need for the relatively few horsemen riding round their square to take them on. A hundred and more mounted barbarians were breaking from the trees in a dark wave.

9

Marcus stared across the half-mile that separated the 9th from the forest's dark bulk, watching the enemy irregular cavalry trot briskly from their hiding places under the trees' canopy. Forming a rough line, the horsemen accelerated to a canter, starting up the gentle slope towards the century's fragile square. He looked about him at his men, their attention focused on the oncoming cavalry, their faces fixed in disbelief at the cruel twist in their fortunes. Even Dubnus seemed diminished, leaning on his pole as if suddenly tired, and for a second the hope went out of the young officer. He stared beyond his men, at the smaller group of horsemen that had drawn away to wait a short distance upslope of their position, just short of the slope's crest, close enough for them to see their mocking grins. Then, with an intensity that shocked him as much as the men he commanded, his temper ignited, firing a burning fury into his voice.

'Ninth Century, spear drill!'

A few men turned to look at him, their faces numb with the shock of their ambush by the horsemen, stoking the fire of his fury.

'Ninth Century, spear drill! Prepare to assault the horsemen to our rear!'

Dubnus came to life with a start, slapping the man next to him across the back.

'You heard the fucking officer. Spear drill!'

The century seemed to shiver for a moment, as if a

powerful wind was blowing through the thin ranks, then snapped to attention. Dubnus's voice boomed again, stirring them with a fresh purpose.

'*On the command form line, form a double line facing the front. Ready . . . Form line!*'

The 9th moved quickly, months of drill practice taking over and dropping them into position without conscious thought. Within twenty seconds they were drawn up in line facing the still-distant oncoming horsemen, their spears held ready to throw. Marcus looked behind him, seeing that the smaller group of cavalry was still in place on the slope to their rear, watching curiously as their enemies apparently abandoned the small degree of safety given by their shields, but still not bothering to do any more than sit and watch. As the last men moved into their places, Marcus drew his sword, turned and pointed it up the slope.

'*About face. Charge!*'

The tribesmen's ponies reared in surprise as the line ran towards them, every man bellowing at the top of his voice. The more skilled horsemen among the Britons managed to wrestle their mounts out of place, and ride away up the slope, but the majority were too slow, struggling to control their beasts. As the soldiers' battle cry died away, Marcus shouted the last command necessary to launch his attack.

'*Throw!*'

The line of men threw almost simultaneously, exhaling a collective whoosh of breath as their spears flew from straining arms, a short vicious arc of wood and metal that slammed a rain of razor-sharp steel into the milling horsemen. Men and horses were impaled by the missiles, their screams blending into a cacophony of pain.

'*Swords!*'

The 9th, barely breaking step, charged in over the fallen,

stabbing at men and animals with the carefree ferocity of victory, offering no mercy to those unable to run. A short, frenzied melee ended the fight, leaving half a dozen soldiers with assorted flesh wounds while almost a dozen of the dead and dying tribesmen and their mounts were scattered across the tiny battlefield.

Marcus turned back to the larger body of horse, their pace accelerating at the sight of their fellows' slaughter, and now barely four hundred paces distant.

'Form square.'

His men nodded grimly at the quiet command, retrieving their spears and moving swiftly into their allotted places, ready to receive the enemy charge and die. As the square formed, Marcus looked about him again, noticing with surprise the few survivors of his men's vicious attack, having galloped away over the slope's crest, now flying past the century in the direction of their fellow horsemen at a breakneck pace. As they passed the oncoming mass of horsemen, a couple turned back and pointed back up the slope, shouting at their fellows.

The tribal cavalry faltered, seemingly losing purpose for a second, and in the moment of their hesitation a sound came to Marcus's ears that puzzled him. It was a distant rumble, as if thunder was grumbling somewhere beyond the clear horizon, but apparent as much through his boot soles as his ears. The rumble swelled in volume, making the soldiers' heads turn as they realised that it was coming from behind them, from the direction of the Wall.

With a sudden explosion of movement and noise, a wall of horsemen came over the crest and charged down the slope, parting to either side of the 9th's tiny square. Armoured cavalrymen bent over their horses' necks and thrust long spears towards the tribesmen, who had already turned to ride for their lives, fighting horses rooted with fear by the noise of the oncoming wave of heavy cavalry. A decurion rose in his saddle, lifting his spear and shouting encouragement to his men as they passed the 9th, their shouted response lifting the hairs on Marcus's neck with its bloodlust.

'*Petriana! Petrianaaa!*'

The cavalry swept past the 9th's square and hammered into the rearmost of the enemy riders while the century stood in amazement, watching the tidal wave of horsemen wash across the open space between the crest and the forest. A scattered detritus of dead and wounded barbarian riders and horses studded the ground over which they passed. The mass of native horsemen became thinner by the second, their blown horses easy prey for the stronger and fresher Roman mounts. Spears were thrust into the backs and necks of the fleeing Britons, making their backs arch at the moment of impact.

A group of horsemen cantered up to the tiny defensive square, pennants below their spear heads fluttering prettily in the strong breeze blowing across the open ground. A long dragon standard, twisting and flapping in wind-blown serpentine twists, rode proudly above the formation, which opened to allow a magnificent grey stallion to approach the 9th. Like those of its fellows', the beast's eyes and long face were protected by a decorated armoured plate that curved around the snout, vision enabled by a delicate pattern of holes drilled into the half-globe bulges over each eye. Its rider searched the ranks, age-wrinkled eyes peering from beneath the peak of a heavily decorated helmet, while the riders of his bodyguard rode out to either side, watching their surroundings with professional wariness. Marcus stepped out from the 9th's ranks, snapping a salute at the prefect while he admired the man's heavily muscled bronze cuirass, secured by the customary linen band. The senior officer jumped down from his horse, passing the reins to an attending trooper before returning the salute. He stared at Marcus with unveiled curiosity, turning to survey the slaughter without any change of expression, speaking without returning his eyes to the young officer, his voice a patrician rasp.

'Y'were lucky that we happened along, young centurion, or your head would be decorating some hairy fellow's spear point by now. I'm Licinius, prefect commanding the Petriana cavalry wing. Your unit?'

Marcus stiffened to attention and saluted.

'Ninth Century, First Tungrian Cohort, Prefect!'

The other man turned back to look at him again, one eyebrow slightly raised. Marcus met his stare directly, noting the experience lines that ran down from either side of his nose and his furrowed forehead. The older man was, he calculated, soldier through and through, an experienced prefect with two or three previous postings behind him before being favoured with such a prestigious cavalry command.

'Tungrian, eh? Y'don't *sound* Tungrian, y'sound Roman, youngster. Look it too. So, how does the Ninth Century of the First Tungrians come to be all on its own on the wrong side of the Wall, getting ready to die on the spears of several times its strength of enemy horse, eh?'

Marcus told him the story of the last two days in quick, economical sentences that reduced their achievements to their bare bones, while the prefect watched dispassionately as his men dismounted to finish off the wounded and take souvenirs. He reached the slaughter of the oxen before the other man interrupted.

'Wait a moment . . . *Decurion!*'

An officer detached himself from the waiting troop of horsemen, trotting across to his commander and saluting precisely.

'Sir?'

'Dispatch a message rider to Cauldron Pool, message to read . . .'

The troop commander fished out his writing tablet, the stylus poised over its wax.

'From Petriana Wing. Rescued First Tungrian Ninth under barbarian horse attack to north of Wall at mile fort twenty-seven. Debriefed centurion. Fifty-plus oxen found ten miles to north-east of the Hill. Cattle slaughtered and burned to deny enemy supply. Number of oxen and enemy horse suggest enemy warband ten to fifteen thousand strong in vicinity, now likely to be falling back for alternative supply. Attack on Wall in this sector temporarily unlikely. Forward to commander Sixth Legion immediately. Ends. Give the rider a twenty-man escort. Go!'

The officer turned away to his task.

'Carry on, Centurion.'

Marcus completed the story, explaining their return to the barbarian side of the Wall in defence of their comrade. The prefect pulled his helmet off and tossed it to a trooper, running a hand through his thick head of hair. Streaks of grey ran through the black. After a moment of thought he turned back to Marcus and his waiting soldiers, nodding with pursed lips.

'Well, Centurion, either Fortuna herself smiles down on you, or you're an exceptionally competent officer. Either way, you have a century to be proud of. Not many infantrymen of *my* experience would have taken the risk your men did in seeking to safeguard your friend. I salute you all!'

And, to Marcus's amazement, he did just that, clapping him on the shoulder in congratulation.

'I would regard it as a privilege to escort you and your men to Cauldron Pool, and to take a cup of wine with you once you've had time to get your unit settled. Trumpeter, sound the recall, those layabouts have had long enough to take every blasted head on the battlefield. Now, young man, I'm intrigued by your accent. Tell me more about yourself.'

Marcus, caught in the full glare of the man's piercing intellect, and unprepared for another explanation as to his origins, thought frantically. Antenoch stepped forward neatly, saluting with a gusto that raised eyebrows throughout the 9th.

'Prefect, sir, excuse me, but our centurion has omitted to inform you that there is a young Roman lady waiting for us at the Wall gate. Your eminence might want to detail an escort to her, to ensure her personal safety in these rough circumstances?'

The prefect nodded sagely, a faint smile creasing his lips.

'Quite so, soldier, and right of you to point out the fact. Let us get back on the road to the east, Centurion, and perhaps you and I can talk further in the more relaxed atmosphere of Cauldron Pool.'

He remounted, pulled his helmet back on and rode away, spurring the magnificent grey into a canter back towards the Wall, his bodyguard wheeling their horses to follow.

By late afternoon Legatus Sollemnis was forced to admit to himself that he felt more relaxed with the circumstances of his command than at any time in the past week. He relaxed in his chair while the 6th Legion's staff officers briefed him on the current situation and felt, for the first time in several days, as if a measure of control over the whole awful mess had come his way. The sounds of tree-felling came distantly into the command tent, as his engineers laboured to perfect the field defences that would protect their flanks and rear, and reduce any frontal attack to a vulnerable crawl. With these defences, and the legion artillery commanding murderous firing arcs, his six thousand men could hold such a well-founded position at the forest's edge against thee times their number.

At length Titus Tigidius Perennis took centre stage as the legion's senior tribune, moving to the map and pointing to their position astride the road to Yew Grove ten miles south of the Wall, then to the auxiliary battle group's location at Cauldron Pool.

'So, Legatus, in summary, we face a loose enemy formation of about fifteen thousand men. Our current dispositions limit the enemy warband from doing very much other than burning a few garrison forts. If Calgus attacks south to attempt a breakthrough towards Yew Grove, we can provide the defensive anvil while Prefect Licinius and his auxiliary cohorts, plus the Petriana and Augustan cavalry wings, swing the hammer into their rear. On the other hand, if he tries a push to the west, the auxiliaries can hold him if they choose the right ground, and we can break from our defensive position and do the hammering. Either way, if he moves to attack either force we'll have him straddled like a Robbers counter, ripe for a battle of annihilation. Our good fortune in the discovery and destruction of the supplies for their presumed western force, and the Petriana's annihilation of their cavalry, has made Prefect Licinius's rear safe for the time being. The only question now is how we should capitalise on this development.'

Sollemnis nodded, staring intently at the map in front of him.

'Yes, we seem to have Calgus in a trap of his failed strategy. Without his western force he's unable to remove Licinius's threat to his flank, and effectively unable to move either west or south without dire risk. And to attack to the east would be both largely pointless and risk hemming himself in between Wall and sea. I think we have him, gentlemen, or at least we've balanced the situation enough to have stopped his rampage for the time being. My opinion is that we keep sufficient measure of the initiative just by digging in where we are, and so forcing Calgus to decide what to do next. If he attacks he puts himself at risk of being assaulted from two sides; if he waits he plays into our hands by bringing the Second and Twentieth Legions into play. Any other opinions?'

His First Spear spoke up.

'I agree, Legatus. We must stay defensive until the other legions arrive. Fighting from behind our temporary defences, with our artillery positioned to support the line, we can hold his barbarians off for long enough to let the auxiliaries strike to flank and rear. Moving forward would be suicide with only our six thousand spears.'

Perennis nodded his support.

'I agree with the First Spear, with one small addition. When Calgus moves back to the north, as he is bound to do given his position, we should follow up smartly and get north of the Wall. I have a perfect location for a forward camp in mind once we're free to advance.'

Sollemnis stood with the decision clear.

'Very well, we hold what we have for now, and push the decision on to Calgus. Let's see what he does with several barbarian tribes baying for our heads but no safe way to give them what they crave.'

The road to the fort at Cauldron Pool was uneventful enough, a gentle stroll by the standard of their regular exertions, but the spectacle of the cavalrymen riding easily to either side, heads dangling from saddle horns and spears, eventually started to rankle. Morban rattled his standard at the 9th Century, leading them off in a spirited rendition of a favourite marching song.

'Oh, the, cavalry don't use latrines.
They piss in their leather britches,
They drag their arse in the tickly grass,
Those dirty sons of bitches!'

Marcus gave the decurion riding alongside him a wry smile as the song progressed into a description of the sexual habits of the cavalry, guessing that he'd probably heard it a few times before.

After a while, as clouds rolled over the landscape and threatened rain, they concentrated on covering ground, eager to rejoin the cohort at Cauldron Pool and get the chance to eat hot food. When darkness fell, finding them still a good five miles from their destination, the horsemen lit torches and illuminated their way, triumphantly escorting them to the walls of the fort, where the First Spear was waiting for them in front of twenty men with torches. He stepped forward, gesturing them to follow him into the temporary defences of a six-foot-high turf wall, within which burned the watch fires of dozens of centuries. The 9th marched into the Tungrian section of the camp with their heads held high, to be greeted by a respectful silence from their peers as they paraded.

Marcus stepped out in front of the century, turned on the spot and saluted the waiting chief centurion, who returned the salute with a grim face.

'First Spear, Ninth Century reporting back from detached duty.'

Sextus Frontinius stared back at him, still deadpan, before speaking.

'Ninth Century, if the reports we have received of your activities are correct, you have reflected much pride on the cohort. For now you will be tired, and in need of a wash, food and rest. Your colleagues will show you where your tents have been erected, and will have washing water and hot food ready for you. Morning parade is cancelled for the Ninth Century, you will parade at midday before lunch. Without your current coating of blood and soil, that is. Dismissed.'

He turned to Marcus, putting a hand on his arm.

'Not you, Centurion. *You* come with me.'

He took Marcus through the darkened camp, threading between the leather tents until they reached the headquarters tent, three times the size of those designed to house a ten-man tent party. Inside, dimly lit by the guttering flames of oil lamps, a large wooden table dominated the space, scrolls neatly stacked across its width indicating that it would be a hive of administrative activity during daylight hours. In one corner a hanging screen rendered the prefect's quarters private, a pair of fully armed soldiers from the 5th Century providing immediate protection for their commanding officer. Frontinius coughed discreetly, the slight noise summoning his superior from behind the screen.

Equitius nodded to them both, indicating the seats that clustered around a low table in another corner of the tent.

'Centurion, news of your exploits travels before you. If I am to believe the dispatch relayed to me by the local prefect, your century, in the course of a simple search mission, found and destroyed not only a barbarian scouting party, but fifty head of cattle that had apparently been gathered to feed an enemy warband. Is this correct?'

Marcus nodded, dropping wearily into the proffered chair.

'Yes, sir.'

Frontinius remained silent while the prefect pulled at his beard in a distracted manner.

'I was afraid of that. You present us, young man, with something of a quandary. On one hand, you are still, had you forgotten, a wanted man, with a hefty price on your head. On the other, you are the hero of the hour, responsible for turning back an enemy warband, which might well have been ten or fifteen thousand strong, for the loss of two men. Prefect Licinius is singing your praises to anybody that will listen, and has already sent me a formal request for an interview with you. Probably wants to offer you a position with the Petriana, something better fitted to the well-bred young man you so obviously are . . . And *there's* the main problem. Once the euphoria wears off it'll take him about five minutes to start asking all sorts of difficult questions, and it doesn't take a top-class mind to see where *that'll* end up. If, however, I refuse him permission to speak to you, his questions will be addressed to a wider, and infinitely more dangerous, audience. I am still undecided as to my best course of action . . .'

Marcus nodded.

'Prefect, I've given it much thought in the last few hours. Perhaps I have a solution, for tomorrow at least.'

He spoke for a moment, gauging the other man's reaction. Equitius mulled over his idea briefly, nodding his assent.

'From first light, mind you. Let's not risk Prefect Licinius being an early riser. Very well, dismissed.'

Marcus and Frontinius stood to leave. Equitius turned away and then back again as a thought occurred to him.

'Oh, and Centurion . . .'

'Prefect?'

'Excellent work. Sleep well.'

Outside the tent, Frontinius put a hand on Marcus's shoulder to detain him. His eyes glinted in the torchlight, his face expressionless in the heavy shadows.

'You took your whole century back over the Wall to save the life of a single soldier?'

Marcus nodded soberly.

'Yes. In retrospect it seems a little far fetched, but yes, First Spear, I did.'

He waited for the storm. To his amazement, the older man looked at him strangely for a moment, nodding slowly.

'In the best traditions of the Tungrians, whether you knew it or not. Very well done, Centurion, very well done indeed.'

Marcus frowned.

'But what if I'd lost the whole century trying to save one man? I've thought of little else since it happened.'

Frontinius looked at him in the torchlight, shaking his head.

'There are two types of successful officer, those that do the right thing, and those that are born with Cocidius's favour. The latter can take audacious risks and get far better odds than just following the field manual. You're lucky, Centurion. Keep it that way.'

Antenoch woke Marcus before dawn, shaking insistently at his shoulder until the centurion stirred, swinging his feet from the camp bed and on to the floor.

'Dawn, centurion, and time you were dressed for the day. Here, drink this.

A beaker of warm honey, diluted by a substantial quantity of wine, opened Marcus's eyes well enough. The tent's interior, lit by a single lamp, was dark and oppressive, while a steady drumming on the tent's oiled leather roof puzzled his senses for a moment.

'Pissing down. A great day for serving out your penalty. The night watch took great delight in pointing out that it'll probably rain until midday at this rate when they woke me up. Fucking 2nd century.'

Marcus groaned softly, struggling to his feet. A swift wash in the bowl of water Antenoch had brought in with him enlivened his senses, while the rest of the honey drink warmed his stomach sufficiently to make the task of getting into uniform a welcome distraction from dwelling on the conditions outside. Antenoch helped him into his cloak, and then went to look out of the tent flap while Marcus took a final deep breath, resigned to being soaked to the skin within ten minutes of stepping out into the downpour.

'Your escort's here.'

Puzzled, he went to look through the flap. Outside, grinning happily through the rainswept grey morning, were four of the 9th's soldiers wrapped in their own cloaks, each man holding a wooden pole attached to some kind of hastily improvised wooden framework, across which was strung what looked suspiciously like the remains of a ten-man tent. The scout they had rescued the previous day was closest to the tent door, solemnly gesturing him under the shelter of their portable roof. Antenoch shook his head in amused wonder.

'Stupid bastards, spent half the night putting the bloody thing together. I told them that standing about in the rain all day might make you think twice about taking on five times our number of enemy horse next time the chance presents itself, but *they* insisted . . .'

Marcus walked out under the sheltering leather, shaking his head with speechless wonder. Cyclops, the one-eyed miscreant, freed one hand to salute.

'Where to, sir?'

Stirring himself, Marcus found his voice.

'To the headquarters tent . . . gentlemen, I really don't . . .'

Another of the soldiers, a gaunt-faced man with a heavy facial scar down one cheek, spoke up gruffly, holding up his right hand to contain Marcus's protest.

'The entire century wanted this, sir, so don't be worrying about us. There'll be another four men along in a while so's we can go and have a warm. Now, lads, on the command march, to the head shed, *march*!'

They paraded through the camp's empty streets, drawing

amazed stares from the guards mounted at each century's section of the camp, men huddled together against the rain peering incredulously in the growing light, until they reached the headquarters tent. Frontinius peered through the tent door, stepping out into the rain with his eyes wide. The four soldiers stared resolutely at the lightening sky, while Marcus squirmed uneasily at the prospect of his superior's opinion. Having walked around the contraption once in complete silence, his immaculate boots beading with rain drops, the First Spear turned to address a nervous Marcus.

'I have to say that for the first time in twenty–two years of service I am quite genuinely amazed. You, Scarface, what's the meaning of this?'

'The Ninth Century cares for its own, sir. We won't be letting *our* young gentleman catch his death of cold . . .'

And he shut up, his face red with the pressure of having answered the cohort's senior soldier back.

'I see . . .'

Centurion and men waited with bated breath for the law to be stated.

'Nothing in the manual specifically states that an officer on administrative punishment can't be sheltered from heavy rain by four soldiers with a tent lashed to a wooden frame. Even if at least one of the soldiers concerned is famous throughout his cohort for holding the opinion that most officers aren't fit to scrape out the latrines after him . . .'

'Scarface' went an even deeper shade of red.

'. . . so, is there room for another under there?'

Marcus gestured to the space next to him. Ignoring the indignant eyes of the roof-bearers, Frontinius stepped in from the rain, taking his helmet off and shaking the drops from its bedraggled crest. He regarded Marcus with a sideways glance, sweeping a hand across his pale scalp to catch the odd raindrops gleaming there.

'And now, Centurion Two Knives, since you have me as a captive audience, you may tell me all about your exploits of yesterday.'

When Prefect Licinius appeared after breakfast, he too came up short at the sight of the rain cover. What put the honey in that particular cake, Morban later confided to Dubnus, was the fact that custody of the four poles was in the process of being transferred from one four-man group to another. The cavalryman had watched, speechless, while the eight men transferred the cover from one group to another with the precision of a legion parading its eagle. When the handover was finished, and the outgoing men had completed the effect by marching smartly around the corner of the headquarters tent before collapsing in stifled laughter, the prefect approached, taking in the silent centurion and his First Spear. The latter was happily chatting away about the fighting habits of their enemy, and affecting not to have noticed the senior officer.

'. . . whereas the warband, you see, is usually a one-shot weapon. The tribal leader points them in the right direction, whips them up into a frenzy, and then lets them run wild. Which can be a problem if they need to be turned around for any reason, since you can't just . . .'

He snapped to attention, shouting to Marcus and the roof-bearers to follow his example. Licinius, having thus been formally recognised, strolled forward, nodding to Frontinius and staring with visible envy at the mobile roof while rain beat at his oiled leather cape.

'At ease, First Spear.'

Frontinius relaxed, throwing the tribune an impeccable salute.

'Prefect Licinius, sir, welcome to the *First* Tungrian camp.'

The prefect returned the salute with casual ease, stepping close enough to gain some shelter from the incessant rain.

'First Spear Frontinius. Might one ask the purpose of this
. . . ?'

He waved an arm vaguely at the scene, raising an eyebrow
at the sober-faced Frontinius.

'Prefect this centurion is under administrative punishment,
one day's parade in full uniform and withdrawal of speech.
For exceeding the remit of written orders specified by Prefect
Equitius in that he took his century over the Wall to rescue
one of his men and ended up having to be rescued by you.'

'And the prefect himself?'

'Out with four centuries, sir, patrolling down towards the
North Road.'

'And *this*?'

He gestured again at the rain cover, its roof sagging slightly
with the weight of water soaked into the oiled leather.

'Simple, sir. It would appear that this young officer has
instilled sufficient pride in his men that they regard the
punishment of one as a collective duty.'

The other man smiled gently, recognising the deflection
of any comment he might have regarding the shelter's legal
irregularity.

'I see. Very well, First Spear, please inform the centurion
that I'm sorry to have missed the chance to meet him properly.
The Petriana is ordered to conduct a reconnaissance in force
to the west, to discover the exact dispositions of our blue-
nosed friends. Doubtless we'll get another chance, though.
Quite amazing . . .'

He turned and walked away, shaking his head in disbelief.
Frontinius waited until he was out of sight, stepping out
from beneath the rain cover and eyeing the steadily lightening
clouds with a critical gaze.

'It'll have stopped within the hour. Very well, Centurion
Two Knives, I hereby commute your punishment to
confinement to your tent until dusk. Get some sleep; your

century has the night guard. Doubtless the Prince will be keen to introduce you to the art of aggressive night patrolling . . .'

Marcus slept soundly, despite the noise of the camp, until Antenoch shook him awake again at sunset; he wolfed down a plate of cold meat and bread and went in search of his chosen man, closely followed by his clerk. Dubnus was detailing the guard roster for the night, counting the century off into tent parties and giving each one a part of the Tungrians' area of the camp to patrol. When he was finished, one last eight-man group of soldiers remained in front of the headquarters tent, a collection of older men, more than one bearing the scars of previous skirmishes. He spoke quietly into Marcus's ear.

'These are the best men for a night patrol, steadier than some of the others. We'll go over the Wall, up into the trees on the high ground, then wait and listen. This is a good camp, but we've used it many times before, so it ought to be known to the enemy. The tribes will have scouts out, and will try to infiltrate men in to watch the camp, perhaps even snatch a sentry or an officer from his tent. We hear them, we stalk them, and we kill them. Simple. You'll learn some new skills tonight. Morban can stand in as watch officer while we're out in the forest.'

He passed Marcus a thick wooden stave and a length of black cloth.

'Your cloak will hide you in the forest and keep you warm. Wrap the cloth around your head until your helmet's full, it'll keep your head warm and offer some protection if you get hit on the head. The club's a lot better for fighting in the dark than a sword, but the other side will be using clubs of their own.'

Turning to Antenoch, standing to one side with a large and distinctly non-regulation sword strapped across his back, he waved a hand dismissively.

'We won't need you tonight. Stay here, and guard your tent.'

Antenoch turned away impassively and disappeared into the surrounding shadows.

'I still don't trust him. Better if we leave him behind, and avoid the risk of a knife in the back.'

He led the party through the gap in the earth wall and up a shallow slope towards the dark treeline at a slow trot. As they reached the trees the patrol flattened themselves against the cold earth, waiting in silence for Dubnus to decide whether it was safe to move. Marcus stared out into the maze of tree trunks, his night vision slowly improving as his eyes became accustomed to the darkness. Dubnus muttered into his ear.

'Look to one side of what you want to see. Seeing in the darkness is better from the corner of the eye than the centre.'

It was true. He looked into the forest, seeing the tree branches sway gently as a breeze lifted their leaves, and heard the distant hoot of a hunting owl. Below them, huddled into the river bend, the camp squatted in its solid bulk, studded with the pinprick light of torches at each guard position. Behind it loomed Cauldron Pool's fort, its whitewashed walls standing out in the gloom to his now completely night-adjusted eyes. At length Dubnus nodded to the patrol, splaying three fingers forward. Two groups of three men moved silently into the trees, heading to left and right, while Dubnus led Marcus and the remaining soldier forward to their own listening position, a hundred yards inside the forest wall.

They padded slowly and quietly through the tree trunks, fallen twigs crackling minutely under their boots. Marcus copied Dubnus's exaggerated steps and slow, cautious footfall, each foot searching for larger twigs as it sank to meet the ground, avoiding making any loud noises. At length they settled into their listening post for the night, a space between two fallen trees that Dubnus had clearly used before from the ease with which he found the sheltered spot. Marcus and the other soldier huddled into their cloaks at Dubnus's whispered suggestion, leaving him to stare out into the silent darkness.

Down in the camp, with the troops asleep for the night, and night patrols padding morosely around the perimeter fence, Annius slipped quietly through the ranks of tents, through the doglegged gap in the six-foot-tall earth rampart and up to the stone-built fort's walls. A pair of soldiers stepped forward with their spears levelled, letting him past and into the fort once it was established that he was on official business. Since the fort was more or less a duplicate of the Hill, he found his way to the supply building quickly enough, and knocked quietly on the door, slipping quickly inside as soon as it opened.

The storeman closed the door behind him, sliding a pair of massive iron bolts into their sockets, turned and silently beckoned Annius to follow him. At the rear of the storeroom he opened another, smaller door, gesturing the quartermaster through in front of him. A small personal room lay beyond, well lit by oil lamps, the walls insulated against the cold air outside by hanging carpets, while a flask of wine and a tray of small honey cakes decorated a delicately carved wooden table. A man lounged on a couch by the room's far wall, nodding graciously to Annius and indicating the couch's companion on the other side of the small table.

The quartermaster arranged himself on the couch in a dignified silence, waiting for his host to speak first. With this, as with any other negotiation, every tiny advantage was to be sought. The other man waited another moment before stirring himself to lean on an elbow, baring his teeth in a cockeyed smile below calculating eyes.

'So, friend and colleague Annius. When your mob marched in yesterday I wondered how long it would be before you and I were doing business. Are you buying, or selling?'

Annius pursed his lips, forcing his face to stay neutral.

'A little of both, my trusted friend Tacitus.'

'Excellent! Here's to a mutually profitable exchange!'

They drank, both sipping politely at the wine rather than risk its effects on their skills. Tacitus gestured to the cakes, and took one himself in the age-old gesture of trustworthiness. Annius nibbled at another.

'These are good.'

'My own baker, in the vicus. You'll take a dozen, as my gift?'

'I'm grateful.'

And down a bargaining point already. He fished in the folds of his cloak, passing the other man a small wooden box.

'Saffron?'

'The best Persian. I remembered your affection for the spice. Perhaps your baker can use it to good effect.'

And up two. The spice had cost him a small fortune, but put Tacitus in his debt by the rules of the game they routinely played.

'Well, if you have more of this to sell, our bargaining will be a memorable event . . .'

'Unfortunately not the case. That was the last of the traveller's supply.'

'A shame. So tell me, brother, what is it you bring to the table?'

'Little enough – we marched too quickly for detailed preparation. Five jars of Iberian wine, a small quantity of a precious ointment from Judaea . . . and money.'

'Money, indeed? You *must* be keen. And what is it that you seek?'

Damn him for a cool bastard.

'Information, Tacitus. I have a small local difficulty to manage, and remembering how good your sources have been in the past . . .'

Tacitus adjusted his position, rising up on one elbow.

'Ah. Problems with your First Spear? I wondered how long he'd tolerate your ways of making money. I . . .'

'No, it isn't Frontinius. He keeps me on my mettle, makes sure that his men have effective equipment, but he tolerates my provision of the better things in life as a necessary evil. *And* makes sure that my business pays a healthy percentage to the burial club. No, the problem's a step lower down the ladder than Frontinius.'

Tacitus's eyes narrowed with the admission.

'A *centurion*? Tell me more . . .'

Marcus woke again when Dubnus shook his shoulder, nodding silently at the big man's silent instruction to watch the arc to their front. The chosen man rolled into his cloak and was still, leaving Marcus alone in the darkness. He watched the silent forest with slow head movements, remembering the instruction to use the corner of his vision rather than looking directly at the subject. After a few moments purple spots started to dance in his vision, making him close his eyes for a moment before starting the process again. After an hour or so a faint sound caught his attention, a tiny click out in the trees, but sufficient to snap his senses alert. A moment later there was another, louder, and then again, the almost imperceptible but unmistakable sounds of men moving across the forest floor.

He reached out with a foot and nudged Dubnus awake, keeping his attention focused on the scene to his front. The chosen man rose silently, moving his head alongside that of his centurion.

'Breaking twigs.'

He pointed in the appropriate direction to back up his whispered warning, then kept silent. Dubnus listened for a moment and nodded, bending close to Marcus's ear.

'They're here. Perhaps too many for us. We'll sound the alarm and get back into camp. The others will do the same.'

Marcus nodded, shaking the sleeping soldier awake and whispering in his ear to be ready to run. While Dubnus prepared to put the signal horn to his lips, ready to blow the note that would alert the camp, Marcus prepared for the short run back through the surrounding trees. He leant his weight on the stub of a branch, readying himself to vault the fallen tree that formed the rear of their hide. With a rasping cough the stump, rotted through beneath the bark, tore away from the trunk under his weight, the noise echoing out into the forest's silence. For a moment the silence returned, but then, with a sudden chorus of shouts and yells, came the sound of men running across the forest floor towards them.

With a curse Dubnus put the horn to his lips and blew one high note that drowned out all other sound, tossing the horn away and hefting his club, shouting into the darkness.

'Ninth, to me!'

Their chance to run was gone, the enemy, alerted by the snapping wood, charging in at them too quickly for flight to be a realistic option. Marcus readied himself, stepping alongside Dubnus and bracing himself for the enemy's assault with his stave held ready to strike.

A body hurled itself out of the darkness, and was met by a vicious swing of Dubnus's club. Two more followed, both men going down under the defenders' blows, and then a torrent of tribesmen assaulted the trio, splitting them into tiny islands of resistance. Marcus swung his stave into one attacker's belly, releasing it as it caught in the reeling man's clothing, swept his sword out and stepped forward to strike at another, hamstringing the man as he shaped to attack Dubnus from behind. A massive tribesman stepped into the fight, swinging his own club in an expert backhand to deal a fearsome blow to Marcus's head. He fell, vision dimming as consciousness slipped away, vaguely aware of a figure standing over him with a sword held high, screaming incoherently as the sword poised for its strike.

Frontinius briefed Prefect Equitius an hour later, once the excitement of a full cohort stand-to was over and the centuries had gone grumbling back to their interrupted sleep. He'd been on the scene in minutes with the duty century, but only in time to greet the 9th's men as they carried their casualties off the hill.

'It was nothing really, just a few barbarian scouts running into our listening patrols. It was too dark for much serious fighting, and what there was seems to have been scrappy. More like a vicus bar brawl than a real fight. The turning point appears to have been one of our lads going into a blood rage in the middle of the skirmish and slicing up several of the barbarians, after which they seem to have thought better of the whole thing. We've got a man dead and two wounded, one light sword wound and a nasty-looking concussion. That's the good news. The bad news is that the man with the concussion is our very own Roman centurion, his helmet stove in by a barbarian with a strong club arm.'

Equitius groaned.

'So now he's stuck in the fort hospital for any and all to see?'

Frontinius shook his head.

'No, I spent a few minutes with the doctor and had him hidden away in a quiet part of the building, away from curious eyes. I've also told the Ninth to keep the news of his injury to themselves. The Prince can run the century for the next day or two.'

Equitius nodded thoughtfully.

'So this might even work to our advantage, and keep him out of sight until it's time to deploy into the field.'

Frontinius snorted a mirthless laugh.

'Yes. And we get to find out if his skull is thick enough to keep his educated brains in one piece, or whether the blue-noses have just solved our problem for us.'

Light pricked at Marcus's eyes as they struggled to open. He could see only a ball of light, with a dark figure floating behind it. Closing his eyes, and surrendering to the darkness again, and whatever it was that was happening, seemed much the easiest thing to do.

When he woke again the metallic taste in his mouth was gone, and the light that greeted his cautious gaze was that of weak daylight, a pale shaft through a window in one wall of the room in which he lay, still exhausted, in a narrow bed. Underneath heavy blankets he was naked, while his head ached awfully. A familiar voice called out from close by.

'Orderly! Orderly, you dozy bastard! Fetch the doctor! He's awake.'

The owner of the voice came back into the room and, fighting his eyes back into focus, Marcus recognised an exhausted-looking Antenoch.

'Lie still, the doctor's coming.'

He sat down in a chair at Marcus's bedside, running a hand through his disordered hair.

'We thought for a while you might not live, you were out of it for so long. Only the helmet saved you, and you should see the dent in *that*! You won't be . . .'

He stopped in mid-sentence, as another figure entered the room. Marcus gingerly turned his head to see the new arrival, blinking at the sunlight, recognising the doctor with a shock.

'You . . . but you're a . . .'

'A woman? Evidently your concussion hasn't entirely removed your cognitive powers, Centurion Corvus.'

It was the woman from the farm . . . an image of her fury at the sight of slaughtered cattle flashed into his mind. Felicia . . . ? His memory grasped for the name, making his brow knot with the effort.

. . . Clodia Drusilla? Felicia Clodia Drusilla! He raised an arm, the limb seeming heavy.

'Water . . . please?'

Antenoch put a cup to his lips, the liquid ungluing his mouth and throat.

'Thank you. Madam, I am . . .'

'Surprised?'

Her eyebrow arched in a challenge that Marcus knew was completely beyond his faltering capabilities.

'. . . grateful for your care.'

He closed his eyes for a moment, feeling his body sag against the bed with exhaustion. Her voice reached him, as if from a distant place.

'And now, Master Antenoch, it's time for you *both* to get some proper sleep. Go back to your unit and sleep for at least ten hours. Here, I'll make it a formal written command . . . there, "to sleep for ten hours without interruption". Give that tablet to your chosen man. And tell him that the centurion will be ready to receive visitors tomorrow afternoon at the *very earliest* . . .'

Calgus stood astride the Wall with his adviser Aed as the sun set that evening, watching his warriors pouring back to the north through the North Road's smashed gates. They were moving in good order for the most part, one or two supporting comrades clearly the worse for drink, but if individuals had overindulged in captured wine it was of little concern to him. Behind them the fortress of the Rock was still smearing the sky with the grey reek of its smouldering timbers, while torches were being lit by his marching troops to provide illumination for the night movement. All things considered, he mused, he had enough reason to be satisfied as his first attack played to its close. At length his adviser Aed spoke, his opinions delivered with the customary candour that Calgus valued, where most others would tell him simply what he wanted to hear.

'So, my king, their Wall is broken, the garrison troops huddle anxiously around their forts to east and west, and their Sixth Legion seems content simply to prevent our advance on Yew Grove. Some of our people see this as victory enough, while others argue for striking west or south and destroying the Roman forces before they can join. We must explain our next moves soon, before the tribes fall to arguing among themselves. A lack of Roman shields to batter will have our peoples at each others' throats before long.'

Calgus spat on to the Wall's flat surface, his face twisting into a sneer.

'I will gut the first men who take swords to their brothers myself, you can let that be known. As for the Romans, I've told the tribal leaders that our cleverest move is the one we're making now, to pull back from the Wall and let them follow into the uncertain lands to the north if they dare. The right move is to pull back, and invite them onwards on to our ground. Of course, it would have been different if our western warband had not failed to break the Wall to the west, behind the traitor cohorts. If we could have put the soldiers waiting to the west between two forests of spears and with no place left to run, that would have been a blade to their guts I would have twisted without hesitation.'

Aed nodded, his face impassive.

'I understand, my lord. Yet I must tell you that at this moment our only real fear is the warband itself, or more particularly its urgent desire for battle. Real battle. The tribes grumble that their war so far has been one of chasing after fleeing Romans and burning empty forts. Lord Calgus, the northern tribes are clamouring for a proper fight, a fight we currently deny them.'

Calgus nodded at the advice. After the council of the tribes the previous evening he was already aware of the problem. He had called the gathering of tribal leaders knowing that he would at the least have to listen to their arguments for their warriors to run amok down the line of forts that garrisoned the Wall. These were arguments made stronger by the speed with which the defenders had evacuated their forts, rather than fight for their homes. Put simply, the defenders seemed ripe for taking, ready to fall under the tribes' attacks. He'd listened patiently until their arguments dried up in the face of his silent contemplation. When silence had fallen and all men in the gathering he'd called were waiting for him to say something, he'd voiced his opinion.

'What you propose is exactly what the legatus commanding that legion down the road to Yew Grove wants, for us to waste our time and strength destroying empty forts. They will simply retreat in front of us, leaving us to spend our energy on pointless destruction. Or worse, they will attempt to pin us between their two forces. I'm not entirely sure our warriors would stand their ground if that happened.'

One of the tribal leaders had stalked forward to stand in front of him, a dead Roman's head held casually by the hair in one hand, a Roman infantry sword in the other. He turned to the assembled chiefs, holding both in the air above his head.

'I say we *fight*! My people have tasted Roman blood, taken heads, taken *weapons*. To retreat now will bring shame upon us in the eyes of Brigantia – who knows whether she will look with anger upon a retreat in the time of victory, and punish us for avoiding battle.'

The gathering held its collective breath, waiting for Calgus to pounce from his chair, perhaps even draw the sword that hung from his waist and take the other man apart with it for the slur. He was more than capable of such sudden violence, as they all knew from experience. After a long silence, allowing time for the suddenly isolated noble to realise what he had done, Calgus laughed softly. A collective sigh of released breath greeted the sound.

'Balthus bids us storm more of the Wall forts, while the legion to our south hide in their camp, and yes, we could easily fire another half-dozen of their camps, knock the gates out of a dozen gateways, kill a few hundred careless Romans, take more swords and spears . . .'

He paused, looking around the gathering, meeting each of the leaders' eyes in turn.

'How many heads have we taken already? Five hundred? A thousand? What good will another five hundred do us? Do any of your men lack for swords, or shields? And as for their weapons, well, I ask you . . . Balthus, would you fight me here and now, man to man, you with that toothpick and me wielding the sword of any other man here?'

He paused again, waiting for the implication to settle in.

'I thought not. If we delay here we simply give the Romans more time to bring their legions together in a massive armoured fist that will smash our warbands. I have information on that subject, and it isn't good news. The southern legions started moving north several weeks ago, anticipating our attack, and will be on the Wall inside a week. And when they arrive, my brothers, the western legions will move through the Wall farther to the west, and move east to pin us here on the wrong side of their defences. And then, in all truth, we will be done for, outnumbered and unable to fall back to join the other warbands, and all because we were desperate to win a few more heads and some Roman spears?'

He turned to encompass the gathered nobles with opened arms.

'We need neither a few hundred heads more nor any number of the Romans' weapons, suited to their tactic of hiding and stabbing and *not* to the way we fight, man to man. What we need is to take not five hundred heads, or a thousand, but *ten* thousand. When a legion's standard lies on the ground before us, when we have the head of a Roman general pickled in a jar, *that* will be a victory! On that day, I am certain, the other legions will think carefully before coming north to punish us, but will instead send negotiators to buy peace with us, at a price of *our* naming. But to achieve that victory, we have to lure that single legion out on to our ground, where we, and not the Romans, choose the place and manner of our meeting. So tell me, my brothers, should we stay for a while here, and win more useless trinkets for our warriors to play with, or shall we follow our intended plan and take a prize worth having?'

He'd prevailed, of course; his argument had been all the more convincing for being correct. Finding the stores at Noisy Valley all but emptied in advance of their arrival had validated the Roman traitor's other revelation, that the western legions would arrive weeks earlier than he had expected. Now the warband was pulling back from the Wall in good order, its leaders happy enough to follow his direction and keep a muzzle on their men's urge to fight. Calgus turned to face his adviser, the older man's face inscrutable in the dusk's failing light.

'Your counsel is true, as always, Aed. I'll give the tribes all the heads they can carry, granted their patience for a few days.'

The Romans could skulk behind their defences for the time being – his warband would have vanished into the north by the time they stirred to follow. The trick now would be tempting the 6th's legatus to follow them on to a killing ground that Calgus would choose with care. That, and a little inside assistance.

IO

Marcus woke again in the middle of the next morning, his head relatively clear, and his stomach growling for food. Clodia Drusilla took one look at him and ordered a bed bath and a meal, both administered by a stone-faced orderly who responded to Marcus's attempts at conversation with monosyllabic grunts. Hot water, a borrowed blade and a clean tunic lifted his spirits, even if he was still weak enough to fall back on to his bed exhausted afterwards, and a small meal of bread, dried fish and vegetables left him replete. He slept again almost immediately, and was woken by a hand gently shaking his shoulder.

It was Licinius, the Petriana's prefect, smiling down at him with a glint of triumph. Dressed in a mud-stained tunic and armour, he had clearly come to the hospital directly from the saddle. The shutter was closed, and Licinius was carrying a lamp, adding its illumination to that of the lamp already burning by the bed.

'Ah, there you are, Centurion.'

Marcus pulled himself up on to his elbows, subsiding back on to the pillow that his superior hastily pushed beneath his straining body.

'The orderly tried to send me away. Now I've seen you, I think I understand why. Are you up to talking?'

Marcus declined the chance to put the conversation off once more, too tired to be bothered with his own safety any longer.

'Yes, Prefect, we can talk, but tell me, what time is it? What's happening out there?'

The other man sat on the short stool provided for the purpose, hunching forward to hear Marcus's tired whisper. As he opened his mouth to speak again, Felicia burst through the door, her mouth a thin white-lipped slash in a face pale with anger. The prefect leapt to his feet, bowing respectfully.

'Clodia Drusilla, my dear, what a pleasure to see you again. I . . .'

She pushed a fist into his face, making him step back in surprise, almost tumbling over the stool.

'You have no right or permission to be here, and as this officer's doctor I'm ordering you to get out. *Now!*'

Marcus raised a hand, forestalling her outburst.

'It's all right, Doctor, just a friendly conversation . . .'

She turned on him, wagging a finger threateningly.

'That isn't *your* decision, Centurion, and besides . . .'

'No more running.'

'What?'

'No more running from the truth. Not from an honourable Roman prefect.'

'But . . .'

Her reproach ran dry, leaving her staring helplessly at the bedridden centurion for a moment. She turned and left the room in silence. Licinius sat down again, raising an eyebrow at Marcus.

'Clodia Drusilla seems very protective of you, young man. Perhaps y'should consider your position very carefully with regard to that young lady. I happen to be acquainted with her husband well enough to know the way he'll behave if he suspects his property is being coveted by another . . .'

Marcus looked at him questioningly, until the older man shrugged his shoulders.

'Never mind. Just watch yourself there. As to the time,

it's late in the afternoon, two days after you took what was by all accounts quite a thump on the head. As to what's happening outside . . .'

He paused, rubbing his tired face with a wrinkled hand.

'Calgus came down the North Road, burned out everything down to Noisy Valley, let his men loose on White Strength and burned that down too, then retreated back up the road and vanished into the landscape, Mars damn him for eternity. I've got patrols out looking for the warband, but for the time being they're off the bloody map. Now that the barbarians have left the scene of the crime, Sixth Legion has come forward from the blocking position they were holding to the south, marched through here at lunchtime and thundered off over the horizon to some secret camp or other they scouted out a while ago. Where the other legions have got to, Mars only knows. But we, young man, have subjects closer to home to discuss, do we not?'

Marcus nodded, giving in to the inescapable.

'Firstly, as to your great secret, don't trouble yourself with the revelation, I've already questioned Equitius and got the truth out of him.'

Marcus's eyes opened wide.

'You . . .'

The officer waved a hand dismissively, shaking his head in amusement.

'Y'clearly don't appreciate my position here, young man. I command the Petriana cavalry wing and I'm the senior prefect of all the Wall garrisons. I'm already a senator as a result of an imperial promotion after a dirty little skirmish a few years ago, and I have some *very* powerful friends in Rome. When I told your commanding officer to spill the beans he did what he was told, related the whole story and offered to resign his command and fall on his sword. Because he's a realist. The man that lives in Yew Grove may nominally command the Wall garrison, executing the governor's orders, but as long as I'm in place these units answer to *me*, right up to the point where Sixth Legion comes forward into the line and he's in a position to take effective control.'

Marcus lay back, strangely relieved at not having to hide from the senior officer any longer.

'Did you take Equitius's command?'

Licinius snorted his laughter.

'Of *course* I didn't, y'fool! I can't afford to go dumping effective officers just because they happen to have an eye for a good officer!'

'But . . .'

The prefect leaned in close, half whispering into Marcus's ear, his patrician affectations suddenly replaced with a harder tone.

'But *nothing*, man. I told you I've got friends in Rome, men of influence and stature. They write to me regularly about the city and what's happening around them, and their letters have steadily become more pessimistic. Some of them even write anonymously, using recollection of our shared experiences as their identification, for fear of their words being read by the wrong person. Our new emperor is in the sway of dangerous men, and is steadily undermining the rules that have underpinned our society for almost a century. Your father and his brother were his victims, murdered for their land and to silence a potential dissenting voice in the Senate. As a loyal citizen of Rome I should, of course, arrest you, and Equitius and his First Spear, and hand you over to Sixth Legion for trial and execution.'

He stopped speaking, and looked away from Marcus, out of the room's window.

'As an officer of Rome, with a prior duty to the defence of this province, it is my judgement that I will do *no such thing*.'

'But you risk losing everything.'

'Centurion, there are two or three warbands out there that amount to about thirty thousand fighting men, all of them fired by the desire to liberate their lands from Roman influence and get their cocks up some nice soft flesh in the process. Against that mass of angry warriors we total ten thousand regular troops and two thousand cavalry, plus another eighteen thousand legionaries − *if* the legions make an appearance in time to join in the fun. If we get it wrong, I could be dead inside the week, in which case my failure to report your presence here will be inconsequential. My duty is first and foremost to the troops under my command, and to the people that depend on our protection to prevent those savages from killing and shagging their way all the way down to Yew Grove.

'And besides, quite apart from yourself, there are two other good men involved at the very least. Your First Spear is an outstanding soldier, and Equitius . . . Equitius has something even more special. It wouldn't surprise me to see him reach very high office indeed, if he comes through this thing intact. You'll understand when you're my age . . .'

He got up and walked to the door, reassuming his former aristocratic bearing.

'Anyway, you're a good officer, "Marcus Tribulus Corvus", good enough to take advantage of your luck. Make the most of that fortune in the coming days, ride it to the best possible advantage. We shall have need of your brand of audacity if we're to prevent this Calgus from nailing our heads to his roof beams. Just don't give me reason to regret this decision.'

He left, raising an eyebrow at Felicia, who glared at his departing back before hurrying back into Marcus's room, appraising him with a frank concern he found touching.

'He knows your secret, then?'

'Yes, he put the question directly to my prefect.'

'And . . . ?'

'I'm to return to duty as soon as I'm fit. It seems that live officers are of more value than dead traitors at this time.'

She exhaled noisily, sitting down at the end of his bed.

'I'm pleased. I've known him for long enough to be aware that he has his own very particular set of principles, but I wasn't sure how he'd react to your situation.'

'He said that your husband . . .'

He stopped, unwilling to embarrass the woman.

'Is a violent man? Would react without thinking if he thought there might be some slur upon his manhood? He's a good judge of character. Not everyone sees through that veneer of "hail fellow, well met" that Prefect Bassus uses to mask his real nature. Did he think that we were lovers?'

Marcus blushed, unable to meet her questioning gaze.

'Yes, I think he did.'

She laughed, putting her head back. The laughter stung Marcus's pride, making his voice harsher than he would have wanted.

'Not so funny, madam, you're a beautiful woman. He can see that any man would find you attractive . . .'

He hoped that she wouldn't detect either his discomfort with her amusement or his almost total lack of physical experience of women. Her laughter died away, and she returned his indignant glare with a gentle smile.

'On the contrary, Centurion, it wasn't *that* prospect I was laughing at. The old proverb came to mind – "Better to be strangled for a sheep than a goat". If you get my meaning?'

She turned and left, the secret smile staying on her face until she was back in her tiny office, making the duty orderly raise his eyebrows in mute curiosity.

Dubnus arrived an hour later, standing awkwardly in the doorway until Marcus beckoned him in. The big man came to attention at the bottom of the bed, in which Marcus was now sitting, reading a borrowed scroll of Caesar's writings on his campaigns in Gaul, launching into a speech he had clearly prepared with painstaking care.

'Centurion, I request permission to be allocated another century, at a lower rank if necessary . . .'

Marcus sat bolt upright, making the ache in his head throb a little harder. He swayed for a second with the pain, causing Dubnus to leap around the bed and steady him by the arm. The pain subsided after a moment. He motioned the soldier to sit down, and took a moment to wind the scroll up, looking into the other man's stonily fixed face. What reason could his deputy have for wanting to leave the 9th?

'*Why*, Dubnus?'

The chosen man knotted his fingers, and his eyes blinked rapidly, betraying the turmoil beneath the surface.

'A chosen man's main job is protect his officer, and . . .'

'*Bullshit!*'

The roar surprised Marcus himself, and sent another wave of pain through his head, but the rush of relief he felt in discovering the cause of his deputy's unease mixed powerfully with his panic at the prospect of losing the man. Dubnus flinched back on the chair, his eyes widening at the sudden display of anger.

'Your *job* is to be my deputy, to stand behind the century with your pole's end in their backs, and ensure that the Ninth moves in accordance with my commands, steady the men when they waver . . .'

He stopped for a moment, and reached for the water cup by his bed, drinking deeply.

'. . . and that's a job you perform superbly well. Think back, Dubnus. When I decided to go out and rescue our runner, without you at the back of the column our men would have turned and run for the safety of the Wall before we'd got two hundred yards out into the open. They were shit scared, and so for that matter was I. It was only your voice behind them that made them keep moving.'

'But in the forest . . .'

'*I* managed to make enough noise to bring the tribesmen down on us. That was nothing to do with you.'

'And I failed to stay with you.'

'We were fighting for our lives, in the darkness, against superior numbers. It's a wonder we aren't *both* stuck in here, or somewhere worse. Look, forget it, Dubnus, it wasn't your fault, and you're not leaving the Ninth. Relax, man, you're making my headache worse! Besides, *someone* stepped over me and held the blue-noses off . . .'

Dubnus winced at the attempted humour, then became serious again, the look on his face stopping Marcus mid-sentence.

'Which is the other reason why I should leave the century. It wasn't me that saved you, it was . . .'

'Yes?'

'. . . Antenoch.'

'*Antenoch?!*'

Dubnus nodded miserably.

'He came out of the trees behind us, jumped over you and fought off the tribesmen until relief arrived. Killed three men, and cut the sword arm off another . . .'

He tailed off, watching Marcus intently.

'Antenoch followed us into the trees without y— us noticing?'

Dubnus nodded again, his face lengthening. Marcus felt his grip on his self-control starting to slip.

'After you refused to let him patrol with us?'

'Yes.'

The reply was no more than an ashamed whisper, and for a second Marcus had the sense of talking to a naughty child. He kept control of a desire to laugh uncontrollably by the skin of his teeth.

'Good.'

'Eh!?'

'I said *good*, and I meant it. Your feud with him has gone on long enough. From now on you'll trust him implicitly, as I evidently have every reason to do . . . where is he now?'

'He'll come to the hospital later. I told him to wait until I was back in camp.'

Marcus lay back, his head buzzing with pain.

'Very well. Tell him to come up and see me after the evening meal, I need to sleep some more now. And Dubnus . . .'

'Centurion?'

'Don't even consider leaving the Ninth again without winning a vine stick first . . . unless you want me to have you . . . have you . . .'

He slipped into sleep. When he woke again the pain in his head was almost gone, and Antenoch was sitting quietly at his side, reading the borrowed scroll. Seeing his centurion awake, he furled the scroll, shaking it in Marcus's face.

'And what sort of reading matter is this for a sick man? Besides, what the *divine* Julius actually knew about fighting the Gauls would probably have fitted on your pocket tablet with room to spare. There's more to warfare than looking good on a horse and knowing when to send in the cavalry. I'd like to have seen *him* stand in a shield wall with the shit flying and retain his famous composure.'

Marcus laughed at him, refusing to be drawn.

'Oh good, you're better. You must be, or the good lady Felicia wouldn't be talking about letting you out in the morning.'

'Don't be so familiar, Antenoch, unless the *lady*'s given you permission to use her forename. One of these days you'll talk yourself into a mess I can't get you out of.'

'Oh, the lady and I are on first-name terms, Centurion, from the long conversations we had mooning over your sickbed, before you got bored with sleeping all the time. Conversations, I might add, that lead me to the belief that Felicia entertains feelings for you that go beyond those that might be expected between doctor and patient. You play it right, you could be hiding the sausage . . .'

Marcus's irritation boiled over, his finger stopping an inch from Antenoch's nose.

'Enough! You'll push me *too* far, you insolent bastard! Credit me with some sense of decorum! She's a married woman, for Jupiter's sake. Whether I want her or not, there are rules by which our lives are run.'

To his dismay, the Briton collapsed against the wall in giggles.

'Rules! Gods above, listen to him . . .'

He wiped his eyes theatrically, shaking his head in mock amazement.

'. . . and you a Roman citizen born and bred? Don't you know you people practically *invented* adultery?'

They stared at each other in angry silence for a moment, neither willing to concede. At length Antenoch spoke again.

'Anyway, be that as it may, the lady Felicia, who I am sure has led the most *blameless* of lives, entertains more than a hint of affection for yourself. And that's *official.*'

Marcus rose to the bait.

'What do you mean, *official?*'

His clerk smiled slyly.

'Her orderly told me so. We shared a mug of beer last night, after he was off duty; call it a scouting mission on your behalf, if you like. He's been with her for a year and a half down at Fair Meadow, helping her put damaged Second Tungrians together again, and he reckons he knows her better than her husband ever will . . .'

Marcus shook his head, aghast.

'I really shouldn't be listening to this . . .'

'But you will, because you feel for her just as much! I *warned* you I'd always speak my mind! She hates her husband because he won't recognise her abilities, and wants her to play the submissive little wife for him. Another fool that thought he could change a woman once they were married . . .

'Anyway, he told me that she gets all misty eyed when she thinks he isn't looking, and he's pretty sure *you're* the cause. Which I can understand, a nice young boy in uniform like you. And what's more . . .'

Marcus raised his arms in mock surrender.

'No more! I've heard all I need to. You're quite impossible, and I'm tiring fast just listening to you. Run along and play your games with the orderly, and leave me in peace. We can discuss this again once I've got a grip of my vine stick.'

Antenoch got to his feet, his smile undaunted.

'You'd only break the stick. Sleep well, Centurion, but remember what I've told you.'

He went to the door, looked out into the corridor and then turned back, as if on an afterthought.

'And if she *does* decide she can't resist, I think you'll owe me an apology. Perhaps we could even have a small wager on the matter?'

He ducked round the door frame, as Marcus threw the scroll at his head.

Annius sat in his tent throughout the afternoon, working through a sheaf of tablets and sending his staff around the camp to find the items he required, until he was convinced that the cohort had all of the supplies required for a deployment into hostile territory. Spearheads had already been purchased from the local armourer, spare swords traded for surplus sets of mail, and generally scarce boots quietly stolen from a neighbouring unit's store. All might be required in the next few days, and he had no intention of inviting the wrath of men he would depend upon to stand between him and thousands of angry barbarians.

Darkness fell, and he worked on by the light of half a dozen lamps, snacking from a plate of cakes purchased from Tacitus's bakery, until a disturbance outside the tent caught his attention. Rising to go to the flap, he received his clerk in the belly, the man literally thrown into the tent from outside. They fell on to his table, scattering tablets, cakes and lamps, plunging the interior into darkness. The flap was pulled open, the man standing in the opening silhouetted in the light of the torches that burned around the camp.

'Stores officer Annius?'

The cohort's guards would notice, would come to his rescue. He gathered his dignity, getting to his feet and trying to make out the indistinct figure at the tent's door.

'Yes. What . . .'

The other man reached into the tent, grasping him by the neck and pulling him out through the door, choking him with the pinch-hold on his windpipe. Close up, in the light of the torches, he was evidently officer class, dressed in cavalry armour, and with a body that Annius would have bet filled his cuirass without any trouble. He leaned in close to speak into the stores officer's face, his eyes shining in the torchlight and a hand sliding down to his waist, gripping the hilt of his dagger.

'I told your clerk, and I'll tell you, shut your face if you want to live. I could slit your throats and be away from here before your guards woke up. Understand?'

His vision greying from the vice-like grip on his throat, Annius nodded limply.

'Good.'

The grip relaxed, allowing him to gulp in some air. His arm was grasped, leaving him no alternative but to accompany the man as he led a winding path through the tents. Without a cloak he began to shiver in the night's cold air. After a minute's swift walk the officer pushed him into a tent, lit brightly by several large lamps, and followed, placing his bulk between Annius and the door flap. A younger man, also in uniform, sat idly in a chair at the tent's far end. A thin purple stripe ran along his tunic's hem, and he was attired in magnificently polished armour. In the lamplight Annius read his face in an instant, finding the intensity and intelligence of a predator under a shock of blond hair.

'Well, storeman, do you know who I am?'

He shook his head, realising that he should speak, and chanced a response.

'A senior officer, sir, a legion tribune to judge from your rank . . .'

'Quite so. And more too. You'll doubtless have heard of our emperor, Commodus?'

'Yes, Tribune.'

Did this have something to do with that young bastard of a centurion? What had Tacitus been broadcasting to the world?

'My name is Titus Tigidius Perennis. My father is the praetorian prefect of Rome. I carry a special commission from the emperor . . .'

He took a small scroll from inside his tunic, and waved it at Annius.

'I've read it so many times I can remember the wording as if it were open in front of me . . . "find and bring to justice any person guilty of treason against the throne, of *whatever* rank, within the Imperial Government of Britannia. Command the services of any man required to aid in this task, of whatever rank, on penalty of death for refusal." On penalty of death, storeman.

'There's more, but it's only detail by comparison. I came to Britain to serve as a tribune in the Sixth Legion, under Legatus Sollemnis, a man suspected of harbouring treacherous sympathies with certain Roman enemies of the state. Enemies since dealt with in ways fitting to their unveiled treason.'

He let the implicit threat hang in the air for a moment before getting to his feet and walking across to Annius, staring him in the eyes before restarting his discourse.

'I found the legion well trained and ready for war, the legatus obviously competent, but curiously reticent on the subject of his emperor, unwilling to discuss a subject he *might* have felt could trip him up. And so I waited, content to work in preparation for a war we were both convinced was close upon us. Then, a few months ago, came word that a young traitor, son of one of the men arrested for treason, had run for cover, and was seeking to join the Sixth as an anonymous centurion. Legatus Sollemnis played it straight, sending the boy back south by night as instructed by the governor, giving my men a chance to deal with him on the road. *Someone*, whether with the legatus's blessing or not, killed a cavalry decurion and two of his men sent to deal with the traitor. Worse, they tortured the decurion for information while he lay dying and then escaped into the open country, almost certainly with the traitor in tow. After which disappointing events nothing was heard of either the outlaw or whoever aided him. Until, perhaps, now . . .'

He turned away, pacing down the tent's length before turning back and speaking again.

'The decurion they killed was a respected man in these parts, first in line for promotion to first spear with the Asturians. Who, you might have heard, have sworn to a man to have their revenge on the killer, whenever and wherever the chance arises. This man . . .' He gestured to the officer filling the tent's doorway. '. . . has a particular interest in taking the killer's blood, since the man was his older brother. Now, a contact of mine within the fort tells me that you have information on the subject which I might find useful. He recommended I speak with you with all dispatch.'

He paced back to the terrified storekeeper, staring into his eyes.

'Now, you are, at this moment, weighing up whether to tell me the truth or not. Let's face it, I'm here tonight and gone in the morning, while your First Spear will always be there, and eager for revenge if he thinks you've betrayed him in such a way.'

He turned to the decurion and nodded. A pale sword slid from its scabbard, the edge winking in the lamplight.

'The decurion here, however, is another matter. He wants revenge on this traitor, and whoever helped him, and he'll be very upset indeed if he feels that you're obstructing his path to justice. So, storeman, your choices are simple – tell me everything you know, here and now, without hiding anything, or they'll find you face down in the river with a rather nasty hole in your back. It's really up to you . . .'

Annius opened his mouth and started talking.

Marcus read quietly through the evening, submerging himself in Caesar's two-hundred-year-old account of his subjugation of Gaul until the shadows lengthened, and the orderly came to light his lamp. After a while straining to make out the characters in the half-darkness became too much of an effort and he rolled up the scroll and slid beneath the blanket, blowing the lamp out to leave the room in darkness. Hovering above sleep's dark waters, his mind easing down to rest, he thought for a second that he felt a gentle touch on his face, soft enough not to pull him back from the brink of rest, enough to hold him there in a state of uncertain thrill.

The touch came again, and a soft voice spoke soothingly to him as a warm body slipped under the blanket beside him. His body trembled slightly with the sudden realisation, as hands caressed his back and neck, lips finding his ear and gently kissing away the fear. He rolled over to meet her kiss with his own, still stunned at the situation, pausing for breath after a long moment.

'It would seem that I owe my clerk an apology.'

Felicia renewed the kiss wordlessly, moving her body over his beneath the blanket's rough folds.

Felicia left Marcus's bed in the early hours, abandoning him to an exhausted, dreamless sleep. He woke long after dawn to the orderly's persistent shaking of his shoulder.

'Centurion, there's a messenger from your cohort waiting outside. Clodia Drusilla grants you her permission to leave the hospital, and has asked me to give you this . . .'

He directed a significant look towards Marcus, making it quite clear that he could guess at the tablet's contents. As he left one of Marcus's men came through the door with a bundle of clothing and equipment tied up in what Marcus quickly recognised as his cloak.

'Sir, First Spear's regards, an' he requests you to rejoin the cohort on the way to the North Road. The horse boys found the barbarians yesterday, an' we're moving to attack them . . .'

Marcus dressed quickly, shoving the tablet into a pocket and grabbing a piece of bread from the breakfast table as he followed the soldier out of the infirmary's quiet corridors and into the fort's orderly hubbub. The rest of the man's tent party were waiting impatiently at the door, their leader saluting smartly at his appearance among them.

'Morning, sir, good to see you looking better. I hope you're up to a run this morning, the cohort marched out at the double almost half an hour ago, along with the Second and the Batavians.'

Marcus nodded grimly, tightening his new helmet's strap until the leather bit into his chin, ignoring the pressure on his still-sensitive scalp, while the men checked that their packs were secure on their carrying poles before hoisting them on to their shoulders along with their spears. A shouted command set them running, a steady trot to which, Marcus was pleased to discover, his body adjusted after only a moment's protest. Five minutes took them across the fort's bridge and out of view of the fort, passing through wooded copses and open fields as they climbed the steep hill to the east of the river. Despite the road's arrow-straight line, Marcus kept a hand on his sword's hilt, aware that a roving barbarian scouting party would see an officer and eight men as fair game.

Half an hour's running brought no sight of the cohort, confirmation of Marcus's mental arithmetic. He had guessed that it would take the best part of another hour to catch the Tungrians, and so it proved, the black snake of men appearing on the horizon as they ran into sight of the crossroads with the North Road.

The tail-end century of the rearmost cohort was clearing the crossroads and heading out through the wall's open gates as the nine men ran up to it, Marcus recognising their companion unit, the Second Tungrians, with a sudden guilty start. They moved to the verge, padding past the marching soldiers without breaking their pace and ignoring the barrage of catcalls and insults that followed their progress up the line of centuries. At the column's head Marcus recognised his own cohort, and quickened his pace in response. A voice rang out from behind him, peremptory in its authority.

'You there! Centurion! A moment!'

He signalled his men to rejoin their colleagues, and then turned reluctantly to face the speaker, walking backwards to keep pace with the column's leading rank. An officer marched forward from his place alongside the column's head, extending a hand in greeting. Marcus saluted before taking the offered hand, turning to walk alongside the other man.

'Quintus Dexter Bassus, prefect, Second Tungrian Cohort. And you, I presume from the look of you, are the First Cohort's illustrious young cattle-burning centurion?'

Marcus drew on his praetorian etiquette training, recalling his instruction on how best to maintain a respectful posture while escorting a walking dignitary, and turned his torso towards the prefect, nodding his head slightly.

'Yes, sir . . .'

He took a deep breath, thinking quickly.

'. . . Centurion Two Knives. I prefer to fight with two swords when possible, and the title seems to have stuck.'

'I've heard it . . . a soldier's name if ever I heard one. Is there a name that you can share with me?'

'With pleasure, Prefect. My family name is Corvus.'

'Well, Centurion Corvus, I can only offer you my inadequate but heartfelt thanks for your rescue of my wife . . .'

They walked in silence for a moment, the massed rattle on the road of hobnailed boots and the jingle and rattle of harnesses and equipment filling what would otherwise have been an uncomfortable gap in the conversation.

'The thanks, Prefect, would more appropriately be offered to my century, but nevertheless I am happy to acknowledge them, and to express my pleasure that we were in the right place at the right time.'

The other man pursed his lips, perhaps, Marcus thought, caught between the need to show gratitude for the act and a curiosity as to what Felicia might have said to him during the their time together.

'You're too modest, young man. The whole army is talking about the way your century denied the barbarians their supplies, and I owe you a debt of thanks I cannot easily discharge. The gods only know what indignities your fortunate arrival spared my wife.'

'Prefect, you may be aware that I sustained a head injury during a night patrol two days ago. Your wife was good enough to administer her medical skills to my wound, greatly assisting my recovery. Any debt is thus well repaid.'

The other man stared at him for a moment.

'A noble sentiment, and more typically Roman than I'm used to from the local officers. I find it refreshing to see a young gentleman accept a position in an auxiliary unit, rather than insisting on serving with the legions. Although I'm surprised that a traditionally minded First Spear like Frontinius would ever accept such a recruit. I wonder, Centurion . . .'

Marcus willed his face to remain impassive.

'. . . if Clodia Drusilla mentioned to you what she was doing over the Wall at such a time?'

Relief flooded his mind at the man's obvious preoccupation with his woman, followed immediately by the realisation that he was still walking on eggshells.

'Ah . . . no, sir, now that you mention it she didn't tell me, and neither did I have the time to ask. I was preoccupied with getting my men away from danger, and . . .'

'And not really your business anyway, eh? Very well, Centurion, since you're clearly a man of discretion, I can see I shouldn't delay you from your men any longer. Good day.'

Marcus saluted briskly and turned, relieved to be away without having to face difficult questions regarding either his own provenance or the other man's wife. Accelerating his pace, he trotted smartly past the tail-end century, the men of the 10th striding along with their axes over their shoulders. As he passed the 10th's front rank Titus stepped out with his fist raised for the tap.

'Good work, young Two Knives, you're the talk of the cohort.'

Marcus reflexively tapped the huge man's fist with his own, shooting a surprised glance at the big man's smug smile. Normally he would now have been running alongside his own men, but the 9th were at the column's head. Otho, striding along beside his 8th Century, simply smiled his battered smile and winked as the young centurion passed. Ahead of him Brutus was walking along backwards at the head of the 7th . . . applauding? He slapped Marcus on the shoulder as he passed, calling after him.

'And I thought I was supposed to be the lucky one!'

Rufius's chosen man was apparently in command of the 6th, and quite sensibly kept his mouth shut and his eyes to the front as a red-faced Marcus hurried past. As he progressed up the column's length shouts of ribald encouragement from the marching ranks accompanied his progress until he reached the standard, carried in the midst of the 5th Century. Julius was marching at the Fifth's head with Rufius striding alongside him. His friend's face widened into a broad smile of welcome.

'Here's the young fellow, fresh from his deathbed. Here, Two Knives, clasp hands with me once more.'

Marcus put his hand out, only for Rufius to grasp it eagerly, rolling his eyes.

'I shook his hand! A real live hero! I won't ever wash it again . . .'

Julius nodded to him, his eyes showing a mix of respect and something else that Marcus was hard placed to identify. It looked almost like . . . concern?

'How's your head, Two Knives?'

'Harder than I thought, thank you, Julius.'

The other man nodded with a sardonic smile.

'It's going to have to be, if you're going to keep on like this.'

Rufius poked Julius in the ribs.

'He's just jealous. We've spent the last three days patrolling and sitting around bored, not tucked up in hospital with a nice lady doctor to look after our *every* need.'

Marcus blushed a deeper shade of red, unable to control the reaction, and Rufius pounced on the display, his bearded face split in a disbelieving grin.

'Ah, so there *is* something to the rumour?! You *lucky* bastard! I swear you could fall into shit and come out smelling of myrrh!'

Marcus bit his tongue to prevent a sheepish grin that was hovering on the bounds of his control.

'A gentleman would never discuss such a question. I'll talk to you later.'

He set off up the column with his ears still hot under the helmet's protection, making a mental note to murder his clerk at the first opportunity. The prefect was nowhere to be seen, but Frontinius dropped back from the column's head as soon as he heard Marcus's voice, returning the younger man's salute.

'You can have your century back now that you've caught up with us. Keep them moving at the double march until the signal for a rest comes, and otherwise take your cue from the Raetians ahead. If you see men to the flank, take a good look before you shout – there's a legion out here somewhere, and I wouldn't want the Tungrians to be the ones to point the spear at our own side. Keep your eyes open.'

Marcus nodded acknowledgement, then ran to the head of his century, settling into the ground-eating double march, a blessed relief after the morning's exertion. Antenoch appeared at his shoulder after a moment.

'Good morning, Centurion, I trust you slept well?'

Marcus's eyes slitted, daring the man to push his question any farther. Antenoch took the hint.

'Er, good. I've got some bread and dried meat if you're hungry after your . . . er . . . exertions?'

'Give me the food, Antenoch, and keep your mouth shut. It seems that there are far too many people in this cohort making assumptions about my behaviour without you making it any worse.'

He accepted the food and chewed quickly, wanting it inside him and not in his hands if trouble developed, gave his clerk another withering stare and then dropped down the line of march to talk to Dubnus at the century's rear.

'How are they?'

The Briton nodded grimly.

'Ready.'

'What was the morning's briefing?'

'There's a lot happened since your bang on the head. The warbands that came south of the Wall didn't stay long to fight once they found Noisy Valley burnt out and a legion dug in between them and Yew Grove. They've retreated to the north, back past Red River apparently. No one knows why. The Sixth Legion followed up and is somewhere north of the Wall. They've got cavalry in contact with the blue-noses, so now we're moving to close them down for a battle. The prefect's gone to meet the Sixth's legatus, to agree the overall plan. There's a big fight waiting for us, and not too far off either.'

Equitius wondered for the hundredth time how Sollemnis had managed to manoeuvre a whole legion through such close country, and, for that matter, why? His escort, a thirty-man detachment from the Asturian cavalry who seemed to have become Tribune Perennis's personal command, looked nervously to either side of the narrow path, into dense forest vegetation that made vision impossible after no more than a dozen yards. Something took fright deep in the undergrowth and bolted away from the path, making his horse prance nervously for a moment.

'This rather reminds me of the accounts of the Teutoburger Forest I read as a boy.'

The comment went seemingly unnoticed by the younger man for a long moment, before he responded over his shoulder, not bothering to turn in the saddle.

'I had the Asturians map this area's paths during the spring, just in case we needed to move one of the legions round an enemy's flank, if the Wall were under threat. I've got this country etched into my head. Varus made the mistake of advancing into close terrain he'd failed to thoroughly scout. *That's* the way to lose a legion or three.'

Equitius scowled at the other man's back, hating his self-assured swagger. And yet his plan had succeeded brilliantly so far, moving the legion from its blocking position behind the Wall into a hidden temporary fortress from where they could strike at the enemy warbands without warning, given the right opportunity. It was this very opportunity with which Equitius was riding to join the 6th, news that the Petriana had managed to pinpoint the warband's location. A horseman had galloped into the Cauldron Pool camp the previous afternoon, with news that his detachment had chanced upon the warband's well-beaten path north of the wreck of the Red River fort. Successful in their stealthy tracking of the enemy formation to its current resting place, they were calling for reinforcement, and quickly, before the warband decided to move again.

That old war horse Licinius had led the rest of the Petriana out an hour later, leaving instructions with Equitius to get the 6th Legion committed in their support as soon as possible. They had been riding ever deeper into barbarian territory since early morning, following the legion's path down what was no more than a hunter's track, and now the sun was close to its zenith. The Asturians kept to themselves, leaving him with nobody to talk to other than Perennis, a young man for whom he was gradually developing a marked aversion.

'So, Tribune, how did you come to be posted to this miserable end of the empire?'

Again the calculated pause.

'I asked for the posting. My father told me that the emperor wanted to send a young man of the equestrian class to serve with the Northern Command, to provide him with a first-hand description of the country and its people . . .'

A thinly disguised reference to his role as an imperial spy which, Equitius sensed, was deliberately sufficiently implausible as to make the real purpose quite apparent.

'Hearing this, I persuaded him to present me to Commodus, and to make the case for my taking the role. The emperor asked me what I would do in the case of my discovering treachery at *any* level of the army. Even that of a legionary legatus.'

And he paused again, letting the silence drag out.

'I told him that I would quite cheerfully condemn the traitor to a public and agonising death, as a lesson to any others of the same mind. It seemed to hit the right note . . .'

Equitius would have bet it did. Commodus's reputation for insecurity and bloody overcompensation was already well established. Perennis turned in this saddle, looking back at him.

'I expect you would have said exactly the same.'

Equitius met his eye, suddenly frightened for the first time in several years, hiding his fear behind a slow smile.

'I expect I would.'

Thirty yards ahead of them, and without warning, half a dozen armoured men stepped from the undergrowth, their spears ready to throw. It was, now he thought about it, perfect country to defend. If a column of attackers were surprised on the path they would be bottled up like rats in a lead drainpipe. He glanced to one side, and saw armoured men moving through the woods, closing the trap. The centurion on the path ahead demanded the password, and waited to receive it from Perennis without a change of expression.

Password given and accepted, Equitius looked down at the men as they rode past, grim-faced veterans who looked up at him with the disdain to which he'd become accustomed as an auxiliary officer. Regulars, as convinced of their superiority over any other fighting man as they were that the sun would rise the next day. Proud, and nasty with it, habitually taking no prisoners and expecting no quarter. Where a captured auxiliary would be slaughtered without compunction, as a traitor to his own people, a legionary would be saved for more exquisite treatment, to be exacted at leisure if possible. To the tribes they were not simply soldiers of the hated oppressor, but enemy citizens, or as good as, and both feared and hated in greater proportions accordingly.

A mile down the track they broke out into the open, a clearing in the forest greatly enlarged by the legionaries' labour in felling trees, the fallen trunks stripped of their branches and converted into a rough log palisade around the temporary camp's perimeter. Their branches had been hacked into thousands of stakes and set outside the wall at angles that would impale a careless night attacker. Tents mushroomed across the open space inside the fence, enough for a full legion at eight men to a tent, men still working at strengthening the camp's defences. Equitius smiled, remembering the old adage – give a legion open ground for a night and you got a field camp surrounded by an earthwork four feet high. A week, and they would pillage the surrounding land for the materials to build a full-blown fort. A month, and the officers' mess would look as if it had been there for a year.

The small party passed through the open gateway, making their way to the camp's centre, where the command tents rose above the lower troop and officer versions. Sollemnis met them at the door of his headquarters tent, accepting Perennis's salute with appropriate gravity before clasping Equitius's arm in a warm greeting.

'My good friend, it's been almost a year!'

Equitius nodded soberly, glancing significantly at the tent.

'And now we meet in a time of war, with little time for talk.'

'But talk we must. Perennis, I would invite you to share our discussion, but you probably have duties to attend to?'

The tribune nodded.

'Indeed, sir. I thought I might take a squadron of the Asturians to the west, and make sure that the barbarians haven't slipped away from the Petriana.'

Sollemnis waved a hand absently.

'Very good. Regular dispatches, mind you. I want to know where you are when we move.'

He turned away, gesturing Equitius into the command tent, past the hard-bitten legionaries guarding its flap.

'A drink?'

An orderly came forward with a tray, pouring them both a cup of wine, and then withdrew, leaving the two men alone. Sollemnis gestured to the couch.

'Please, my friend, sit down, you must be tired after a day in the saddle. Now, firstly, tell me what you think about my tribune.'

'Freely?'

'Of course. You're not overheard, and you and I are old friends. Your opinions have always been important to me, never more so than now. So, tell me what you think.'

Equitius weighed his words.

'On one level he seems the most complete soldier. Was this location really his idea?'

'Oh yes, he spent most of last summer cataloguing the ground. He has a sound grasp of tactics, and an understanding of war fighting and strategy that puts men twice his age to shame. And on the other level?'

'He's . . . dangerous. Do you trust him?'

'Trust his abilities? Absolutely. You'll have heard the stories about our great victory over the Twentieth in last autumn's manoeuvres? That was our Perennis, using the Asturians to scout a way around their flank patrols and bring us down on their supply train like wolves on the flock while the shepherd was away. The senior centurions recognise a kindred spirit, and they worship the ground he walks on. Trust the *man*? Not likely! He was imposed on me by the governor and on him by the emperor, for the purpose of ensuring my loyalty, but for a young man his ambition burns exceedingly brightly. Too brightly for my liking, I'm afraid. His father's influence, I suppose.'

'So why tolerate him?'

'I refer you back to my first answer. His skills will be invaluable to the legion in this campaign, after which I'll send him back to Rome as a hero to report our victory, and recommended to take command of a legion of his own, with promotion to senatorial rank. In the meantime I'll do everything possible to keep *our* secret from him. Now, I believe another young man's been making something of a reputation for himself in the last week?'

Equitius smiled wryly.

'Yes. His adoptive father did too good a job of the boy's training, turned him into a bloody assassin. We paired him with an experienced chosen man, in the hope that he'd temper the boy's lack of experience, instead of which they went storming around the countryside at the first opportunity, burning out Calgus's supplies and taking on his cavalry at suicidal odds. But for old Licinius you'd have no son now.'

'Licinius. *Gods!* How long did it take that old bastard to see through the matter?'

'He didn't have to. He asked me for the truth and I gave it to him. You lie to that man at your peril.'

'Hmm. And his verdict was . . . ?'

'That the boy's too good a soldier to throw away. If the emperor's men discover him, Licinius will of course disown the pair of us as traitors.'

'So we're not discovered . . . yet.'

The legatus blew a long breath out.

'You have my thanks for your risk. I'll find a way to make amends once this is all dealt with. The Twentieth comes up for command rotation early next year. My recommendation will be for you to take the rank of legatus . . . not that the position is guaranteed to be in my gift. I never quite understood why it was that you didn't get command of the Twenty-second Primigenia in Germania. You were senior tribune, after all . . .'

'The legatus and I didn't entirely see eye to eye. He thought it was appropriate for the senior officers to benefit from a variety of incautious frauds against official funds. I didn't. I was caught between two fires – I either informed on him and earned a reputation as a toady, or ignored the situation and paid the price with the rest of them when they were found out. I managed to get the appropriate information to the governor, but I didn't want promotion into the shoes of a man I'd effectively condemned to death, so I asked him to send me to Britannia instead. Being appointed to an auxiliary cohort was the closest thing to a promotion I could have expected under the circumstances. Command of a legion would be a very fine thing indeed, but I'm happy enough with the Tungrians.'

His friend nodded.

'Well, if I get my way you'll have a legion soon enough. In the meanwhile, we should probably concentrate on more pressing business. Tell me about this new development with our esteemed adversary . . .'

The cohort went north at a fast pace, twice marching past burned-out forts. The smell of charred wood stayed with them long after the ruined outposts were out of sight, as had an altogether more disturbing odour. Marcus was kept busy until after sunset once the cohorts turned off the line of march for the day. Since the prefects had decided to avoid the previous marching camps which abounded in the frontier area, their locations likely to be known and watched, there was a four-foot turf wall to be built and no time to waste. One tent party was drawn by lot and sent to form part of the guard force, an important precaution even if the enemy could not be expected to find their encampment this late in the day, even less attack it. Another tent party was set to prepare the cohort's evening meal. With all tasks distributed and under way, and their section of the rampart growing steadily under Dubnus's expert eye, Marcus suddenly found himself lacking any worthwhile task. Knowing looks were exchanged a moment later as his wiry figure joined the working party to carry cut turfs from the increasingly distant cutting gang to the wall builders.

Antenoch, one of the more skilled rampart builders, threw down the turf he was holding in disgust, watching his officer's more or less clean mail shirt swiftly deteriorate under his first muddy load. He nudged Dubnus, who had graciously made a great show of accepting his presence in the century, who in turn set out to intercept his centurion, but a raised hand forestalled his comment.

'The more bodies involved, the quicker we finish. I can't supervise the wall building, and I can't cut turf or build the rampart with any expertise. The century is all working, I'll bet most of the officers are working, and I'm damned if I'll stand by and watch. Get on with making that rampart sound, and you can teach me the basics later.'

Frontinius walked past on an inspection a few minutes later, searched without success for the centurion's distinctive crested helmet, and was about to ask Dubnus where his officer was when he made out just who the slightly grubby figure delivering turfs to the wall-building gang was. He stood and watched as the tired centurion headed back out to the turf cutters, nodded to himself and then, with a raised eyebrow to Dubnus, went on his way.

With the wall declared complete, high enough to slow an attacker's charge to a walking pace and make excellent spear targets of anyone crossing the obstacle, the cohorts went to dinner, with the exception of the guard units, who paid for their inactivity during the building work with a later meal. Fed, the men turned their hands to their domestic chores in the flickering torchlight, making hurried repairs to clothing and equipment, well-worn jokes and insults flying between the working men in equal measure as they relaxed tired limbs and minds. Their last task was to remove the worst of the day's dirt from their uniforms and faces. A delegation from the 9th promptly demanded Marcus's dirt-caked mail, which they brushed out and returned with a polished gleam.

As the troops turned in for the night, huddled into their blankets and packed tight in their eight-man tents, the officers were called to the headquarters tent for their briefing. Equitius, who had returned just before sunset, ordered the tired centurions to stand easy.

'As you know, I met with the Sixth's legatus early this afternoon. Our situation is more than stabilised – it has become, on the whole, favourable. The Sixth is camped in this forest *here* . . .'

He pointed to a point on their rough map twenty miles distant.

'Second and Twentieth Legions have reached the Wall and are marching along the main road to join us. They'll probably arrive some time the day after tomorrow. Sollemnis plans to tackle the warband during that day with everything we can throw at it, and as quickly as possible, before it can gather any more spears. Even if it means starting the attack before the Second and Twentieth arrive. So, we break camp in the morning and march with all speed to join the Petriana and Augustan cavalry wings, which are currently holding position ten miles to the north-west. The Sixth will also move tomorrow, with the intention of joining our forces together and forcing a decisive action. Once we have their position fixed we'll gauge how best to bring them to battle but, and I emphasise this, we'll only fight if we can bring the legion *and* our own spears to bear, and on the right terrain for our tactics. Together we're twelve thousand men with the cavalry wings, quite enough to make a mess of twice our number of undisciplined barbarians on the right ground. So, go and get some sleep and have your men ready to move at first light. We've got a long marching day in front of us tomorrow.'

Marcus headed back to his tent, eager to roll up in his blanket and snatch a few hours' sleep. As he took his boots off something poked him in the ribs, and he remembered the tablet the orderly had given him that morning, hastily pushed into a tunic pocket and then forgotten in the rush of the day. Opening it, he leaned over close to the single lamp, straining to read the stylus marks on the tablet's hard wax.

'*Marcus, thank you for last night. If I were not already taken, you would be my choice. It's cruel how the fates conspire to make this clear only after it's too late. With my love.*'

The next day dawned to a thin summer drizzle, accompanied by a sharp wind to mercifully cool the hard-marching cohorts. Goaded by their centurions to a brisk pace, and for once grateful for the absence of unobstructed sunlight, they headed up the North Road towards the abandoned outpost fort at Red River. In the 9th, half a mile ahead of the leading units since the Tungrians were leading the column, nobody was in any doubt as to what they should expect.

'Roaring River Fort burnt to the ground, although I dare say they scoured the place for weapons first. Red River won't be any different.'

Dubnus nodded grimly at Morban's words as they marched, remembering the scene as the cohorts had marched past the shattered remnants of the Roaring River Fort the previous day. In peacetime the fort had been home to a sizeable detachment of auxiliaries, usually rotated out of the Wall units for six months at a time. Positioned north of the Wall, it also attracted more than its share of hangers-on – prostitutes, thieves, merchants and pedlars, all keen to part the soldiers, separated from their usual environment and loved ones, from their money in any way possible.

The warband had evidently come down the North Road fast enough that the evacuating troops had found little time to worry about the occupants of the fort's ramshackle settlements, who had themselves either taken swift flight or paid a severe price for their collaboration. Fifty or sixty men had been nailed to the remaining standing timbers at Roaring River, another twenty farther south at Fort Habitus, all of them smeared with tar and then set ablaze. Only the blackened husks of their bodies had remained, along with an overpowering stench of burnt flesh. Of the women there'd been no sign, although their fate wasn't hard to imagine. There wasn't a man in the cohort that hadn't imagined the same fate for his own fort and shuddered. Already the mood among the troops had changed, from one of concern as to what they might come up against in the field to a hunger to get some revenge, spill barbarian guts and take heads.

The same thought was obviously on Equitius's mind, for he ran forward with Frontinius and a twenty-man bodyguard from the 5th and caught up with the 9th at the milestone three miles before they reached the Red River fort.

'It's off the road here, I think, and time for you scouts to start earning your corn. If this Calgus is half the commander he's cracked up to be they'll have Red River under watch, and I'd rather stay incognito for the time being.'

He looked to either side, then pointed off to their left, at rising ground stretching up to a distant line of trees.

'We'll wait here on the road until you report that the path ahead to that forest is clear.'

The 9th went in the direction indicated, off the road to the left, and started up a narrow farmer's track that led to a rude hut, the abandoned farmer's dwelling, then on up to the treeline. The woods, three hundred yards distant across the abandoned field, were an uncertain refuge, however. Morban took a good hard look and spat derisively into the dust.

'Cocidius above, the entire warband could be in that lot and we'd never know it.'

Marcus turned back to grin at the standard-bearer.

'That's what the prefect meant when he said it was time to earn our corn. Want to take the standard back to the main body?'

'And risk getting jumped on my own on the way back? No, thank you very much, sir, I'll risk it here with a few dozen swords between my soft flesh and the enemy.'

'Very well. Chosen, we'll have a party of scouts up that path as soon as you like, the rest of the century to observe from here until we know what's behind the trees. Nice and steady, no need for shouting or rushing about.'

Dubnus nodded, walking through the troops and picking his scouts by hand, briefing them in measured tones rather than the usual parade-ground roar. The five men chosen shook out into an extended line across the field, then started climbing the slope at a measured pace, slow enough that they had time to strip ears of corn from the standing crop. They nibbled at the immature kernels as they moved through the thigh-deep green carpet.

'Look at those lucky bastards, just strolling in the country and chewing some poor bloody farmer's wheat.'

Morban spun to glare at the speaker, the soldier Scarface, shaking the bagged standard at the man, then whispered at him sotto voce.

'Shut your mouth, you stupid sod. Firstly, it's them risking a spear in the guts, not you, so a few nibbles of corn isn't exactly a great reward. Secondly, if your bellowing brings a fucking great warband down out of those trees before the rest of the cohort gets here to die with us, I am personally going to stick this standard right up your arse before they cut my head off. Statue end first!'

Scarface hung his head, red faced. Tongue lashings from Morban, while not exactly rare, were usually less vehement.

The scouts progressed up the slope, vanishing into the trees together as if at some preordained signal. After a moment a man reappeared at the wood's edge, waving them to come forward with some urgency. The century went up the track at the double, Marcus leading the way in his eagerness to see what had animated the man. Antenoch drew his sword and stayed close to his centurion, his eyes moving across the trees with hard suspicion as they ran up the slope. Morban, hurrying along behind them, muttered an insult at the clerk's back.

'What's the matter, Antenoch, hasn't he paid you yet this month?'

Inside the wood, in the shade and quiet, Marcus found two of the scouts conferring over something, while the other three were dimly visible fifty or sixty yards distant, moving deeper into the trees. There were flies swarming in the still air, their scratchy buzz sawing at his nerves as they criss-crossed the scene. The man who had waved them up the track, now recognisable as Cyclops, gestured to the ground with some excitement.

'They were here all right, sir, a day ago, perhaps two.'

Marcus looked. In a small pit, dug a foot or so into the earth, a pile of human excrement and small animal bones formed an untidy still life, a small cloud of buzzing flies still feasting on their find. He turned to find Dubnus at his shoulder. The chosen man looked down into the pit, then squatted down and poked at one of the stools with a twig.

'These men got lazy, didn't bury their leavings properly. Cyclops, look for other pits, probably filled in. See how many you can find. Two Knives, you need to brief the prefect. This is a day old from the feel of it, no more, or the flies would have lost interest by now. These were probably the men that torched Red River, set an ambush here in case there were Roman forces in the area to come to the rescue. These woods would easily conceal a whole warband, and hide their fires . . .'

'Sir!'

The call came from the scouts deeper into the woods. Marcus shot a glance at them.

'Dubnus, you brief the prefect, I'll see what's got their attention.'

He went on into the woods, the century spreading out to either side, spears and shields held ready. The scouts beckoned him on, pointing to the ground. Now that he took the time to look he saw that the damp earth was pressed flat for a hundred yards in all directions, the marks of many boots. Most of the prints, the most recent, were pointed in the same direction. West.

I I

The cavalrymen's horses fretted at their reins, impatient to be away from the plodding infantry column and free to run. The prefect had a dozen horsemen, his escort from the 6th's camp, to use as swift messengers in the absence of the Petriana's courier riders. Four were to be loosed now, tasked to ride north-east and find the oncoming legion, to warn them that a second warband was in the field. The headquarters clerks finished coding the message with the day's cipher and a centurion whisked the tablets out to the waiting horsemen.

Equitius scratched his beard, increasingly itchy as the spartan field regime of cold-water washing took its toll on his cleanliness. He'd manoeuvred the column off the road and into the woods, then dropped his five cohorts into a swift defensive posture while he composed his message to Sollemnis. Another warband on the move gave Calgus much greater ability to threaten any advancing Roman force, manoeuvre to strike at a flank or rear while the first held their attention. Even more than before he knew the critical importance of adding their four thousand spears to those of the legion, for both their sakes. He raised an eyebrow questioningly at Frontinius.

'And now, First Spear, before I call the other prefects to confer, your advice, please. Do we push forward to our meeting point with the legion, or make a more cautious approach? There could be ten thousand or more spears waiting for us out there.'

Frontinius pondered, rubbing his scalp.

'I say we hump forward to join with the Sixth as quickly as we can. Better to be part of a combined force than wait about out here for the barbarians to find us. The Ninth can scout forward half a mile in advance, make sure we don't fall into any nasty little traps.'

Equitius nodded his agreement, turning to walk away.

'Very well, I'll get the other cohorts ready to move. You'd better get the Ninth on the job.'

The day's advance was for the most part a non-event. The 9th went forward at a steady pace while individual tent parties were directed to any feature of the rolling ground capable of concealing an enemy. Every copse, every wrinkle in the ground, was investigated by nervous soldiers, their caution easing as the day grew older and still no sign of the enemy was found. The beaten path left by the warband's passage had turned gradually away to the north-west, while the cohorts' meeting point with the 6th lay directly to the west.

By the middle of the afternoon the wind had died away to nothing, and the soldiers were starting to get hot and irritable under the burden of their armour. Helmets were removed and hung around the troops' necks, allowing the sweat to evaporate from their scalps rather than soak into their helmet liners, and water skins became an increasing source of temptation when a centurion's back was turned. One of the questing tent parties, investigating a small clump of trees just off the line of march, beckoned Marcus and Dubnus forward with frantically waved hands, the rest of the century deploying to either side in guard positions. In the middle of the copse was a grim scene, already busy with flies and stinking of decay's onset. Half a dozen men lay dead, one with his throat cut untidily wide open, the others with combat wounds. Dubnus examined the bodies, looking at each one's blue tattoos with care.

'They're from the same tribe, but four of the bodies are from one family group, two from another. They must have quarrelled . . .'

He moved one of the bodies with his foot, pulling a hunting bow from an indignant cloud of flies, a quiver of a dozen heavy iron-tipped arrows tied to the weapon.

'. . . and they must have been in a hurry to leave to have missed *this*. I'd guess that some of the losers escaped, and the winners headed for the warband, eager to get their version of events in front of their tribal elders first.'

He strapped the bow across his back, having tested the tautness of its string. Frontinius came forward with the runner sent to fetch him, and surveyed the scene unhappily. He looked hard at the bodies, then nodded agreement to Dubnus.

'You're right, a family squabble by the look of things. This could have been a scouting party, or just a group of men on their way to join the warband, but either way, it tells us that we're too close to the main force for my comfort. We'll push on as planned, but I want extra vigilance from here.'

The rest of the afternoon, however, passed without incident, at least until the 9th spotted a line of horse-drawn carts against the dark green mass of the next line of hills, and a row of machines made tiny by the distance.

'Legion artillery train,' Morban grunted. 'The rest of them'll be on top of the hills digging out a camp while those lazy bastards sit on their arses.'

They stopped to wait for the cohorts to catch up with them, unwilling to advance out towards the line of bolt throwers and catapults until everyone knew exactly who they were. Legion artillerymen were notoriously quick to fire at almost anything that moved, and their weapons were capable of punching a bolt through a man at four hundred paces.

Once the cohorts had advanced to their position Frontinius took the 9th forward at a cautious pace, until a detachment of the legion's cavalry galloped over to investigate them. Their decurion nodded recognition, saluted Frontinius and pointed up the hillside.

'The Sixth's up there digging in, First Spear, and you're invited to join them as soon as possible. There's probably twenty thousand enemy spears within a half-day's march of here, and the legatus's keen to get everyone into defensive positions for the night.'

They marched past the supply train, eyeing the evil-looking bolt throwers, painted with names like 'Maneater' and 'Ribsplitter', and their lounging crews, then climbed the hill's long slope until they reached the crest, where a scene from a hundred field exercises greeted them. The legion's six thousand men were labouring like slaves, a steady flow of cut turfs flowing to the rampart building gangs. The 6th's camp prefect strode out to meet them, pointing over the temporary fort's rising walls to a point on the far side.

'Glad to see you, prefect, your last message put the wind up everyone. We'd like your cohorts on the eastern face, since that's the side where the slope's shallowest.'

Equitius shot a wry smile at Frontinius before replying.

'I'll take the fact that you want us to protect the most vulnerable face of the camp as a vote of confidence, Prefect. I presume that if we come under attack you'll consider yourselves invited to the party?'

Later, dug in and fed, their artillery placed around the camp and their watch fires set twice over to delude enemy scouts as to the size of their force until the camp seemed ablaze, the troops sat uneasily in their tent parties and centuries, mulling over the likelihood of action the next day. The older men passed down their wisdom, such as it was, to the younger troops, while officers and their chosen men circulated their commands, each seeking in his own way to bolster their morale. The circulation of officers was not restricted to the junior ranks either. Late in the evening Legatus Sollemnis walked into the Tungrians' lines, a dozen-man bodyguard walking about him with jealous eyes. He clasped hands with Equitius, and joined him in the headquarters tent for a cup of wine.

'So, are your men ready for tomorrow? We'll get our chance to measure our skills against theirs very soon now if I read the signs correctly.'

'Signs?'

'Didn't the camp prefect tell you? Sometimes I wonder how that man ever made it past centurion . . . Our cavalry scouts have the warband you've been following located, and under close watch, about ten thousand men strong. They've occupied an old hill fort, but without their own scouts they're blind, and we have freedom of tactical manoeuvre I never thought I'd enjoy on hostile ground. The original warband, the one Perennis located two days ago, is still thirty miles distant, and not showing any signs of moving yet. It's a chance to defeat the warbands piecemeal before they join together, and one I intend to take with both hands. We have the bastards that razed every fort on the North Road in our grasp my friend, and in the morning we'll give them a taste of the hammer and anvil.'

He unrolled a rough hand-drawn map of the area.

'We're here, about ten miles from the barbarian camp. Tomorrow I shall send your five cohorts and four of my own, under your command, around their left flank by *this* route, and send you into their rear. I will take the main body of the legion forward in frontal attack, with an approach to contact across *this* open area, using these two large woods as cover for as long as possible. Calgus will find spears whichever way he turns, and we shall have them bottled up for the slaughter.'

Equitius frowned.

'It's aggressive, that's clear enough. What about a reserve?'

Sollemnis nodded his understanding.

'I know, I've thought long and hard, but for a start we've got the Petriana, and your formation will act as a reserve of sorts. The simple truth is that this thing's balanced on a knife-edge – we need to get at them before the first warband joins up and makes them too big to tackle without the other legions. If we can exploit their lack of scouting ability to hit them without warning, we can get the job done quickly and efficiently.'

The other man frowned again, uncomfortable at having to tell his friend his misgivings about the plan.

'And you're basing all this on the reports of our scouts. Who presumably are still under the command of your senior tribune . . . ?'

'Yes, and the answer to your unspoken question is just as it was before. Do I trust him not to play a dangerous game once all this is over? Of course not! But he's proved adept with his Asturians, better than the Petriana since he took over the task to let Licinius rest his men. He's put me in a position to cripple this revolt with a single decisive blow, and if I fail to take that opportunity I'll find myself recalled to Rome before you can say "imperial death warrant for failing to put down barbarian uprising". What would you do?'

Equitius nodded his agreement, although his face lost little of its pensive cast.

'If you want an honest opinion, Gaius, I'd say it's risky. There's no proper reserve, the advance to contact takes your force past two large woods that could hide thousands of men, and it's all based on reports from a man I wouldn't trust for a second . . . but I take your point about the risks of delaying.'

'And if we catch them in the open, without time to form

up, we can grind them to shreds between our shield walls. It's a risk, but it's one I have to take. Will you take it with me?'

Equitius put a hand on his friend's shoulder, looking hard into his eyes.

'As if you even need to ask . . .'

Sollemnis nodded, his lips pursed with gratitude and emotion.

'Thank you. And now, I would appreciate a tour of your unit. You'll understand that there's one officer in particular I would appreciate meeting, if only briefly. I haven't seen the boy since he turned twelve apart from a brief meeting under difficult circumstances . . .'

The prefect raised an eyebrow.

'Are you sure that's wise? It might be better to let that sleeping dog lie.'

'I understand your concern. Look, it'll do your boys good to see that I'm out and about, and I'll only be with each century for a minute or two. I'd just like to see him once more before we confront the barbarians. By this time tomorrow one or both of us could be face down in the dirt – I'd prefer to have seen my son the way I want to remember him, rather than the way circumstances might force upon us. Please.'

Equitius relented, shaking his head slightly.

'Being too damned persuasive got you that particular problem in the first place, I seem to remember. You always were too good at getting what you wanted. I'll have Frontinius walk you around the cohort, a brief tour of inspection. Don't give the lad any reason to suspect the truth, though. The last thing I need on the night before a major action is a centurion wondering whether his dead father really was his father, wouldn't you agree?'

The First Spear met the legatus outside the cohort's

command tent as bidden a few minutes later. He saluted formally, and then stood to attention.

'Legatus, I believe you have requested a tour of my cohort?' Sollemnis smiled at him, waving a dismissive hand.

'Relax, First Spear, I just want to see what state my troops are in for tomorrow's fun and games.'

'We attack tomorrow, sir? Without waiting for the other legions?'

'Yes, and I've just had this conversation with your prefect. There are some aspects of the plan which are less than perfect, but if we destroy this one warband then we can put Calgus on the defensive. And we might well find that a disheartened barbarian army melts away in the face of a successful outcome tomorrow.'

Frontinius kept his mouth shut and Sollemnis, sensing his disquiet, extended a hand to point into the camp.

'So, shall we have a look at your men?'

They walked into the camp, heading for the closest watch fire.

As arranged at their last meeting, before the warband's rampage to the south, Calgus went to the hill fort's eastern entrance shortly after dark had fallen. His army was gathered inside the tall earth rampart's wide perimeter, taking full advantage of the protection afforded by the massive earthwork. He had, with some trepidation, agreed to the Roman traitor's suggestion that he bring the warband to its fullest possible strength in this ancient place, knowing that his army would be in deep trouble if the three enemy legions took them by surprise. Now he waited in the torchlit darkness with his bodyguard clustered close around him, eager to see if the man was as good as his word.

After a few minutes' wait a voice called softly out of the darkness.

'Bring him to me. Don't damage him.'

Four men walked forward into the night with torches, finding Perennis waiting for them fifty yards down the road, his open hands raised to show that he was unarmed. He walked back to where the barbarian leader waited, seemingly as relaxed as ever despite the spears pointing at him from all angles.

'Calgus. I see your hunger for victory has overwhelmed the risk that I might be leading you into a trap?'

'I have more than twenty thousand men at my back, Roman. I doubt there's a trap you could spring that I couldn't batter to pieces.'

Perennis smiled, the gesture half hidden in the torchlight.

'I warned you a week ago that the southern legions were farther advanced in their progress than you believed. Now I can tell you that they've reached the Wall, and are hurrying to join with the Sixth Legion. Once they've joined your chance to take advantage of my plan will be at an end, and you and I will be firm enemies rather than allies of convenience. I estimate that you have until noon tomorrow in which to strike, and no more time than that. We must conclude our business quickly if you're not to find yourself rudely interrupted by the Second and Twentieth Legions. So what's it to be, bloody victory or an ignominious retreat back into the hills? You know you can't face them in open battle.'

Calgus turned away, staring out into the darkness, his features unreadable.

'What do you propose? Even a single legion will cause my people grievous losses if I allow them to face us in line of battle with the support of their auxiliary cohorts. Have you brought my army here just to tell me we've no alternative but to run, or give battle in the very way that has always resulted in our defeat? Because if you have . . .'

The Roman interrupted him impatiently.

'I *propose* the ambush that's been in my mind since the first time I scouted this ground six months ago. I *propose* your warriors taking the legion by surprise while it's still deployed for the march. That way you can strike from both sides, and avoid the danger of the cohorts getting into line. There's a place not far from here that fits the bill perfectly, funnily enough.'

Later on in the evening, with most of the troops bedded down if not actually sleeping, and the legatus safely back among his own men, Equitius invited Frontinius to join him in a cup of wine, as was often their habit in the field. They sat in the flickering lamplight and talked as friends, the artificial restrictions of their ranks temporarily abandoned.

'So what did Sollemnis say while you were out walking the cohort with him?'

Frontinius took a sip of his wine.

'After we'd spoken to a couple of the centurions he asked me what I really thought about his intention to attack Calgus tomorrow.'

Equitius grimaced.

'And you said?'

'I told him that his role of late seems to consist mainly of putting my cohort in harm's way.'

Equitius grimaced again.

'Ouch. And what did he say to that?'

'He apologised for sending young Marcus to us, explained how he had no option under the circumstances. Then he asked what I thought of the boy. I told him that it was an unfair question *under the circumstances*, and that he should form his own opinions when he met him. Well, we walked into the Ninth's area just after that, got challenged very smartly, had a chat with young Two Knives and a few of his men, made our excuses and moved on. We can't have been there for more than two or three minutes, but it was enough for the legatus. He stopped to wipe his eyes in the shadow of a tent. When he spoke to me again he was obviously choked up by seeing his boy again. And, bearing in mind that he might not get to see him again, that seemed understandable. Now, Prefect, show me exactly what it is that our august leader plans for the morning.'

He stared at the map spread across the table in front of them, putting a finger on the position where the barbarian warband was reported to be camped.

'They're here . . . ?'

'As reported by the younger Perennis, yes.'

'Hmm. We break camp at dawn, make a swift march to contact . . . can't be more than six or seven miles . . . and if they're in the same place when we arrive it should be a reasonably straightforward fight unless they decide to run away. Our ten thousand men against their ten thousand men, and us with the advantages of at least partial surprise and able to fight on our own terms.'

'Yes. Although you've failed to guess one aspect of the plan. He intends splitting his force into two parts, hammer and anvil. We're not going to let them run away, we're going for a battle of annihilation.'

Frontinius's eyebrows rose.

'And you think that's wise? Risk them catching and defeating each of our smaller forces in turn?'

'He's set on it. The fact that Perennis's scouts have set the whole thing up for him doesn't leave him with much alternative from his point of view.'

Frontinius shook his head.

'Well, that goes against the style of warfare that I was taught. If it all goes right we could kill lots of barbarians tomorrow, but if anything goes wrong, if they've moved since the last scout report, or if there's more of them around that we haven't found, we could both be decorating Calgus's roof beams in a week or two. I'd better go and treat this tired old body to a few hours' sleep.'

The legion and its supporting cohorts snatched a hasty breakfast in the dull grey light of dawn, and were on the march less than thirty minutes after the sun had cleared the horizon. Taking another calculated risk, Sollemnis had decided that they would camp in the same place that evening, and thus avoided the lost time of actually striking camp, leaving their tents standing ready for the legion's return. The long column of men snaked north, led by a detachment of the Asturian cavalry who had returned from their place watching the warband late the previous night. Only Perennis and a few picked men had remained in place, and they would have pulled out at first light, heading for a prearranged meeting point to provide the legatus with a last-minute briefing on the warband's dispositions.

While the Tungrians were far back down the order of march, back behind the 6th's last cohort, Equitius had ridden away with Sollemnis's officers to participate in the final orders group that would start once Perennis and his scouts rejoined the column. As the legion moved forward he stopped his horse for a moment to take the sight in, turning in the saddle to stare back down the line of soldiers marching four abreast up the rough track that had been chosen as their approach route for the battle to come. Sollemnis ranged up alongside him, his horse steaming slightly in the chilly dawn air. He recognised a cohort's senior centurion and saluted gravely, getting a brief nod and hurried salute back from the officer as he passed.

'It isn't often you'll see a whole legion bashing along this fast. Even on exercise the centurions have to lay the vine stick on pretty hard to get their boys really sweating, and yet just look at them this morning . . .'

The hard-bitten legionaries were slogging past them at a pace reserved for those times when the legion needed to be somewhere else very quickly indeed, and some of them were clearly already suffering from the exertion. They had been forbidden to sing this morning for fear of making too much noise – any song would in any case have quickly been blown out by their blistering pace. Equitius could already see faces in the ranks that were stretched by the effort of sucking in enough air to keep men and their sixty-pound load of armour and weapons moving so quickly. Another century passed, the officer ranging easily alongside his men with one eye on the road and the other on his people, sparing a quick glance and a sardonic smile for the officers sitting comfortably on their horses. Other glances lacked the hint of humour and were simply surly in the face of such relative luxury.

'My officers were about as happy with the prospect of today's battle as you were last night. They also asked about our lack of a defined reserve, and some of the senior centurions were quite vocal on the subject. If anything goes wrong, Mars protect us, there'll be a long queue of them ready to testify that they warned me about the dangers.'

Equitius nodded sagely.

'Quite possibly including myself, if you have the misfortune to end up with your head on the end of a spear. But if we succeed . . .'

'Ah, if we succeed, the old saying comes into play. You know, "victory is a child with a thousand fathers . . ."?'

'So, first father of today's triumph, where are we holding the orders group before splitting into two forces?'

'Two more miles up the road, if Perennis is at the spot he's chosen to meet us.'

They rode on and, as expected, Perennis was indeed

waiting for them at the preordained place, a fork in the road. His Asturians tarried a short distance away, an evil-looking decurion and half a dozen horsemen, while he walked forward and saluted Sollemnis with precision. For a man who had spent the night at best rolled in his cloak and sleeping in a ditch, he looked fresh and ready for the day.

'Legatus, I have a report for you from the point of decision.'

Sollemnis nodded, gesturing his officers to gather round before motioning Perennis to begin.

'Sir, the barbarian warband is still in the same location and apparently suspects nothing. Their strength is estimated at ten thousand men, and when we left they were waking up for the day, with cooking fires lit and no sign of preparation for combat. If you still intend attacking, I would say that our chances of success are almost total.'

Sollemnis looked at his other officers as he replied.

'Thank you, Tigidius Perennis this is good news. Gentlemen, I have decided to attack as we planned last night. The first six cohorts of the Sixth will advance in column across the open valley to the enemy's front, using the woods to the right and left as cover for the move. This advance will be carried out at the battle march. On my command we will deploy into battle line and assault the barbarian hill fort. The legion artillery will accompany us, and will provide support from the flanks, if it can be deployed quickly enough.

'At the same time, the Sixth's remaining four cohorts, plus our five auxiliary cohorts, this force to be commanded by Prefect Equitius, will advance around the right flank. This force will take position ready to strike at the barbarian left and rear once the main force is engaged. The signal for them to attack will be three loud trumpet blasts followed by the advance signal. If the flank force is detected, or sees anything to indicate an alerted enemy, Prefect Equitius will sound three blasts followed by the stand fast signal, and will deploy into line ready for battle. In this case I will judge a response from the tactical situation to hand. My intention is to draw the barbarians into a battle and then close the door behind them. Gentlemen, we're not just going to defeat this collection of savages masquerading as soldiers, we're going to rip them limb from limb. Tell your men that this is going to be a victory that they'll sing about for many years to come. That is all.'

His officers turned to go back to their places.

'Ah, one more thing.'

They turned back to face him again, faces expectant.

'I hear there's talk in the legion about what happened when the North Road forts fell – Roman citizens, soldiers and civilians, tarred and torched, and the gods only know what indignities carried out on them beforehand. I expect that you've all heard men calling for equally harsh treatment to be given in return whenever we get the opportunity . . . ?'

They waited expectantly.

'I have to say that I agree wholeheartedly. Tell your commands that there will no mercy shown to any of the enemy attempting to surrender or escape. Any prisoners that *are* taken will be processed to my headquarters, and will be crucified this evening. Their legs will *not* be broken and they will be left to die slowly with no exceptions save one. If we take Calgus alive, he'll be paraded through Rome before he feels the strangler's cord tighten at his windpipe. That is all.'

Equitius saddled up and rode back down the long column of resting legionaries, most of them lying on their backs, recovering from their exertions of the previous hour, until he reached the 7th cohort and called for the senior centurions of the last four cohorts in the column. With the officers gathered around him he confirmed the orders from Sollemnis, and told them to get their men moving. The cohorts got ready to move without any of the shouting and chivvying usual in some legions, their air of quiet determination and competence reassuring Equitius that his temporary command would perform well enough when battle was joined.

The nine cohorts headed up the track past the remainder of the 6th, past Sollemnis, who watched them pass with a pensive expression, turning right at the fork on to another track. If their scout's intelligence was correct, this road would take them along the edge of the shallow valley through which the 6th would advance to battle, round the barbarian left flank and into the position from which their attack could be launched. Equitius scanned the horizon until he saw the landmark he'd been told to look for, then reined his horse in alongside the senior centurion of the leading cohort.

'Head for that wood on the horizon, and keep your eyes open for barbarian scouts. If we're compromised I'd rather have some time to do something about it. I'm going back down the column for a chat with the auxiliaries. If you get to the wood before I'm back up here, break the march for a ten-minute rest.'

The other man nodded his understanding, and Equitius turned his horse to ride back down the column. He found the Tungrians sweating away in their place behind the last legionary cohort, and rode alongside Frontinius for a moment.

'Is the cohort ready?'

His bald head beaded with moisture, Frontinius grimaced up at his superior.

'As ready as we'll ever be. Let's just hope the scouts have got it right.'

Turning again, Equitius rode to the column's rear, stopping to talk to his fellow prefects. Each of them was grimly determined, their men looking much the same as did his own, a combination of warlike posture and underlying nerves. In the distance to their rear he could see the main force column snaking away from its rest position, heading for the side of the nameless shallow valley. Back at the front of the column the wood was drawing closer, and when it was less than half a mile away he spurred his horse forward to investigate before his men arrived.

The trees were silent and empty, with no hint of an enemy presence, and Equitius climbed down from the horse to take in the scene in the valley below, creeping cautiously to avoid making his silhouette stand out above the steadily brightening skyline. The wood was positioned at the valley's head, a small stream flowing down through it and across the almost flat expanse below. Two larger woods half filled the space, one to his right half a mile distant down the slight slope, the other half as much again to his left, and he stared intently at them for a long moment. If there were to be any threat to the 6th's approach march, it would surely come from within the densely packed trees. Nothing moved. Indeed, the landscape was preternaturally still, without even birdsong, and a vague sense of unease permeated his thinking as he watched the shadows imperceptibly shortening under the rising sun's gaze.

He turned back to look for the approaching column, and saw the leading troops less than four hundred paces distant. Remounted, he cantered the horse across to them and ordered the senior centurion to rest his men there rather than risk having them appear on the skyline and alerting any zealous barbarian foot scouts. As the first centuries fell out for their breather, a party of horsemen came into view, hurrying up the line of soldiers, pursued by the inevitable obscene catcalls. As the group approached, he realised that it was Perennis and his Asturian escort, headed by the glowering decurion. The legion tribune rode up and, without preamble or greeting, launched into his orders.

'A message from the legatus. He's received new intelligence

and has therefore changed the plan. The Sixth Legion cohorts are detached from your command, as are the Second Tungrian, Raetian, Aquitani and Frisian cohorts. I am to lead these units to form a blocking position to the rear of the main force, while your cohort is to remain here and provide a watch on the woods to the right of the main line of march. You're to keep the cohort well away from the valley's edge, at least four hundred paces, and you personally are commanded to watch the valley from cover. Any enemy movement to the rear of these woods, which you will see before the main force, is to be alerted to the legatus by the triple sounding of a trumpet followed by the stand fast signal as previously agreed.'

Equitius stared at the man in disbelief. To change a battle plan halfway through the approach to contact was downright dangerous, and went against everything that both he and Sollemnis had been taught. Questions flooded his mind.

'What new intelligence? What could have changed so dramatically as to invalidate the original plan?'

Perennis looked at him with irritation and urgency, pulling a tablet from the tunic beneath his armour.

'Prefect Equitius, I am neither granted the time nor ordered to explain what's going on. Time is of the essence now, and I must carry out my orders without delay. Read this, and you will see that my orders are lawful.'

He wheeled his horse away, calling to the 7th Cohort's senior centurion.

'Decimus, you old bastard, get your grunts ready to march right now. We're heading to the west to get into position to guard the Sixth's backside!'

The officer looked at Equitius and shrugged, entirely used to the legion way of doing business.

'They're legal orders, right, Prefect?'

Equitius scanned the tablet carefully. While the writing

could have been anyone's, the mark of Sollemnis's seal was unmistakable.

'Yes, First Spear, they are.'

'In that case, sir, we'll see you later. Seventh cohort, *on your feet!*'

The long column started moving again, the line of march swinging back to the west as it reached the place where Equitius was sitting unhappily on his horse. The Tungrians fell out of the column as they came up ten minutes later, the other auxiliary prefects stopping briefly to sympathise as they passed, and then the column was gone, marching out of sight behind a small hill.

Frontinius walked up to Equitius with a perplexed expression.

'All I heard was that we were to stay here. What the fuck's going on, Prefect?'

Equitius climbed down from his horse, passing the message tablet to his deputy.

'You tell me. One moment we're marching to take part in a pitched battle and massacre ten thousand blue-faced savages, the next I'm standing here with my phallus in my hand just in case something that those scouts assured Sollemnis couldn't happen does happen. Something smells very wrong here. Anyway, you'd better brief your officers, pull the cohort back to four hundred yards from the crest. I'll stay here to watch the valley.'

He walked unhappily away.

Frontinius took a good look around, taking in their new surroundings, and then called Marcus to him.

'Right, Centurion, you can take a tent party and scout out that wood for me. I want to be sure there are no nasty little surprises waiting for us in there, and I want to know anything else that's worth knowing about it. Keep below the skyline and don't go anywhere near the edge of the trees, I don't want anyone spotting you. Dismissed.'

Marcus gathered Dubnus and a tent party to him, leading them along the edge of the wood with deliberate care. Dubnus took the hunting bow he'd found the previous day from its place on his back and nocked an arrow, the cruel barbed head glinting in the sunshine. Close to the narrow stream that flowed down into the trees they found a path, two men wide but showing no recent sign of passage by either boot or bare feet. Thorns and branches grew across it at intervals.

'Hunter's path . . .' Dubnus mused. '. . . there must be a source of game near.'

Marcus took a look down through the archway of trees, down a path that ran arrow straight to the thumbnail-sized speck of daylight at the far end.

'Chosen, you're best at this sort of thing, scout forward for us. Cyclops, you come with me to provide the chosen man with support if he needs it. The rest of you squat down here and keep out of sight. If I call, get down this path as fast as you can and be ready to fight. Otherwise, *don't* move!'

Dubnus slid into the trees, deep shadow still covering the wood's floor out of the thin early light. The smell of pine needles filled the air, and insects buzzed lazily at the intrusion. He stepped softly down the path, sweeping the arrow's head slowly from side to side as if using the point to sense for enemies. Fifty yards down the path the wood was utterly silent, the trees undisturbed by animal or breeze, the exit at the far end of the path a coin-sized arch of light. Something moved off to the right, almost imperceptibly, and the arrow tracked round to cover that arc, holding steady as Dubnus bent the bow back the last inches to its full tension, with only two fingers stopping its explosive release of energy. A hare bolted from cover, weaving across the needle-coated floor, twisted in mid-leap and fell to rest transfixed by three feet of hunting arrow. Marcus and Cyclops, following up ten yards behind, breathed out long sighs of released tension.

Dubnus plucked out another arrow and nocked it to the string in one fluid motion.

Five paces from the path's end he stopped, motioning the other men forward. Marcus squatted behind him, peering over his shoulder. Through the arch of trees he could see most of the valley, but was sure that they would be invisible inside the path's dark tunnel. The long grass that grew across the valley waved in idle ripples in the gentle breeze, while the trees in the large woods to right and left waved their branches fitfully. Dubnus stared intently at the scene, something as yet unidentified nagging at his sense of what felt right. To their left a sudden movement caught the eye, men coming over the side of the valley and spilling out on to the slope, a column of men moving fast and with purpose.

'The Sixth.'

Marcus nodded, watching their progress while Dubnus scanned the valley again, his gaze coming back to the woods that were piquing his suspicion without providing a basis for real concern. The legion ground across the valley at a fast pace, almost running now, centurions urging their men on with encouragement and imprecation, desperate to close the distance and get into line, knowing the vulnerability of a column in the face of a determined attack. The woods rippled their branches blamelessly in the breeze, catching his eye again, and as he stared at them the realisation hit him with a force that turned his legs to stone for a long second.

'The trees.'

Marcus looked over his shoulder, seeing only massed greenery.

'What?'

'Look at the branches. They're in the fucking branches!'

He leapt to his feet and sprinted back up the path, leaving a bemused Marcus looking for something his chosen man had spotted, but he could not work out what it was. Then Cyclops whistled low behind him.

'The branches, Two Knives, they're not moving together. The bloody barbarians are in the trees!'

'This is the point of decision, sir, these next two or three minutes.'

The 4th Cohort's First Spear wiped a hand across his sweat-beaded forehead, his legs pounding away on the soft grass to keep up the legion's pace. Sollemnis nodded gravely, recognising the truth in the panted words. A legion in column in close country was a notoriously vulnerable situation. Varus had proved it at the Battle of the German Forest by advancing three legions into a massive and well-prepared ambush by German tribesmen, red-haired giants not unlike the present enemy, and had paid with his own life and eighteen thousand other men's besides. Deployed into line, the legion could quickly reorient to meet any threat, could employ its disciplined fighting power against an enemy and exchange lives at a rate of three dead barbarians to one lost legionary. In column, with heavy cover to either side, a clever enemy could attack the legion's rear no matter which way the marching men turned to fight. As long as Perennis was right, and they could reach the line of attack undetected, all would be well . . .

He turned back to look down the marching column. The 6th Cohort had cleared the valley side. The head of the column was now level with the wood to their left, and was swinging to take full advantage of the cover of the one to their right.

'Five minutes, I'd say, then we'll be out of the cover of that wood and start deploying.'

He'd ordered that the column break out into two three-cohort-long lines four men deep, with the rearmost line ready to feed men into the grinder as barbarian axes and swords progressively ate into the front ranks.

'Anyone from the front rank that survives the day will be awarded the assault medal. With ten thousand barbarians to hack through and a hill fort to storm, I'd say they'll have earned it.'

His senior centurion nodded agreement. The defeated barbarians were likely to fall back into their fort, and even with the bolt throwers set up on the flanks a few hundred yards back, spitting their foot-long bolts into the hill fort to discourage the barbarian archers, it was going to be an unpleasant day for the men going face to face with the warband.

The column's head was approaching the right-hand wood now, three minutes of vulnerability left, and then he'd take a victory that would stamp out this rebellion and put fear into the barbarians that would keep them quiet north of the Wall for another generation. Calgus, if he were taken alive, would be carried off in chains and paraded in front of the emperor before a staged execution. If not, his head would have to do. He knew of native scouts who understood the art of preserving a dead man's head for years, and he would have Perennis take it to Commodus with the 6th's Legion's badge stamped on to the dead man's forehead, cement his place in imperial favour and kill the rumours of disloyalty for good. He smiled to himself at the image. Perhaps he ought to have Perennis dealt with too . . .

From the ridge-line to the north of the advancing legion cohorts a trumpet note sounded, catching the attention of every man in the column, repeated itself, then sounded a third time, the note switching into the stand fast call and making his guts contract. It was the signal that he'd ordered Equitius to give if they were detected, or found an alerted enemy, but it was coming from the wrong place.

With a sudden rattling hammer of iron against armour plate hundreds of arrows ripped into the legion's ranks, dropping dozens of unprepared legionaries in writhing agony or sudden death. The column dithered for a moment, another rain of arrows striking home, and this time Sollemnis saw what he'd missed in the surprise of the first volley – that they were being fired from above head height, negating the defensive protection of the legionaries' shields. A legionary near him spun and fell, an arrow lodged deep in his throat, another jerking and then toppling stiffly backwards to the ground with a feathered shaft protruding between the cheek-pieces of his helmet. The hissing passage of an arrow past his left ear warned that he was the archers' target.

'They're in the trees!'

At least one centurion had come to the same conclusion, and several centuries started to form testudos, shields held to side and overhead to frustrate the attacks, getting ready to charge into the trees and dig out the barbarian archers at close quarters. Then, as the situation started to stabilise after the first shock of attack, a thick wave of tribesmen bounded from the woods to either side of the stalled column with a berserk howl that lifted the hairs on the back of the legatus's neck, pouring out of their cover in an apparently unending stream of rage to charge into the nearest cohorts. Swinging swords and axes with hate-fuelled ferocity, the barbarians smashed into the unformed line, in an instant exploding the legion's carefully trained fighting tactic of shield wall and stabbing sword into thousands of individual duels. Sollemnis knew only too well that these were fights in which an infantryman armed with a short infantry-pattern sword was at a disadvantage faced with a weapon of twice the length.

He regained his wits, drew his sword and bellowed above the din.

'Defensive circles! Form defensive circles! The flank force will take them in the rear if we can defend long enough!'

The 4th cohort's senior centurion, his men suffering under the iron rain of barbarian arrows, but as yet not engaged, bellowed to his officers to follow the order, and Sollemnis walked into the protection of their shields with his bodyguard as the circle closed, looking across the battlefield to see two other cohorts fighting to achieve the same result under a press of barbarian attackers. The rest of the legion was already fighting in broken order, with little hope of regaining any meaningful formation before the battle's end.

Inside the circle a dozen wounded legionaries were being seen to by the cohort's medical officer, most with arrows protruding from their throats and faces. The medic looked closely at a stricken chosen man, took gauge of the wound's severity, shook his head decisively and moved on to the next casualty. The dying man, with an arrow's shaft sticking out of his neck, and blood jetting from the wound, put a shuddering hand to his sword's hilt, half drew the weapon, then stopped moving as the life ran out of him. Sollemnis wrenched his eyes from the scene, striding to the First Spear. The veteran soldier was calmly scanning the battle around them with a professional eye, looking for an advantage despite their desperate situation.

'Situation?'

'There's more than ten thousand men out there, more like twenty. We've been *had*! Looks like the last three cohorts are already in pieces. Ourselves, the Fifth and Sixth managed to get into defensive formations, but once the others have been polished off they'll make short enough work of us, or just stand off and let their archers pepper us until we're too weak to resist. If the flanking force doesn't get stuck in soon we're all going to die . . .'

The legion's eagle standard-bearer stood close, his own

sword drawn, clearly determined to sell his own life in defence of the emperor's eagle. An arrow clattered off his helmet, another hitting the standard's eagle with a hollow *thwock*, making the man duck reflexively, his eyebrows raised at his legatus in mute comment. Sollemnis nodded grimly, then turned to stare up at the ridge-line where the alarm signal had sounded. A few figures stood silhouetted on the crest, apparently watching the battle below. The standard-bearer, a man of seniority in the legion and well known to the legatus, pushed his way to Sollemnis's side, disdaining the stream of arrows directed at the eagle.

'Why don't they attack, sir? There's another nine cohorts up there, and in good order.'

The legatus shook his head in puzzlement, hearing the screams of his command's dismemberment from all around.

'I don't know, but how Tigidius Perennis and his Asturians scouted this ground as safe for the approach is . . .'

A sudden insight gripped his guts hard, testing his sphincter with a sudden push that he barely managed to control. Perennis. Of course. The other warband had clearly never stayed in place as he'd been briefed, the brazen lie tempting him into a move whose audacity would clearly be judged as suicidal with the luxury of hindsight. He drew his sword and picked up a dead man's shield, tugging down his ornate helmet to be sure the back of his neck was protected.

'Very well, gentlemen, if we're going to die today, let's make sure we give these blue-faced bastards a decent fight to sing about. Wounds of honour, Sixth Legion. *Wounds of honour!*'

Watching the slaughter below, Equitius shook his head with fascinated horror.

'There must be something we can do.'

Frontinius replied in tones dulled by resignation to the facts.

'Yes, we can parade on the crest and in all likelihood the men down there will look up, laugh at us and get on with butchering the Sixth. Or we can advance down the slope into the battle and be dead inside ten minutes. You're looking at a doomed legion, Prefect, something few men have seen and even fewer have lived to describe. The Sixth's standard will be carried away into the northern mountains and become an object of wonder for the tribes, most likely with your friend Sollemnis's head to accompany it. He made the decision to attack across that valley; he changed our role at the critical moment; now he's paying for those mistakes the hard way . . .'

Equitius nodded unhappily.

'I just don't see how he could have got it so wrong. The man was a senior tribune in the war against the Marcomani, took command of a legion with a battlefield promotion when his legatus dropped dead in the middle of an action, and fought them brilliantly to rout twice his own strength of barbarians. It isn't a mistake he ended up running Northern Command . . . so how the bloody hell do we end up with *this*?'

The 6th's remaining three cohorts were creeping together, now under attack by thousands of barbarians and seeking to combine their strengths. A horn sounded, and the attackers drew back from combat, leaving the field clear for their archers to pour arrows into the compressed masses of legionaries. After a dozen volleys from the archers the horn sounded twice more, and the Britons charged in again, swords and axes glinting brightly in the morning sun as they went about their destructive work. Even at that distance the smell of blood and faeces was now reaching the watching soldiers, as the scale of the slaughter mounted. Equitius heard the sound of approaching hoofs, and turned to see Perennis and his escort approaching again. The tribune reined his horse in and took in the view from the valley's edge for a moment before speaking.

'Well, well. It would seem that our legatus has got himself into a bit of a pickle.'

Equitius stared up at him with narrowed eyes, seeing the sardonic smile playing about his face.

'Shouldn't you be worrying about bringing up the reinforcements, Tribune?'

The other man sat back in his saddle, sharing an amused glance with the decurion.

'It might have made a difference when the barbarians first attacked, a few thousand armed men piling down into the battle from up here, but not now, thank you, Prefect Equitius. Those six cohorts are all but finished, and I don't think that tossing another nine after them would be a particularly positive step, do you? At least this way I still have most of a legion's strength to command until the reinforcements arrive from Gaul.'

'You? A junior tribune? An equestrian in command of a legion?'

'Oh yes, didn't I mention my imperial warrant?'

He reached into a pocket and pulled out a scroll, tossing it down to Equitius. The prefect read it, taking in the imperial seal and the wide range of power it bestowed upon Perennis.

'I particularly like the sentence that says I should take command of the Sixth Legion should Legatus Sollemnis be found incapable of his task. I'd say he'll reach a state of incapability some time quite soon, so while I may not be of senatorial class, I will be exercising the power granted to me by the Emperor . . .'

Frontinius leaned over to Marcus, muttering quietly into his ear.

'Get yourself back over to the cohort. Be ready to bring your century over here in a hurry.'

'. . . And so, from this moment I'm assuming command. I'll incorporate the auxiliary cohorts into my legion to bolster our strength, but not *your* cohort, Prefect. You and your people have a special place in my plans. Stay where you are, Marcus Valerius Aquila, no trying to creep away when you think nobody's looking!'

Marcus stopped, turning slowly to look up at Perennis.

'Yes, I've known that you took refuge with these half-savages and their disloyal prefect for a while now. Your supply officer was very forthcoming one night in the camp at Cauldron Pool, when the decurion here applied the tip of a dagger to his throat. Did you really think that you could hide with these bumpkins for ever? All that you've done is bring your own disaster down on this entire cohort. Just as Legatus Sollemnis has paid the ultimate price for his treacherous attempt to hide you, so will this collection of semi-barbarian traitors!'

Dubnus put a hand behind his back, and muttered the word 'axe' quietly over his shoulder to Cyclops. The weapon slid from its place in the small of his back, the handle slapping unnoticed on to his palm, its comfortingly familiar wood rubbed smooth by years of handling. Perennis nodded to the stone-faced decurion, who jumped down from his horse and drew his sword. The other cavalrymen watched intently, arrows nocked to their bows, ignoring the single tent party of men standing in a huddle to their left. Perennis leant out of his saddle, pointing towards the wood that Marcus and his men had recently scouted.

'And now, gentlemen, your orders. The First Tungrians will establish a defensive position on the slope below that wood, and prevent the barbarians from breaking out of the valley by that route for as long as possible. There is to be no retreat from the position, which must be held at all costs and to the last man. You, First Spear, will command the cohort, since I am now declaring a sentence of death on your prefect for his treachery in harbouring an enemy of the emperor and the state. I could be more thorough in my punishment, but the rest of you will obviously be dead soon enough.'

Equitius scowled up at Perennis, full realisation of the true nature of the last hour's events striking him.

'You've just thrown six legion cohorts into a barbarian trap to get rid of one man that was in your way? And now you'll casually toss away eight hundred more spears because one innocent victim of Rome's descent into despotism takes shelter among them?'

Perennis smiled broadly.

'Your friend Sollemnis is reaping the crop he's sown, and so will you all, soon enough. The rest is detail. We'll go on the defensive for a while, Rome will send in a legion or two from Gaul, the Sixth will be reinforced back to full strength, and all will be as it should be. Besides, *you've* got more pressing matters to worry about. Decurion, execute the prefect.'

Frontinius half drew his sword, stopping as half a dozen drawn bows swung in his direction. Equitius put his hands on his hips, and straightened his back in readiness. The decurion took a step forward, raising his long cavalry sword for the executioner's blow before his eyes widened with shock as Dubnus's throwing axe smashed into his back. The heavy axe blade's weight punched through his armour, chopping through his spine and into the organs clustered behind it. A gout of blood spilled from his open mouth in a scarlet flood as he sank forward on to his knees, his hands helplessly seeking the source of the sudden rush of enervating pain. Before any of the cavalrymen could react, Dubnus was among them, his sword flashing as he struck at one and then another. Marcus and Frontinius drew their swords and charged in alongside him.

One of the horsemen loosed an arrow at Frontinius, the missile's iron head flicking off his helmet just as Marcus hacked at the man's leg with a fierce downward cut, his sword severing the limb just above the knee and chopping into the horse's ribs with the force of the blow. The animal reared up, tossing the crippled cavalryman from his horned saddle, then kicked out hard with its back legs in protest at the pain, catapulting another Asturian from his mount with his chest caved in.

Marcus was knocked to one side as Cyclops jumped in front of him, raising his shield to block an arrow from a horseman the young centurion had failed to notice in the melee. At less than twenty paces' range the missile punched through his shield's layered wood and leather, the iron head transfixing his shield arm and drawing an agonised grimace from the one-eyed soldier. Pivoting on his left leg with a swelling bellow of rage, Cyclops slung his spear with deadly accuracy into the horseman's chest as he reached back for another arrow. The throw's huge power punched through a weak point in the cavalryman's mail shirt, scattering a handful of broken rings from the point of impact and thrusting the spear's steel point deep into the horseman's lungs. Eyes rolling upwards, he fell backwards over the side of his horse and vanished under the hoofs of the horses surrounding him. Cyclops pointed to his one good eye, shouting over the fight's swelling volume.

'Less stabbing and more looking, young sir.'

He drew his sword, nodding to Marcus before charging into the whirling melee in search of another target for his wrath. Perennis kicked his horse's sides hard, galloping out of the knot of infantrymen which was growing bigger and nastier by the second as the rest of the tent party took on the Asturians with their spears. He was thirty paces distant when Dubnus's arrow slammed through the back of his neck an inch above the top of his cuirass's protection, and stayed in the saddle for another five seconds before collapsing stiffly over its hindquarters to land in a heap on the turf. The few remaining Asturians bolted, thrashing their horses to escape as the fastest of the 9th Century's men arrived on the scene seeking targets for their unblooded spears. Marcus was the first man to reach Perennis, coming up short when he saw the arrowhead protruding from the tribune's throat, and the man's desperate attempts to breathe. Frontinius ran up a moment later, took one look and turned away with a grim smile.

'He's got two minutes, five at the best. Say hello to the ferryman for us, Perennis, you'll be across the river a while before we get there.'

Equitius walked up to them, a haunted look on his face. Frontinius slapped him on the arm.

'Cheer up, Prefect, it isn't every day that you're condemned to death and then reprieved inside a minute.'

'Not such a reprieve, First Spear. I . . .'

His head lifted as he spotted a movement in the middle distance, horsemen moving through the waving grass, a long white banner twisting proudly in the breeze. He smiled wanly at the sight.

'I see Licinius retains his impeccable sense of timing . . .'

A single decurius of the Petriana rode up to them, Prefect Licinius dismounting before his horse had stopped moving. Grim faced, he stared down at the fighting below for a moment before turning back to speak, taking in the scene in front of him as he did.

'Gentlemen, I . . .'

The sight of the slowly choking Perennis left him speechless for a moment.

'Who shot him?'

Frontinius shook his head imperceptibly at his prefect before speaking.

'We did, sir, or rather one of my men who's a finer shot than I'll ever be did, and at my command. Tribune Perennis had just admitted to an act of stupidity and treason whose result you can see down there, and was attempting to murder Prefect Equitius.'

Licinius looked around him carefully, fully digesting the scene.

'Which would explain the dead Asturians scattered around? Not to mention the fact that several of your own men seem to have arrow wounds?'

'Sir.'

'You can imagine how *that's* going to look if it's reported back to Rome. Where is the legatus, by the way?'

Equitius stepped forward, pointing down the slope.

'He's down there, Licinius. That young bastard suborned the Asturians, or at least enough of them to be able to carry out his plan. He must have passed a message to Calgus in some way while he was supposed to be shadowing the warband. They let the Sixth get into the open and then rushed them while the legion was still in column. He's got some sort of warrant straight from the imperial palace, empowers him to take command of the Sixth if necessary, so the bastard wanted to make sure Sollemnis wouldn't survive.'

Licinius leaned in close and half whispered his next question, glancing significantly at the unsuspecting Marcus, who was busy with his wounded.

'*Does he know yet?*'

Equitius shook his head.

'*No. Nor should he, under the circumstances.*'

'Agreed. What a fucking mess. So apart from the fact that half a legion is being taken apart under our gaze, what's the local situation?'

Equitius pointed in the direction that Perennis had taken his command.

'Four cohorts of the Sixth, the Second Tungrians, Raetians, Frisians and the Aquitani are somewhere over in that direction. They were supposed to be the other half of a plan to attack the warband, but *bloody* Perennis took them away to where they'd be no use when this happened.'

Licinius pursed his lips.

'My boys are half an hour's ride back that way, and I met a messenger a while back who said the Second and the Twentieth are ten miles down the main road. The only problem is that that lot will have gutted the Sixth and buggered off into the hills long before we can bring them into the action . . .'

He walked to the edge of the slope and stared down for a long moment. Equitius sighed deeply and followed him.

'Licinius, before my tame Brigantian prince demonstrated his marksmanship with the hunting bow on Perennis, the little shit ordered us to make a stand on the slope here, just in front of this wood. He wanted to destroy us for harbouring the boy, you understand, but in his desire to see us all dead he actually issued the only order appropriate under the circumstances. An order that I and my men will follow if you ask it of us.'

Licinius turned to face him.

'You'll likely all be dead within the hour, unless I get lucky and find the other legions a lot closer than they ought to be.'

Equitius returned his gaze.

'And you think that these men don't know the meaning of a Roman soldier's honour?'

Licinius looked him straight in the eye, seeing the other man's resolve in his steady stare.

'My apologies to your command. Very well.'

He walked quickly across to where Perennis lay panting his last few breaths, searching his body with swift efficiency until he found the imperial warrant scroll, then leant over to speak into the dying man's eyes.

'Listen to me, Titus Tigidius Perennis. You thought what you were doing was clever, that the emperor would thank you for removing a traitor from imperial service. You might well have been right. Your father, however, may not be so sanguine at the loss of his family's honour. I will make it my sworn task to make sure the full story reaches Rome, to tell him how you connived to destroy half a legion, and how, when the time came, another full cohort volunteered to face the same barbarians and give me a fighting chance to take revenge for those betrayed men. And how I executed you to avoid your suffering anything that might be said to resemble an honourable death . . .'

He drew his dagger and slit the dying tribune's throat wide open, watching with satisfaction as life ebbed away from Perennis's amazed eyes.

'Well, that at least feels a little better. Prefect, I'm off to find the other two legions. Best of luck.'

He stood up and saluted Equitius, who gravely returned the gesture, then vaulted back on to his horse and rode furiously away, barking orders at his men. The prefect watched him go for a moment, then turned to address Frontinius.

'Well, Sextus, now it's our turn to earn our corn.'

The First Spear smiled grimly.

'Don't think I'm immune to the irony of our situation, Prefect. Young Perennis should be laughing now, wherever he is.'

Equitius put a hand on his shoulder.

'Wherever he is, First Spear, we're quite likely to see at first hand soon enough.'

12

Frontinius led his centurions down the hunter's path at the trot. In a minute or so their centuries would follow them down the through the trees, and in those few seconds he needed to lay the foundations of a successful defence. If, he mused humourlessly, while his mind worked on their options for defending an apparently hopeless position, the entire cohort not simply dying in the first barbarian assault could be termed a success. Ten yards from the forest's edge he stopped and gathered his officers around him, their faces betraying the same grim determination fixed in his own mind.

'Brothers, there isn't time for any inspirational stuff or exhortations to heroism. Put simply, we've been sent to fight and likely to die in order to buy time for the other legions to jump those blue-nosed bastards from behind and put it to them the old-fashioned way. Your men are going to realise that soon enough, when they see thousands of men coming up the hill for their heads. They will look to you for an example. Give them one. Show them a grim face, but not despair. Lead your centuries with aggression, but keep them disciplined. If we do this right we can still pull a victory out of this disaster, but that depends solely on us. We are now the most important ten men on this battlefield – so let's live up to that burden in the next hour.'

He paused, looking at each man to take a gauge of their resolve. Good enough.

'Orders. The cohort will come down this path in number

order with the Fifth at the rear and the Ninth in their place in the centre, the prefect will make sure of that. Take your centuries down the slope to the line I point out to you and set up for defence, two men deep and no more, three-foot spacing per man. We're lucky that the wood curves down on both sides to meet our flanks, so we can anchor the line off the trees. Get the ground in front of you dirty as quickly as possible, and get your caltrops out straight after that. Speaking of trees . . . Bear?'

The big man stepped forward.

'Your axemen will be last down the path. Take them to left and right and make me an abatis as fast as you can, three rows of fallen trees deep all the way from each end of the line back round to the path, but leave the path clear of obstruction. When the obstacles are in place, widen the path enough to let four men down it abreast. In the unlikely event of our being reinforced I'd like the way in behind us wide enough for a cohort to move down it at speed. Everyone clear? And remember, brothers, win or lose, this day will be sung about long after the rain washes our blood away. Let's make it a story worth telling.'

The Tungrians exploded out of the wood on to the open ground, the centuries hurrying down to the line pointed out by Frontinius as they cleared the trees. The First Spear barked at his centurions to speed up their deployment as he pointed each century to its place, aware that the tribesmen, pausing in their assault on the shrinking remnant of the Sixth Legion to watch the new development, could turn and charge towards them at any second. The wood behind the cohort echoed with the growing racket of eighty axes working furiously on the tree-felling that would defend their flanks and rear. Each tree was under attack by two of the 10th Century's men, as they laboured with expert blows to drop it neatly into position with its branches facing outwards, presenting an impassable obstacle. Once the line was established, each end anchored in the trees to either side as the wood curved around their defence, he gave a small sigh of relief and shouted his next command.

'Get that slope dirtied up!'

The cohort's long line marched a dozen paces down the gentle slope, then stopped, the troops fishing under their groin protectors to urinate on to the grass. Selected men ran to the small stream that ran through their new position and filled their helmets with water, carrying the load carefully back to their places in the line before emptying the liquid on to the ground. On command they stamped and twisted with their hobnailed boots, digging at the wet ground beneath their feet, ignoring the spray of acidic-smelling mud that spattered their lower legs and retreating gradually back towards their former positions to leave a five-yard strip of ground in front of their line an oozing mess. Frontinius ignored the drama taking place below them as the 6th Legion's surviving troops huddled into three ever dwindling groups. With the ground to their front made treacherously slippery, he called for the last element of their defence.

'Obstacles and tribuli!'

The centuries mustered the heavy five-foot-long staves each man had carried from the camp, each one sharpened to a fire-hardened point at both ends, and lashed them into giant obstacles, each formed of three stakes tied together with rope. Bags full of the small iron tribuli were strewn around the obstacles, presenting sharp points to the feet of the unwary attacker. Julius, standing with his 5th Century behind the main line of defence, both escort to the cohort's standard and tactical reserve, turned to speak to his chosen man.

'You can keep an eye on this lot. I'm going down to the front to get a better view and have a chat with my young

Roman friend. I see no reason why he should get all the fun.'

He strode down the slope, clapping an arm around Marcus's shoulders and pointing out across the warband's presently scattered force. Lowering his head to the younger man's ear, he spoke quietly, a gentle smile on his face.

'Well, Centurion, there they are. Twenty thousand angry blue-faced men who will very shortly come up this buttock of a hill to take our heads. Are you ready to die with your men?'

Marcus nodded grimly.

'Ready enough. But before they take my head, I'll send a good number to meet Cocidius before me.'

Julius laughed, slapping him delightedly on the back.

'And you don't mind if I stay for the fun? I can't stand being stuck back guarding that bloody statue while you get all the glory. And I might be of some use when the shit starts flying . . .'

Marcus nodded, but raised a finger in mock admonishment.

'As long as you contain your contribution to swordplay, and the occasional piece of advice, it's a deal. If you want to command the scout century, make sure you come *second* in the competition next year.'

A horn sounded far out across the battlefield, and the milling tribesmen hacking at the remnants of the 6th Legion's cohorts pulled back in temporary truce. Silence gradually fell across the field, the panting Britons taking an opportunity to get their breath, tend to their wounded and remove their dead and dying from the bloodied grass. Trapped behind the unmoving wall of tribesmen, the remaining legionaries did what they could for their own wounded, little enough in the circumstances.

Sollemnis squinted up the hill over the heads of the barbarians surrounding what was left of his command, making out the auxiliary cohort arrayed in defence across its slope. He tapped his First Spear on the shoulder, pointing at the Tungrians.

'What . . . what do you think they're about up there?'

The other man grimaced as he drew breath, the broken shaft of an arrow protruding through his armour from his abdomen, the price of taking his turn in the cohort's rapidly contracting perimeter.

'You've got me. Looks like a suicide mission. We'll be welcoming them to Hades soon enough.'

Sollemnis laughed grimly, hefting his sword.

'No doubt about that. These bastards are just having a breather, they'll be back for our heads once they've got their wind back.'

He glanced about him.

'I need to hide this sword, hope that it stays concealed from the blue-noses. Those are Tungrians up there, I can see their banner. My son's up there with them, and if he lives I want it found and passed to him.'

The other man nodded blankly, too shocked to wonder at the legate's revelation.

Sollemnis took up a dead soldier's gladius, testing its balance.

'This should serve well enough. So many dead men . . .'

The First Spear coughed painfully and pointed to their dead standard-bearer. An arrow had ripped into the man's windpipe a few moments before, dropping him to his knees as he choked out his life. The eagle standard still stood proud above his corpse, gripped in lifeless fingers.

'You'd best stick your sword under Harus's body . . . Yes, that ought to do it. They'll take the eagle, but likely leave his head if you strip away his bearskin. Unlike you and me. We'll go to our graves in separate pieces . . .'

Sollemnis smiled again, with genuine amusement this time. 'It seems we're to be collector's items, then?'

'Roman officers' heads. No mud hut should be without one.'

A horn rang out with a sudden bray that jerked their attention back to the warband surrounding them. The warriors charged into their pathetic remnant with a revived purpose, their swords rising and falling in flashing arcs as they butchered the exhausted survivors of the 6th Legion's cohorts. Seeing the man in front of him go down under a powerful sword-blow that cleaved his right arm at the shoulder, Sollemnis stepped into the fight alongside the few men of his bodyguard still standing with a snarl of frustration, striking fast and hard at the man responsible and tasting brief satisfaction as the man's blood sprayed across his cuirass. The feeling was short lived, his appearance marking him out as a senior officer to the men facing him. He landed one more blow, putting his gladius deep into the chest of another warrior before the man's comrade thrust a spear deep into his unprotected thigh.

The First Spear, already felled by a sword thrust into his spine, and numbly inert as the barbarians fought to strip him of his fine armour while his life ebbed away into the puddle of blood soaking the ground around him, watched the scene with the unique detachment of a dying man. Sollemnis went down on one knee, helpless to defend himself as the warriors around him gathered for the kill. A sword skidded off his cuirass and sliced into the meat of his right arm, and a vicious blow from a club cracked the elbow joint and left his borrowed sword dangling useless at his side.

'He's *mine!*'

A loud voice sounded over their clamour, a magnificently armoured giant of a man stepping out of the attackers' midst and calling a halt to their attacks with a simple bellowed command. He batted aside a despairing sword-thrust from the last of the legatus's bodyguard with his huge round shield, contemptuously smashing the exhausted man to the ground with another punch of the shield's heavy boss and stabbing down into the space between his helmet's cheek-pieces. The other warriors backed away, clearly too scared of the man to deny him the moment of triumph. His helmet and armour were coal black, inlaid with intricate silver patterns befitting his obvious status as a tribal champion, heavy iron greaves protecting his thighs and calves to make him almost invulnerable as long as he could carry the weight. Only his booted feet lacked protection.

Sollemnis teetered on the brink of falling on to his face, only willpower keeping him on his knees as he looked up into the swordsman's face.

'Go on, then . . . get it over with, y'bastard.'

His voice was no more than a croak, the words bringing a smile to the big warrior's face. He hefted his sword in flashing arcs, luxuriating in the pleasure of letting the legatus see what was coming for a long moment before swinging the blade to sever Sollemnis's head from his shoulders. A warrior retrieved the grisly trophy and carried it back to the legatus's killer as the Roman's headless torso toppled slowly sideways to the bloody grass.

As the First Spear's consciousness slipped from his faltering grasp he saw the big man lift the legion's eagle standard from the standard-bearer's lifeless fingers. Stamping down on the standard to separate the spread-winged symbol of imperial power from its pole, he tossed the broken shaft away, took the foot-high statue by one wing and stalked away from the legatus's headless corpse, back into the warband's seething mass of men.

As the cohort stood helplessly and watched the final

destruction of their beleaguered colleagues in the valley below them, a keen-eyed Tungrian called out a sighting, pointing at the valley's far slope. There, made tiny by the distance, moved a party of three war chariots, accompanied by some fifty native cavalry cantering steadily across the battlefield. A great dragon banner flew proudly in the wind of their passage, its forked tail whipping eagerly from side to side. The prefect stared out at the oncoming horsemen, raising his eyebrows in question.

'The infamous Calgus, coming for a look?'

Frontinius snorted.

'Probably wondering what's going on. I doubt Perennis actually told him that he intended to send us to our doom here, and *we're* on rising ground and in good order. Eight hundred spears could make a medium-sized mess of his warband before they roll over us, and slow up his next move. If he's the strategist I believe him to be, he'll be worried, keen to take his prizes and get his men away before Second and Twentieth Legions come over the horizon baying for blood. I'd suggest that we might look a little more confident, just to reinforce that nagging doubt. Perhaps we could make some noise?'

Equitius smiled.

'Hail, Calgus, those about to die salute you?'

'Something like that.'

'Very well. Trumpeter, sound "Prepare for defence".'

The notes sang out sweetly, hanging for a moment over the hill, piercing the continual hammering of axes. After the shortest of pauses Frontinius heard his centurions shouting their commands, then the soft rattle of spears being readied. Frontinius strode forward in front of the cohort, as was his right, drawing his sword and raising it above his head, polished steel shining in the mid-morning sun, then turned back to face the ranks of grim-faced soldiers. He swung the weapon down to waist height, rapping the blade's flat on to his shield's scarred surface, repeating the blow to establish a slow but steady rhythm that was easy for the soldiers to follow, as they rapped their spears against the metal bosses of their shields. The noise built quickly, until the pulses of sound echoed distantly back from the slopes about them, a basic, intimidating noise that put heart back into the more timid troops, and swelled the anger of the rest as they stood and waited for the chariots and horsemen to draw close. The dragon banner snaked across the valley floor, drooping limply back on to its standard as the horsemen came to a halt two hundred paces from the Tungrian line.

After a moment a rider came forward, cantering within shouting distance and then stopping to stare across the lines of hard-faced, lean-framed soldiers before calling out his message over their noise.

'The Lord Calgus suggests negotiation. Man to man, no others to attend. Safety is guaranteed.'

He wheeled his horse, riding back to the knot of barbarian cavalry without a backwards glance. Frontinius glanced over at the Prefect, seeing the Roman's jawline tighten as his lips pursed to a white line.

'Well, Prefect, shall we go and meet the man that tarred and torched the inhabitants of Fort Habitus and Roaring River?'

The prefect stared at the distant dragon banner, fitfully prancing in the gusts above his enemy's bodyguard, for a long moment before responding, putting a hand on his First Spear's shoulder.

'The invitation was for one. I'll go. You'll stay here, and lead the cohort if this should be some sort of device to distract us, or to capture a senior officer.'

'And if it is . . . ?'

'I'll probably be joining my father rather sooner than I've

previously thought would be the case. As might "the Lord" Calgus.'

He walked on down the slope, watching his step on the treacherous strip of glutinous mud and stepping carefully to avoid the tribuli's eager spikes, and came to a stop halfway between his own troops and those of his enemy. A figure had stepped from their ranks as he had, and paced towards the field towards him, carrying a bundle wrapped in a bloodied blanket, until they were close enough for spoken conversation, although beyond sword-thrust.

They stared at each other for a moment, the prefect eying the other man's bundle with unhappy certainty as to its contents until the Briton chose to break the silence, his Latin unaccented.

'Well then, Prefect, I am Calgus, lord of the northern tribes. I broke the Wall, I *despoiled* your forts from Three Mountains all the way south to Noisy Valley and I,' pointing a thumb back over his shoulder, 'caught your legatus in a trap of my careful making, *with* his legion. And now I have something to show you.'

He allowed the bundle to fall open, its contents dropping to the grass at his feet. The highly polished bronze eagle from the 6th Legion's standard gleamed prettily in the morning sun, its defiant spread-winged pose incongruous under the circumstances, while the helmeted head rolled slowly across the grass and came to a stop on its side, Sollemnis's dead stare facing out towards the waiting Tungrians. Equitius sank to his haunches, staring intently into his friend's lifeless eyes. Calgus put his hands on his hips and waited for a response, while the prefect took a long moment before rising silently to his feet. The Roman nodded, still staring down at his friend's severed head, his face stony, then lifted his gaze to stare back at the waiting Briton.

'This man was my friend, for more years than I care to

recall. We drank together, chased women together in our younger days, and we fought Rome's enemies together too. Men like you. We tasted the barbarity of combat with men like *you*, and we rose above it. We kept our humanity, but we always won those battles by doing whatever we had to. So if you're hoping to unman me with this display you're going to be disappointed. It's nothing less than I expected, and nothing less than I would have done in your place. But it changes nothing.'

He took a deep breath, and squared his shoulders.

'So, Calgus, let's get this over with. I am Prefect Septimus Equitius of the 1st Tungrian Cohort. I found your cattle in front of the Hill and burned them to deny your men their flesh and prevent your attack on my fortress. I lured your cavalry from the cover of the forest for the Petriana to destroy, and *I*,' and he in turn pointed back over his own shoulder, 'am going to keep your warband here for long enough that the rest of our army will fall on them and utterly destroy them.'

'Tungrians? Tungria lies over the water, Prefect, closer to Gaul than to Britain. Those men are Brigantes, *my* people, not yours.'

'I think you'll find otherwise if you're unwise enough to send warriors up that slope to meet them. Local born they may be, but their training and discipline are Roman. I think you know what that means.'

They shared a quiet smile, a spark of communication across the wind-whipped ground. The prefect pulled his cloak tighter about him, seeking to keep out the wind's questing fingers.

'Come on, Calgus, let's drop the bombast. You're an educated man, Roman educated if the stories are true. I don't think you believe in shouting insults and arse-slapping any more than I do.'

The other man nodded, his face staying neutral.

'Go on.'

'In truth I am more impressed than I expected to be. Your control of those tribesmen is better than I've seen before, and your recruitment of a Roman tribune to lure his legatus into your grasp was a clever stroke. Or more likely he recruited you, eh?'

Equitius paused for a moment, allowing the fact of his knowledge of Perennis's treachery to sink in. Calgus's green eyes narrowed with unasked questions.

'So, now that we've established that you've done a reasonable job so far, let's get down to business. You could just have sent that rabble to die on our swords, but you chose to talk first, and while I'd like to think that's because our reputation goes before us . . .'

Calgus smiled again, shaking his head in amusement.

'Never let it be said you lacked a sense of humour, Prefect of the First Tungrians. I came to offer you the chance to leave this battlefield intact, before you force me to send my men to slaughter yours. Will you save those lives? My aims in making this war have always been limited to the goal of a negotiated peace with Rome, certain *reasonable* concessions for my people and honour for both sides. After all, without a settlement, this war could last for several campaigning seasons, and consume tens of thousands of Roman lives, soldiers and innocents both. This victory, combined with the threat my warbands pose to the frontier, should be enough to bring your governor to the negotiating table. Our demands are simple enough, and do not threaten an inch of Roman territory, so there should be no need for further loss of life. After all, I am, as you suggest, an educated and civilised man at heart.'

The prefect wondered what the tribes' demands were, if not for some retreat from the frontier. Money in tribute and improved trading terms probably, removal of all Roman troops from their forts north of the wall for a certainty.

'So you ask me to walk away from the fight? And let you away from this place before the other two legions and the *rest* of the Sixth arrive? I think not, Calgus. I think you know that the time you'll need to break my line greatly increases the chance of our being rescued, and by overwhelming force. At the least we can buy your deaths with our own. I think you know you already have the victory, and want to save your own men's lives for another fight. You know there are other legions out there, but you don't know where, because you haven't got any mounted scouts to send out. Your mounted bodyguard alone wouldn't stand a chance, not with the Petriana roaming about looking for heads. Without that knowledge, and now that I have your traitor, you know you should disengage, and get away cleanly, but I'd guess that the tribal leaders won't let you walk away from a fight this unbalanced. If we don't leave the field we force you to fight just by standing there. True?'

The Briton smiled easily, gesturing back towards his waiting warriors.

'Perhaps. The one certainty is that if you and your men don't leave immediately then you will shortly pay the price for frustrating the will of a man with twenty times as many warriors as your entire cohort musters. Think about that, while you walk back to your command. You have a few minutes in which to spare us both further spilt blood. Otherwise the next time we meet your head will be stuck on a spear's point.'

The prefect nodded solemnly.

'Perhaps. But you'll have climbed a high wall of your own dead to enjoy the sight.'

Calgus walked back to his bodyguard, his mind moving over

the calculations. He guessed at ten centuries in the Tungrian line, a full cohort. Given time they would make the thin line's flanks impossible to turn, protected by impassable barricades of hastily felled trees and rows of sloping wooden spikes to impale the unwary attacker. Attack now, or pull his men away to safety, the victory already under his belt and a Roman legatus's probably dead?

He stopped and looked up at the Tungrian line again, musing on the grim faces that had stared back at him. His own people, so familiar, obdurate in defence, incandescent in assault, but with the overlay of Roman discipline to temper their courage, which made each one of them the equal of his best warriors in terms of simple killing power. The difference, the key difference, was that no matter what the provocation, the situation, little would persuade them to break their wall of shields, from behind which their short stabbing swords would flicker like the tongues of hundreds of deadly snakes. Refusing to enter the chaotic swirl of man-to-man combat, the Tungrians could afford to fight several times their number, the more numerous enemy without any means of applying that superiority in numbers. Just one cohort, though, eight hundred men against thousands of his own. How long could that take? Even if he lost as many as he killed, or even twice as many, it was an exchange that made more than adequate sense.

He walked on, jumping back into his chariot as he reached his bodyguard. Eyes turned to him, awaiting his command, the men ready to put their lives at risk.

'They will not withdraw. Their prefect was disappointingly resolute.'

Aed raised his eyebrows, indicating a desire to speak.

'Then we must fight, my lord. No warrior will willingly walk away from that many heads begging to be taken. Besides, many are not yet blooded . . .'

'I agree. But it must be fast. The Roman spoke of other legions, and at the very least the other cohorts commanded by their legatus must be close at hand, and their bloody Petriana too. Handled properly, their cavalry and even one full legion could carve us to ribbons if they caught us here, even though we would be more than twice their number. Send a rider to Emer and Catalus's warbands – they've stood and watched the others kill Romans, they must be raring to get into the fight.'

The tribal bands moved forward at the run, eager after watching their fellows rip the guts out of the hopelessly outnumbered cohorts. The younger men joshed each other as they ran, boasting breathlessly of the heads they would take, the older warriors straining to catch a glimpse of their adversaries and take their measure. The two leaders met as they ran, agreeing swiftly on a simple left and right split, nothing fancy in the amount of time they had, a straight forward charge and hack, using their superior strength in numbers to overwhelm the auxiliaries.

On their slope the Tungrians stood impassively, still hammering out the menacing rhythm of spear and shield, the noise numbing their senses to any fear, replacing the emotion with an incoherent sense of common identity. The cohort had ceased to be a collection of individuals, and had become an engine of destruction ready to strike. The relentless pulse of its fighting heart had stripped away the feeling of self from its members and left them in a state of detachment from reality, ready for the impersonal fury shortly to be required for their survival. They watched, still pounding out their defiance, as the enemy advanced quickly across the open ground to their front, forming up into lines that roughly matched their own, one hundred and fifty paces down the slope, out of spear's throw. Another brief command rang out from the trumpeter, silencing the drumming and bringing their spears into the preparatory position for the throw. In the sudden silence the slight noises of weapons and armour were suddenly magnified, the dull clink of equipment ringing out across the slope as both sides made ready.

In the 9th Century's front line Scarface and his mates braced themselves for the fight to come, the veteran soldier talking quietly to the men around him. Even the tent party's watch officer deferred to the scarred soldier's twenty years of experience.

'Now, lads, this is going to be a right gang fuck once they get up the slope, so here's how it's going to go. When Uncle Sextus gives the order we'll sling a volley of spears into them. Aim for the men who've lost their footing, the ones too distracted to see your spear coming until it's tickling their backbone. You've carried the bloody thing on your back since the day you joined, and never really had the chance to use it properly, so make the fucking thing pay you back for all those miles you've carted it. That'll be one less blue-nose to wave a sword at you. Once the spears are gone we air our blades double quick and get the shields set strong, ready for them to hit the line with everything they've got. You lads at the rear, you get a good fucking grip of our belts and brace us to hold firm. We're on a nice slope, so it shouldn't be too hard to hold them if we work together. After that you just concentrate on the same old drills, board and sword, parry and thrust. Put your gladius into a blue-nose's guts, twist the fucker, kick him off it and get back behind your board. Don't fucking stand there watching him die, or his mate will carve you up just like you would if you was him.'

He paused, swelling his chest with a great draught of air.

'Breathe deep, lads, you'll need all the air you can get in the next few minutes. And just remember, any of you bastards turn from this fight before it's done and you'll have me and my blade to deal with once we're done with this shower of unwashed hairy arseholes. We stand together.'

Along the Tungrian line a few men quailed and were swiftly dealt with by the officers and their older comrades, slaps and kicks putting them back into the line. The majority listened to the cohort's veteran soldiers tell them how to deal with what was coming and stared impassively down the slope at their enemy, prepared to kill in order to live, a stark equation both understood and accepted. In order to live through, to see their women and children again, they would have to slaughter the tribesmen in great numbers. Almost to a man, the soldiers were ready to start the butchery.

In the tribal ranks men swiftly made their last preparations, discarding heavy items of clothing that would restrict their movements in the coming melee, muttering hasty prayers to their gods for victory. The older warriors, alive to the possibilities of the coming combat, sensibly added the hope for a clean death should their time have come. Without the time to indulge in any lengthy diatribe against the invaders, the chieftains looked to each other, nodded their readiness, then charged forward up the slope, hurling thousands of warriors at the flimsy Roman line.

The Tungrian centurions looked to Frontinius at the line's centre, waiting for his signal as the barbarian horde surged up the gentle incline. Waiting with one arm raised, he watched the shaggy warriors storm towards his men, thirty yards, twenty-five, the usual range of the initial spear-throw, twenty, until at fifteen yards from the shield wall they hit the strip of greasy mud that his troops had painstakingly stamped into bubbling ruin. The leading wave of attackers slowed, fighting to stay on their feet as they bunched to avoid the giant wooden obstacles' sharpened points. Crowded from behind and perilously close to falling headlong into the mud, more than a few suddenly shouted their pain as the scattered metal caltrops, half hidden in the mud, pierced their feet. The tribesmen's attention was suddenly focused more downward than forward.

Scarface raised his spear, shouting encouragement to his comrades, easing the weapon back and forth in readiness to throw, as he searched for a target among the mass of tribesmen struggling towards the Tungrian line.

Frontinius whipped his hand downward in the pre-agreed signal. A volley of spears arced flatly into the struggling tribesmen, finding targets unprotected in their struggle to stay upright. The front ranks shivered with the impact, men screaming as flying steel spitted them through limb and trunk, their flailing bodies adding to the chaos as the barbarian charge faltered.

The veteran soldier found his mark, a big man carrying a six-foot-long sword momentarily distracted by the greasy footing, and stepped forward to throw his spear, arm outstretched as he followed the weapon's flight through to his point of aim. The barbarian jerked as the spear's cruel steel head punched into his belly, blood jetting from the wound as he sank to his knees. Drawing his sword with a smile of satisfaction, Scarface backed up the slope until he felt hands grab his belt to steady him, lifting his shield into line with those to his right and left.

Along the line the centurions bawled new commands, their men drawing their swords and crouching deeper behind their shields as the barbarian wave regained some of its momentum, shrugging aside the dead and dying to struggle towards the silent Tungrian line. Seeing their momentary difficulty, Frontinius made a snap decision, lifting his sword and pointing at the barbarians with its blade, bawling the order that unleashed his men down the slope.

With a shrill of whistles from their officers the cohort lunged the few remaining paces down the hill into their enemy, smashing into the struggling barbarian line with their heavy shields and bowling the enemy front line back into the warriors behind, then stepped in with their swords.

Scarface heard the whistle, kicked back to disengage the soldier held fast to his belt and bounded down the slope alongside his comrades with a blood-curdling howl, punching his shield's metal boss into the face of a warrior with his sword raised to strike, then stabbing his sword's point into the man's guts and kicking him off the blade in one fluid motion. He shouted to his mates as he raised his shield into position.

'Line! Reform the line!'

The cohort's front rank snapped their shields back into place, presenting the barbarians with an unbroken wall to frustrate their attacks. The soldiers repeatedly punched the metal bosses of their shields into the faces of the oncoming men, upsetting their precarious balance, then stabbed their short swords into their chosen targets, aiming for the body points that centuries of experience had taught would kill a man in seconds. Blood flew across the gap between the two lines in hot sprays as men fell back from the point of combat, weapons falling from their hands as they sought to halt the flow or hold intestines into torn bellies, or simply explored agonising wounds with shocked bewilderment as life ebbed from their bodies. The ground beneath their feet, doused with a mixture of blood, urine and faeces, became steadily more treacherous. The Tungrian rear rank's role became one of keeping the men in front on their feet, and not exposed to an enemy blow on the ground. Punching and thrusting at the seething throng that railed desperately at their shield wall, parrying enemy sword and axe strokes and striving in turn to murder their deliverers, the Tungrians fought as men who understood that their only survival lay in slaughter, cold blooded and clinically efficient.

In the 9th's front rank Scarface crouched behind his shield, his left arm shuddering with the shock of sword-blows against its scarred wooden face, watching the barbarians intently through the gap between his helmet and the shield's top edge, looking for any chance to strike. The long-haired warrior facing him, hemmed in by the men around him, raised his sword to chop the blade downward in the only attack open to him, and presented a fleeting opportunity that the experienced soldier took without hesitation. Stepping forward one pace, he thrust his sword between the other man's ribs and dropped him, doubled over with the sudden awful pain, into the blood-spattered mud.

A tribesman already fallen with a spear through his thigh gathered his strength to strike at the Roman's extended leg, but the wily soldier simply slammed the sharpened metal edge of his shield down across the man's sword arm, slicing down to the bone before stepping quickly back into his place in the shield wall. The man next to him slipped on the mud, going down on to one knee and opening himself up to the blows of his attackers. Without conscious thought, Scarface shifted his shield to protect his mate for the critical seconds required for him to regain his footing, ignoring his own peril. The man to his right killed a tribesman shaping to attack the momentarily unprotected veteran, ripping open his throat with a swift stab of his gladius. Within seconds their wall of shields was complete again, steady against the barbarians railing at its unyielding face.

To Marcus, standing behind the double line of his men with a tent party of soldiers ready to thrust into holes hacked in the line, it looked like a hopelessly unequal battle. As the seconds passed he realised that most of the dying was being done on the other side of their shields. Relatively few of his own men had gone down, despite the thick throng of enemy pressing up the slope.

'Stand fast, Ninth century, parry and thrust!'

Dubnus's familiar booming voice gave him heart, and he shouted his own encouragement above the screams and shouts of the battle. A gap opened in the line in front of him, a pair of men felled by the same massive axe blow, and he instinctively pushed the replacements aside and stepped into the breach before any of the enemy could surge through. The tribesman wielding the axe stamped down at his victim, attempting to wrench the blade from deep in his victim's chest, then gaped as Marcus's powerful chopping blow hacked away his right arm, a heavy boot striking him under the chin. The maimed man fell back into the wall of frenzied blue-painted faces that confronted Marcus and was lost to view, replaced by another, who, seeing Marcus's rank, leapt forward in attack, only to be spitted by the cavalry sword's length. Twisting the blade in a savage half-circle inside the barbarian's scrabbling hands to loosen it within the body cavity, he punched forward with his shield at the dying man's chest, ripping the sword free in a shower of gore that painted both the shield and his chest dark red.

To his left a man from the neighbouring century suddenly leapt forward into the mass of the enemy, thrusting about him in a blood frenzy, killing one then another barbarian, then sank blood-soaked into the throng of the enemy, screaming as a dozen battle-crazed warriors bludgeoned him to death. The century's chosen man pushed a man into the gap, bellowing at his men to keep their heads and hold the line.

To their front, Marcus reckoned, as he parried and stabbed at the enemy in front of him with his men, the onslaught was easing, as the tiring tribesmen found it harder to stay on their feet with so many of their own dead and wounded underfoot. One of the less seriously wounded attempted to cut at his ankles from the ground, provoking a hacking stroke that neatly removed his arm at the elbow. The man rolled back under his comrades' feet, tumbling two of them on top of him with his agonised writhing.

The mass of tribesmen in front of Marcus parted without warning, allowing a tall and heavily armoured man to step out into the gap between the two lines. His black helmet and chest armour were intricately decorated with silver inlays and already coated with dried blood, his thighs and calves protected by iron greaves. He eyed the young centurion with cold appraisal for a moment, then with a sudden lunge sprang to attack the officer. Three savage hacking blows from his heavy sword smashed into Marcus's shield, their power numbing his left arm and putting him on the defensive. The big warrior paused in his attack, laughing down into Marcus's face, his voice a grating boom over the noise of the battle.

'I've already taken the head of a legatus today, so I won't bother with yours, I'll leave it to the crows. Are you ready to die, little Roman?'

Marcus held his ground, ignoring the taunts, and readied himself for the next onslaught. The big man sprang forward again, but this time Marcus met his sword not with his shield but blade to blade, turning the blow aside and stepping close in to slam his shield's iron frame down on the warrior's unarmoured foot, feeling bones crack under the impact. As the warrior fought to control the pain he attacked again, stabbing downward with his sword and spearing the blade through the man's shattered foot and into the soft ground below before twisting it savagely and ripping the sword free. Then, while the huge warrior staggered where he stood, paralysed by the crippling pain, Marcus raised his shield to the horizontal and chopped its harsh metal edge into his attacker's undefended throat with all his strength. With a stifled gurgle the tribal champion fell back from the shield wall, fighting for breath that was never going to reach his lungs through a ruptured windpipe. The barbarian line shivered and inched backwards away from the cheering Tungrians as their hero fell to the ground, his face darkening as he twisted in his death throes.

Along the line the gap between the two forces widened a little, as the tribesmen paused to regain their wind in dismay at the failure of their initial assault. The Tungrians straightened their line, one eye for the man next to them, one on the enemy. Horns blew to the warband's rear, ordering the tribesmen to pull back and reform, and they backed reluctantly down the hill, still shouting defiance at the Roman troops. No command was given to follow their retreat.

On the slope before the panting Tungrians lay hundreds of enemy warriors, some dead, some dying, all spattered with blood, some moaning pitifully with the pain of their wounds, others screaming intermittently in their agony and distress. The men of the 9th stared bleakly down at the scene, some, those few among them familiar with the sights and sounds of a full battle, with numb indifference, most simply wide-eyed at the horror of the scene. One or two made ineffectual efforts to wipe away the gore that had blasted across armour and flesh with each sword stroke, but most restricted themselves to wiping the blood from their eyes and mouths, knowing that there would be more to replace whatever they removed from their bodies and equipment soon enough. Julius sought out Marcus, pulling him from the front rank with a rebuke softened by the young officer's wide-eyed look of astonishment.

'That's a good place to get killed. Stay *behind* the line next time, and put your soldiers into the fight. We've got a short time before they come back. It would be a good opportunity for the century to drink some water. I'll check for casualties . . .'

He looked down at the two men killed by the axeman,

one without head and right arm, the other cloven a foot down into his chest.

'Best you remove these two. They're already with Cocidius . . .'

Marcus pointed down at the wounded tribesmen to their front, almost within touching distance.

'What about them?'

The reply was dismissive.

'They're dead, they just haven't realised it yet. Leave them there; they'll slow down the next attack.'

The young officer nodded jerkily, calling for the water bottles to be passed along the line, and commanding the closest men to carry the ruined corpses of their dead into the forest at their rear.

In the Tungrian front rank Scarface leaned on his shield, grateful for the chance to get his breath back and take a mouthful of water to swill away the coppery taste of blood.

'That was good enough. We must have done twenty or so of the bastards and lost, what, two of ours? Who came forward to replace them?'

The promoted rear-rankers raised their hands sheepishly.

'You two, eh? Welcome to the front rank, boys, this is where the corn gets earned the hard way. Keep your heads for a few minutes more and you'll have a place here for the rest of your time.'

He laughed at their comical expressions as both men realised that their lives as soldiers had just changed for ever.

'Oh yes, all that piss-taking the front rank always gives the girls at the back? That'll be you giving rather than taking from now on. Welcome to *my* army.'

The 9th drank gratefully, the more composed soldiers discussing the fight almost conversationally, leaning tiredly on their shields like pottery workers taking a break from the kilns. Some, the more experienced and perceptive, knowing the danger of the less experienced men losing themselves to the battle rage when the fight renewed itself, worked on the men next to them, coaxing them back to reality with words of home and family. Morban found Marcus checking the edge of his sword with a careful eye, and offered him a drink from his bottle.

'Nicely fought, Centurion, you took that big bastard's arm off like lopping a sapling, and the way you did the boy in black armour with your shield was nothing short of poetic. The lads're already talking about the way you jumped into the line and got stuck in!'

Marcus nodded, sheathing his sword and holding on to the hilt to hide the shaking of his hand.

'Thank you. I hope your son escaped injury?'

'Indeed, I think so, the little I could see of him from here.'

A shout from the line of troops grabbed his attention, pointing arms guiding his stare to the edge of the valley a mile or so to their right, past the small forest's edge. There, silhouetted against the skyline, a mass of horsemen was moving into position, perfectly placed to sweep down the slope and into the barbarian flank. Their long lances were held vertically, the points making a winking glitter of razor-sharp steel in the mid-morning sunlight.

'*Get the blue-faced bum-fuckers!*'

'*Give them the eight-foot enema!*'

A chorus of shouts implored the riders, identified as the Petriana and Augustan cavalry wings by their twisting white banners, two thousand men strong, to attack the mass of men below, but their inaction once their deployment was complete was just as Equitius had expected. An unsupported charge against so many warriors could end only in a glorious failure. All the same, anything that gave Calgus one more thing to worry about, and heartened his own men, had to be good. Even as he watched a force of some five thousand men detached themselves from the barbarian mass on the plain below, wheeling at speed to form a rough defensive line of archers and spears, ready to absorb any charge.

He walked on, to the point where his command ended and Caelius's started, hailing his brother officer. The other man strode down the line of barbarian corpses, keeping one eye on the ground against the risk of being surprised by a wounded man feigning death.

'Hail, Two Knives, freshly blooded, from the rumour passed down our line, and from the blood painted across your mail. I hope you offered that prayer for me?'

Marcus smiled wryly.

'I was a little busy at the time. I'll be sure to mention you next time I can get to an altar.'

'Good enough. What do you think they'll do now?'

Both men stared downslope at the milling horde, order gradually returning to their mass.

'If I were leading them? Keep the cavalry safely at arm's length, put some archers and slingers out front, harass us with darts and stones to keep our heads down, and pull the rest away before two full legions take them dry from behind . . .'

Equitius was weighing the same question.

'We came down here as bait, to keep the warband in place until the main force can be moved up. I don't believe we've been here long enough to have achieved that aim, do you?'

Frontinius shook his head with pursed lips.

'Another hour at least, I'd say. I presume you'd like to attract their attention some more, rather than letting them slip away into the hills?'

'Yes. They can break into family bands and worm their way into the folds in the land. We might only take a tenth of them if that happens . . .'

The First Spear called a man to him, muttered instructions in his ear, and then turned back to the conversation.

'I have a way to hold them here, but it won't be pleasant. Especially since they'll come back up that slope like wild animals.'

The prefect nodded slowly.

'As long as Calgus doesn't pull his men away to safety, the price will be justified. Do whatever you have to.'

The First Spear nodded impassively and turned away, walking down the cohort's line at the high-tide mark of barbarian dead, inspecting the troops as if on peacetime parade, giving an encouraging word here and there. The man he'd sent to help him search for a particular corpse had succeeded, running down the line of shields with a freshly removed head dripping blood on his leggings.

The First Spear took it from him, examining the slack face with an intensity that was almost feral. The owner's hair was long and greasy, the seams of his face dark with the grime of long days on the march. His eyes stared glassily back, their animation long departed along with the man that had formerly watched the world through their windows.

'How do you know he was a chieftain?'

The other man held out his hand, showing his superior an impressively heavy torc stained dark red with blood, the gold wrapped in a serpentine arc that had previously been around the dead man's neck. Frontinius took the heavy piece of jewellery, weighing it in his hand and remembering the one like it that Dubnus's father had always worn, even after his dethronement.

'Somebody *was* important.'

He turned to stare down at the barbarian warband, quiet now, waiting for a command, and spoke again, without taking his eyes off the mass of warriors.

'Go to the prefect. Warn him to be ready.'

He stood silently on the slope for a moment, the head dangling almost forgotten from one hand, the torc in the other, until the men below him, alerted by those at the front, grew silent at the sight.

Calgus came to his decision with his usual speed and insight. At his rear waited the bulk of his warband, rested and ready to move. To his right were the enemy cavalry, at least temporarily neutralised by the screen of infantry and archers he'd thrown out to cover that wing of the warband. Their spears stood out above them in a forest of wood and steel, a full cohort from their density. In front of him, arrayed on the bloodied slope, the Tungrians stood motionless at the high-tide mark of a thick carpet of dead and dying men, waiting for his next move. Between them, slowly regaining a sense of order, the depleted tribal bands were reforming under new leaders, preparing to storm the hill once more.

'Pull them back.'

Aed raised his eyebrows.

'My lord, they are not yet successful. We . . .'

'I know. But there are two more legions marching in these hills. That prefect was far too relaxed for that cohort to be far from friendly spears. If they come upon us here, with the advantage of the slope, and with those fucking horsemen, we'll be dead meat. No, we leave now, break into tribal bands and go back to the muster. Then we can . . .'

A shout rang out across the open space, some leather-lunged Roman officer shouting the odds. Except . . . Calgus strained to hear the words, a fresh premonition of disaster stroking the hairs on the back of his neck.

Frontinius lifted head and torc, the former dangling by its greasy hair, the latter glinting in the early afternoon sun.

Inflating his barrel chest, he bellowed out across the mass of men below, silencing their growing noise.

'Leave this place now, or we will kill you all! *Warriors?!* You have failed once, and you will fail again like the children that you are compared to *real* soldiers.'

He paused for breath, and allowed the silence to drag on for a long moment.

'We killed your leaders and threw you back down this insignificant hill with ease. You came seeking heads and left your own by the hundred! If you come back up again, we will do the same to you. See, the head of a *defeated* chieftain!'

He swung the dead man's head in a lazy arc by its hair, resisting the temptation to hurl its obscenity away from him and into the seething tribesmen, raising the heavy torc to glint in the sunshine and be recognised as a symbol of authority.

'You were weak, and we punished you. Now run away, before we treat you all like *this*!'

Feeling queasy, he put the head to his crotch and pushed his hips at it in an unmistakable gesture, then threw it high into the air above their heads. With an angry roar the tribesmen surged forward, charging up the hill in their mad fury. Frontinius ducked back into the line of soldiers, shouting for them to ready their spears.

To the warband's rear, Calgus closed his eyes for a moment as the realisation hit him.

'My lord . . .'

'I know. I have no choice. I must kill the prisoners and send the entire warband up that hill. But not on *their* terms. Get me the tribal leaders.'

The Tungrians loosed their second and last volley of spears, plunging the barbarian front rank into chaos once more, then huddled into their own shields with swords ready. The oncoming rush slowed to a walk across the slippery ground, to a crawl over the wall of their dead and wounded, until the tribesmen arrived, in ones and twos, in front of the Roman shield wall. With Frontinius disdaining a charge against such disorganised opposition, preferring to keep his men on firm ground, they waited for their enemy to stagger exhaustedly on to their shields, then began their slaughter with a professional ease. Even when more men had struggled through the obstacles in front of the cohort's line, building the attacking force to a more respectable size, the anger that had burnt out of them was replaced by a wary respect, most of them holding off from the Roman swords, content to shout defiance at the Tungrians.

Scarface's tent party crouched ready to engage behind their shields, sensing that the fight had gone out of their opponents but unwilling to believe the battle could end so easily. A single man leapt from the barbarian line, a huge warrior swinging a six-foot-long blade around his head and bellowing abuse at the Tungrians. Stripped naked and possessed by a mighty rage, he swung his long sword over the top of the shield wall and opened the two new front-rankers' throats with the blade's end before whipping it back above his head to hack down into the Tungrian shields. Scarface's neighbour, caught beneath the sword's descending blade, raised his shield two-handed in self-defence. He staggered backwards as the savage blow chopped through the iron frame and sank the razor-sharp blade deep into his shield's wooden layers. Both Scarface and the soldier on the far side of the attacker stepped in and stabbed their swords deeply into the naked warrior's sides, Scarface backhanding his stabbing stroke into the man's side and ripping the blade out through his stomach muscles to release a slippery rope of guts. Releasing the long sword's hilt, the warrior staggered back from the shield wall with blood pouring down his legs from his dreadful wounds. The two men whose throats he had slashed died where they fell, bleeding out from their severed arteries in less then a minute. They were unceremoniously dragged away behind the line, two more rear rankers taking their places.

The prefect and Frontinius had little concern for their front, however, their attention being fixed on the mass of men gathering at the slope's foot.

'He'll put more men in to threaten our flanks to fix us, perhaps throw in some skirmishers to keep our heads down, then throw that mob up the middle and look to crush us under their numbers . . .'

The prefect nodded unhappily.

As they watched, the warband's bulk split into three groups. Two smaller groups split to left and right, and began climbing the slope with grim purpose, while a larger third body of men, perhaps ten thousand strong, started moving up to reinforce their attackers.

'What would you advise?'

Frontinius shook his head unhappily.

'All we can do is reposition some of the weakened centuries from the centre to the flanks and hope they can hold off the fixing attacks, then strengthen the centre with our reserves.'

'It isn't much of an option.'

'Prefect, it's no option at all. Either way we'll all be dead quite shortly unless Prefect Licinius manages to get some troops here within the next ten minutes.'

The other man drew his sword, glaring down at the mass of men moving up the hill to either side of their embattled position.

'Very well, take the Fourth and Seventh out of the centre and put the Fifth and Tenth in to replace them. I can't see a reserve being much use when this comes to knife fighting.

Good luck to you, First Spear. Let's hope we meet again under more promising circumstances.'

They clasped hands, then Frontinius strode down the slope, bellowing orders to his centurions and setting their last desperate plan in motion. The 5th and 10th Centuries streamed down the slope to reinforce the centre of the line.

Marcus and Julius stood together behind the thin line of their men, watching as their attackers, beaten back once more by the cohort's swords, gathered their strength. Rufius had strolled across to join them for a moment, his vine stick now tucked into his belt and his sword drawn and bloody. More and more men were clambering over the wall of dead and dying warriors, to swell the numbers facing them. To make matters worse smoke had begun to blow across their line, from trees set ablaze in the forest upwind to their right, making it harder by the moment to see their enemy. The barbarians were hammering on their shields, screaming abuse at the Tungrians, who, understanding the depth of their situation, were increasingly casting nervous glances to their rear rather than to the front. Julius stared out at the clamouring horde dispassionately.

'If they attack in that strength we'll have to abandon the line and fight in pairs, back to back.'

Marcus nodded, his mouth dry. As he squinted through the smoke, it appeared that to either side of the position the battle was yet to begin, the thousands of warriors in the flanking warbands apparently content to threaten the Tungrian flanks and hold the bulk of the cohort in position, rather than commit to an attack.

'Why don't they attack along our whole length? Surely they could push both flanks in and turn to roll us up with those numbers.'

Rufius answered him without taking his eyes off the advancing barbarians.

'Calgus wants to blood the men that haven't fought yet, give them back their manhood after Uncle Sextus put them down so cruelly. The main attack will come through the middle, right here, and we're the men that will have to stop it.'

'An interesting life and a short one, eh, brothers?'

They turned, finding Frontinius standing behind them.

'I thought your men might be feeling a little exposed, so I've come to share in the fun and show them that we're all in the same shitty boat. Julius, it's time your century stopped sitting about and actually did some fighting, so I've brought them down to strengthen the line.'

He pointed to their left, and Julius turned to see his men coming out of the smoke, his chosen man guiding them into the gap opening up as the 4th Century went to ground to let them through and into the line. Caelius, so far unscathed, pulled back with his soldiers, shot Frontinius a quick salute and then led the 4th off down the line, following the First Spear's pointed direction. Julius smiled broadly at the sight of his men.

'And about time. Excuse me, brothers. *Right, ladies, get your shields up and your spears ready to throw. Let's show these bluefaced bum-fuckers the entrance to Hades!*'

He trotted away to rejoin his men, shouting encouragement as he ran. To the right, beyond Rufius's 6th, the big men of the 10th Century were replacing the battered 7th. Rufius nodded grimly.

'That's going to be a nasty shock for the blue-faces. A century of axes is a terrifying prospect when they start lopping off arms and cleaving heads. The Bear's boys will be painted black from head to foot before this is over. Right, I'd best go and get my lads ready.'

He headed off to his century, leaving Frontinius and Marcus alone behind the 9th. The First Spear watched the enemy massing to their front impassively from behind his borrowed shield, keeping his eyes on the enemy as he addressed Marcus for what would probably be the last time.

'Well, Centurion, whether you be Tribulus Corvus or Valerius Aquila, I think you can take comfort in the fact that you've proved an exemplary officer these last few days. If I have to meet Cocidius in the next few minutes I'll be honoured to do so in your company.'

Marcus nodded.

'Thank you, sir.'

An arrow sailed past his head, as a sudden barrage of missiles made the soldiers hunch deeper behind their shields. The barbarian archers, using the wall of corpses for cover, began sending a continuous rain of missiles against the two centuries. Steel-tipped arrows hummed and whirred through the line, accurate shots punching into shields and clicking off helmets. Frontinius stood straight in the face of the barrage, raising his voice to continue his monologue.

'They'll keep this up for a moment or two; pick a few of us off with lucky shots, then charge in for the kill. When they do, you fight in pairs with your partner. If he's dead, find another, or fight in a three. Watch each other's backs, and *don't* leave your partner. If your partner is wounded, concentrate on killing blue-faces, not looking after him, or you'll be next . . .'

And he stopped, his eyes suddenly wide with the impact of an arrow between the greave that shielded his calf and the chain mail that ran down to mid-thigh. The missile had skewered his leg above the knee, toppling him unceremoniously on to the grass with a rivulet of blood seeping around the shaft. With a delighted roar the barbarians that had crossed the wall of bodies surged forward en masse, eager to take the one head that mattered to them above all.

The line disintegrated into a whirling melee, Marcus and

Dubnus going back to back over Frontinius as a tide of tribal warriors washed past them. Several men moved to encircle them, drawing a tightening circle of swords around the three men, gathering themselves for the kill. With an incoherent, berserk scream, Antenoch hit the men facing Marcus from behind, thrusting his sword through one's back and stamping him off the blade before swinging fiercely at the other's shield. Marcus and Dubnus went on to the offensive, killing two men and putting the other two to startled flight.

Across the century's frontage knots of men were fighting their own personal wars, still parrying barbarian swords and thrusting back with their short swords, but the fight was descending into a deadly mass brawl, and without the disciplined protection of the shield wall the soldiers were horribly outnumbered. Ten yards in front of Marcus two barbarians had a single soldier cornered, one hammering at his shield while the other outflanked him and sank his sword into the beleaguered man's neck in the gap between helmet and mail. The soldier crumpled instantly, just as the sprinting centurion hit his attackers from behind, running one man through with his cavalry sword and leaving the weapon sheathed in his back, smashing the other to the ground with a shield swipe and drawing his gladius to finish the stunned warrior where he lay.

As the struggle hung in the balance, and quite without fanfare, a wave of fresh troops charged down the slope into the battle, suddenly equalising the odds and chasing off the startled barbarians. Marcus and Dubnus stood panting over their wounded superior as the reinforcements finished off the enemy wounded around them with swift unconsidered efficiency. Following the bellowed commands of their officers, the new arrivals slotted into the line between the cohort's decimated centuries, bolstering the defence to more than its original strength.

The men of the 9th Century jeered as they recognised their new companions in adversity.

'It's the fucking Second Cohort. Well done, lads, you managed to find the battlefield at last, then?'

A solidly built watch officer muscled his way into the front rank, his spear held ready to throw. He shot Scarface an indifferent glance, his attention riveted on the regrouping warband.

'That's better, all front-rankers together. Just about now one of those blue-faced boys would have been hacking your head off to take home to frighten his kids with when they wouldn't go to their bed at night. But some idiot officer said we had a duty to pull your knackers out of the fire, what with you being our sister cohort.'

He spat on the ground noisily.

'Sisters being just about right. Anyway, here we are and here we stand. No reason why you lot should get all the fun. When does the next session start?'

Where the line had been thinning to the point of desperate vulnerability there were now three unbroken lines of shields, the newcomers' strength giving fresh heart to the desperately tired Tungrians. Those of the cohort's survivors with the energy shouted the time-worn insults that had always been exchanged when the 1st and 2nd Tungrians met in the field. An officer walked out of the smoke that still drifted across the slope in pale grey curtains, his sword drawn, searching for the First Spear. Frontinius winced as Dubnus finished lashing a broken spear shaft to his wounded leg as a makeshift splint, raising a weary hand in salute as the other man stopped in front of where he lay.

'Prefect Bassus. I can honestly say I've never been quite so pleased to see the Second Cohort . . .'

The prefect laughed, looking out over the rampart of bodies.

'We heard your trumpet calls on the wind, so faint that some men swore it was only the wind, but the stand fast was clear enough for those with ears to hear it. The other prefects insisted on following their orders, but I never liked that greasy little shit Perennis, and seeing this lot proves I was right. Beside, Tungrians never leave their brothers dangling.'

Frontinius nodded, climbing to his feet with Marcus's help.

'I fear all you've achieved is to dangle alongside us, but I appreciate the company while we wait to die. And now, if you'll excuse me?'

The First Spear hobbled off up the slope to make his report to Equitius, using another broken spear to support his weight on the wounded leg. Bassus looked to Dubnus, raising a questioning eyebrow.

'Excuse us for a moment, Chosen.'

He waited for the big man to walk out of earshot before speaking to Marcus, his face suddenly dark with anger.

'I received a message yesterday night, a tablet from my wife, respectfully asking me for a divorce. It seems that she has tired of my company and, I can only presume, wishes for that of another. While this is hardly the time for such a discussion, I will be expecting a frank conversation with you once we have these barbarians running.'

He turned on his heel and walked away to attend to his command. Julius strolled back across the slope with a sidelong glance at the senior officer.

'Trouble?'

'Nothing I haven't earned.'

The other man smiled easily.

'I don't think he'll be troubling you after the battle. Not from what I've been hearing his troops say in the last couple of minutes.'

Marcus stared at him uncomprehendingly.

'Never mind. Everything in its time.'

The two men took stock as corpses and the seriously wounded were carried away up the slope by the walking wounded, counting another twenty casualties between their two centuries as their line clung to its ground with what was, even with the reinforcement of another eight hundred men, a tenuous hold. Through a gap in the smoke Marcus saw the Petriana waiting still on their ridge-line, the sparse forest of their spears unreduced and unmoving. Julius followed his gaze, then spat on the bloodied grass.

'No help to be expected from that direction. Bloody cavalry are all the same, good for the chase once the battle's won, just never around when the shit starts flying.'

Marcus nodded grimly, watching the barbarians working themselves up for another charge. Julius spat on to the scarred turf again, examining his sword's edge.

'This is it. This time they'll throw everything they have at us, here, on the flanks, everywhere, and that will be it, Second Tungrians or no Second Tungrians. Are you ready to die for the empire?'

'For the cohort. The empire can kiss my hairy arse.'

The older man laughed with a dark delight, his eyes wild with the fight.

'Spoken like a real Tungrian. Let's get into the line and get ready to go out in style.'

Up the slope, the prefect was weighing his options, watching as a medic carried out field treatment on Frontinius. The medic, having cleaned the entry and exit wounds around the arrow's shaft with water and a clean cloth, took an exploratory grip of the feathered end that protruded from the First Spear's knee. The prefect winced with his friend's obvious pain. Frontinius leant back on the grass wearily, closing his eyes as the bandage carrier took a firmer grip of the arrow. With a sudden twist, the medic snapped the arrow's shaft, then swiftly pulled the barbed end out of the back of the officer's knee. Frontinius watched with narrowed eyes as he expertly bandaged the wound, winding the cloth tightly as blood blossomed through its weave.

'You can stand, First Spear, but you have to keep the leg straight. And keep your weight off it.'

Frontinius struggled to his feet, accepting the prefect's offered hand to pull him erect.

'I'll be separated from my head quite shortly, sonny boy. The knee can . . .'

His retort trailed off as movement up the slope, at the wood's edge, caught his eye.

The Tungrians watched the wall of barbarians slowly wash up the hill towards them, picking their way carefully across the wall of their dead. There was no headstrong charge this time, only a steady advance by the thousands of men to their front, confident in their numerical advantage but made cautious by the sight and smell of the dead and dying littering the ground around them. Facing them, men from both cohorts stood in an ordered line, calm in their resignation for the most part. A man close to Scarface whimpered with fear, quietening as the veteran soldier glared down the line at him and barked out his name. The 2nd Cohort watch officer nodded approvingly.

'Too late for second thoughts now, my lads. If you can't take a joke then you shouldn't have joined in the first place. Just make sure you take some of the bastards across the river with you.'

With certain death at hand, men tightened their sweat-and-blood-slickened grip on swords and shields, waiting to kill for the last time.

The barbarian line passed over the wall of dead, speeding

up to walking pace with the obstacle crossed, the lack of spears in Roman hands having reduced it to a hindrance rather than the death trap it had been earlier in the morning. Twenty yards from the Tungrians they stopped at a shouted command, allowing Calgus's messenger to step into the gap between the two forces.

'Tungrians, the Lord Calgus offers you one last chance to live. Surrender now and you will be well treated . . .'

His voice tailed away as Julius stepped forward, his armour painted with the blood of a dozen men, his shield scored and notched by swords, the shafts of three arrows protruding from its wooden face.

'One step more and I'll send your cock back to the *Lord* Calgus while the rest of you stays here. You want these . . .'

He raised sword and shield into their fighting positions, backing carefully into the line as the men to either side readied themselves in similar fashion.

'. . . then fucking well come and get them, cum stain.'

The messenger shrugged indifferently, then turned away and was absorbed into the barbarian mass. The warband's fresh warriors began banging their swords and shields, creating a wall of sound that bore down oppressively on the Tungrians, first advancing one step, then another, some swinging their swords in extravagant arcs and screaming of the slaughter to come. The Tungrians waited, hollow eyed, for the barbarian line to charge across the narrowing gap and finish the unequal contest.

The barbarian line gathered itself to pounce, the mass of shaggy-haired warriors baying for blood as the Tungrian cohorts waited grimly for their assault. Frontinius's voice rang out over the din, his command the last Marcus would have expected.

'Tungrians, on the ground! *On the ground!*'

The line went to the ground after a second's bewildered pause, the brighter soldiers realising what it meant and twisting to look back to their rear as they fell. The barbarian line wavered at the sight, as a line of hard-faced soldiers, fresh and unblooded, came out of the smoke. These men were different to those in the Tungrian line, their armour fashioned from overlaid plates rather than chain mail, their javelins topped with slender iron shanks sprouting viciously barbed points. Scarface and the 2nd Cohort watch officer exchanged looks of amazed glee.

'Legionaries? Fuck me, it's the Sixth, or what's left of 'em. They must be gagging to get into this lot.'

The watch officer nodded as he hugged the blood-sodden grass.

'They do look a tiny bit pissed off.'

'Halt!'

Prefect Licinius's voice was authoritative above the warband's din, all urbanity lost in the harsh command. The newcomers' force stretched all the way across the small battlefield behind the Tungrians, three lines of men with spears held ready to throw. More men were advancing out of the smoke behind them. A lot more men.

'Front rank, *throw!*'

The advancing soldiers took an unhesitating three-step run-up and launched a volley of spears into the warband's front rank.

'Front rank, kneel! Second rank, *throw!*'

Another rain of spears showered on to the barbarians.

'Second rank, kneel! Third rank, *throw!*'

The warband shuddered under the third volley, hundreds of men having fallen in the previous few seconds. Licinius's voice hardened.

'Sixth Legion, on your feet. Form line for attack.'

The legionaries were on their feet with their line dressed and ready in seconds, a wall of shields and swords suddenly presented to their amazed enemy.

'Sixth Legion, for the honour of your fallen dead . . .'

The hairs on the back of Marcus's neck lifted with the emotion in the prefect's voice. A sudden silence descended on the battlefield as the warband grew quiet with apprehension, their presumed easy victory suddenly impending disaster. Only the cries and moans of the wounded broke the silence. Licinius growled into the hush the last command that would be needed to start the slaughter, his harsh voice audible from one end of the line to other.

'. . . no . . . *prisoners!*'

The depleted legion's centurions echoed the command, ordering the surviving cohorts forward in a deliberate advance. Their determined tread took them over and past the Tungrians, the supine bodies trampled by men fixated with the view to their front. As the warband's front rank quailed at their remorseless advance, unable to retreat owing to the sheer mass of men packed in behind them, the legionaries closed the gap between them and started their slaughter with ruthless efficiency and barely restrained fury.

'Find the officers!'

Marcus recognised the voice, and stood up in the shelter of the legion's line.

'No need, Prefect, we're here.'

Licinius nodded impassively, then switched his gaze to stare out across the valley.

Through the smoke's dying efforts Marcus could just make out a mass of men emerging from the cover of the wood to their right, a cohort at the least. The thick column kept on coming, pouring on to the slope like a monstrous armoured snake. Julius, staring at the mass of troops with eyes that seemed unfocused, pulled off his helmet and scratched his sweaty scalp.

'How many?'

The prefect smiled grimly.

'Six thousand. That's the entire Twentieth Legion. And to our left is the Second, the other half of the nutcrackers. These barbarian bastards are going to pay in blood for what they've done today.'

From the cover of the wood's other arm another tide of men was washing down the other slope, another legion in full cry. On the crest above them the cavalry's armour still glittered in the morning sun, but as Marcus's eye found them they started to pour down off the hill, the Petriana on the move at last, seeking targets for their lances. The warband, in severe danger of being encircled by the legions, shivered under the shock of their sudden appearance on its flanks, then broke into hundreds of family groups, falling over each other in their haste to escape the battlefield. Marcus bent over, putting his hands on his knees to provide support for suddenly weak limbs, and was abruptly, violently, sick.

★

Postumius Avitus Macrinus, legatus of the Imperial 20th Legion, stepped on to the blood-soaked slope with a grim face, the two centuries advancing up the hill ahead of him systematically butchering any of the wounded that had survived. A stroke of luck had brought a Petriana messenger to him as his own legion and the 2nd were marching less than five miles distant. His leading cohorts had been driven forward towards the distant smoke of the battle at a merciless run by their centurions, their exhaustion turning to cold purpose as they crested the final slope and saw thousands of the enemy below. The barbarian warband had scattered like chaff under their combined attack, put to flight in their tribal and family groups and pursued by a dozen cohorts with murder in their hearts and the guidance of questing cavalrymen, eager for heads.

He'd met with Licinius briefly when the Petriana's prefect had found the oncoming legions, and had guided them in to attack from either side of the wood before taking the 6th's remaining cohorts down through the trees to reinforce the Tungrians. He'd been unsurprised to have his request for the prefect to take over the remnants of the 6th legion refused without hesitation.

'Absolutely not, Legatus, I was brought up on horseback and this style of fighting doesn't suit me. Besides, you need the Petriana out in front of your legions, and I'm the best man to keep a foot firmly up their idle British arses. Go and talk to the man that made this possible.'

He'd pointed up the hill behind them, at a cohort-sized group of warriors arrayed behind an impressive rampart of dead barbarians, and told the legate in swift, economical sentences the story of Titus Tigidius Perennis's betrayal of the 6th and the Tungrians' stand on the hillside. Both Perennis's treachery and his parentage had come as a shock to the veteran officer.

'Jupiter! Sextus Tigidius Perennis's son did this? The son of the praetorian prefect lured an imperial legion into a barbarian ambush? Every time I think I've seen it all . . .'

Nodding his understanding, and clapping the tired prefect on the shoulder, he'd called a senior centurion to his side, pointing up the hill.

'I'm going up there. You might want to send a few men with me in case any of those dead barbarians is faking.'

Behind him, mute testimony to the effectiveness of Perennis's betrayal, thousands of Roman bodies lay in untidy bloodstained heaps around a series of unseen diminishing circles, the successive defence perimeters of the hopelessly outnumbered and disarrayed 6th Legion cohorts taken in Calgus's trap. He had already seen Sollemnis's body for himself, needing to know that the man was really dead and not carried away as a hostage. The legatus's sword had been hidden under another man's body, concealment sufficient to foil the brief search of the fallen for valuables that had been all the ongoing battle had allowed the barbarians. The weapon now rested in its scabbard once more, carried by one of his staff. He would have the difficult honour of passing it on to the man's oldest son.

He should have been at home himself, his age advancing towards a mature fifty more quickly than he cared to consider after a lifetime fighting Rome's enemies. The throne, however, or those behind it, trusted him too well to leave him in retirement. He'd been called from his fireside to command the 20th barely three months before, with instructions to look for signs that senior officers in the province were not to be trusted.

'I won't be the imperial informer, Prefect Perennis,' he'd told the praetorian guard's commander flatly, pointing a thick finger at the emperor's right-hand man, with whom he'd served twenty years before in Syria. He'd been respectfully summoned to dine with the imperial favourite, a private dinner served by slaves who appeared deaf, so little was their interest in the proceedings.

'And no one expects you to, Senator, least of all me. I don't care if some of the younger and impressionable idiots believe all they hear from Rome, and take it into their stupid heads that Commodus isn't fit for their respect. Every young emperor has to earn the regard of the army, and he will, given time. What I want from you is hard intelligence on the British situation, who's effective and who isn't. The rumours reaching us here are that the governor is playing a foolish game, not sending all of the gold intended to keep the northern tribal leaders happy to the right places, and we'd rather know the truth with enough time to act on it. Gods above us, the last thing we need is another bloody revolt on the edge of the world. On top of that, you'll provide us with a tested senior officer in place if anything does happen.'

He'd nodded, able to accept the task he was bidden to take on. Perennis had smiled quietly and sipped his wine, then put the cup down.

'One thing, though, you could keep an eye open for the late Senator Valerius Aquila's boy. There are rumours that he might have buried himself out of sight in the Wall army.'

He'd given the other man a darker look, as unresolved as to his views on young Aquila then as he was now. He'd known the senator in happier days, and had viewed his death with a sickened resignation as one of the small dramas that play out across every change of power. If the lad was still at large, and not dead or enslaved, he was mindful not to take too close an interest. Ignoring the misdemeanours of the men that surrounded the young emperor was one thing, abetting them was quite another.

Before him, in increasing numbers as he climbed the incline, slipping more than once on the treacherous footing, were arrayed barbarian dead, the leavings of the auxiliary cohort's defiant stand at the valley's head. At first they lay alone, wounded men killed as they had crawled away from the battle, then in twos and threes. The ground, previously scattered with the blood of the wounded, became slick with blood and faeces, the earth pounded into a greasy bog under thousands of feet, and the dead suddenly outnumbered the living. An eye-watering stench pervaded the air.

Unable to avoid committing the indignity of stepping upon the fallen, the legatus climbed a wall of corpses three feet high, men hacked and torn by grievous wounds, dropped in their hundreds to form a rampart for the defenders to shelter behind. A soldier to his right spotted some minute movement among the mangled warriors, and stepped in to strike with his gladius. The legatus returned his gaze to the front, seeing auxiliary troops among the dead for the first time, their bodies neatly laid in rows by their fellow troops and covered with their capes. He winced at the number of their dead, looking to the remaining troops to gauge their fitness for further action.

The cohort was standing to attention, neatly paraded across the hillside by century, a good sign in itself, as was the fact that they had already washed most of the inevitable blood spray of battle from their faces, if not their black-caked armour. The cohort's prefect stepped forward to meet him, the man's grasp shaking slightly. Shock or fatigue? He kept his demeanour brisk, hoping to help the man a little with his battle weariness.

'Prefect Equitius? I'm Legatus Postumius Avitus Macrinus, Twentieth Imperial Legion and, with the death of our esteemed colleague Legatus Gaius Calidius Sollemnis, now general in command of this whole sorry mess.'

He paused, looking out across the sea of corpses.

'You, Prefect, seem to have gained us a victory. The

Petriana's commander tells me that you held this place against many times your own number in order to keep Calgus busy until reinforcement could arrive. You paid a heavy price for that success, I see . . .'

The other man nodded, his eyes far away.

'You could consider this ground bought and paid for, Legatus.'

A burly man passed them without recognition, his hollow eyes fixed on the body cradled in his arms.

'Another casualty. As you say, bought and paid for.'

The prefect watched Morban deposit the corpse alongside the cohort's other dead with gentle care.

'His son, I fear.'

'Ah . . . a difficult moment for any man.'

The senior officer waited a moment, watching the other for signs of mental defeat, but saw none.

'I'm sorry, but I'm new enough to this country not to know your unit by anything other than name. Forgive the question as simple ignorance of your men's resilience, but can they fight on?'

The prefect nodded slowly.

'We have an overall casualty figure of one hundred and fifty-eight dead and another one hundred and three seriously wounded, of whom at least half will die, plus a couple of hundred with minor wounds, cuts and bruises, who can be treated in the field. I am three officers short, one dead and two wounded, plus a First Spear with an arrow wound that he's determined to ignore, and I've lost half a dozen or so watch officers. So it isn't pretty, but yes, we can fight, given time to bury our dead and get some food into the troops.'

'Good. And yourself?'

The other man raised an eyebrow.

'I'm in better condition than most of my men. They did the fighting here, not me.'

'And yet your quick thinking, coupled with their prowess, made amends for what would otherwise have been a total disaster. With Calidius Sollemnis dead I'm the only general officer left in this command, which gives me the undisputed right to make battlefield promotions I feel are justified. I'm also a recent appointment from the imperial court. Even the governor wouldn't consider challenging my authority on a question of promotion. You're the man I need, Prefect, to take what's left of the Sixth legion and rebuild it.'

'Legatus, with respect . . .'

The senior officer silenced him with a raised hand.

'No, Prefect, the respect comes from this side of our short relationship. Your auxiliaries fought like praetorians here. You know how to manage soldiers, and you come with a ready-made reputation. With Perennis dead, my only other option would be to promote a young man from my own staff, and there's none of them your equal. The Petriana's prefect told me not to bother asking him, and since they're our most potent weapon I'm happy to leave him in post. I can't guarantee you the position in the longer term, but you'll lead the Sixth for the rest of the summer, and you'll have the title and status that go with the responsibility. You'll be able to retire to a nice civil job even if you're not confirmed in position, and in the meanwhile your family will be quartered in the Yew Grove headquarters. So, don't tell me you won't accept my offer, because I'm not minded to let you refuse.'

The prefect closed his eyes for a moment, wearily considering the options.

'Who succeeds me here?'

'I presume your First Spear's competent?'

He nodded.

'Then there's no urgent need to find a man of the equestrian class to replace you. Let that wait for calmer days. For the time being your men need a familiar face to look up to, not a new one they didn't see on this bloody hillside today.'

'Very well, Legatus, I will accept your generous offer.'

'Good. Take a few minutes to brief your people and then take command of the Sixth at once. You'll find them regrouping at the far end of valley if my order to halt their pursuit reached them. I'll let you have the Frisians and the Raetians as temporary reinforcement to bring your legion up over half-strength. Oh, and have the two Tungrian cohorts pull back to the Wall. I want some rear-area security on the road between here and Yew Grove, besides which it will give them a breather. We'll need them back in the campaign soon enough.'

'Sir.'

The new legatus turned to go, then turned back.

'I presume that you've found Legatus Sollemnis's body?'

'Yes, he died on his feet, it seems. He'd been beheaded, though. I hear these wretched people sometimes preserve the head of an enemy in the oil of the cedar. Perhaps when you recover his lost eagle you'll be able to bring him some peace too.'

'Did you find his sword?'

'Indeed, my First Spear has it. I'll return it to his family when I go back to Rome at the end of the year.'

'I know Sollemnis's son better than most people. It would be my honour to return the weapon to him . . .'

The legate called his senior centurion over, took an oilskin-wrapped package from him and presented it with obvious relief.

'I'm happy to have the responsibility off my shoulders. I've never once enjoyed seeing the faces of the relatives when I pitch up with their loved ones' personal effects . . . Anyway, Legatus, away and get your new command pulled into shape. I'll see you at tonight's commanders' conference.'

He turned away and picked his way gingerly down the hillside, watched by the remaining Tungrians. Frontinius hobbled over to the prefect, a question on his face.

'I'm a legatus, Sextus, new commander of the Sixth, or what's left of them . . .'

Frontinius congratulated him with genuine warmth, delighted for his friend.

'You will always be able to count on our support, Legatus. Might I enquire as to your replacement?'

'For the time being you're in command here. In the longer term I expect there'll be a queue of suitable candidates . . .'

Frontinius nodded.

'Then I'll make the most of my brief moment in the sun. Our orders?'

'Get your dead underground with dignity and then move to join the legions. They'll be camping back on the hill we used last night, I believe. I suggest that you use the Sixth Legion's supplies since they're several thousand men down on their establishment. Tomorrow morning you'll be marching for the Rock as fast as you can alongside the Second Cohort, and will secure what's left of the fort . . .'

Equitius's face creased into a frown.

'. . . and no, it isn't a quiet option for you, or any sign that I consider your command as unfit for battle. There are probably several thousand barbarians still milling about to our rear in a variety of groupings, and while I expect them to take to the hills once news of this action gets out, some of them still might be tempted to try a run south instead. In truth we've little enough between here and Yew Grove that we can trust to get in their way. Securing the crossroads south of the Wall is my first priority, after enjoying the sight of Calgus's head on a pole and seeing the Sixth's eagle back in the hands of a bad-tempered standard-bearer. I'll ask for a century of cavalry from the Petriana to scout ahead of you, and to maintain contact with the main body of the army . . .'

The new prefect nodded his understanding.

'. . . and now I must leave. Before I go, I need one favour from you.'

Frontinius nodded.

'Legatus?'

'I need a bodyguard, just a few tent parties. These men don't know me, and I don't know them. I'd feel safer with a few close friends between me and the blue-faces.'

'Got anybody in mind?'

Equitius looked out over the battlefield, still amazed at the slaughter committed across the valley's green slopes.

'I thought I might ask you for the Ninth Century, or what's left of them. Young Corvus ought to be safe enough with Perennis out of the way . . . and at some point I need to give him this.'

Frontinius peered inside the oilskin package as Equitius opened it to display the weapon inside, taking in the sword's fine workmanship.

'Very pretty. Sollemnis?'

'Yes. Tradition says it goes to his oldest son . . .'

'And now might not be quite the right time for that story to be told.'

'Exactly.'

Frontinius nodded.

'Very well, Legatus, the Ninth it is. Just remember we want them back.'

For the 9th the next month passed as quickly as the previous week. Sixth Legion, reinforced by the addition of the two auxiliary cohorts, giving it an effective strength of six cohorts, marched into the north, while the 20th and the 2nd legions pulled back to hold the Wall and start the task of rebuilding its shattered forts. The legions' task, carried out day after unremitting day, was to sweep the open countryside for tribal bands on the run after what had quickly became known to both army and the unwilling populace through which they moved as the Battle of the Lost Eagle. After the first week, with the weather turning sour and wind-driven drizzle working its way into armour and equipment, bringing the scourge of rust without constant care, the experience soon began to pall.

Waking before dawn, often in driving rain as a succession of cloud banks swept across the country, the legion was routinely on its feet until after dark, an eighteen-hour day at that time of the year and longer for men standing guard in the night. Moving into the increasingly mountainous country in search of the fleeing barbarians exposed them to likely ambush and inevitable pinprick attacks, knives in the dark and snatched bow shots from hidden archers who frequently escaped their clutches.

Intelligence gathered by their native scouts told Equitius that the captured eagle, and with it Sollemnis's head, went before them, tantalisingly close to recapture, and for the sake of his dead friend he pushed its pursuit for longer than might have been judged prudent. Each village and farm they encountered greeted their passing with forced indifference, as if neither side knew that refugees from the battle were hidden close by. Even the petty revenges of searching the rough dwellings, stealing any valuables their inhabitants were stupid enough not to have hidden, and the confiscation and slaughter of the farm animals for food, did little to lift the spirits of men who knew their enemy was laughing at their failure to retake the legion's precious standard.

Marcus's men held up well enough, helped by the distraction of keeping Morban from dwelling on his loss. The burly standard-bearer didn't sleep, lost weight and volunteered for guard duty at every opportunity, seeking activity to prevent opportunities to brood over his son's death in the battle's last minutes. Some of the century attempted to use humour to keep his spirits up. Marcus overheard two of his men attempting to lighten the standard-bearer's mood in camp late one evening.

'Morban, how many legion road-builders does it take to light a lamp?'

'No idea.'

'Five – one to light it and four lazy bastards leaning on their shovels to watch!'

The other soldier chipped in.

'Morban, how many stores staff does it take to light a lamp?'

'Go on.'

'Ten – one to light it and nine to do the paperwork!'

The first man started back in.

'Morban, how many prostitutes does it take to light a lamp?'

'Look, just . . .'

'Looks like one, but she's only faking it!'

Morban smiled sadly as he stood to leave.

'Look, lads, I know you're just trying to cheer me up, and that last one wasn't too bad, but just give it a rest, eh?'

Dubnus spoke darkly to Marcus on the subject, an unusual frown on his face.

'The next action we see, he'll take his first chance to jump into the blue-faces and get killed. Which is bad enough, but I wouldn't trust some of the lads not to jump in behind him and try to save him . . .'

They agreed to keep an eye on their friend, and in the event of impending battle to make sure he was kept away from the shield wall. Marcus knew it could only be a temporary solution.

With the legionnaires visibly losing their edge under the constant strain, and without any indication that they might regain the legion's badge of honour any time soon, Equitius was forced to bow to the inevitable. Standing in camp late one evening, watching the troops labour over yet another turf wall in the orange light of the setting sun, he turned to Marcus and looked at the young centurion properly for the first time in over a week.

'You look tired, Centurion, in need of a decent bath and a cup of a decent red . . .'

Marcus straightened his back reflexively, opening eyes that had narrowed to slits in anticipation and need of sleep.

'Relax, I wasn't finding fault. The gods know *I* could sweat a helmet full of dirt given the chance. And as for a decent drink . . . anyway, I've come to a decision. Tomorrow we'll have a rest day, give the cohorts a chance to get their tunics clean and polish the rust off their swords.'

Marcus nodded gratefully.

'And the day after?'

'We turn south. Four or five days' march ought to see us back to the Wall.'

'We're giving up the hunt?'

'Yes. They're playing with us, you know, spreading rumours to lead us round the countryside like a bull being pulled round the farmyard by the ring in its nose. Soon enough Calgus will lure us into some nasty ambush or other, cost us more men we can't afford to lose, and I don't intend to give him the satisfaction. It's time to go home and wait for reinforcements from Gaul.'

A shaft of orange sunlight lit the camp, and Equitius stretched luxuriously in the warm glow.

'Share a beaker with me, Centurion?'

They sat in Equitius's private tent, pitched alongside the

massive command tent, and sipped their wine. For a while neither spoke. At last Equitius broke the silence.

'I don't suppose the last year has been anything other than a waking nightmare for you. If it's any consolation, you've acquitted yourself better than I could have imagined when we took you in, back in the month of Mars. With hindsight, though, you were never going to fail this test. Not with your blood. I've been waiting for the right time to give you something, and now seems as good a time as any . . .'

He pulled the oilskin package from under his camp bed, putting it in Marcus's hands with a smile.

'It belonged to Legatus Sollemnis. He wanted you to have it . . .'

Marcus unwrapped the sword, looking closely at the hilt's ornate decoration and inlay before pulling it from the scabbard and testing its fine balance.

'It's a beautiful weapon . . .'

'So it should be. I was with him when he bought it and it cost him more money than *I* would ever have spent on a sword. It served him with honour too, right across the empire in the service of the Emperor Marcus Aurelius.'

'I'm honoured. But why me?'

'He spoke to me the night before the Battle of the Lost Eagle. Perhaps he had a premonition, I don't know, but he asked me to make sure that the sword went to you if he should be killed the next day. I'd say he wanted it to go to someone that will bring it further honour. Besides, you're about the right age to have been the son he always wanted . . .'

He hovered close to breaking his promise to Frontinius at that moment, resisting the urge to tell Marcus the truth only with an effort of will.

'And now, Centurion, you can get that lamp fuel down your neck and fetch the senior centurions to come and see me. The sooner that lot out there know they've got a day of rest tomorrow the happier we'll all be.'

The depleted legion turned south the day after next as promised and, with thoughts of home in their hearts, made the journey back to the Wall in four days. At Noisy Valley, where buildings were being thrown up to replace those burned out to deny the warband their supplies, the other legions had set about building a temporary camp to house them until they could march south to their fortresses at the campaign's end. Equitius went looking for the 20th's legate to make his report, taking Marcus and a tent party of his men as close escort. They found the Northern Command's new general in his freshly erected wooden principia, a clutch of legion tribunes and senior centurions gathered around him as they planned the campaign's next moves. Dismissing his escort for the time being, Equitius approached Legatus Macrinus and made his salute before joining the group.

Marcus took his men outside to wait for the legatus, sitting them down in the early afternoon's warmth with a quiet order to Dubnus to keep them busy polishing their helmets, and to call him when Equitius had completed his duties inside, then headed for the infirmary. The legionaries guarding the hospital confirmed that there were Tungrian wounded inside. He found a couple of dozen of them, including five of his own men, sporting bandages and, in a couple of cases, fracture splints. Their delight at the visit was obvious, and they sat him down on a bed and plied him with questions on the state of the campaign.

It soon became clear that they knew more about what was going on than he did, and the consensus was that there was another advance to the north planned before the end of the summer. The Tungrians had been sent back to the Hill a few days before for a week's leave and to do whatever recruiting was possible locally to boost their strength, but were scheduled to return to the swiftly growing legionary fortress that Noisy Valley was becoming for further duty. Yes, they were all well enough, although several of their mates had died in the difficult days of the march south from the battlefield, too badly hurt to survive for the most part, but the care in the hospital had saved several others, particularly that from one doctor, the last said with much rolling of eyes and significant nods.

Marcus, knowing exactly where the conversation was going, smiled weakly and took his leave, promising to remember them to their friends and, if time allowed, to send their mates in to see them. In truth he'd forced himself to forget her, assisted by the strains of the last month, and being reminded of her existence was like having an ice-cold dagger twisted in his soul. Turning away, he came face to face with Felicia, who had been standing watching him with his men with a small smile on her face. He froze with uncertainty, blushing uncontrollably.

'Centurion. I trust you find your men in good condition?'

Recovering his wits, he bowed formally.

'Yes, ma'am, I'm told that almost everyone that made it here survived. The Tungrian cohort is in your debt.'

She smiled, and Marcus's heart leapt in his chest.

'That's probably no recommendation for our care. Anyone that survived that journey was probably going to live anyway . . .'

The more vocal of the Tungrians butted in indignantly on her behalf, one of them volunteering to remove his bandages and show Marcus the truly horrible wound the doctor had cleaned with delicate care three times a day, picking out the dead flesh so carefully that he hadn't even felt her working, until Marcus's irritation overcame his embarrassment, and he shooed the men back to their beds.

With order restored, he turned back to Felicia with fresh confidence.

'If their exuberance is any guide, I'd say you've done a fine job on them, Doctor. Perhaps we could discuss their likely further treatment somewhere a little quieter, and I'll pass your diagnosis on to their prefect when I see him next.'

She smiled a secret smile, beckoning him down the ward and into her tiny office. In the small room, lit by the sun's light through an open window, he noticed that her tunic was not dark blue, as he'd supposed in the less well-illuminated ward, but simple black. She followed his gaze and pursed her lips.

'My husband was killed in that battle you fought against the barbarians.'

Marcus frowned, confused.

'He was alive the last time I saw him.'

'It happened later in the day, apparently, during the pursuit. His cohort cornered a barbarian band which turned and fought them to the death. He was found dead after the fight. It was a spear apparently, although the circumstances seem to have been confused . . .'

'I'm sorry. I mean . . . I read your tablet . . . and he told me that . . .'

'I know. I hated the man for the last year of our marriage, and his death has freed me to do whatever I want, within reason, but I still feel guilty about what happened.'

Marcus leaned back against the wall, looking closely at her face.

'I'm . . . I . . .'

'Yes, Centurion?'

'I would prefer it if you would call me Marcus. And I'd like to think, given time, of course, that we might . . .'

'Be together? Yes, I thought so too. I think I still do. But I *do* need time to let all this work itself out. Come and see me next time you're in camp. I won't be going anywhere in the meanwhile.'

He nodded his understanding, turning for the door.

'Centurion . . . Marcus?'

'Ma'am?'

'Firstly you could stop calling me "ma'am" as if I were some Roman matron. You know my forename . . .'

He managed a smile in return.

'Yes, Clodia Drusilla. But, if you'll forgive me, I won't use it until I know whether we're to be friends or something more. Call it superstition. And secondly, ma'am?'

'You could hold me for a moment. Remind me what male affection feels like.'

He took her in his arms, holding her slim body against his armour and stroking her hair with his right hand. After a long moment she pulled away, smiling again.

'Next time we do that, I'll make a point of your not being dressed in twenty pounds of chain mail. We don't *all* have a compulsion for men in uniform. Now, off with you, I've got work to do.'

Marcus ran the gauntlet of the wounded Tungrians, all of whom had stupid smiles on their faces and some of whom went so far as to wink and nod vigorously at him, pulling his helmet on as he walked out past the guards to cover up his own stupid smile. From the knowing looks and sideways glances he got from the men waiting for him outside the principia, he guessed that the wounded had found some way of passing the news to their colleagues. Thinking what he would have to put up with from Antenoch, he shook his head, only making his men smile more widely behind their hands.

When Equitius emerged from the building half an hour later, the look on his face was neutral, neither happy nor troubled.

'I'm in command for the rest of the summer, at least, and then we'll see what happens. There's still the small matter of a lost eagle to be dealt with, of course. Entire legions have been cashiered for losing their standards, broken up for reinforcements, so who knows what'll happen when the news reaches Rome . . .Twentieth and Second Legions are going to camp here for three weeks, since the barbarians will be too busy getting the harvest in to worry much about fighting us for the rest of the month. I'm taking the Sixth south to Yew Grove, to collect three cohorts of reinforcements that are expected there from Gaul within the week. So, you can head west to the Hill and rejoin the cohort. Give Uncle Sextus my thanks for the loan of your men, and tell him that I'll have a couple of centuries of replacements put to one side for him for when he brings his people back to Noisy Valley. That should get him back to full strength. There's a troop convoy expected into Arab Town soon with initial reinforcements, *real* Tungrians from northern Gaul, apparently.'

One more surprise awaited Marcus before he turned his men west. Rounding a corner on his way to the stores, he bumped into a squat man in uniform, his hair cropped short in the military style.

'Young Marcus!'

'Quintus!'

They embraced with delight, Rufius standing back to look his friend up and down.

'A bit thinner, a bit more muscle . . . and a scar or two, I'd bet. Not to mention an attachment to a rather attractive and recently widowed lady doctor, from what I've heard.'

Marcus shook his head in mock anger.

'Isn't there anyone in this bloody camp that can mind their own business? But why are you here, and not at the Hill?'

'I asked Sextus for some leave, and a chance to sort out some of my business affairs. It's amazing, you go missing for a month or two and suddenly you have to get the money people owe you at the point of a sword. Anyway, tell me what you've been up to in the hills since we turned south, you young puppy.'

The older man backed away as Marcus prodded him playfully in the belly with his vine stick.

'Not so much of the *puppy*, Centurion, I've done a good deal of growing up since we met on the road to Yew Grove.'

Rufius inclined his head gravely.

'Indeed you have. Do you have time for a drink and a natter?'

They repaired to the officers' mess and drank local beer while Marcus related what had happened since their parting after the Battle of the Lost Eagle. At length Rufius sat back, nodding his head sagely.

'You have been busy. At least all this excitement has taken everyone's mind off looking for a young man called Marcus Valerius Aquila for a while. Let's hope that bastard Perennis and his Asturian cronies were the only people that knew enough about you to be dangerous. You know that Annius died soon after the Battle of the Lost Eagle? Apparently he was found with an issue spear stuck right through him. Somebody strong must have taken a dislike to him . . . Anyway, you're safe now.'

'That's to be seen. I hardly look like one of the locals, do I?'

'True, but you're among friends. Anyway, I must go. I'm due back on the Hill by nightfall tomorrow, and there's still a nasty little shopkeeper that owes me three months' rent on his premises.'

He stood to go, offering his hand to Marcus.

'One question, Rufius.'

'If I can answer it.'

'You were Legatus Sollemnis's man. Why would he leave me this?'

He tapped the sword's hilt, raising an eyebrow in question. Rufius looked at him with calculation.

'Lad, the legatus was a good friend of your father. Think of the risk he took to look after you the way he did. Surely that's enough reason? Don't go looking for what isn't there to be found . . .'

From the thoughtful look in Marcus's eye, he wasn't sure that his bluff had succeeded.

The next day, eager to see the Hill again, the 9th took their leave of the legion and headed west along the road behind the Wall, a day's easy march bringing them to the fort. Marcus dismissed his men to their barracks and a well-earned rest, and went in search of Frontinius. He found the prefect enjoying a moment of quiet relaxation in the cohort's bathhouse, sitting quietly in the deserted steam room in the quiet of the evening. His wounded knee had healed well enough, although he was careful to hold it out straight in front of him, occasionally flexing the joint experimentally.

'Well, Centurion, it's good to see you back from the wilds! How did the Sixth fare after we parted company? Sit down for a sweat and tell me your story. Are you back with us to stay?'

'The Ninth Century is detached from service with the Sixth Legion, Prefect, with forty-nine effectives and five men still in the Noisy Valley base hospital. Legatus Equitius wants us all back at the Valley by the end of the month, for reinforcement and in case the barbarians decide to have another try. As to our story, there's nothing much to tell really. We marched round the mountains of the north chasing shadows and lies for a month, and hardly saw a man of fighting age.'

'All hidden away from reprisals, no doubt. How are your men?'

'Tired and homesick. Most of them just need a few days' rest: twelve hours' sleep a day and no parades . . .'

'What about Morban?'

'He's still in pieces. His son's death seems to have robbed him of the will to live.'

'Hmmm. You might want to get yourself down into the vicus in that case. His son's woman died suddenly a few days ago, and I hear her mother's come to collect her grandchild. If Morban's been knocked sideways by his lad's death I'd imagine he'll be devastated when he finds he's about to lose his grandson as well . . .'

Marcus took his leave, dressed hurriedly and headed down to the south gate, stopping a retired soldier in the vicus's street to ask for directions. At the door to the small house indicated he stopped, hearing voices from within.

'No, Morban, the boy has to come with *me*. Who's going to look after him if he stays here? You won't be around most of the time, and what sort of example will *you* set to the boy. By all accounts you drink, you whore and I know for a fact that you swear all the time. He comes with me!'

'But the lad . . .'

'Will be well cared for. What's your alternative?'

Marcus knocked respectfully at the door, standing back and taking off his helmet. It opened, an older woman, wiping at tear-filled eyes with the hem of her sleeve, standing in the opening.

'Centurion?'

'Ma'am. I'm Morban's officer and I heard he might be here. Could I come in for a moment?'

She ushered him in, the four of them practically filling the room. Morban's grandson crouched in a corner, his knees pulled up to his chest and his head buried between them. Marcus squatted down to his level, putting out a hand to touch the boy's face, lifting it with one finger under his chin. Guessing the boy's age to be nine or ten, he looked into his wet eyes and felt the loss and loneliness he was suffering. Memories of another little boy of the same age flooded over him, reminding him of a past happiness he hadn't given thought to for many days. He stood up again, turning to the woman with a small bow.

'Ma'am, so that you can understand my position regarding this unhappy situation, my parents were both killed earlier this year, as were my older sisters and younger brother. If anyone in this room has an understanding of what that boy's going through, it would be *me*.'

The woman's face softened a little with the words.

'You both think you've got a claim on the boy, one through blood, the other through an ability to provide the upbringing he needs. Now, I *could* simply enforce the law and tell you that the cohort has first claim on the lad, simple as that. And, ma'am, there would be nothing you could do to stop me. However . . .'

He put a hand up to quell the rising concern he saw in her face, shaking his head at Morban as his mouth started to open.

'*However* . . . from my unique perspective, I happen to believe that there's only one person in this room that can make the decision as to what should be done with him. I also think you should both stop to consider the effect your argument is having on *that* person.'

Morban turned his head to look at the wall, a single tear running down his face. Marcus squatted down again.

'What's your name, young man?'

The boy lifted his tear-streaked face, his voice quavering.

'My mother called me Corban. Dad used to call me Lupus for a nickname . . .'

'Very well, little wolf, you have a choice to make. It isn't an easy one, but nobody else can make it for you, no matter how good their intentions might be. You grandmother wants you to go home with her, and live in her village. There'll be other boys of your age to play with, and you'll be able to learn a trade of some kind as you get older. Your grandfather wants you to stay here on the Hill, and grow up to be a soldier like him and your father, but you can't join until you've seen fourteen summers, which is still a long time away, and you can't stay here without anyone to look after you. Before you choose, I'll give you a third choice. I'll take you on as my servant, which will mean that you have to keep my clothes clean and polish my boots and armour every day. I'll have you taught to read and write and, when you're old enough, you'll be able to choose whether you want to become a soldier or not. Also, I'll make sure that you go and see your grandmother twice a year. So, which do you choose?'

The boy thought for a moment.

'I want to be a soldier like my dad.'

'Well, you can't, not yet. You're too young for one thing, and I don't think we have any armour in your size. You can either take my offer or go back to your grandmother's village. Either way you can volunteer for service when you're old enough.'

'I'll work for you.'

'Centurion.'

'I'll work for you, Centurion.'

Marcus stood up, turning to face Morban and the old woman.

'He's made his decision. You, Morban, will be responsible for his good behaviour, and for ensuring that he isn't corrupted by bad language and poor behaviour. You will also be responsible for making sure that he spends time with his grandmother as promised, when the cohort isn't on campaign. And you, ma'am, should be aware that he's now effectively on imperial service, albeit as a civilian. I guarantee that he'll be educated by the time he's old enough to volunteer for the military, and that he'll have the best possible start in life we can give him. I've got at least one man in the century that has more learning than I do, and we'll make sure he pays attention.'

Morban turned to face her, putting a hand out to hold hers.

'He'll have fifty parents in the Ninth. I swear he'll come to no harm.'

She thought for a long moment, and then nodded with resignation.

Marcus looked her in the eyes, feeling tears of his own distorting his vision.

'If there's one thing I understand, ma'am, it's how that youngster's feeling right now. I'll be his big brother for as long as he needs me. After what these people have done for me, it's my chance to repay some of my debt.'

He bent to the boy, putting a hand out while the other wiped his eyes dry.

'Come on, then, wolf cub, let's be about our business. We've got a century to get into shape.'

The pair walked out of the door hand in hand, turning up the street towards the main gate, drawing surprised glances from a pair of passing soldiers. They turned to make a ribald comment from the security of the shadows, saw the look on Morban's face as he emerged behind them, and immediately thought better of it. The standard-bearer watched his officer and his grandson from the doorway as they progressed up the hill, losing sight of them as they passed the soldiers on guard. He turned to follow them up the road, muttering quietly under his breath to himself with a determination he hadn't felt for many days.

'Don't you worry, Centurion, my lads are going to follow you any fucking place you command. Or I'll know the reason why.'

EMPIRE

The story began in

WOUNDS *of* HONOUR

It continues in

ARROWS *of* FURY

I

The Tungrian centurions gathered round their leader in the warm afternoon sunshine, sharing a last moment of quiet before the fight to come. Marcus Tribulus Corvus winked at his friend and former chosen man Dubnus, now centurion of the 9th Century, which Marcus had previously commanded, then nudged the older man standing next to him, his attention fixed on the ranks of soldiers arrayed on the hillside behind them.

'Stop mooning after these legionaries, Rufius, you're a Tungrian now whether you like it or not.'

Rufius caught his sly smile and tip of the head to Julius, the detachment's senior centurion, and picked up the thread.

'I can't help it, Marcus. Just seeing all those *professional* soldiers standing waiting for battle takes me back to the days when I stood in front of them with a vine stick. And that's my old cohort too . . .'

Julius turned from his scrutiny of their objective and scowled at the two men with an exasperation that was only partly feigned. Rufius nudged Marcus back, shaking his head solemnly.

'Now, brother, let's be fair to our colleague and give him some peace. It's not his fault that it's taken all morning and half the afternoon to get two thousand men and a few bolt throwers into position. Even if my guts are growling like a shithouse dog and there's enough sweat running down my legs to make my boots squelch for a week.'

Dubnus leaned over and tapped the veteran centurion on the shoulder.

'I think you'll find we call that wet stuff "piss" in this cohort, Grandfather.'

The older man smiled tolerantly.

'Very good, Dubnus. Just you concentrate on taking your lads into action as their centurion for the first time, and I'll worry about whether I'll be able to hold my bladder in a fight for the fiftieth time. Youth, eh, Julius?'

Julius, having turned back to his study of the defences looming before them, replied in a tired tone of voice that betrayed his growing frustration with their prolonged wait in front of the tribal hill fort they would shortly be attempting to storm.

'Might I suggest that you all shut the fuck up, given that it looks like we'll actually be attacking soon? Just as soon as those idiots have been cleared from the top of their wall that'll be us on the march, and ready for our starring role in Tribune Antonius's great victory over the Carvetii tribe. When I send you back to your centuries you get your men ready to advance, you repeat our orders to them all one last time, and remember to keep your bloody heads down once we're on the move.'

Julius cast a disparaging glance at the batteries of bolt throwers ranged alongside his four centuries, their sweating crews toiling at the weapons' hand winches as they ratcheted the heavy bowstrings back ready to fire. He tugged at the strap of his helmet, the crosswise crest that marked him as a centurion ruffled by the breeze as he turned back to stare at the wooden walled fort to their front.

'I don't trust those lazy bastards not to underwind and drop the occasional bolt short. And when we do attack, let me remind you one last time that our objective is to break in and take the first rampart. Just that, and only that. Tribune Antonius has been crystal clear on the subject.'

Marcus managed to keep a straight face despite Rufius's knowing smile. It was an open secret among the officers of the 6th Legion's expedition against the rebellious Carvetii tribe that the legion's senatorial tribune, the legatus's second-in-command, was desperate to prove his readiness to command a legion of his own before his short tenure in the position ended to make way for another aspiring general.

'Once the way's clear to the second gate we let the legionaries through to take their turn, got it? So, clear any resistance behind the first wall and then hold your men in place. No battle rage, and no trying to win the fortification crown. Not that any of us would ever be so favoured with two cohorts of regulars all vying for the honour. Once we've done our bit I'll call the bloody road menders forward and they can do the rest.'

The officers clustered around him turned to watch as the bolt-thrower battery to the right of their soldiers loosed a volley of three missiles at the hill fort's outer wooden palisade, barely two hundred paces from the ranks of their soldiers. At such close range the weapons crews were taking full advantage of their weapons' accuracy, and another of the barbarian warriors lining the fort's wooden walls was plucked away by the bolt's savage power, most likely dead before he hit the ground behind the palisade. After a moment the remaining defenders ducked into the cover of the fort's thick wooden beams, and the artillery crews grinned their satisfaction as their officer shouted at them to get back on their weapons' hand winches and prepare to shoot again. Julius nodded.

'That'll be it; their heads are down. Get back to your centuries.'

The four centurions saluted him and turned away, heading for their places in the two columns of auxiliary infantry waiting to either side of the heavy wooden ram that was key to their assigned task of breaking into the hill fort. Dubnus, the leader of the century that led the right-hand column, a tall and broad-shouldered young centurion with the frame of an athlete and a heavy black beard, spoke quickly to his chosen man, who in turn set the century's watch officers to one last check that every man was ready to fight. While they fussed over armour and weapons for the final time Dubnus shouted the century's orders across their ranks, repeating Julius's command to take the first rampart and then hold to allow the legions through with their assigned task complete. That done he drew his gladius and picked up a shield he'd left on the ground in front of his men, smiling wryly at Marcus, who stood at ease beside him in front of the century with his helmet hanging from one hand.

'When I got my vine stick last month I assumed I'd never have to carry a shield again in all my days . . .'

His friend's eyes were alive with the prospect of the impending action. He was as tall as Dubnus, and if his body was less massive in its build it was still impressively muscled from the months of incessant conditioning since he had joined the cohort in the spring. His hair was as black as a crow's wing, and his brown eyes were set in a darker-skinned face than was usual in the locally recruited auxiliary cohorts. A long cavalry sword was sheathed on his left hip, while the shorter infantry gladius, which usually hung on his right hip, was in his right hand. Its ornate eagle's-head pommel gleamed in the afternoon sunlight, the intricately worked silver and gold polished to a dazzling brilliance.

'. . . and yet here you are, hefting a painted piece of board again as if you were still in the ranks? Perhaps you'd rather go forward with just your vine stick for protection, eh, Dubnus?'

'No, I'll put up with the burden this once, thank you, Marcus. Those blue-nosed idiots aren't going to keep their heads down for long, and they'll throw everything but the water troughs at us once we're through the gate. If we get through the gate. Now, you're sure you don't want to lead the Ninth Century forward one last time?'

His friend shook his head, gesturing to the front rank of the century arrayed behind him.

'No, thank you. These are your men now. I'm only along for the ride. After you, *Centurion.*'

A sudden bray of trumpets stiffened their backs, calling the waiting centuries to readiness for the inevitable command. Marcus pulled on his helmet, his features suddenly rendered anonymous by the cheek guards' brutal lines, then took up his own shield.

'Infantry, advance!'

Julius turned back to face his men from the head of the left-hand column, drawing his sword and pointing it at the fort.

Tungrians . . . *advance!*'

At his command the detachment's two columns marched steadily forward down the gentle slope that ran down to the hill fort's perch high above the valley below. Three sides of the fort's position were utterly unassailable owing to the heavily forested and precipitously steep slopes that fell away from the pinnacle to the north, south and east. The only possible approach to the hill fort was from the west, where a flat and treeless ridge angled up to meet the hill on which two legion cohorts and their supporting artillery were gathered, ready to follow up on the advance of their Tungrian auxiliaries. Bordered on both sides by the wild forest of oak and birch that made the hill fort's steep approaches so difficult, the space beneath the trees thick with holly, alder and hazel that made it practically impassable, the ridge's wide path led arrow straight down to the fort's massive outer gates. Only here was there any realistic prospect of an attacker's advance meeting with anything but disastrous rebuff, but in anticipation of such an obvious approach, the fort's occupiers had long since constructed an elaborate series of defences across the fort's western face. Three successive palisades of thick wooden beams defended the innermost point of the fort, the hill's flat summit.

The Tungrians hunched behind their shields as the fort's wooden rampart loomed in front of them, casting nervous glances at the thirty massively built barbarians striding purposefully between them. An iron-tipped battering ram fashioned from a tree trunk hacked from the surrounding forest hung between the two ranks of prisoners, and swung to and fro as they marched down the ridge's slope. Each pair of men on either side of the ram was shackled together at the wrist, their chains wrapped around the tree trunk to remove any chance of flight, and every man was naked from the waist up, while a legion centurion and a dozen hard-faced soldiers marched alongside them in grim silence with drawn swords. The legion officer barked a command into the oppressive silence that greeted their advance.

'When we reach the gate you barbarian bastards will swing that ram as if your lives depend on it. Which they do!' He waited a moment to allow the men among them that spoke some Latin to translate his words for the others. 'When the gate's breached you will be released from your chains, and you will then go forward into the fort and take on the defenders with any weapon that you can get your hands on. Any man that runs will be put down by the soldiers alongside you or behind you without a second thought, so if you think that's a better choice than going through the gates you can think again. Those of you that survive the attack will be freed to return to your villages with your second brand.' Some of the men glanced down at the mark crudely burned into their right forearms, 'C' for '*captivus*'. 'Let me remind you that if you decide to run, and in the unlikely event that you actually get away with it, the lack of that second brand to cancel out the first one will get you crucified when you're recaptured. And that, my lads, is not a pleasant way to leave this life. Far better to die cleanly here in the sunlight than choking out your last miserable breaths in agony, and with your back opened up like a side of bad meat.'

Dubnus nudged his friend.

'Keep your eyes open for them once we're inside. I'm pretty sure that half of them fought us at Lost Eagle, I even recognise a couple of them, and they'll probably be only too happy to take one or two of us with them. Especially men wearing crests on their piss buckets like you and me.'

Marcus nodded grimly as the attacking force came to a halt in front of the massive wooden gates.

'Archers, ready . . .'

He glanced back, seeing the century of Syrian archers arrayed behind their small force taking up positions from which to shower the ramparts with arrows if the defenders were sufficiently unwise to show themselves. The legion centurion commanding the ram's conscripted bearers pointed at the gates, bellowing the command for them to start their assault. With a collective grunt of effort the ram-bearers swung the tree trunk backwards, then heaved it forward with a collective lunge, the iron head's arc ending against the gates' timbers with a rending crash, sending a shower of dust cascading down on to the leading Tungrian soldiers waiting alongside them. A tribesman popped up from behind the wall and lifted his arms to hurl a rock down on to the ram's bearers, but fell back with an arrow in his neck and a dozen more studding the palisade's wooden wall before the missile even left his hands. Twice more the ram swung back and hammered into the gate's creaking timbers, and with the fourth blow the left-hand gate sagged tiredly on to the ground, ready to fall. Julius barked an order back into the expectant silence.

'*Tungrians, wait for my command . . .*'

The ram's fifth collision with the fort's defences ripped away the left-hand door; its shattered remnants fell back into the gap between the fort's first and second palisades in a cloud of dust and splinters. Without the strength of its support, the right-hand gate surrendered after another two blows of the ram's massive iron head, leaving the gateway open and empty. The waiting legionary guards tossed keys to the barbarians' chains to the shackled men, waiting behind their shields with drawn swords as the prisoners freed themselves from the ram. Some of the barbarians gathered their chains to use as crude weapons, while others simply looked about them at the Roman troops gathered to all sides in a combination of hatred and simple terror. With the last of them freed, the centurion pointed his sword at the gateway.

'Go! Go and earn your freedom!'

For a moment longer the prisoners hesitated, until a shaggy-haired giant who had hefted the ram's heavy nose with straining muscles bellowed his defiance and loped forward into the fort, triggering a collective howl of anger and a sudden mad charge from the men behind him. As the last of the barbarians vanished through the gateway, Julius flashed his sword down.

'Advance!'

The four centuries trotted quickly towards the smashed gate's opening, flinching involuntarily as the bolt throwers on the hill behind them spat their heavy missiles over their heads in a salvo of shrieking iron. As Marcus rounded the gateway and stepped over the fallen gates' shattered timbers a falling man rebounded from the palisade in front of him and hit the ground with a wet crunch of shattered bones, a bolt buried deeply in his chest. He stepped forward and hacked reflexively at the dying man's head to make sure of the kill, then stared up and down the curved face of the inner wall. There seemed to be no other target for his sudden urgent need to take his blade to another enemy, only the half-naked barbarian prisoners milling about between the walls to either side of them and a few scattered corpses of the bolt throwers' earlier targets. He started as a scream sounded from the rampart to his rear, suddenly feeling horridly vulnerable to whatever was happening above and behind him. Instinctively raising his shield as he spun to face the outer wall, he felt a clanging thud as a spear intended for his back found only the iron boss in the shield's centre. The spearman howled his frustration at the miss, then staggered forward off the wall and turned a neat half-somersault to the ground with an arrow buried in his neck, the price of standing to make the throw.

A flicker of movement caught Marcus's eye, a mob of a hundred or more barbarians streaming round the fort's inner wall from his right, waving swords and axes in the air as they charged towards their attackers with berserk howls. They ripped through the barbarian prisoners without mercy, clearly aware of their former allies' need for redemption through victory and taking no chances with their loyalties. For whatever reason, and whether it made sense or not, the defenders had committed most of their strength to meeting the Tungrian attack head on. Any chance that the legion cohorts would be bearing the brunt of the battle once the auxiliaries had broken the fort's first line of defence was clearly no longer a reality. Dubnus had seen the barbarian charge, and stepped forward with a bellowed command that cut through the moment's confusion.

'Form a line!'

A good part of the 9th Century was through the gate already, and in seconds they had an unbroken wall of shields raised across the gap between the first and second palisades, the other centuries clustering to their rear in the thin space between the walls. The wave of attackers crashed into them, hammering at the shield wall with swords and axes, while the Tungrians held them at bay and stabbed back at them with practised skill, aiming killing blows at their throats, bellies and thighs. Stuck behind the line, Marcus craned his neck to see what was happening behind the fort's enraged defenders. As he watched, the massively built prisoner who had headed the first wave of attackers through the gateway got back to his feet a dozen paces behind the rearmost enemy warrior. A red smear across his forehead indicated that one of the defenders had clubbed him to the ground without taking the precaution of checking that the blow had been sufficient to put him out of the combat. He was pointing to something that was out of sight to Marcus around the inner wall's curve, bellowing words that were inaudible over the battle's cacophony of screams and curses. With a sudden flash of insight Marcus realised what he must be pointing at.

'The next gate . . .'

He turned to Dubnus, pointing urgently past the seething mob of barbarians on the other side of their shield wall.

'The second gate's open! Give me ten men, quickly!'

He sheathed his spatha and tossed the shield aside, climbing nimbly up the rough wooden ladder that led on to the wall's wooden fighting platform with a sudden burst of energy born of his realisation that the way to the heart of the fort had been left open behind the mass of warriors throwing themselves on to the Tungrians' shields. Climbing on to the narrow platform, he looked out for a moment across the ridge, back to the legion cohorts waiting in the afternoon's sunshine, their standards gleaming prettily in the sunlight. He waved down at the Syrian archers with the agreed crossed-fists gesture to indicate that the wall was taken, the signal to stop shooting at anything that moved along the wall's length. The archers' centurion waved back, barking to his men to stand down, and another man joined Marcus on the rampart, his face dimly remembered from his time commanding the 9th Century earlier that summer. Their eyes met, and as Marcus raised a hand to beckon him on down the wall in his wake a hot spray of the soldier's blood stung his eyes. A heavy bolt had opened his throat with the precision of a surgeon's scalpel, the man's blood fountaining across Marcus's mail armour as the soldier toppled choking back into space and fell on to the men fighting below them. Another bolt slammed into the timber an inch below the top of the wall, directly in line with Marcus's stomach, and the third screamed past his head with a hand-span to spare and no more, burying itself in the rough timber of the second palisade. Another man climbed on to the wall, and Marcus recognised Scarface, a 9th Century soldier with little respect for the cohort's officers.

'Best keep you fuckin' head down, Centurion, or those legion tosspots'll put a dart clean through it.'

Marcus nodded, ducking below the rampart and beckoning the other man on.

'Follow me!'

He scuttled off down the line of the rampart bent almost double, slipping and almost falling on a patch of still-wet blood, and looked back to make sure that the men who had climbed up after him were following. Thirty paces around the outer palisade's curve from the point he had climbed up he dropped from the platform's eight-foot elevation to land beside the massively muscled prisoner, drawing both swords as the man spoke in rough Latin, his voice a bass rumble.

'Gate open. We close, they trap.'

Marcus nodded, beckoning his men to jump down.

'What's your name?'

The Briton spoke without taking his eyes from the open gate.

'Lugos.'

'Come with me, Lugos. I may need someone that speaks

the language, and you'll be safer with us than staying here. If this works you'll be a free man by the end of this fight.'

The big barbarian nodded curtly, and Marcus led his small party along the curve of the inner palisade to the gate, still open despite the obvious risk to the fort's security. Marcus peeped round its timber frame, seeing a cluster of a dozen warriors standing next to the much smaller opening in the fort's third and last wall. He pulled his head back, speaking quickly to his men.

'There's only one more gate. It's still open, and they've only left a few men to guard it. We've already captured this one, and if we can stop them closing that one we've got the fort at our mercy. Are you with me?'

The three 9th Century men who had followed him nodded readily, Scarface glaring round at his comrades in a way they knew only too well, while the three others, from other centuries and therefore less used to his way of doing things, stared back with a mixture of uncertainty and apprehension. It would have to do. The barbarian had acquired a spear from somewhere, and stared down at him without any visible expression.

'Very well, gentlemen, let's go and win ourselves a fort.'

He threw himself round the gate's wooden frame and shouted a challenge at the warriors guarding the last gate, wanting them to see the small number of men charging along the wall at them with a single officer at their head. They dithered for a moment, caught between the need to deny the Romans the gate they were entrusted to guard and the opportunity to kill their enemy, and in that time his sprinting pace halved the distance between them. Glancing back, he saw that only the barbarian, his three former soldiers and one other man had joined him, but it was too late to do anything but face the enemy warriors, suddenly confident as they realised that they outnumbered their Roman attackers by two to one and came forward with their swords drawn.

Jinking to right and left, Marcus batted aside the leading warrior's sword-thrust with the long blade of his spatha and hit the man hard with his right shoulder, punching him back into the men behind him and gaining a moment's confusion in which his small group could gather their strength. Spinning away from the tangled knot of barbarians, he readied himself to take on another warrior, only to see Lugos leap at his intended victim with a blood-curdling howl, spitting him through the guts with a downward lunge of the spear he had found and leaving it buried deep in the man, taking the sword from his nerveless fingers. He raised the weapon over his head and hacked it down into another warrior's unprotected head, his eyes bulging wide with the bloodlust. Marcus dragged his gaze from the spectacle in time to parry a sword-blow from his left with the gladius' short blade, spinning to his right and chopping the spatha's heavy blade through his attacker's spine, severing the man's head in a shower of gore. The headless corpse toppled stiffly backwards to the turf. The other Tungrian soldiers were in the fight now, crowding in behind Scarface's lead, and the gate guards were abruptly on the defensive as they found their strength almost halved.

Marcus looked beyond them to the last gate, knowing that their unexpected run of luck could still end in stalemate if the men remaining inside managed to get it closed. The eight-foot timbers of the fort's innermost palisade were more than stout enough to hold off the attackers for long enough for the remaining occupants to have time to make their escape over the walls on the fort's far side, and down the steep slopes into the surrounding wild forest, whose secret paths only they knew.

'Scarface, hold them! You . . .'

He pointed at the panting Lugos, hooking a thumb at the last gate.

'. . . with me!'

The other man nodded, understanding the Roman officer's purpose if not his words, and the pair burst past the knot of fighting men and ran hard for the gate. A single man hurried through the gap just as they reached it, drawn by the sounds of battle, and died on the barbarian's sword without ever quite comprehending how badly the fort's defence was undone, the slippery rope of his guts falling through his torn stomach wall as Lugos pushed him back against the timber rampart and lunged at him again, shoving the sword's blade up into his chest to skewer his heart. Marcus burst through the gate and stopped, his swords held ready to fight as he took in the scene before him. A wide-open space crowned the hill's crest, perhaps fifty paces in diameter and surrounded on all sides by the final wooden palisade. A single timber-built hall stood against the enclosure's far wall, and the open space between gate and building was studded with smoking cooking pits and the scattered remnants of their last meal. A single warrior stood outside the hall, and as Marcus stood breathing heavily in the gateway he shouted something through the door behind him. A massively built warrior stalked through the doorway, a fighting axe held in one hand and a round shield in the other, the thick gold torc around his bull neck marking him as the tribe's king. He stood for a moment, taking in the sudden reality of his defeat before setting off towards Marcus at a lumbering trot with his bodyguard running alongside him.

The centurion looked back at the gateway behind him, seeing that the prisoner was still the only man to have reached as far into the enemy's defences. He stabbed his spatha's long blade into the grass at his feet, pointing to the gate and chopping at the air with a bladed hand.

'Destroy the gate!'

Fiona Walker is the author of fifteen bestselling novels – most recently *The Woman Who Fell in Love for a Week*, which is also published by Sphere. She lives in Worcester with her partner and two children plus an assortment of horses and dogs.

Visit Fiona's website at
www.fionawalker.com

Follow Fiona @fionawalkeruk